PRESIDENTIAL MISSION I.

TIMELINE

World's End	1913 - 1919
Between Two Worlds	1919 - 1929
Dragon's Teeth	1929 - 1934
Wide is the Gate	1934 - 1937
Presidential Agent	1937 - 1938
Dragon Harvest	1938 - 1940
A World to Win	1940 - 1942
Presidential Mission	1942 - 1943
One Clear Call	1943 - 1944
O Shepherd, Speak!	1943 - 1946
The Return of Lanny Budd	1946 - 1949

Each book is published in two parts: I and II.

PRESIDENTIAL MISSION I.

Upton Sinclair

Simon Publications

2001

LCCN: 47030286

ISBN: 1-931313-08-3

Dis tributed by Ingram Book Com pany

Printed by Light ning Source Inc., LaVergne, TN

Pub lished by Si mon Pub li ca tions, P.O. Box 321 Safety Har bor, FL

An Author's Program

From a 1943 article by Upton Sinclair.

When I say "historian," I have a meaning of my own. I portray world events in story form, because that form is the one I have been trained in. I have supported myself by writing fiction since the age of sixteen, which means for forty-nine years.

… Now I realize that this one was the one job for which I had been born: to put the period of world wars and revolutions into a great long novel. …

I cannot say when it will end, because I don't know exactly what the characters will do. They lead a semi-independent life, being more real to me than any of the people I know, with the single exception of my wife. … Some of my characters are people who lived, and whom I had opportunity to know and watch. Others are imaginary—or rather, they are complexes of many people whom I have known and watched. Lanny Budd and his mother and father and their various relatives and friends have come in the course of the past four years to be my daily and nightly companions. I have come to know them so intimately that I need only to ask them what they would do in a given set of circumstances and they start to enact their roles. … I chose what seems to me the most revealing of them and of their world.

How long will this go on? I cannot tell. It depends in great part upon two public figures, Hitler and Mussolini. What are they going to do to mankind and what is mankind will do to them? It seems to me hardly likely that either will die a peaceful death. I am hoping to outlive them; and whatever happens Lanny Budd will be somewhere in the neighborhood, he will be "in at the death," according to the fox-hunting phrase.

These two foxes are my quarry, and I hope to hang their brushes over my mantel.

Author's Notes

In the course of this novel a number of well-known persons make their appearance, some of them living, some dead; they appear under their own names, and what is said about them is factually correct.

There are other characters which are fictitious, and in these cases the author has gone out of his way to avoid seeming to point at real persons. He has given them unlikely names, and hopes that no person bearing such names exist. But it is impossible to make sure; therefore the writer states that, if any such coincidence occurs, it is accidental. This is not the customary "hedge clause" which the author of a *roman à clef* publishes for legal protection; it means what it says and it is intended to be so taken.

Various European concerns engaged in the manufacture of munitions have been named in the story, and what has been said about them is also according to the records. There is one American firm, and that, with all its affairs, is imaginary. The writer has done his best to avoid seeming to indicate any actual American firm or family.

...Of course there will be slips, as I know from experience; but *World's End* is meant to be a history as well as fiction, and I am sure there are no mistakes of importance. I have my own point of view, but I have tried to play fair in this book. There is a varied cast of characters and they say as they think. ...

The Peace Conference of Paris [*for example*], which is the scene of the last third of *World's End*, is of course one of the greatest events of all time. A friend on mine asked an authority on modern fiction a question: "Has anybody ever used the Peace Conference in a novel?" And the reply was: "Could anybody?" Well, I thought somebody could, and now I think somebody has. The reader will ask, and I state explicitly that so far as concerns historic characters and events my picture is correct in all details. This part of the manuscript, 374 pages, was read and checked by eight or ten gentlemen who were on the American staff at the Conference. Several of these hold important positions in the world of troubled international affairs; others are college presidents and professors, and I promised them all that their letters will be confidential. Suffice it to say that the errors they pointed out were corrected, and where they disagreed, both sides have a word in the book.

Contents:

BOOK ONE

So Nigh Is Grandeur to Our Dust

1

Humanity with All Its Fears

LANNY BUDD'S heart was high as he drove northward along the Palisades. Hardly a day during the past six months had passed that he had not imagined this hour when he would make his report to the Big Boss—what he would say and what the Boss would answer. Six months is a chunk out of any man's life, and Lanny's had been crowded with new experiences. He had been all the way round the earth, and most of the trip near the equator, where the distance is greatest. Meantime that earth had been witnessing events of pain and terror, cataclysms so momentous that men would continue to write and talk about them so long as there was anybody on the planet able to know what had happened in its past.

The sun was shining warm on this early April afternoon. Small white clouds drifted across the blue sky, above apple orchards wreathed in pink satin blossoms, to welcome a world traveler home. The well-paved highway wound irregularly along the wooded cliffs, dipping now and then into hollows, or coming out upon open places where a driver could observe the broad sweep of the river, the railroad on the opposite shore, the villages, and the hills dotted with farmhouses and country mansions. Lanny, who delighted in motoring, had not had a steering wheel in his hands for half a year. He had come from the snows of Archangel and the fogs of Newfoundland; and here was warmth, sunshine, beauty, comfort—all the gifts of nature and of civilization which an American of the leisure classes takes for granted and appreciates only after he has been traveling in wild and poverty-stricken lands, or amid scenes of war and destruction.

The warmth seeped in through the traveler's skin, the orchard scents through his nostrils, and the beauty through his eyes. His subconscious mind absorbed these while his conscious mind was busy with the great man he was going to see, the story he had to tell him, and what questions would be asked and what answers given. Lanny had missed so much, in these days when significant events came piling one on top of the other, hardly giving people time to realize any of them. America had been at war for a matter of four months, and it had been one defeat after another, with not a single success. Bataan had just surrendered, and the Japanese were close to India; the Germans were close to Leningrad and to the Suez Canal. Lanny thought: F.D.R. is the man who will know about everything. How much will he tell me. and what will he want me to do?

II

After a drive of an hour and a half the motorist came to the high Poughkeepsie bridge and crossed over to the east bank of the river. He drove through the spread-out city with the queer Indian name and on up the post road to the north. This road was wide and fairly straight, arched by tall elm trees and lined with the fences and gates of country homes. Soon it was a village called Hyde Park, and then it was an estate called Krum Elbow, for the past nine years the "summer White House." Lanny had been here just before setting out upon his long journey. That time he had been smuggled in by the back door in the night and had seen his Chief lying in bed, wearing pongee pajamas. and a blue crew-necked sweater, which he wouldn't part with even after the moths had devoured parts of it. Only once had the visitor entered this estate in the normal way, the first time, before he had become a secret agent for the most powerful man in the world.

At the little sentry-box by the entrance gate there had formerly been a State Trooper; now it was wartime, and the United States Army had taken over. The driver stopped his car and gave his name to the sergeant in command. The sergeant had a list, no doubt, and knew it by heart. He surveyed a conventionally dressed gentleman in his early forties, wearing a tropical worsted suit of brown, a tie and a homburg hat to match; a little brown mustache, a friendly smile, and a sun tan not entirely lost in the snows of Russia. "I have to see your driver's license, Mr. Budd," said the man; and then: "I have to look in the trunk of your car." It was a sport car with a rumble seat, and anybody who had been hidden there would have had to be of jockey size. Lanny said: "It isn't locked." The sergeant took a glance and then said: "O.K., sir."

The car sped up the drive, through a lane of shade trees which their owner loved—he was pleased to describe his occupation as "tree grower" instead of President of the United States, a less dependable job. The mansion was something over a hundred years old, two-and-a-half stories, partly brick and partly stone; it had been added to now and then, each time in a somewhat different style of architecture. At the front entrance was a semicircular portico with four white columns, and here was a sentry who gave Lanny an informal salute but did not stop him. His coming must have been announced by telephone, for the door was opened without his having to ring, and a Negro butler took his hat; a woman secretary greeted him cheerfully.

III

In front as you entered this family home was a grandfather's clock, and at the right a circular stairway with carved banisters. The way to the library was at your left, and as you turned in that direction you were confronted by a statue of the President as a youth, a life-size seated figure rising out of a square block of stone. There was a passageway, and a descent of three or four stairs, and at one side a ramp on which a wheel chair might be moved. Wherever the President sat, the wheel chair was near, and a button which he might press to summon his Negro attendant.

· The library formed the left wing of the building and was of generous size. There was a fireplace at each end; in front of one was a large flat-topped desk, and sitting behind it was the man Lanny had come to see—a large man, with large shoulders and head and a frank, cheerful face known to most of the world. He was on the alert for his visitor and did not consider it necessary to pretend to be preoccupied; his face lighted up and he held out a welcoming hand from a distance. "Hi, Marco Polo!" In the dozen visits that Franklin Roosevelt had received from his secret agent he had never failed to think up some fancy greeting, and this time it was for a man who had traveled all the way across China. He added: "By golly, I can't tell you how I have missed you!"

"You have had enough to occupy your mind." The visitor smiled. He looked with curiosity at this great, crippled man who carried an Atlas load upon his broad shoulders. F.D.R. was a little thinner, a little more careworn, but never more cheerful, for he liked people to come to see him, especially when they had interesting reports to deliver.

"Make yourself at home," he said and signed to a tall chair beside his desk, one of two "gubernatorial chairs" which he had earned, one for each term he had served in his native state. Lanny saw that the desk had toy elephants and donkeys, billikins, snake rattles, all sorts of odds and ends that admirers sent him; also a formidable stock of official documents which he would have to dig his way through, but not this afternoon. He had come to Hyde Park for a week end of badly needed rest, and talking to Presidential Agent 103 was one of his ways of diversion.

"You are able to get about all right?" was his first comment. "Tell me just what happened."

"My plane cracked up in a terrific storm, and when it hit the sea both my legs were smashed. But they're all right now, and ready for duty."

"I thought to myself when I heard about it: he'll be one man who can understand *my* plight!"

"Believe me, Governor, there wasn't a day in the hospital and afterward that I didn't have that same thought."

"You were luckier than I, you could hope for a comeback."

"I was more lucky than any man had better count on. I don't know if I ever told you that an astrologer had predicted that I would die in Hongkong. I had several close calls there, and almost got converted to a belief in the stars."

"Alston tells me that you were married instead." Then, with a chuckle: "You know the jingle about needles and pins?"

"Plenty of trouble began there, but it wasn't due to getting married. Quite the contrary."

"I wish you happiness, Lanny. You must bring your wife to see us sometime."

"That will give her pleasure indeed. She is, as you may have heard, a writer of short stories, and has given the Nazis some sharp digs. The Russians were delighted by them."

"Send them to me and I'll be glad to read them. Did you see much of Russia?"

"Only Kuibyshev and Moscow, but I had some worth-while talks. You will want to hear first about Stalin, I imagine." Lanny brought up the subject at the first moment, being aware of his Boss's fondness for chatting. The caller didn't want to get diverted, say to the President's great-great-uncle or great-grandfather or whoever it was that was suspected of having been an opium smuggler in the China Seas; or perhaps to the model of his Yankee Clipper which stood in a glass case against one wall of this ample room.

IV

Lanny Budd launched himself upon a subject which he could be sure was of importance to the Commander-in-Chief of the American Armed Forces. He reported on a two-hour conference with the mystery man of the Kremlin—not so mysterious if you would read some of his published writings and those of his master, Lenin. But many people find it easier to contemplate a mystery than to read a book, and Lanny doubted Franklin Roosevelt's ever having seen one of Stalin's tomes. He described the oval room which was the Soviet chief's office, and the interview late at night, and the fur coat and boots which had been presented to the emissary from the White House.

"The Embassy here at Washington made inquiry about you and I gave you my O.K.," said F.D.R. To which the visitor replied: "I guessed that must have happened, because Stalin was so frank and gave me several messages for you."

"The thing we want to know most of all, Lanny, is whether they will stick it out in this war."

"As to that I am sure you need have no fear. They have seen too much of Nazi brutality, which is really quite insane. A Russian would as soon trust a Bengal tiger as take the word of a Hitlerite. Stalin's reply to my question was prompt and decisive. They are in this war to the finish, and only beg that you will get help to them as quickly as possible."

"We will do our best, Lanny, but we have almost nothing at present. Our shortage of shipping is paralyzing, and the U-boats are playing the very devil with us. The Russians expect a heavy attack this spring, I assume."

"They do, and cannot be sure where it will come; that is the disadvantage of defensive warfare. The best guess is that Hitler will concentrate on the south because of the oil, which is his greatest need. It will be an overwhelming attack; he has not been nearly so heavily hit as the Soviet communiqués would have us believe. His retreat was strategic, to prepared winter positions, and not many of his troops were sacrificed. He will no doubt throw in everything he has as soon as the ground is dry. There are millions of Russians, now strong and happy, who will be food for the wolves and the kites when the steppes are dry."

The smile had gone from the President's face, and instead there was a mask of grief, which silenced his secret agent. "You know, Lanny, I never dreamed I'd be a war president. It is a thought I could hardly have faced."

Lanny did his best to meet this mood. "Lincoln didn't want it, Wilson didn't want it, I doubt if any of our war presidents ever did or will. You are in the hands of fate, sir; and history will record that you did your job well." Lanny guessed that this was what Roosevelt lived for, the fountainhead from which he drew his courage and confidence; he was making history that men would study and from which they would renew their faith in democratic principles.

The visitor went on with his story. He told everything the Red dictator had said, including the assertion that he was not a dictator. He repeated the questions Stalin had asked about Roosevelt; questions all to the point, revealing a knowledge of America that extended even to Hearst and Colonel McCormick and their newspapers, whose main purpose appeared to be to misrepresent the Soviet Union. Then Lanny underwent an inquisition similar to the one he had gone through in Moscow. What did Stalin look like, what was his manner, what appeared to be the state of his health? Lanny reported that he spoke quietly and paid close attention to every reply. He was in his sixties, but only gray hair and mustache betrayed his age.

"A curious thing," the President said. "I had the impression that he was a big man, but they tell me this is not so."

"I would guess him to be four inches shorter than I, and I am five-ten; but he is sturdily built. His training has been that of a revolutionary, a hunted man under the tsardom, and it must be hard for him to imagine the free institutions which you and I take for granted. It must be hard for him to realize that men born to wealth and comfort like ourselves can be genuinely interested in the abolition of their own privileges. But when I proposed a toast to the progress of democracy throughout the world, Stalin drank to it without hesitation. Of course he has his own definition of the word, and his own idea of how to attain the goal. If he is to be persuaded that our way is better, it will have to be by actions, not by words."

V

Everything about the Soviet Union and then everything about China. F.D.R. stuck another cigarette into the long thin holder which he affected, lighted it with a patent lighter, and started another inquisition. He wanted to know what life was like in the interior of a land which had been at war for ten years. How did the people appear, and what were they doing and saying? Had the travelers seen any signs of starvation, and what had they used for money, and how much did the common people know about what was going on in the outside world? "They all know about *you*," Lanny said with a grin, "and they are all sure you are going to send them several thousand airplanes by next Tuesday."

"Alas, I would not dare tell them how few planes we have, Lanny. I won't tell even you. It will be impossible to get anything to them for some time."

"The intelligent ones realize that. They say they are worse off since we entered the war. They used to get some goods by smuggling or by bribing Jap officials. Now they get nothing."

"It is of the utmost importance that China should not collapse, Lanny. We can only make promises, but we do this with real sincerity. We are surely going to smash the Jap warlords, and then it will be possible for a peaceful and democratic China to exist."

"That is what I told them everywhere. I took the liberty of saying that I was a special emissary of yours, sent to give them assurances."

"You are that wherever you go, Lanny. I understand that you were in Yenan. Tell me about that. I hear such contradictory reports."

So this "Marco Polo" described "Red China," the land in the north and northwest to which the Communist armies had marched when expelled from the rest of the country, and where they were now building a crude, pathetic utopia, mostly in caves chopped out of cliffs where the Jap bombers couldn't reach them. Lanny told of the odd impression this life had made on him; it wasn't Marxist and certainly not Leninist, it was early American utopian; it was a "colony," a "phalanstery," a "commonwealth." Its people did not talk about class struggle; they talked about co-operation and brotherhood and worked at it with apostolic zeal.

"Then they are not trying to socialize industry?" asked the President. The answer was: "It was carefully explained to me that their theoreticians have decided that at this stage they must promote private industry as a means of overcoming feudalism."

"A sort of N.E.P.," commented the other. "That ought to make it easy to get along with them."

"One might think so. But unfortunately the Chungking government wants to perpetuate feudalism under the label of democracy. They maintain a strict blockade of Yenan, and we were told that it would be impossible to get there. We did manage it, but it was an uncomfortable journey, and not without its dangers."

"Every nation wants to continue its civil wars, it appears, even while it is being crushed by the Japs or the Germans."

"Even after it *has been* crushed, Governor. That is the situation in France, and among every group of refugees I have met anywhere."

"It is sad," was the reply. "But the problem seems very simple. We are going to fight Japs and Germans and break their military systems. That is the only thing that counts with us, and we are not going to fight anybody's civil wars, not in China, nor in France, nor in Italy, nor wherever our troops may go. When it is over, we'll see that all the countries have a fair democratic election, and after that they will be on their own."

"Is that the formula, Governor?"

"That is it. Paste it in your hat and look at it every once in a while. Everybody who is willing to help fight Japs and Germans, and Italians, of course, is our ally, and everybody who wants to fight anybody else will have to be sat on for the time being."

"I'm glad to hear it from your own lips, Governor, for I know from previous experience how it is going to be. All sorts of cliques and causes will try to use our armies for their schemes."

"The watchword is democracy. That means government of the people, by the people, for the people—and it means all the people, not just General Whoosis and Prince Highupsky."

"Don't forget to mention that to your State Department and to your generals," was the visitor's dry suggestion.

VI

The busiest man in the world lighted still another cigarette and proceeded to "talk turkey," as he called it. "Tell me, Lanny, what do you want to do next?"

The visitor had prepared for this and replied promptly: "I want to do whatever will be of the greatest help to you."

"We are building a big, and I hope an efficient, Intelligence service. I can turn you over to 'Wild Bill' Donovan, a shrewd and loyal man, and he will make you one of his right bowers."

"If that is where you think I can do the best work. But I was rather hoping you might have some personal mission for me. You know how I feel—my contact with you has been half the fun of all this."

"It's not a thankful sort of job, Lanny. It has no future."

"You mean that I won't get titles and a salary? I have never wanted those. My reward is to sit in this gubernatorial chair and tell you my story, and hear from you what is coming next and what I can do to help it along."

"You would rather go on as a free lance, then?"

"I have never learned to be anything else, and I'm not sure I could become a cog in a machine. I have been thinking about it, and here is the difficulty: the contacts I have in Europe are personal and I am bound by pledges; before I could tell Colonel Donovan anything of importance, I should have to go back there and persuade my friends to give their consent."

"Surely you don't expect to go into Germany any more!"

"I can't see any way to do it. But I have a contact in Switzerland that has proved valuable in the past, and I hope to find the man still alive and on the job. It is the same with an old friend who is working with the underground in Toulon. There should be code letters waiting at my mother's home on the Riviera."

"The situation has been altered greatly since we have been forced into the war. What will you use as your camouflage now?"

"I have given much thought to that all the way across Asia and Europe. I believe I can still get along in neutral countries in my role of art expert. My clients have money, and they will buy paintings if I can find them and get them here."

"But it surely won't seem plausible for an art expert to be rambling about Europe carrying on business in wartime!"

"It will seem more plausible than you might like to believe, Governor. There is plenty of bootlegging and black marketeering going on, and most high-up people still believe that there are special privileges. In London I was offered opportunities to speculate in French industrial shares—I mean, of industries in Occupied France, strictly illegal. I could tell you scores of stories along such lines. All I have to do is to smile knowingly and remind my friends that my father is president of Budd-Erling Aircraft and an influential man in his own country. To those who are sympathetic to our cause I can drop a hint to the effect that I am able to assist my father in getting information. The slightest hint will suffice, for people will realize that such matters would be strictly hush-hush."

"Shall you continue to pose as a secret sympathizer with Fascism?"

"I have worked out a rather complicated technique in the course of the years, and I vary it according to the person I am with. Most of the time I am the art lover, the ivory-tower dweller, the lotos-eater, careless of mankind. Something that will amuse you—I was wearing that role the evening I met the lady who is now my wife, and she gave

me a fine dressing down, called me a 'troglodyte.' But most of the time
that role satisfies people in the *haut monde*."

"I've an idea you may find it different now that we're in the war,
Lanny. People have taken sides."

"I have learned to shade my statements and put on a little smile
which makes me enigmatic and mysterious. With those who are Fascists at heart, or without realizing it, I can take the attitude of my
former wife, Lady Wickthorpe, who has become a pacifist and hu-
manitarian; she deplores mass slaughter, and perceives so clearly that
it cannot help anybody but the Reds. These lofty sentiments break
nobody's bones."

"I am told that conditions are changing fast, in France especially.
The Germans are making themselves bitterly hated, and the underground is spreading fast."

"I am prepared for that, and I may feel free to make the real truth
known to more persons than in the past. I had to use extreme care so
long as I was going into Hitlerland; but I've an idea that my visit to
Stalin has put an end to all that. It is hard to believe the Nazis wouldn't
get a report of it. Indeed, I decided that my goose was cooked last
September, when I was brought into Halifax after the plane crash.
The hospital people found two passports on me, one of them under
an assumed name. The nurses knew about it, and it must have been
whispered all over the town. I am bound to assume that the Germans
would have agents there, and that the story would get to Berlin. So far
as I know, the Führer never had but one American friend, and if that
one was revealed to be a spy, it would make a tremendous scandal
among the insiders. I rather think I may get echoes from it when I
meet the old-time Social Democrat and labor leader who is my contact in Geneva."

"I get your point, Lanny," said F.D.R. "Let it be understood that I
don't ask you to go into any German-held territory, or Italian. We
have many others who can do that, and at less risk."

VII

They had come to the crucial part of their talk, about which Lanny
had been dreaming for half a year. The Big Boss fell silent, looked at
him steadily, and began in a grave voice: "I am going to share some
information with you, Lanny—top secret. You will understand without my saying it, you are not to drop any hint of it to any person."

"Of course, Governor."

"I have to specify, not even to your wife."

"My wife has never asked me a question, once I had told her that I was pledged."

"Churchill came here just before Christmas, as you probably heard; he brought a large staff, and we threshed out the problems of world strategy. We both agree that Germany is our principal foe and must be beaten first; but we differ as to the best way to get at him. I would like to cross the Channel and seize the Cherbourg peninsula. I would do it this summer, even poorly prepared as we are. The Russians are pleading for a second front; they are in desperate straits, and we fear they may be knocked out of the war. But Churchill won't hear of it; he is afraid of another Dunkerque. He keeps talking about what he calls 'the soft underbelly of Europe.' He is hypnotized by the idea of breaking in by the back door. As you know, he tried it in the last war."

"I have heard him explain his failure, to his own satisfaction."

"I doubt very much if I'll be able to change him. In any case, I am determined that we shall fight this year; and if it can't be Cherbourg, then it'll be French North Africa. In either case, it will be the largest expedition ever to cross an ocean and will involve a colossal amount of work; something like a thousand ships, with landing craft, artillery, air support. Have you picked up any hint of all this?"

"I haven't been any place where there were hints, Governor. I can see the strategy—to make the Mediterranean safe, shorten the route to Suez, and be in a position to take Rommel in the rear."

"Just so. And if we can take Tunis we shall be able to cross to Sicily, and then to Italy."

"Italy would be dreadful country to fight in, Governor. I have motored through it, and it is a bootful of mountains."

"We shall have command of the sea, and soon, I hope, of the air. If we can take the airfields in southern Italy we shall be in a position to bomb southern Germany and the munitions plants which Hitler has built in Austria, imagining them safely out of reach."

"That all sounds fine to me, Governor."

"The main point is that we shall be doing something, and giving our troops actual battle practice, the only way they can learn. Also, we shall be showing the Russians that we mean business; every division that Hitler has to send to stop us will be one more missing from the eastern front."

"You want me to go and spy out the land?"

"Go first to Vichy and meet the leaders, as you did before. Let them talk, and tell you how they feel about us, and what they expect us to do, and what they will do in reply. Then you might meet your friend in Toulon and get acquainted with some of the underground people. Sound them out on the all-important question of their Fleet, and what we have to expect from both officers and men."

"They won't talk to me, Governor, unless I reveal the truth about myself."

"Use your own judgment. If you can meet the right people and get anything of value, you may tell them that you have been sent by me. Tell them that our armies are coming, and soon, but don't say where or when. Give them money, if they are dependable and can use it to our advantage. We must have a new arrangement about money, Lanny, for we are spending it, really spending now. Nothing counts but saving the lives of our men and furthering our objectives."

"I see what you mean, Governor. I don't want any money for myself—"

"I am paid a salary, Lanny, and so is everybody I am putting to work. You are a married man now, and you have to think about a family."

"My wife is very proud of earning all she needs, so put me down as one of your dollar-a-year men. But when it comes to distributing money to the underground, I'm willing of course. I have the good fortune to know one absolutely reliable man, and have no doubt that he will be able to lead me to others."

"I will arrange to have a hundred thousand dollars put to your account in your New York bank. I shall not expect any accounting, except in a general way, when we meet. When you can use more to good advantage, let me know."

"What the underground needs, Governor, is not so much money as arms and explosives."

"When you come back, bring me the names of such persons as are willing to be known to us. I will turn them over to Donovan, and his agents will get in touch with them. We have many ways of getting supplies into France now, and we shall have more. However, I don't want you to go deeply into that sort of thing, which is bound to be dangerous. What I want from you is information from the top people, with whom you have had so much success. It's all right for you to go to Switzerland and see what your German man is doing, and give him whatever money he can use; but don't stay long. I'd rather you would go to North Africa and meet the top people there, and find out what their attitude is now and what it's likely to be when we come. I don't need to go into details, you will understand what is needed."

VIII

So there were the orders, not very different from what P.A. 103 had received in the past and what he had expected now. His quick mind started thinking up questions, but before he could speak his Boss began: "Do you know Robert Murphy?"

"I met him in Vichy, but only casually. You may remember, you advised me to keep away from Admiral Leahy and the rest of our staff because they might suspect that I was the mysterious 'Zaharoff' who was sending reports through the Embassy."

"I have sent Bob as our counselor to North Africa. He has been provided with a staff of vice-consuls, about a dozen. They are carefully chosen men, mostly young; they know French, and of course their consular duties are nominal; they are there to prepare the way for a possible invasion. You will inevitably meet them and form an impression of what they are doing. I am not sending you to watch them, but if you see anything that I ought to know, you will tell me about it; that goes for good things as well as bad, their successes as well as their inadequacies."

"I understand, Governor."

"You will find Bob Murphy a delightful fellow, warmhearted and genial—perhaps too much so for the sort of people he will be dealing with. He is one of what you have called my 'striped-pants boys.' "

"Your cookie-pushers, Governor." Lanny grinned.

"Also, he is one of those liberal Catholics whom you find it hard to believe in. But you will recognize that he is the sort I have to send to Vichy France and to their colonies. You will like him personally, and will discover that he has a nasty job. I need not tell you that the enemy agents are swarming in that region and are pretty well in command of its affairs."

"I realize that. Do you wish me to approach them secretly and pretend that I am still their friend?"

"I leave that to your judgment. I doubt if you could get much from them, because they will naturally assume that you must be their enemy now. I am more interested in what you can get from the French, of all groups. They are bound to know that we are coming sooner or later, and they will be trimming their sails to the new wind. You will encounter many varieties of intrigue."

"Algiers will be a nest of rattlesnakes, Governor; I'll do my best not to get bitten. Am I to give Murphy any hint of what I am doing?"

"Not at the outset, I think. He'll no doubt have his suspicions. Tell me this, can you manage to work your camouflage in that part of the world? Is there any art there?"

"Wherever there are wealthy French residents, there are always paintings, and maybe good ones. I have come upon old masters in unexpected places, and to be looking for them in those colonies would be as natural as looking for spinning wheels and grandfather's clocks in Vermont or New Hampshire. There must also be Moorish art preserved there. I don't know much about it, but I could bone up in the library and be an 'authority' in a week or two. I'll try to interest one or two of my clients in the idea, and then I'll be able to write letters and send cablegrams from the field. That impresses the censors, and of course they inform the authorities, and presently they begin to think that I may really be what I pretend to be."

"Fine!" said the President. "I am beginning to believe it myself."

"But of course I won't be able to interest the State Department gentry in Moorish art. It's up to you to see that I get a passport to all these places you have suggested."

"I'll have Baker attend to that at once. How soon do you think you can go?"

"I ought to have a week or so to attend to personal matters. I want to get my wife settled in New York, and take her to Newcastle and introduce her to my father and his family. My father may have some request to make of me—and that's important, because it provides an extra camouflage and enables me to meet influential people. I suppose you will want me to talk with Professor Alston about this project?"

"By all means. He will have many suggestions to make. Take your time, but no more than is necessary."

"Am I to send you reports in the usual way?"

"Through our chargé when you are in Vichy, through Harrison in Switzerland, and through Bob Murphy in North Africa. I will instruct Bob that letters for me marked 'Zaharoff' are to be forwarded by diplomatic pouch, unopened."

"By the way, Governor, that reminds me—an odd thing. As you know, I amuse myself by delving into psychic phenomena. Most of my friends take it as a sign that I am slightly cracked, but they can't explain the things that happen."

"I have known of such experiences, Lanny, and am· not surprised that you are interested in the subject."

"At my mother's home on the Riviera there is an old Polish woman who is a medium. She has been a family pensioner for the past fifteen years. Whenever I go there, I never fail to try a few sittings, and one of the 'spirits,' or whatever they are who never fail to announce themselves, is old Zaharoff. He fusses and frets because I won't pay a debt he owes a man at Monte Carlo, but he never tells me any way to get the money. The last time I was there, about a year ago, he gave me quite a shock by announcing that he was greatly displeased by the way I was making use of his name. You understand, I have never mentioned that fact to a living soul, and I thought you and I were the only two persons who knew that I was 'Zaharoff.' Of course, it may be that the medium got that out of my subconscious mind; anyhow, it makes me uneasy about having other people experimenting with Madame. My stepfather does it continually, and he might talk about it, simply because he wouldn't have any idea how important the secret is."

"I get you," said F.D.R.

"It set me to thinking about the name. The old munitions king didn't have many intimates before his death, and if one of my reports were to fall into the hands of the Gestapo, they might set out making inquiries among the old man's heirs and business associates and thus come upon my name. So I think we had better have a new deal and bury old Sir Basil."

"All right," said the President, "choose a new name." Then, before Lanny could speak, he added: "A North African landing is known as 'Operation Gymnast.' That is top secret, but if ever you get into a spot and want to convince one of our people that you are an insider—somebody like Bob Murphy—you can use it."

"O.K.," replied Lanny. "It might be a good idea for me to have a name along the same line. Suppose we say 'Traveler.' I seem to be earning that fairly."

"So let it be, and I'll give the necessary instructions. Also, I'll list the name with my private telephone service, and any time you call the White House and give the name, you'll reach me if I am available."

"Fine, Governor! Thanks a million."

"The thanks are all yours. And one thing more. Get me a visiting card out of that desk drawer."

Lanny had done this once before and knew where to look. The President took the card and wrote on it with his fountain pen: "My friend Lanny Budd is worthy of all trust. F.D.R." He handed that to the secret agent, saying: "Better sew it up in the lining of your coat or some safe place, and use it only when you are sure it is needed."

The agent replied: "If I get into a jam with the enemy, I'll chew it

up and swallow it!" Little did he guess what a seer he would prove
to be.

IX

Business first, then pleasure. "If you can spare the time," said the
Boss, "you might stay for tea and meet some of the family. You don't
have to be so carefully hidden from now on."

Lanny said he would be glad to stay. A button was pressed, and an
amiable Negro man appeared, the same Prettyman whom Lanny had
seen many times dozing in a chair just outside the President's bedroom
door. The master was wheeled from the library, up the ramp, and
along the hall to the drawing-room at the other end of the house.
There was a tea service waiting, and Lanny met for the first time the
tall, active person whom the newspapers were wont to call the "First
Lady of the Land," and whose picture he had seen so many times.

The First Lady was splendidly dressed in a pale blue panne-velvet
gown, adorned with "diamond clips" in many places. She had the same
delicate blond coloring of eyes and skin which had once caused Lanny
to say of Bernard Shaw that he was the cleanest-looking person he
had ever seen. In her story of her own life she had stated that since
she had not been blessed with a pretty face she had had to cultivate
other gifts. But Lanny thought her opinion of her own face was certainly a mistaken one; she was not only pretty, she was an exquisite
person. Her blue eyes smiled constantly, even when she was occupied
with the tall silver tea service. There was no trace of that gaucherie
in gestures and posture which news-camera men somehow managed to
put into her photographs. Perhaps their employers always chose the
worst!

Eleanor Roosevelt had been her name before her marriage—she
was Franklin's cousin. She had married him and brought up five children, whom her mother-in-law considered she was spoiling. Her political enemies had considered that these children wanted too much
money, and too many divorces; but now the four tall sons were in the
service and doing their painful duties, so that clamor was for the most
part stilled.

The young Eleanor had played tennis, and the mature Eleanor
played politics, and in that game half the country finds fault with
whatever you do and attributes it to the worst motives imaginable.
The conservative half considered that Eleanor gadded about too much,
especially in wartime; they insisted that woman's place was the White
House, and that it was a deplorable thing for a President's wife to be

filling the place up with all sorts of riffraff—movie actors and dancers and labor leaders and even Negro singers. They found it intolerable that she should go flying about the country, making speeches to women's clubs and "radical" conventions and what not; they didn't like the sound of her voice, rather high-pitched and tremulous over the radio, nor anything that she had said over a period of ten years. They insisted that she made too much money, and refused to pay attention to the statement that it all went to charity. In short, they just didn't like her; and the worst of it was, she didn't appear to mind it in the least, but went serenely ahead to manifest her able personality and give pleasure and advice to millions of the plain people who wanted it.

Now here she was, seated behind a tea-table, smiling brightly. She knew that this caller had been in her husband's service without pay, and was going off again on a dangerous mission. She set out to be agreeable to him, and he had no trouble in believing that it was because she really liked him and was interested in what he had to say. She had heard of his escape from Hongkong, and who wouldn't want to hear about that? Lanny, who liked to talk, told about it; then he told about Ching-ling, the widow of Sun Yat-sen, founder of the modern Chinese Republic. She was another gracious lady, born just halfway round the globe, yet her social ideals and political program were in complete harmony with those of the First Lady of the Americans. So powerful are the forces which are making the modern world, and are making it one world, whether or not anybody wants it so.

Lanny told about the cruise from Baltimore on the yacht *Oriole*, which had taken him to the Orient, and how on the night of the Japanese attack on Hongkong it had endeavored to steal out of the harbor. Four months had passed, and the yacht had never been heard from, so it must be presumed to be lost. The President remarked that of the many vessels which had made that attempt, seventeen were missing. Of course some might have been captured. "We may not know until the war is over, for our barbarous enemy pays no attention to the Hague Convention."

Mrs. Roosevelt asked about Reverdy Holdenhurst, owner of the yacht. She had never met him, but had heard of him. He was one of those "economic royalists" whom F.D.R. had pilloried, and who had responded with bitter hatred. "A strange, unhappy man," Lanny said. "He was not equal to the battle of life, and he knew it, and clung to his money as his one form of distinction. I never gave him any hint concerning my attitude to the New Deal. It was enough that he put his money into Budd-Erling stock and enabled my father to expand more rapidly."

"Let him be admitted into heaven on that basis," remarked the President.

Lanny knew how to make himself agreeable, and also when to take his departure. When he arose, Mrs. Roosevelt said: "Tell your wife that when she is settled I shall be happy to call upon her." Nothing could have been kinder, and he said so. As he drove back to New York he reflected upon the subject of how much a woman could do to make or mar the life of a public man. In how many of his crucial decisions had this man been guided by his wife's advice, by the facts she put before him, and the people whom she introduced to him? What would he have been without her by his side? Would he even have survived his illness? Lanny, who had called himself "a feminist" from his boyhood, found confirmation of his creed.

2

Between Love and Duty

LAUREL CRESTON'S friend Agnes Drury had shared Laurel's apartment in the East Sixties, just off Park Avenue. Now Laurel had been around the world and come back with a husband; they could make room for him, but it was crowded. Laurel had said: "I'm afraid he'll be leaving very soon." Her unmarried friend replied: "I am curious to see what a man is like."

When the man returned from his errand up the Hudson, Agnes was in the kitchenette, preparing the evening meal. The new wife came and put herself in her husband's arms. "Lanny," she whispered, "I have been to the doctor."

"And what?"

"He says it has happened."

"Sure?"

"Absolutely."

"Oh, *grand!*" He held her tightly, and she hid her pleasure in his coat. She was a little woman, and the top of her head just about came to his shoulder. He kissed her soft brown hair. "I am tickled to death," he said. And when she asked: "Really? Truly?" he declared: "It will be an adventure for both of us, and make sure that we have to appreciate each other."

He had a twelve-year-old daughter in England, but hadn't seen her for almost a year, and he had the sad belief that she would mean less and less to him as she grew up. She was Irma's daughter, and Lanny was bored with Irma and her friends and everything they said and thought and did. But a child of Laurel Creston's could grow up to be interested in what Lanny himself said and thought and did. He led his subdued bride to the sofa and put his arms about her, whispering delightful nothings to cheer her up and give her courage for woman's long ordeal. He put off saying: "I have to leave in a week," and instead remarked: "I ran into Mrs. Roosevelt, and she offered to call on you."

Laurel was surprised, and objected: "That wouldn't be proper. I ought to call on her. She is the older woman."

"Well, drop her a line at Hyde Park and fix it up the way you think best. She is worth knowing, and some day you may want to write about her."

The wife didn't say: "Where did you meet her, and how?" If Lanny wanted to tell that, he would do so; if he didn't, she had to assume that he was bound by his orders, and she was bound not to "fish." She was rigid about all duties, an ethical person. She didn't even ask: "Have you found out when you are leaving?" Perhaps he wasn't free to let her know that meeting the First Lady and getting his marching orders had any connection with each other. She had married him with the understanding that he was not free to tell her anything about his job.

II

Their next adventure was to be a visit to Newcastle, Connecticut. Lanny said: "How about driving up this evening? It only takes an hour or two."

The answer was: "I am a little tired and I'd rather rest and start fresh in the morning. I had to get some clothes, you know."

"Haven't you a closet full?" he countered.

"How manlike! Don't you know how fashions change in half a

year? And don't you realize how much your own happiness depends upon my managing to please your family?"

"Really, darling, you don't have to worry about that. They will be delighted with you."

"Their delight may be increased if I look the way they think I ought to. For a man forty-two years old, you are still naïve, Lanny. You told me for how long they tried to get you married to an heiress."

"They gave up that hope long ago. I am sure they will be willing to settle for a bluestocking." He chuckled.

"Maybe so, but all the same I'm taking no chances. Whatever you think of them, I'm sure they think of themselves as very grand people."

He chuckled again. "They surely don't think themselves any grander than your Uncle Reverdy thought *himself*. They wanted me to get married, and when they hear that I am 'expecting,' they will welcome you as the vessel of the Lord."

"We will go the first thing in the morning, and I'll have a chance to make friends with your stepmother before I meet your father. One at a time!"

Lanny telephoned to Newcastle and announced this program, and incidentally gave his father the medical tidings. He had announced their safe arrival on the previous evening, as soon as they had stepped off the plane from Newfoundland. Early the next morning Robbie had sent them a car for their use. That was Robbie's way.

Lanny inspected the spring costume which his wife had purchased, a blue frock and hat to match; he had told her that he liked her in blue, and so she had adopted it. She would take along the very grand fur coat which had been presented to her in Moscow, for you couldn't count upon New England weather in early April. Lanny duly praised her taste, and then they went in to the supper which Agnes Drury had got ready—mostly out of cans, according to the custom of apartment dwellers in Manhattan. Agnes was a trained nurse whom Laurel had met in a boarding-house when she had first come to New York; they had teamed up and got along perfectly, because one went out to a job while the other sat at home and pecked at a typewriter. It would be still more convenient later on, for when Laurel needed help, she would become Agnes's job, and Lanny could be sure that his wife was in competent hands.

Only after they were alone in their room did he tell her: "Darling, I have to be leaving for Europe in about a week."

He saw her blanch. She had known it was coming, but that did not spare her the pain. He added quickly: "I am not going into Germany or any enemy-held country. I have positive orders on that. So there won't be much danger."

"Yes, dear," she forced herself to say. "Do your best to take care of yourself, for my sake." She had had fair notice what she was marrying, and what her lot would be. She would never torment him with grief.

"Millions of men are going into danger," he reminded her, "and mine will be of the least."

"I know. I know, Lanny. I have my job, and I'll do it and not allow myself to brood."

"My headquarters will be at Juan-les-Pins. Write me there; but of course nothing of a confidential nature. The Vichy censorship will read everything. Remember, I am an art expert."

"I understand. When do you expect to return?"

"Usually I stay two or three months, depending upon what I run into. I will write to you frequently, and I may be able to drop you a hint by references to paintings I discover. Be on the watch for a double meaning in any names of painters or their subjects." He didn't say: "That is my code."

III

Next morning they set out on their drive, by one of the bridges across the Harlem River and along the boulevard which borders the Sound. The weather favored them, and the fur coat stayed locked in the rumble seat of the car. They drove to what had once been the little town and now was the crowded port of Newcastle, and onto the higher ground where the masters of the community had their homes. Esther was out in the rose garden, waiting for them, and Robbie, busy though he was, came home at lunchtime to meet his oldest son and newest daughter.

They were pleased with Laurel—how could they be otherwise? She was thirty-three, a settled woman who knew what she wanted, and presumably Lanny was it. She was what is technically known as a "lady," and shared his peculiar ideas and interests. She was going to give him a child, and that was what all his parents wanted—the pair in Connecticut and the pair on the French Riviera. The former got their claim in first, inviting Laurel to come and live with them; but Laurel, forewarned, made it plain that the way of life she had established was necessary to her work. In New York she met the editors and publishers and got their advice. She was going to write several articles about what she had seen in China and Russia and then resume work upon a partly completed novel. Pregnancy wasn't going to make any difference in her life, at least not for some time. A lady who knew her own mind!

There was a whole flock of Budds and Budds-by-marriage who had to drop in and satisfy their curiosity; and there had to be a hurriedly got-up reception for all the friends at the country club. The visiting bride had to be driven to see that vast new fabricating plant which was turning out fighter planes, a new model every two or three months, the way things were going in this mad war. For a year or more the Budd-Erling had lagged behind the Spitfire, but now it was ahead, Robbie proudly announced, and marched his daughter-in-law through drafting rooms and "mock-up" rooms where it was being made absolutely certain that never again would American flyers have to fear anything in the skies. There was a new phrase, "jet propulsion," which Robbie barely whispered; he couldn't show any of that because he had hidden it away somewhere in the deserts of the far Southwest.

Laurel had heard about the Budd-Erling Aircraft Corporation, not merely from her husband but from her Uncle Reverdy. Now that he was presumed to be lost, she, as one of his heirs, would become a stockholder—another way of being important among the Budds. She was seated in a sort of little handcar and was run through the immense plant, amid a considerable racket and what looked like confusion but · wasn't. She saw parts of planes coming down from overhead and being welded together; she saw them roll out of doors, taxi under their own power, and take off on test flights. That would be going on all day and all night, while she ate and while she slept and while she finished an anti-Nazi novel. It was part of the immense and horrifying price required to put three dictators out of business; and much as she hated war, she had to reconcile herself to it, and be glad that her new father-in-law had foreseen it for half a century, and had had his own way at least for the past half-dozen years.

She had heard a lot about him, and she now put her shrewd mind to understanding his. He was nearing seventy but refused to make any concession to age. His hair was gray, but his frame was sturdy and unbowed. He was kind and generous to everyone he liked, but he was limited in his interests and set in his opinions, as hard as the concrete of his runways or the steel in the engines of his planes. The world was a place of battle, and his country was going to get on top, and he, the master of Budd-Erling Aircraft, was on top in his country and going to stay there. The way to get along with him was to take those things for granted.

As to Esther Remsen Budd, Lanny's stepmother, the problem was even simpler. Esther, too, was an ethical person, a daughter of the Puritans. The great lady of her town, she took her duties seriously, supported all worthy causes, and would not permit the Republican Party boss to bring to prominence in public life any man who neglected his family or got drunk in public. She quickly decided that this shrewd woman writer was exactly the proper person for her problem stepson, and had a long confidential talk with her, telling about Lanny as she had known him since his youth, and about men in general, and the necessity of managing them. When after a visit of two days the couple set out for New York, the gray-haired woman kissed the brown-haired one and told her that she was a member of the clan and free to call for their help at any time.

IV

Back in the city, Lanny visited the bookstores and found a couple of works on Arab and Moorish art, which he learned was mostly architecture, because the Prophet, seeking to put an end to idol worship, had banned all "images," and the zealots of his faith had interpreted that to include painting. Lanny visited the Public Library and spent a couple of mornings reading diligently and making notes concerning arabesque doorways with carved interlacements, and mosaic floors with designs representing flowers, vines, and geometrical forms made out of pious sentences from the Koran.

Also, there was his friend Zoltan Kertezsi, his associate in art matters for a couple of decades. Zoltan had never met Laurel, nor indeed heard of her; he was astonished when his friend dropped down out of the blue with a wife, and of course he wanted to meet the lady. A lonely old bachelor would stop in at the little apartment now and then, and when he had come to know this woman writer well, he told her a story that he had never told Lanny, the story of his losing the great love of his life. She had been a lady of high degree in Hungary, his native land, and had decided at long last that she did not care to marry a commoner.

This gracious and cultivated art lover, now in his late fifties but still youthful at heart, had been handling the paintings of Beauty's deceased husband, Marcel Detaze, which were stored in a bank vault in Baltimore; he now had accountings to render and suggestions to make.

Also, he could tell Lanny about art in North Africa, French, Spanish, and Moorish, for he had traveled in those regions and had made many acquaintances there. He had long ago got over his surprise that his colleague was able to travel in wartime; he pretended to consider it quite normal, even though he knew that he, Zoltan, could never have got such permissions. A tactful person, he had never questioned Lanny, and would never question Lanny's wife; he would pretend to take it as proper that some persons should enjoy privileges.

Did Lanny's clients have any suspicion concerning his ability to gad about in a severely restricted world? They were all wealthy persons who were accustomed to having their own way. They knew about Budd-Erling and wouldn't be surprised to hear that the son of Budd-Erling enjoyed the confidence of State Department officials. They wouldn't question their art expert, any more than they had questioned their bootlegger in times past, or would question their black-market operators in times soon to come. If somebody brought you what you wanted at a price within reason, you would pay him and take possession, whether it was an old master, an automobile tire, or just a few pounds of butter or cartons of cigarettes.

Lanny didn't have the time for his usual trip to Chicago and points in between. He used the long distance telephone, and had a chat with his plate-glass friends in Pittsburgh and his hardware friends in Cincinnati; with old Mr. Hackabury, the soap man of Reubens, Indiana, and old Mrs. Fotheringay, who filled her Lake Shore mansion with painted babies. He drove out to Tuxedo Park, and discovered that his friend Harlan Winstead was not interested in Arab or Moorish art objects, but thought that a neighbor might be. This Mr. Vernon was invited to lunch; he was building a villa for his favorite daughter, and was charmed by the descriptions Lanny gave of arabesque doorways and mosaic floors with interlacing designs made of Arabic scripts. He suggested that it might be a unique idea to take up such mosaics, carefully numbering each piece on its under side, and restore them as features of a loggia or a patio in an American suburban home.

Lanny pointed out that Algeria was full of ancient Roman ruins, whole cities, and that the Romans also had gone in for mosaics, and without being afraid of either polytheism or nudity. The best of these ruins had been made national property by the French government, but others were on private property and the mosaics might be purchased. Mr. Vernon authorized this well-recommended art expert to make such purchases for him up to a total cost of twenty thousand dollars. He wrote a letter to that effect, which Lanny said would help him in getting a passport from the State Department, though its real purpose was to lull the suspicions of officials in Vichy France and its African possessions. He knew from long experience that there was no baggage so well worth its weight as letters from American millionaires.

V

The President's confidential man, Baker, telephoned to the apartment, and Lanny went to the man's hotel room and got his passport. He made sure that it covered all the places to which he might have to go.

Baker said: "I hope you have better luck than you had with the last ones, Mr. Budd. I can get you passage on a Clipper to Lisbon by way of Puerto Rico and Brazil on Saturday."

Lanny said: "Fine," and that was that.

The time was short. He had to have a conference with Professor Alston. He was ready to fly to Washington for this, but Alston telephoned that he was coming to New York and that Lanny should wait. Meantime there was Jim Stotzlmann, who was F.D.R.'s friend as well as Lanny's. The President had hinted that Jim was another P.A., but had told Lanny not to ask, and Lanny hadn't. This genial fellow, big and yet gentle as a girl, was only a couple of years older than Lanny, but while Lanny had been playing with the fisherboys on the beach at Juan, Jim had been dining with most of the crowned heads of Europe, on board his father's "palatial" yacht—as the newspapers always called it.

In World War I the scion of the Stotzlmann clan had enlisted as a private, and later had become an Army Reserve officer. Now he was a Major, and stationed in New York, busy with mysterious matters having to do with docks and shipping and the prevention of sabotage. They had dinner at Jim's hotel, and Lanny told the story of six months' misadventures. Jim, for his part, told of goings-on in what had become the busiest port in the world. "You can have no idea of the scale on which we are going into this war, Lanny. It fairly takes one's breath away."

"What I want to know about is the junta," Lanny said. That was their name for the group of powerful persons who for the past year or more had been discussing a plan for putting the New Deal out of business by taking physical possession of its principal exponent and keeping him under their control.

"They are still at it," Jim said. "I still can't sleep at night because I can't get the Governor to take it seriously enough."

"I had hoped that since we got into the war their patriotism might have come to the fore."

"Patriotism, heck!" responded the Major. "That gang knows nobody but themselves."

"Do they expect to make a deal with Hitler?"

"They expect to do anything that will keep them from having to fight for Stalin. I'm not free to go into details, Lanny, but that remark was made by Harrison Dengue to a friend of mine barely a week ago. I personally reported it to the Chief, but he just smiled and said: 'Well, his money is fighting, and that's all we care about.'"

"Dengue said he wanted to see me again after I had talked to Hitler and his crowd; but I doubt if I'm ever going into Germany again. This war has been most inconvenient for me." Lanny said it with a smile, and his friend smiled in return; they had met only two or three times, but their points of view were so nearly the same that they could talk in shorthand, as it were.

"Dengue is in Chicago now, and that is one of the headquarters of sedition. I wish you could go out there and make friends with them, Lanny."

"I wish I could, but I have to fly overseas in a couple of days. I turn our great Chief over to your keeping."

"He has promised me to have Hyde Park taken out of the New York Military District and put directly under the care of Washington. That will help, I hope."

"You know, Jim," said Lanny, "the story you told me has haunted me; I doubt if I'll ever get it out of my mind. We've read about how the Roman Republic was overthrown, and so many others in history, but we just can't bring ourselves to realize how easily the same thing might happen in this country. Just imagine that in the next industrial crisis the labor crowd, or what are called the 'radicals,' carried an election, and our big business masters wanted to keep them out; suppose there was an Army cabal, and these men backed it with their money and their newspapers and their radios; suppose they were to seize the newly elected President, hold him incommunicado, and issue orders in his name—what could the rest of us do?"

"That is just what I keep hammering into my friends, Lanny. They all say: 'The people would rise.' But what can the people with shotguns and pitchforks do against modern weapons of war and modern organization? With bombing planes and poison gas a few men could wipe out a whole city; and I know men who are ready to do it—they have said so in plain words."

"I could compile a list of a hundred such," responded Lanny. "It is a danger we shall not be free from so long as capitalism endures; and it is going to die a hard and nasty death."

VI

There was one other man in New York with whom Lanny wanted to have a talk. That was his friend Forrest Quadratt, who had been head of the Nazi propaganda service in America. Forrest knew what was going on, and when he got going he would spill many hints. Lanny telephoned the ex-poet's home, and, as usual, the soft silky voice revealed warm pleasure. "Where on earth have you been all this time?"

"I've been all the way round the world and had a lot of adventures."

"Will you come up to dinner? I'll be alone."

Lanny had been planning to take Laurel and Agnes out to dinner, but duty came before pleasure. He walked uptown and over to Riverside Drive, to the familiar apartment with the study full of books and photographs and other literary trophies. Forrest Quadratt was in his fifties, and had made it his business to meet many of the writers of his time. In his youth he had been a flaming erotic poet, a self-proclaimed genius, and he had become embittered because his word was not taken by the critics. Now he was a self-registered Nazi agent—because the law required this frankness. He had collected large sums from Germany and expended a part of them to pay for a flood of books, pamphlets, and papers. He had written speeches for congressmen to deliver and put into the *Congressional Record*, and then he had them mailed out to the extent of hundreds of thousands of copies free of postal charges.

Lanny told the story of his plane smash-up, his sojourn in the hospital, his yacht trip to the South Seas, and his escape from Hongkong. "I couldn't imagine what had become of you!" exclaimed Quadratt. "So much has been happening in the meantime—the wrecking of all our hopes of peace. Have you heard what has happened to me?"

"I saw no newspapers between Manila and New York, a period of more than four months."

"I have been indicted and convicted, and am under a jail sentence of from eight months to two years."

"Good Lord! What for?"

"They framed me on a preposterous charge. I registered myself as in the employ of German magazines, and they undertook to prove that I was in the employ of the government."

"*Herrgott, noch einmal!* Don't they know that German magazines are government institutions?"

"Of course they know it; but they pretended not to, and so did the jury."

"Well, but you're not in jail!" Lanny looked about him at the elegant apartment.

"I am out on bail, pending an appeal. I have every hope that some court will set aside the conviction. The conduct of the prosecutor was so outrageous that he should be the one to serve the sentence."

"You know how it is in wartime," remarked Lanny sympathetically. "The country goes crazy."

"But this was before Pearl Harbor, Lanny. At any rate, the indictment was. It has been an intensely disagreeable experience."

"I sympathize with you, Forrest; and certainly I hope you get a reversal of the verdict." It was hard for Lanny to put the proper amount of feeling into his tone, for he knew what would have happened to a German citizen in Berlin who had made a fortune by serving American magazines or American government agencies in circulating pro-Allied propaganda throughout the Fatherland. That was the advantage which the ruthless men had over the mild and honorable in this world; and how the balance was to be righted was a problem indeed!

Lanny sat watching the rather small man with the round, smooth-shaven face, the thick spectacles, and the hesitating manner. He saw that the convicted agent was a worried man indeed. He spoke with great rapidity, as if he were afraid he would not be allowed to finish; but Lanny let him pour out a stream of troubles. All his German friends in this country were interned and incommunicado, and all activities had come to a stop. Forrest didn't say what they weren't able to accomplish, but left the son of Budd-Erling to make queries as to his meaning. The Americans who were in sympathy with his ideas were many of them no longer working, because it was so difficult to get money. The unscrupulous F.B.I. agents were dogging everybody's footsteps, trying to get something on them. "I have reason to believe they are going to try to frame something else against us; possibly a sedition charge, which carries a much heavier penalty. They are after Father Coughlin now and seem determined to put him out of business."

In short, the skies over Forrest Quadratt's head looked black. He had failed in everything he had attempted, and his appetite for an excellent dinner was spoiled. The might of the Western world was going to be thrown against the Fatherland, and the only hope the ex-poet could see was in the forthcoming spring offensive against Russia, which might wipe out that nest of vipers soon enough to save Germany from a two-front war. Lanny tried subtly and carefully to find out if there might not be another hope, that of replacing Franklin D. Roosevelt as Commander-in-Chief of the American Armed Forces. Lanny mentioned that he was getting in touch with that powerful personality, Mr. Harrison Dengue, but Forrest didn't take the bait; he wasn't going to discuss the junta, even if he knew anything about it.

Could it possibly have occurred to him that the son of Budd-Erling might have changed his point of view when he discovered himself under the Japanese bombs and shells? Certainly Forrest must have known that Budd-Erling was now turning out a superior type of fighter plane, and he must have been warned that the Federal Bureau of Investigation was employing many sorts of agents and disguises in its secret war on American Nazism. It might be that Berlin had informed him that Lanny had visited Stalin. Lanny waited for some hint on the subject, but none came. He decided at last that he was wasting his evening. He excused himself, went home, and took his two ladies out to a late supper.

VII

Charles T. Alston came up from Washington, and Lanny went to his hotel and took him for a drive in the park, a safe place for a confidential talk. This quiet little gray-haired man was much sought after by reporters, for he had been one of the members of the original "brain trust," away back in the days when a former Assistant Secretary of the Navy was elected Governor of New York State, and had the unprecedented idea of inviting some college professors to join his cabinet and advise in the management of the most populous and wealthy state of the Union. Later Alston had been taken to Washington, where he became a "fixer," charged with settling the wrangles of jealous bureaucrats, and later on of statesmen, generals, and admirals who got into one another's hair.

Earlier in his career this professor of geography had served on the staff of advisers which Woodrow Wilson had taken to the Paris Peace Conference, and there he had become Lanny Budd's first and only employer. Lanny had been nineteen then, and now he was forty-two, but he still addressed Alston as "Professor" and still looked up to him as an authority on all affairs of government and politics. Alston, for his part, still thought of Lanny as the brilliant and fashionable youth who had chattered in French with generals and duchesses, while Alston had painfully studied the language from textbooks and wondered how to find out whether you pronounced the final "s" in Reims, and what was the difference, if any, between the sounds of *dedans* and *des dents*. The geographer from the "sticks" had felt the same secret awe of Lanny that Lanny had felt for him.

First Lanny had to repeat the story of his adventures on the plane trip and in Hongkong and Yenan and Moscow. He had had to tell it to F.D.R., and to Robbie, and Zoltan, and Jim, and the end was not yet. Alston wanted to hear everything that Ching-ling had said, and Mao Tse-tung, and Stalin, and others in the Soviet Union. He asked questions, and incidentally imparted a few secrets. "We have to be sure that what we are sending the Russians actually reaches the front; for we are sustaining grave losses on the route to Murmansk, so great that we may have to discontinue it."

"Of course I didn't see anything with my own eyes," responded the younger man. "I can only tell you what Stalin and the others said. They beg for everything we can spare, and are certain that they will be pushed to the uttermost this summer."

"Did they give any hint of the possibility of having to quit?"

"All the way through China and Siberia and Russia proper, we never heard any word but of resistance to the last gasp. You can count upon that as a gift from Hitler. He is the most hated man that has appeared upon the stage of history for many centuries."

VIII

After Alston was through asking questions, it was Lanny's turn, and he had accumulated quite a list. "Professor," he began, "there is something that has been troubling my mind for nearly half a year. You telephoned me at the hospital in Halifax that you had received the information you wanted from Germany. Did you mean that, or were you just putting my mind at rest?"

"I meant most of it, Lanny. We got some information and expect to get more."

"Are you free to tell me anything about it?"

"The rule still holds, that we never speak the words atomic fission except when it is absolutely necessary. But I can say this: we are ahead of the Germans and expect to keep ahead."

"But you can't be absolutely sure?"

"Nothing can be absolutely sure in matters of scientific research. We know what the signs are at the moment, but nobody can know what some German physicist may have hit upon last night."

"I keep thinking there may still be something I can do about it."

"The Chief was quite positive that he didn't want to send you into Germany again, Lanny."

"He told me that. But I told him about my German contact in Geneva, and he was willing for me to go there."

"It would be foolhardy for us to risk taking *any* German into our confidence in this matter. The outcome of the war might depend upon it, and the whole future of humanity."

"Let me tell you a little about this man. I have known him since before Hitler. He was vouched for by the woman who later became my second wife. I have never told you about her; not even my mother or my father knows about her. She was a devoted Socialist Party member, and her first husband was murdered by the Nazis; she became a worker in the underground, and died in Dachau concentration camp, in spite of my best efforts to save her. The man I am talking about helped me in trying to rescue her; before that he was in Spain and proved his loyalty in the fires of that civil war; he rose to be a *capitán*. That surely ought to be enough evidence of his trustworthiness."

"I grant you that, Lanny. But what can he do now?"

"He had quite an extraordinary contact in Germany, apparently someone in Göring's own headquarters. He was able to give me the date of the invasion of Holland and Belgium, and later that of Norway, and I sent this information to the President. The last time I saw this man, about a year ago, he told me he had lost that contact but hoped to get another. He might have it now."

"That is just where the trouble comes in, Lanny. He may have a new contact that he trusts, and it may turn out to be a Gestapo agent playing with him. We simply cannot take such chances with the atomic bomb."

"I grant you that, Professor. But let us consider whether there might not be some information my man could get without having to know what it is for."

"That would be difficult, for the reason that the information is so highly technical that any scientist would know at once what the man was after and could infer what stage we had reached in our research."

"Let me make a suggestion or two. If we could find out whether the Germans have increased their production of graphite, wouldn't that tell us something?"

"In the first place, the fact that we are using graphite to moderate the speed of neutrons is one of the most priceless of our secrets; and second, German production wouldn't tell us much, because graphite is used for many war purposes and comparatively little of it is needed as a moderator.".

"Well, then, how about heavy water? That, as I understand it, is difficult to produce and not much of it exists."

"That is true. If your man could find out if and where the Germans are making heavy water in large quantities, we should have a number-one bombing target."

"And how about Professor Schilling? Can his name be mentioned?"

"I fear we have to say no to that. Schilling is a nuclear physicist and nothing else, and we know that the Nazis have him at that job. We cannot risk having anybody know that he is on our side."

"If I could find out where a number of such physicists are employed, wouldn't that be important?"

"We already have that information, I believe; but I do not know what use is being made of it. I am only admitted to the fringes of these ultra-secret matters."

"This is true, is it not, that the quantity production of fissionable material would require a large plant; and if my man could find out where such a plant is located, wouldn't that be worth while?"

"I have to admit that that would be a major achievement."

"This is the way it appears to me: the Germans must know that we know the possibility of atom splitting, and they would certainly expect us to try to find out about what they are doing. I don't have to give my man any hint that we are working on the project. Can't I just tell him what has been in the scientific journals prior to the war, and ask if he can find out any more on this subject?"

"I should say there would be no harm in that; but it would be an exceedingly dangerous matter for your man and for his contacts."

"That is up to him. I will tell him the facts, as I have always done, and leave it to him to use his judgment. I suppose the same thing goes for jet propulsion, which Robbie tells me he is working on very secretly; and for rocket projectiles, and so on. The Germans are known to be working on these, and it surely wouldn't be any news to them that we are trying to catch up."

"If your man were able to get us real news about these matters, we'd award him a D.S.M. when the war is over."

"To award him American citizenship might be more to the point," opined Lanny. "We shall see."

IX

They talked about the presidential agent's own job, what information he might get in Vichy territory, and what use was likely to be made of it. Alston said that he agreed with the Chief in thinking that they ought to open a second front across the Channel in the summer of 1942, if only for the sake of its effect upon the Russians. "Even if we could do no more than establish a bridgehead, it would pay us in the long run, however costly. But between you and me, Lanny, I don't think we are going to be able to budge Churchill on this issue. I appreciate him as a propagandist, but he fancies himself also as a military strategist, and I fear he is somewhat vain on the subject. Certainly I have found him hard to argue with; he does all the talking."

"I can imagine it," responded Lanny with a grin. "He was so glad to get his troops off that shore, no doubt the idea of sending them back again gives him nightmares."

"He argues that our American troops are utterly untested, and who can be sure they would stand the punishment they would get from the Panzers and from the overhead strafing?"

"To say nothing of the subs on the way across, Professor. You can be sure that Hitler would throw in everything he has to make good the promises he has fed to his own people. It would be a life and death matter for him."

"I have listened to the arguments of the military men on both sides; there is very little agreement among them. We shift in our discussions from Cherbourg to Dakar, to Casablanca, Algiers, and Tunis. Then Churchill takes us to Salonika and the Vardar valley, and even to his old stamping ground of Gallipoli. Then we come back to Cherbourg. But this much I can tell you quite surely: no information that you bring us and no contacts that you make in Unoccupied France and in North Africa will be wasted. We shall surely be landing there before this war is over, and meantime we have to defend ourselves there, to the extent of keeping Laval out of power and Franco properly worried."

"The Governor seemed to think there was no longer any danger of a German attack upon Gibraltar."

"It would appear that the time for that has passed. Franco's demands were more than Hitler was willing to meet; and now, I think, Franco has been brought to realize that we mean business, and he will continue to hold his precarious seat upon the fence."

"F.D.R. didn't seem very clear in his mind whether I am to be an American patriot or a sympathizer with Fascism in my secret heart. It will hardly be possible to play both roles, at least not for long."

"Nobody can tell you about that, Lanny. You will have to go and find out what changes a year has made, and what your probable sources of information are, and then make your own decision as to which side of the fence to be on. A lot of Frenchmen will be doing the same, I fancy."

"No doubt about that!" agreed the P.A. with a touch of bitterness.

X

Parting time was at hand. On Lanny's last day at home Agnes went off to her work, and thoughtfully arranged to dine with a friend and go to a movie so that Laurel might be alone with her husband. But when they were alone they found that they didn't have much to talk about. Lanny couldn't talk about his work, and neither of them wanted to say how unhappy he or she was. Romeo had told them that "parting is such sweet sorrow," but neither found it true. Their hearts ached, and there was nothing sweet about it.

Lanny felt free to say that he was going to Vichy France, to see what the Pétainists were doing and planning. There was no danger about it—that tottering regime was doing its best to remain friends with America, and besides, they all thought that Lanny was one of them. So there was nothing for a wife to worry about; she would do her work, and Mother Nature would do Mother Nature's work, and by midsummer at the latest Lanny would return and perhaps be able to stay and see her through her confinement. Meantime they mustn't make things hard for each other. Laurel agreed, and when tears stole into her eyes she turned her head away and found an excuse to slip out of the room.

She had used the few days to make a rough draft of an article about what she had seen in "Red China." Lanny read this, and they had a subject to occupy their minds. For the past year or two few Americans had been able to get past the blockade which the Central Government maintained against their Yenan rival, and so this article would be something of a scoop; but its political point of view would work against it, because Laurel had been fascinated by the new life she had seen in that half-barren mountainous land, and editors of big-circulation magazines didn't fancy telling their readers that the outcome of this war might be a socialized world. Nor was it in accord with Allied

propaganda to suggest that supplies being flown to Chungking at
heavy cost were not being used against the Japs but were being saved
for use in a future civil war. Laurel said: "I won't doctor the article.
If the big-circulation editors don't want it, I'll give it to one of the
small-circulation editors." Not so good for the future of a budding
novelist!

As soon as Lanny left she was going to Baltimore to visit her aunt,
Millicent Holdenhurst, and tell the story of the *Oriole* so far as she
knew it. That would be a sad duty, and they talked about what she
would say. Once more they discussed the possibility that the passengers and crew of that yacht might have got off in small boats and be
stranded on some one of the thousands of islands large and small which
pepper the map of that part of the world. It had happened to many
people, and every now and then you read in the papers about some
castaway who had found his way back to civilization. The natives took
care of them and did not eat them—or, at any rate, those who were
eaten did not get reported.

Inevitably that led to the strange experience which had befallen the
newly married couple, flying from Yenan to Ulan-Bator over the
great Gobi Desert. Laurel had fallen into a spontaneous trance, the
only time that had ever happened to her. Or perhaps she had just been
talking in her sleep, who could say? Anyhow, Lanny had heard what
purported to be the voice of Lizbeth Holdenhurst, saying that the
yacht had gone down with all on board. Could you believe that? Certainly you had to think about it, after so many strange psychic experiences had come to you.

XI

Lanny had a desire to try a séance with his wife but had refrained
from suggesting it. She had had a warning of danger in advance of his
last flight overseas, and he was afraid that might happen again and
leave her possessed with fear. Now, on this last evening, she told him
that her curiosity was greater than her fear, and she wanted to try one
more trance. There was nothing he could say to that; if he were to
invent some pretext for objecting, she would know that his fear was
greater than his curiosity.

They shut off the telephone and plugged the doorbell, and Laurel
stretched herself out on the couch and closed her eyes. Lanny sat by
with notebook on his knee and pencil poised in proper psychical-
research fashion. Laurel moaned and sighed several times and then lay

still; and presently there came stealing into the room, from eternity, or God only could say where, a voice—what the researchers have labeled a "control." The most urbane and agreeable of controls imaginable was the lately deceased Otto Hermann Kahn, former senior partner of the international banking firm of Kuhn, Loeb and Company. Why he had picked Laurel Creston for his manifestations he did not say, and probably did not know; he professed to be skeptical about the whole affair. A weird joke upon himself as well as upon them!

"Well, well, here we are again!" chuckled the voice. "The last time was Hengyang, if I remember correctly. How people do get about nowadays! It is all I can do to keep up with you."

"Tell us how you do it," countered Lanny, for when you are dealing with the "spirits" you have to enter into the spirit of their occasion.

"I would tell you if I could;" was the reply. "But I am as much at a loss as yourself. Will you pardon me if I refuse to believe any of this?"

"Of course. I don't believe it either. But here we are, Mr. Kahn."

"Do call me Otto," suggested the voice. "Surely we do not have to stand on formalities at this late date."

"With pleasure, Otto. But you will understand that I think of you as being older than myself."

"You will catch up in due course, and you will discover that you are neither so wise nor so important as you appear to your fellow men."

So they bantered, as they would have done if they had met in the drawing-room of that opera *diva* who had been Otto's dear friend in the happy days when it had been the custom for international bankers to take the good the gods provided them. Lanny listened with one half his mind, while with the other half he thought: Could this really be Otto Kahn, or was it just the subconscious mind of Laurel Creston at play, or possibly a mingling of Laurel's with Lanny's and perhaps others? Laurel was a novelist, and her mind was perfectly capable of making up light drawing-room conversation; if you dived into her subconscious mind, her memory mind, her racial mind, who could guess what masses of material might be hidden there, and what connections it might have with other mindstuff, either living or supposed to have "passed on"?

Presently the voice remarked: "There is an old man here whom I used to know well and who says he used to know you. Do you remember Zaharoff?"

"Oh, very well indeed. How are you, Sir Basil? My very best wishes!"

"He says he cannot summon the energy to speak to you directly.

He is worried about his money; he always thought too much of it and didn't get any fun out of it, as I learned to do. He breaks in to say it is somebody else's money, and he wants it paid."

"Yes, I know all about it, Otto. You will have to explain to him that the international banking system has not yet been extended to the spirit world. Perhaps you and he can work up something of the sort. Let me suggest another partner, a friend who has just come into your world, an active capitalist with whom you used to do business. That is Reverdy Johnson Holdenhurst. Have you seen anything of him?"

"I haven't, but I remember him well and will inquire for him. However, I am not interested in money any more. I have musical and artistic friends who have come over, and they are much better company, now that they are not always looking for subsidies or financial aid from me. You know how it was. I used to be an 'angel.' And now I am a ghost! How odd!"

"Tell me about yourself, Otto. You will understand, I am sure, how curious we are about the future world, and how hard we find it to understand."

"What you will find hardest to understand is that I don't understand it either. One moment—here is an old lady who asks to give you a message. Her name is Marjorie."

"Oh, yes. She was my wife's grandmother."

"She still is, she wishes to inform you. She wants you to know that she is better pleased with your conduct of late. It is nice indeed that one gets along with one's grandmother-in-law. I congratulate you."

"I have no fewer than eight grandmothers in the spirit world. You see, I have been married three times. Oddly enough, I never met a single one of those ladies and cannot even recall their names. If you meet any of them, give them my regards and tell them that I am a tireless experimenter with psychic matters and should be happy if they would present themselves and give me an opportunity to exchange information."

This was in the modern drawing-room line of conversation, as anyone should perceive; but apparently it gave offense, for Lanny suddenly heard a severe old lady's voice: "Young man, you are being flippant!" and then silence. Lanny sat wondering: Was that Marjorie's voice, or was it by chance that of Robbie's mother, or Beauty's mother, or one of the grandmothers of Irma, or of Trudi in Germany? As the silence continued, he wondered what had become of Otto Kahn; had Marjorie by chance hit him over the head with a lump of ectoplasm? Not a sound, until Laurel began to moan and sigh, and presently she came out of her trance and opened her eyes and inquired: "Well, what happened?"

Lanny read her his notes and they had some good laughs; they could both take comfort because there had been no prophecies of doom or destruction. So it would be just an ordinary plane trip, and a visit to Lanny's mother on the Riviera, and some chats with French politicians, generals, capitalists, and other "V.I.P.'s"—very important persons, as the Army was calling them. Then Lanny would fly back again, not precisely with the wings of a dove, but he would come to his beloved and be at rest. So he told himself, and her.

In the morning came a girl from Robbie's office who would ride in the rumble seat of the car while Lanny drove with his wife to the airport. She would drive Laurel back to the apartment and then take the car to Newcastle. Laurel exchanged a last embrace with her husband, and stood on the pier at the great airport and watched the gray-painted plane glide out into the Sound and lift itself into the air. She told herself that everything was all right, it was one more trip, like thousands and tens of thousands of others. She held back her tears and conversed politely with the girl. But when she got back to the apartment and was alone, she wept copiously into the pillow which bore the impress of Lanny's head.

BOOK TWO

Now Is the Winter of Our Discontent

3

And Only Man Is Vile

I

P.A. 103 had been placed in the care of "Pan-Am," with his expenses mysteriously paid. He was not being routed by way of Bermuda because he was in the black books of the British government, which had become suspicious of his intimacy with Rudolf Hess and other leading Nazis. Lanny's route was via San Juan in Puerto Rico, and thence to the port of Belém in Brazil; he would cross the ocean to a place called Bolamo in Portuguese West Africa, and from there go on to Lisbon. It wasn't as roundabout as it looked on the maps, and anyhow, distances aren't so important when you rise eight thousand feet into the air and there are no enemy planes to bother you.

He was traveling in a million-dollar contrivance, one of mankind's most surprising achievements. He was one of thirty-three passengers who were provided with every comfort and were looked after by nine young men and one young woman, all carefully trained and clad in natty blue uniforms. Each passenger had an upholstered seat, which at night was made into a bed. There was a buffet where you might help yourself to a variety of tasty foods; there were magazines to read, and a push button which would bring you the services of the good-looking young stewardess. The cabin was soundproof, so you might chat with your fellow passengers, or play cards, checkers, or dominoes. If you were restless you might stroll in the long corridor, and sometimes members of the crew would come down into the cabin and let you ask them foolish questions.

When you travel on land planes you don't see much of the places where you alight; you see only the airport, and each is much like the previous one. But on a seaplane you have a good look at harbors and their shipping, and the vast improvements being made in wartime. If the weather is at all rough, it may take a while to bring the rather fragile machine up to the dock; if the reports from the next station happen to be unfavorable, you may have a wait of a day or two and have time to stroll around. So Lanny learned about parts of the earth which he had never seen before; and while up in the air he diligently acquired information about Moorish art and architecture in their period of greatest flowering. He was genuinely interested, so business and pleasure were one and the same.

The title of the book Lanny was reading attracted the attention of a well-groomed young gentleman who gave his name as Faulkner and said he was an instructor in archeology at the University of Chicago. He was on his way to Volubilis, to investigate new excavations which had recently been made there. Lanny doubted it from the first moment and guessed that he was working on "Operation Gymnast," perhaps under the orders of "Wild Bill" Donovan. But a P.A. asked no questions, and they chatted about the traces of Carthaginian ruins which are to be found in North Africa. Possibly Dr. Faulkner was as good in guessing about Lanny as Lanny about him; but he, too, kept away from dangerous subjects. When they parted in Lisbon, Lanny said: "My business may bring me to Volubilis before long, and if so, we'll meet again." And they did.

II

The traveler had been told to report to the consulate in Lisbon, where arrangements were made for his plane passage, first to Madrid and from there to Vichy. He had to wait a couple of days, and this gave him time to observe what another year of neutrality had done to the spy center of Western Europe. The dictator who ruled Portugal was taking no chances, especially since the vast indefinite power of America had been thrown into the scales. The former college professor saw to it that his newspapers published an equal amount of Axis and Allied news, side by side, and he allowed all parties to spend their money in his capital, provided they did not call names or engage in fisticuffs. British and American and German and Italian planes came in at the same airport, and their flyers drank at the same bars, but without speaking. Refugees of all nations and all creeds ate in the cafés while their money lasted, and when it was gone they tried to find someone to take pity on them. Wages were fifty cents a day.

Not a happy place, not a beautiful place, but one that was useful to a great many people. Lanny avoided the spies and played his own game, visiting the art museum and making inquiries as to private collections and old masters that might be on the market. As an art expert he was no pretender; he knew what to look at, and what prices should be; if he found anything good he might cable, and meantime he could be sure that careful note was being made of his activities and that word concerning them would go to Paris and Madrid and Vichy, London and Berlin and Rome. Dossiers would be compiled, and wherever somebody might wish to make use of him, his hobbies and his weaknesses would be known, and a list of his family connections and friends.

Then to the great city of Madrid, which in Lanny Budd's view was surely the most unhappy place in all Europe. Here had been committed the first wholesale murder of the modern age; the murder of a nation, of a free people and their hopes. Lanny had been here several times. He had seen the beginning and the progress of this crime, and his soul ached with longing to see the end of it. In the best hotel in the city, where he spent the night, the hot-water spigot ran cold and the water was stained with rust. In the elaborately gilded dining-room the meal cost twenty-five dollars and was none too good, but the band played American jazz and the ladies were loaded with diamonds and pearls and the men with gold lace and jeweled decorations. The food choked Lanny, because he knew that in the back alleys of this phony capital the poor were dropping dead from malnutrition, and millions of the enemies of the regime were in prisons and concentration camps. More than three years had passed since the ending of the civil war, but the idea of amnesty was unknown to Franco, and wholesale shootings went on in the prison courtyards night after night. Soldiers were everywhere, and a surplus of swaggering officers and strutting armed Falangists, the Party gangsters.

Lanny knew art collectors here, and high-up personalities whom it was his duty to call upon. General Aguilar would receive him even though his country was now at war with the General's dear friends and patrons, Herr Hitler and Signor Mussolini. Over the usual *copitas de manzanilla* the white-whiskered old *conquistador* told Lanny about a very beautiful Madonna and Child by Murillo, which a friend of his might be willing to part with; incidentally the General did his best to persuade Lanny to part with information about what America was planning to do in aid of the Bolsheviks and against the defenders of the Faith. A son of Budd-Erling Aircraft couldn't pretend to be ignorant on the subject, so Lanny gave figures—slyly exaggerated—as to the output of his father's plant. He added that he was ashamed of these activities and had done everything in his power to persuade his father to reject the filthy lucre which the fanatical Roosevelt was pouring into his lap.

"What does that *Presidente* of yours think he can do?" demanded
the General. "Does not a man have to be truly mad to imagine that he
can conquer the whole continent of Europe? Even Napoleon couldn't
do it from France, and Roosevelt is three thousand miles across the
sea!"

III

The plane which took the traveler to the small capital of Unoccupied France was in no way up to American standards of comfort, but
it flew, and it set him down safely on the broad plain of the Allier
River. Springtime was in full flood and the country was so beautiful
that its inhabitants were a shame, or so Lanny thought. Into this small
watering place and summer resort a good part of the *haute bourgeoisie*
of Paris and other cities of northern and northwestern France had
been driven by bombing and terror. Here they pawned their jewels
and furs and lived the same wasteful lives that had brought their country to ruin. Food was supposed to be rationed, but the black market
ruled, and a corrupt and enfeebled government was powerless against
it. The Germans left enough food for those who could buy it, for
they wanted the help of that same *haute bourgeoisie*.

Lanny found lodgings, not without difficulty, and surely not without price. He did not ask official favors, but set to work at his private
business of exchanging American dollars for French works of art. He
had established contacts on two previous visits and knew where to go;
he could be certain that his arrival would be noted and that politicians
and officials would seek him out. They might guess that he was there
for ulterior purposes, but they couldn't prove it and would treat him
with French courtesy. Wonderful is that power called "social position"; the elegance, the aloofness, the assurance that come with the
possession of wealth—and not crude wealth, but wealth that your family and your friends and your class have possessed for generations, so
that it is like the air you breathe and do not have to think about.

From the newspapers of Vichy, Lanny gathered that he had arrived
in the midst of great events. Pierre Laval had once more become head
of the government; the aged Marshal Pétain had been reconciled with
him again, something Pétain had vowed, a little more than a year ago,
he would never do. Lanny knew enough about this puppet world to be
sure that the political pot must be bubbling furiously; the wretched
newspapers and radio of Vichy wouldn't tell him about the real events,
but he was sure to find out soon.

Sitting in one of the little iron chairs at a round iron table of one of

the sidewalk cafés, sipping a poor imitation of coffee, Lanny heard his
name pronounced in eager tones, and turned to see M. Jacques Benoist-
Méchin, journalist-snob and little brother to the rich. He had risen by
eager subservience to the Nazis, and was named in the papers as a member of Laval's new cabinet. Lanny had seen a good deal of him on
previous visits, and now was prepared to have him demonstrate that
success had not turned his head and that he still remembered old
friends. *"Est-ce bien vous, M. Budd!* What brings you to town?"

They had a chat; brief, for the new minister had pressing duties, but
to the point. He was in a position to speak with authority. He declared
that Herr Hitler had established a New Order for the tormented old
Continent, and it was nothing short of imbecility to fail in recognizing
that fact. France's only future lay in loyal collaboration, and men who
persisted in resisting this course were to be treated like poisonous ser-
pents. *"Écrasons l'infâme!"* exclaimed the cultivated M. Jacques. He
was tall, slightly stooped, wore spectacles, and smoked a pipe; his manners were airy and elegant in the extreme.

Lanny assented promptly. He said he was heartsick over the part
which his country was playing in this situation; and that he had come
back to France, where he had lived most of his life, because he could
no longer stand the atmosphere of violence and fanaticism which he
found in his own America. Lanny rather guessed that this wretched
careerist might not believe what he said, any more than Lanny believed
what the careerist said; yet he put on a tone of ardent friendship—such
a pleasure to see you again; won't you come to my soiree and meet
some of my friends? So men and women lived in this dog-eat-dog
world.

Lanny knew that Benoist-Méchin was one of Darlan's men, and it
was Lanny's desire to see the Admiral, but without seeking the meeting. He asked after the great man's health, and Benoist-Méchin said he
was sound as a nut. "I notice that he is not in the new cabinet," Lanny
ventured. And the other replied: "He did not wish to be. He remains
commander of all the land, sea, and air forces, and retains his title as
heir apparent to the Maréchal. He has always preferred to be the
military man and to leave the world of intrigue to the politicians."

Lanny would have liked to add: "To you!" but he doubted the
journalist's sense of humor.

IV

The visitor could feel quite certain that an intriguing politician would
not fail to inform his powerful military patron that the son of Budd-

Erling was in town, loaded with information concerning affairs in Yankeeland. There came to Lanny's lodgings a messenger with a note from the Admiral, very cordially inviting him to call, and that, of course, was equivalent to a royal command. Lanny strolled through the pleasant sunshine to the Hotel Belgique, where the Ministry of Marine was quartered—all the summer hotels had been turned into government offices, and officials had their headquarters in bedrooms and filed important documents in stacks on the beds. But of course the Commander-in-Chief of the Armed Forces of France had rooms in accordance with his dignity, and his visitor was ensconced in a comfortable chair beside a large flat-topped desk.

Jean Louis Xavier François Darlan was his name, and he came from Brittany, which is a Catholic and Royalist corner of France. He had hated the Republic which he had sworn to protect, and which among his friends he had referred to as *la salope*, the slut. As a loyal Frenchman he had hated the Germans also; but now that they had won, they represented law and order for Europe, so it had not been too difficult for the Admiral to transfer his loyalty to the new masters and his hatred to the British, who had treacherously attacked and in part destroyed his Fleet in an action which the British called Oran and the French Mers-el-Kébir. Darlan would say that his policy was for the protection of France, and France alone; that was what Pétain tirelessly repeated in his radio talks. But when you spoke with them privately you would discover that they did not love France so much as they hated and feared the Soviet Union and the collectivist ideas which were spreading over Europe. It was a continuation of the political point of view which Lanny had heard expressed in a hundred French drawing-rooms prior to the outbreak of the war: "Better Hitler than Blum."

Now this policy was working itself out; Hitler was saving France from the Bolsheviks, and Frenchmen who didn't like it were being thrown into concentration camps or shot at once. When an act of sabotage was committed, the Nazis would seize twenty or fifty perfectly innocent Frenchmen who had the misfortune to live in the neighborhood. A week after Pierre Laval took power, thirty such "hostages" were executed by a firing squad at Rouen, and the very next day twenty more were shot at St. Nazaire. A government of Frenchmen had to stand this, and even defend it! No wonder the land was a seething caldron of hate! An American art expert who had dropped down out of the skies had to watch every step and guard every word.

He told the Admiral that he, Lanny Budd, was a man of peace, and

therefore hated and feared the Red terrorists and their dupes who
were making America a land impossible to live in; he was returning to
his mother's home in France because he believed in the New Order
and wished to live under it. He was going to disregard the request
which the American State Department had just issued that American
nationals in France return to their native land at once; he was confident
that his mother, too, would pay no attention to this request. While he
was saying this, Lanny was wondering, with cold chills running over
him: Does Darlan know that I have been to Russia and talked with
Stalin? If this should be brought up, Lanny had his story ready—that
he had promised his friend Rudolf Hess that he would try to use his
father's influence to get into the Red Empire and find out what he
could about conditions there and the intentions and plans of its masters. Hess was one man with whom Darlan would be unable to check!

But no such question was asked. The fact that Lanny's mother had
lived for more than forty years in France, and that Darlan had met her
some twenty years ago and remembered her well, made it seem natural
that she and her son should love France; also, the idea of a "parlor
Pink" was less familiar to a Frenchman than to an American. The pipe-
smoking Admiral listened while this American told him of the rage
against Roosevelt's policies which was seething in the hearts of a great
number of Americans, and of the possibility that some of them might
take drastic action to draw their country out of the mess before it was
too late. When the Admiral asked if M. Budd had any idea where the
Americans were planning to attack, Lanny tried no evasions, but answered quite truthfully that he had heard on good authority that the
American military leaders were in a state of confusion, and that their
discussions ranged all the way from the English Channel to Dakar and
from there to the Vardar valley in Greece. The Frenchman said that
was in accordance with his own information, and this, naturally, raised
the value of Lanny's stock.

Darlan was a man of medium height, solidly built, smooth-shaven,
alert, and with bright blue eyes. When his pipe was not in his mouth
it was in his hand or on his desk. People described him as having a
"poker face," but perhaps that was only when he was negotiating with
opponents; certainly Lanny had never found it so in their social relations. The host brought out a bottle of his favorite Pernod Fils brandy,
and when he had had a couple of swigs his eyes lighted up with the
fires of *la gloire,* and he said just what Benoist-Méchin had said, that
France was going to have its own kind of New Deal, *la Nouvelle
Ordre,* and from now on traitors and the dupes of traitors were going

to have a hard time of it. This referred especially to the puppet government which the British had set up in London under that archtraitor, Charles de Gaulle. "Seadogs" are supposed to have their own special brand of profanity, and Darlan produced it both in French and English when he named this abhorred personality.

"You hear fools discussing what is going to be done with the French Fleet, M. Budd," pronounced Admiral Darlan. "Well, you may tell them for me, its master, that the French Fleet is going to defend the honor and the glory of France. It is not going to be surrendered, and it is not going to run away, and it is not going to be scuttled. To the last vessel and the last man, it is going to fight whatever enemies may dare to interfere with it."

And there was something for "Traveler" to put into a report, marked "Personal for the President"!

V

Having been accepted as a friend of the great Darlan, the American visitor was *persona grata* to the busy politicians and pullers of wires such as Pierre Pucheu and Fernand de Brinon and Paul Marion and Joseph Barthélemy—collaborators all, who had cast their lot with the Nazis and had risen to power and importance in their service. Now they were basking in the sunlight of success, but at the same time a chill of doubt was shrinking their hearts. When they had taken the gamble of making friends with Hitler, they had assumed that Britain was done for and must soon quit; but Britain had refused to quit, and now, nearly two years later, had the help of the great new power overseas. What was that going to mean? The collaborators listened gladly to an American who told what they wanted to hear, that it wouldn't be long before the American people awakened to the fact that in trying to oppose Herr Hitler they were merely helping Comrade Stalin.

In return for the pleasure of hearing such words, these gentlemen invited Lanny to their homes and introduced him to their ladies. M. de Brinon, a Secretary of State to the Premier, had a charming *amie* whom he had put on the public payroll with the title of "Chief of the Private Secretariat." In her salon Lanny listened to a buzz of gossip that was like the sound of a large hive of bees at swarming time. France had been deprived of most of her wealth and power, but it appeared that the more her resources were reduced, the more furiously her public men fought over what was left. M. Leroy-Ladurie, member of the new cabinet, told the visiting stranger his grave doubt as to the capacities of M. Pucheu, a fellow member, and M. Pucheu, without being informed of this, murmured to Lanny some of the charges which in past times had been made against the character of M. Leroy-Ladurie. M. Benoist-Méchin abhorred M. de Brinon, a rival journalist risen by treachery to a post equal to his own; and so it went. Lanny came away from this evening affair comparing the company to a flock of buzzards he had observed while on a motor trip through the American Far West, squabbling over the carcass of a donkey which had perished in the desert.

However, this state of affairs was convenient for a secret agent, who had no trouble in getting the information he had come for. He heard from the lips of Fernand de Brinon himself the story of how that worthy had brought about the restoration of Pierre Laval. The Nazi governor of Paris was Otto Abetz, red-headed German intellectual who had a French wife as well as a French mistress, and who made a specialty of posing as a friend of Latin culture. Lanny had known him well in the old days when Abetz had lectured in Paris to the elegant, fashionable ladies on how France and Germany must unite to save Europe from Bolshevism. *"Le Couple France-Allemand"* was the slogan. Now this dear friend of Marianne had fallen into disfavor with the Gestapo and the Schutzstaffel, because France wasn't contributing her fair share to the defense of Germany. Herr Hitler was demanding more food, more manufactured goods, more French workers for the factories of Germany, more fighters for his Anti-Bolshevik Legion. The good and kind Herr Abetz was about to be replaced by some such man as Jacques Doriot, one-time Communist agitator who had turned against his gang and was now the most ruthless of Fascist bullies. And instead of the noble-minded old Maréchal, Vichy would have a *Gauleiter* such as now was ruling Poland.

It had been M. de Brinon's duty to bring this information to the old Maréchal and to persuade him to restore Laval to power. It had taken much running back and forth of collaborators between Paris and Vichy, but at last the victory had been won, and the patriotic gentlemen who had saved *la patrie* for a second time were now reaping their rewards.

They were going to make a thorough job of the "coupling" this time. There would be no more nonsense of trying to serve two masters, no more provocation to those upon whom the future of France depended. The French workers who were so desperately needed in the German factories would be forced there by shutting down great numbers of factories at home; and to keep them in order meantime, there would be a new police force, special troops trained by the Germans, who had learned the job with their own SA and SS.

All this Lanny learned from Benoist-Méchin, another Secretary of State to the Premier, whom he invited to lunch and provided with a bottle of the best wine to be found in the town. This high cabinet member revealed that he was going to be entrusted with the presidency of a committee to organize the "Tricolor Legion" and put down once for all the traitorous movements which the puppet De Gaulle was seeking to spread throughout France. The nucleus of the new body was to be the already-existing "Anti-Bolshevik Legion" organized by Jacques Doriot and Eugène Deloncle. "Believe me," said Benoist-Méchin, "these are fighting men, and they mean business."

"I know, I met Deloncle years ago," replied Lanny, "at the home of my old friend Denis de Bruyne."

"Oh, you know De Bruyne?" inquired the cabinet minister. And when Lanny replied that the family were among his oldest friends, the other said: "Then you know Charlot, too."

"He is practically my godson. I have lost track of him since the armistice."

"He is in Vichy now; a *capitaine*, and one of my helpers in the organizing of the new Legion."

"That is indeed pleasant news for me, M. Benoist-Méchin. The last I had heard of Charlot, he was reported captured by the Germans."

"They released him, as they have done many others for whom we were able to vouch."

"I have known him since he was a little chap," Lanny explained. "His mother was one of my dearest friends. It is hard for me to realize that four or five years have passed since I was trying to save him from the French police, when he and his father and brother were charged with taking part in the activities of the Cagoule."

"Thank God those dreadful days have passed!" exclaimed the new minister. "France has found her soul again!"

VI

Lanny lost no time in getting into touch with Charlot. They embraced and kissed each other in French fashion, and it wasn't altogether hypocrisy on the secret agent's part. A strange duality and duel in the human heart; Lanny loathed everything that Charlot believed; he wanted to see it exterminated from the earth; he wanted to see the advocates of it killed, so long as they were bearing arms in its defense,

and here was Charlot, wearing one of its uniforms! Yet, he was Marie
de Bruyne's son, and Marie had been the first woman Lanny had loved
with all his soul. On her deathbed she had committed her two boys to
the joint care of Lanny and her husband—a curious scene, possible
only in predominantly Catholic countries.

Lanny still thought of Charlot as the boy he had first met in the
lovely garden of the Château de Bruyne; a boy well brought up, so
polite that it would have seemed odd to an American, but not to
Lanny; a boy studious yet full of fun, gentle, affectionate, and adoring
Lanny Budd as a model of what a gentleman ought to be. Charlot had
been taught all those things which a member of the "two hundred
families" should believe, and if Lanny had tried to teach him otherwise
he might have broken up the home, which he had no right to do. He
had felt obliged to let those boys work out their own destiny, and the
result had been that Charlot, ardent and impetuous, had become one of
the young French aristocrats who were determined to overthrow *la
salope*. His father had helped to finance the organizing of the reactionary secret society called the Cagoule, and in the fighting which
had taken place in the streets of Paris some years ago Charlot had got
a slash across the cheek and still bore the honorable scar.

It was hard to realize that he was thirty-five years of age. He still
looked young, and his step was springy, his expression intense. He
hadn't had to fight the Germans, having been stationed in Alsace,
where the armies had been surrounded and immobilized until the
armistice. "They treated us officers reasonably well," he said. "And of
course it didn't take *le père* very long to make them realize that I had
been working for Franco-German understanding from a long way
back."

"How is your father?" Lanny asked. The answer was: "Physically
as well as you could expect for a man over eighty; but he is in a situation that is painful to talk about—" Charlot stopped and hesitated; he
saw a look of concern on his old friend's face and added: "You have a
better right to know than anybody else, Lanny. He has fallen into the
hands of an unscrupulous woman who is plundering him unmerci-
fully."

"That is truly sad, Charlot. He has had a weakness that way most of
his life. It caused your mother great unhappiness."

"I have known about that for a long time. It seems to grow on some
men with age. I suppose it is nature's way of punishing them. Anyhow, there is nothing I can do, for he will not let me talk to him about
it. Perhaps if you could go to Paris you might have better success."

That led to the subject of Lanny's attitude to the unhappy world situation. "A dreadful thing, Lanny, that your country should have got into the war on the side of Bolshevism. Do tell me that you have not gone over to that greatest of enemies."

"You know my attitude, Charlot, and I cannot change. I am a man of peace and do not take part in any wars. I am here looking for paintings worthy to go into a great American collection."

"I am so glad to hear that, Lanny. I could not bear to think of you as an enemy. But if your country helps the Bolsheviks to take all Europe, what will become of the art of painting?"

"I hope that we shall have enough specimens safe in America, where the Bolsheviks cannot get at them. So the art can be revived."

VII

The *capitaine* talked for a while about his important assignment, the Tricolor Legion. Lanny perceived that Pierre Laval was planning the same thing in Vichy France that Hitler had done in Germany, the organizing of a private army, a military force of his Party, to replace the army of his country and make permanent his personal grip on power. It was to be a complete outfit, including a youth movement, with banners and slogans and songs. The grown men would have machine guns and hand grenades and rubber truncheons with which to beat their prisoners in the barracks and jails. Charlot's eyes lighted up with fanatical fervor as he told about it; at last they were going to put down the labor unions and their revolutionary propaganda, and make sure that the traditional France would survive and dominate Western Europe. Lanny found the German Nazis strange and terrible people, but he found even more fantastic these Fascists of the Spanish and French Catholic pattern, who were building this machinery of repression in the name of Jesus Christ.

Of course he wouldn't give a hint of all that. He would be warmhearted and sympathetic, as he had always been with the De Bruyne family. He asked about Charlot's older brother, Denis, *fils*, and here was another family tragedy difficult for the younger to talk about. Lanny had known for some time that Denis did not put the same trust in the Germans as his brother did; Denis had thought it his duty to defend his country against the invader. He had fought and been wounded, and had escaped to the south, hoping that France would go on fighting in North Africa. Said Charlot with grief in his voice: "Lanny, I am afraid he has fallen under the spell of the Gaullists. The last I heard of him, he was in Algiers. I wrote, pleading with him, but have not had any reply."

"It is something that happens in civil wars, Charlot." Lanny knew that, as a traditionalist, the *capitaine* would be impressed by precedents. "I know how in the American Civil War brothers argued with each other; some went north and some went south, and more than once it happened that they met on the battlefield."

"I know, Lanny, but think of the disgrace of this! After the wanton attack which the British made upon our unprepared and unresisting Fleet! Now they have set up this wretched puppet, a man who was a mere major general, and yet presumes to constitute himself the government of France!"

"I understand how you feel, Charlot. Let me tell you that I am hoping to go to North Africa. I have an assignment from a client who is collecting Moorish art. If I do, I will make an effort to find Denis and see if I can do anything to influence him."

"Oh, please do!" exclaimed the younger brother. "I cannot talk to him, but he has such respect for your judgment! It is not too late. He might come back here and see what we are doing. I can arrange for him to meet the Maréchal and hear from his Commander-in-Chief personally where his duty lies."

"I'll let you hear from me without fail," Lanny promised.

VIII

The visitor didn't make an attempt to see the old marshal himself. He knew that pathetic figure only too well, and everything that he could and would say. Nothing useful, nothing new, for at the age of eighty-five he did nothing but repeat what he had been saying all his life. If you disagreed with him he would become greatly excited and his attendants would interrupt to protect him; if you just listened, he would pause, and his head would begin to nod and he would fall into a doze. Now he had surrendered all real power to the evil Laval, and would serve as a figurehead to make the masses of the French people, who adored him as the hero of Verdun, believe that *la patrie* was in the hands of an all-wise and all-benevolent father, a deputy of God.

What Lanny wanted to do was to make his report and move on from this health resort before it became unhealthy for him; before his visits attracted too much attention from the Gestapo and caused them to look up his recent doings. But just as he was making inquiries about travel accommodations to the south, he ran into Count René de Chambrun, descendant of the Marquis de Lafayette and husband of Pierre Laval's only daughter. He was sitting in one of those iron chairs in front of a café, an agile little man who always made Lanny think of a jockey. He was a lawyer and a tireless errand boy for his great *beau-père*.

Now he said: "By the way, M. Budd, I mentioned your presence in town to the Premier, 'and he expressed the hope that he might see you before you depart."

That, of course, was an honor, and Lanny responded: "I know how busy he must be, and feared that I might be breaking in on important matters of state."

"He always finds time for his old friends, M. Budd, and especially those who bring news from abroad."

Next morning Lanny received a telegram requesting him to call the Premier's secretary, and when he did so he was invited to be on hand at the end of the working day, to be taken out to Chateldon for the night. He accepted with pleasure. Sitting in the well-cushioned seat of a custom-built Daimler and speeding over the Allier plain toward the mountains, he listened while Pierre Laval poured out his indignation against Franklin D. Roosevelt, Cordell Hull, and Sumner Welles, be-cause of the extreme discourtesy with which these gentlemen had re-ceived the news of the change in the Vichy government. Really, it was as if Laval thought his visitor had had something to do with it, or could do something about it. Lanny broke in, laughing: "Écoutez, cher *Maître*, you must understand that these statesmen are at the opposite pole of thinking from myself. If I could have my way, they would be bounced out on their behinds. Since I cannot do that, I have come back to live in my fosterland, my godmotherland, if you like, the place where I used to be happy and hope some day to be again."

"Yes, yes, I understand, M. Budd. I just need somebody to tell my troubles to. It is incomprehensible to me why those Americans should feel such bitterness toward myself, and should persist in a policy which can help nobody but the Red dictator."

"I can only guess at the minds of the commercial gentlemen who control America's policy. My father is one of them, and even him I cannot understand. It appears that they fear the rivalry of Germany, and the system of government control of foreign trade."

"But it was the Russians who devised that system and taught it to the Germans. And surely the trade rivalry of Britain is a greater men-ace than that of Germany!"

"Big businessmen do not see very far ahead as a rule. Their motto is, one at a time. I suppose that Russia will be next, and then Britain—who can guess?"

So a smooth-talking agent soothed his victim, and presently the new Premier was telling the wonderful plans he had for the restoration of all France—of course in loyal collaboration with the Germans, for that was the cornerstone of policy. "I desire a German victory," declared Pierre Laval. "Indeed, I consider that a German victory has been achieved, and that to reverse it would involve the total destruction of Europe."

Accordingly, he went on to declare, the government of French North Africa was furnishing food to the army of General Rommel in Italian North Africa and intended to go on doing so regardless of anything that America might say or do. Accordingly, the government had worked out elaborate plans for making the French workers want to go to Germany, and for sending them whether they wanted to or not. Pierre Laval clenched his hairy fists and used the language of a butcher's son in expressing his hatred of the men who were secretly trying to thwart this policy and his determination to stamp their faces into their own excrement.

IX

Just as Lanny addressed Roosevelt as "Governor" because he had once been Governor of New York State, so he addressed Laval as *"cher Maître"* because Laval once had been a practicing lawyer in Paris and liked to look back upon those days when success had somehow been more successful than now. The son of the village butcher and tavernkeeper had found out how to make money by showing the rich how to evade their income taxes, and by getting a "cut" in many great enterprises which wanted to break the laws of the Republic safely. He had come back to the place of his birth and had had the satisfaction of buying the ancient Château de Chateldon which dominated the scene. The estate included a comfortable manor house in which Pierre lived with his long-suffering wife, their adored daughter, and the daughter's noble husband, who had been purchased at a price which some placed at seven figures and some at eight.

Here they were, and they were glad to see the agreeable art expert after the lapse of a year. He had an interesting story to tell about his plane wreck and his yachting trip through the South Seas. He said that he had come out by way of China and didn't mention the Soviet Union, nor did he take too long with his tale, for he wanted Laval to do the talking, and he knew that this family didn't really care very much about anything in the world except the intrigues by which they had got power and the menaces and bribes by which they were keeping it. The greedy and vulgar man with the dark complexion and the slanting eyes, which had caused his enemies to call him "the Mongolian rascal," had not one word of reprobation concerning the wholesale murders of French men and women which the Nazis were carrying on all over the occupied portions of the country. He justified their scheme of compelling the French to print and give to them three hundred million paper francs every day, including Sundays and holidays. This was supposed to be for the upkeep of the German army of occupation, but the Nazi economic commissions were using it to buy up the most important industrial properties of the captive land. Laval was following his old practice of getting a rake-off on many of these—for his services in browbeating the owners into giving way.

The tactful Lanny didn't mention any such aspects of the "collaboration" program. What he said was: "They tell me you gave your enemies a drubbing at Riom while I was making my way through China." That was enough to start the ex-butcher boy off and keep him going all through a dinner *en famille*. Laval didn't say so, but he knew perfectly well that the world considered him to have got much the worst of the proceedings. He had put Daladier and Reynaud and Blum, and the rest of his opponents in the prewar government of France, on trial for their lives. He had done it against his own judgment, for he knew how much he had to hide. Hitler and Abetz and others of his new masters had demanded it, hoping to prove these men guilty of causing the war. Instead, the trial had turned into an effort to prove the defendants guilty of losing the war, a different matter and no crime in Nazi eyes. They had put up such a vigorous defense of their public course that the trial had dominated the news of the world. The Nazis had ordered it stopped, and those too eloquent public men were shut up in fortresses—whether guilty or innocent.

Pierre Laval hated them more than ever now, and his language concerning them was more fitted to the village tavern than to the dinner table of the head of *l'État Français*. The spectacle of a furious man stuffing food into his mouth and then pouring out vituperations, pausing now and then to mop his greasy black mustache—this was one which the fastidious Lanny Budd would not have chosen for his own enjoyment, but only in the line of duty. His well-trained memory was taxed to remember all the secrets of Vichy France—vicious France was an almost inescapable pun. When he was shown to his room he did not dare make a single memorandum, but lay on the bed for an hour going over what he had heard in the course of the long evening.

And back in the town next morning, he sat at his little portable and typed off the most important details—no carbon copy—and sealed the sheets carefully in an envelope marked "Traveler: Personal to the President." This he put in a larger envelope, addressed to the Chargé d'Affaires at the American Embassy—Admiral Leahy, the Ambassador, having been summoned home as a gesture of repudiation of the new government. This missive Lanny had delivered by a messenger, watching from the street to see it handed in at the door. Then his job was done. He went back to his room, packed his few belongings, and set out for the south.

X

The trains were running again—it was the classic boast of Fascism that it caused the trains to run on time. They were jammed with people who were trying to get to some place where they hoped that life would be a little less hard than they had found it where they were. They squatted on the floors or in one another's laps, and slept that way if they could. Lanny had learned in China that the conductor of a train keeps some compartment locked on chance that somebody will pay him a *cumshaw* for the use of it; in France it is called a *pourboire*—for a drink—and Lanny paid enough to keep any conductor properly alcoholized for a week. It was his fate in life to be comfortable while other people were miserable, and he made up for it by having his conscience troubled. Manifestly he couldn't go into fashionable society if he slept on dirty floors, and he couldn't be an alert and capable secret agent if he stinted himself on food. If he wanted to meet the rich and powerful he had to look like one of them, and they are watchful and severe in their judgments.

When he stepped off the "Blue Train" at the famous resort city of Cannes, he was the glass of fashion and the mold of form. He had telegraphed of his coming, and there was his mother waiting to welcome him with the mild enthusiasm permissible to a lady on a public platform. More than a year had passed since she had seen him, and there had been parts of that year when she had given up hope of ever seeing him again. But here he was, cheerful and sound as ever, her adored only son, her own handiwork, yet so different from what she had ever imagined. A man of mystery, and never more so than now, when the world seemed to have gone entirely mad—and what part was her Lanny playing in it?

He was forty-two, and his mother almost sixty; she shuddered at the very word, but had to face it. For half her life she had had to worry about what the ladies politely called *embonpoint.* Now the Vichy government had helped her by rationing food, and instead she had to worry about wrinkles. When you have been "plump," and then lose ten or twenty pounds, you have more skin than you need to cover you; and when you come out into the sunlight, how dreadfully the folds do show! You just have to make up your mind that you are an old woman, and get along with such love as you have been able to win in a world where the young are selfish and pleasure-seeking.

But Lanny loved her! He took her in his strong arms and kissed the powder off her cheeks and exclaimed: "Well, well, old girl! Here we are again!" And how was Parsifal, and how was Baby Marcel, and had she heard from Marceline, and had she got the letters he had written from various parts of the earth? And then it was Beauty's turn: How was Robbie, and how was his family, and where had he left Laurel, and what was she doing, and was it really certain that she was pregnant? "Lanny, I want you to know right away, I think you have made a good choice. She is just the woman for you."

"Yes, dear, I am glad to hear you say so. She is wise and sensible and understands me very well." He refrained from extreme praise, being wise himself in matters where "the sex" was concerned; his mother was a jealous goddess, and it wasn't easy for her to see her place taken by another female—and especially one whom she hadn't picked out. But it is the way of nature, and if Laurel was going to give Beauty another grandchild she would be forgiven for having once called Lanny a "troglodyte," and caused Lanny's mother to want to scratch her eyes out.

Essence being almost unobtainable, even to the rich, Beauty was driving herself in an ancient buggy with a middle-aged horse. They looked extremely odd trotting down the splendid Boulevard de la Croisette; they had almost the only vehicle, for traffic was confined to official cars. The small city was packed to the roofs with refugees; they walked in the two lanes of the wide drive, separated by palm trees; they sunned themselves in near nudity on the beach below. "The Côte d'Azur will never be the same again," said Beauty Budd sadly. "But we take what we can get and are thankful to be alive."

"Are you thinking of going back to the States?" the son inquired, and as he had guessed, she told him no. People of all nations had always been polite to her and she couldn't bring herself to be afraid of either Germans or Italians. This was her home, and who could say that she had ever done any harm here?

XI

Always a pleasant thing to come back to Bienvenu, the lovely old place which had been Lanny's home for as long as he could remember. It was his headquarters and repository; his books were here, his piano and accumulation of music scores, his treasures of one sort and another. It was always his dream that some day he would be able to live here again and do the things he really liked. But that couldn't be so long as gangsters threatened mankind. Lanny had been forced to the conclusion that it couldn't be until the world had been made over according to the principles of justice and co-operation.

Meantime here was a place of retreat, a shelter where the gangsters had not yet intruded. The dogs came running out, barking their welcome; following them came a lovely little dark-haired boy, Beauty's grandson and Lanny's nephew, whom they called Baby Marcel, but they would have to change that before long. He was the son of Marceline Detaze, and when she had divorced his father she had had his name legally changed to Marcel Detaze; an honored name, that of his grandfather, the French painter, long since dead. The little one remembered his Uncle Lanny from a year ago, with Beauty's help, of course; Uncle Lanny had taught him dancing steps and would teach him more, and now he leaped into Uncle Lanny's arms with a cry of delight.

And here came Beauty's husband, her third, as she wished the world to believe, and it obligingly did so. Parsifal Dingle's hair had grown snow-white, and if he had his way it would have grown long, for he was too busy with God to bother with barbers. But Beauty wouldn't let him be any more eccentric than necessary, and now and then she would pin a sheet about his neck and trim him herself. It was so hard to get about nowadays that people revived the home industries, reverting to an earlier stage of culture. Parsifal was no trouble to anybody. He adored his beautiful wife—she was still that to him if not to herself—and he asked nothing but to sit in the court reading his "New Thought" books or to stroll about the grounds of the estate, keeping himself in tune with the Infinite. A more harmless man never lived, and he was always delighted to see Lanny, who shared his interest in psychic matters and would go over Parsifal's notes and join in speculation concerning what had happened.

There was "Madame," the elderly Polish woman who had lived on this estate ever since Parsifal had discovered her in a dingy "medium

parlor" on Sixth Avenue in New York. At a time when bankers and
brokers had been throwing themselves out of top-story hotel windows
because they had lost everything in the world, this man of God had
been busy with the next world, or, as he would say, the world in
which yesterday, today, and forever are the same, and which is in us
and around us, whether or not we choose to become aware of it.
Madame Zyszynski didn't have any ideas of her own on these abstruse
matters, but she accepted whatever Parsifal said; she loved this kind
gentleman as if he had been her father, and Lanny as if he had been her
son.

XII

How delightful the son would have found it to stay here and teach
Baby Marcel to dance and to swim, and let Beauty cut the hair of both
of them, and let Madame summon the spirits from the vasty deep, and
let Parsifal sit by as sage and interpreter, and as healer in case of need.
Beauty would have pleaded for it, save that she had tried so often and
knew that it was no use. There was something that called Lanny away,
and it hadn't taken her shrewd mind many years to guess what the
thing must be. Always the call came by mail; there were letters post-
marked Toulon which took him westward, and others from Geneva
which took him northward. Beauty had studied the handwriting and
guessed that the former came from Raoul Palma, whom she had known
for twenty years or more as one of Lanny's Leftist friends; the other
writing she did not know, but it had peculiarities which were German,
and she had noted that Lanny generally went into Germany after getting one of these letters.

She knew much more about this strange son than he guessed. She
had become certain that he had never changed his political coloration,
as he gave the world to understand; if he had, he would never have become a friend of Laurel Creston's—to say nothing of marrying her. The
idea that he was a secret Leftist terrified her, for she knew what danger it
meant in times like these. The fact that he refused to take her into his
confidence hurt her, but she had to accept his cryptic statement: "A
promise is a promise, old darling." She had kept these speculations
hidden in the deepest corner of her mind, and even her best friends
believed that she believed her son to be an art expert, traveling about
the world only in search of beautiful paintings.

Beauty's instructions were never to forward his mail, because of the
uncertainty of his movements and of communications in wartime. She
put the papers and magazines on a closet shelf and locked the letters

up in her escritoire. There was a considerable packet after a whole year, and she didn't make him ask for them, but put them into his hands without delay. He would not look at them in her presence, but would take them off to his study to read and perhaps answer. He would never entrust the replies to the postman who delivered mail at the estate every day, but would find some excuse to go into Cannes and there presumably drop them into an inconspicuous box. All this she had observed for years and had tactfully pretended to observe nothing.

Alone in his study, Lanny set aside a number of unimportant letters and tore open those which had to do with a P.A.'s job. There were three which had come from Raoul, all mailed in Toulon and signed with the code name "Bruges." According to their practice, the text had to do solely with the purchase of paintings; when Raoul wrote that he had located an especially fine Meissonier, it meant that he had important news about the war; when he said that the painting could be purchased for eighty thousand francs, it meant that he wanted Lanny to bring him that amount of money. In the last of his letters, mailed over three months ago, "Bruges" said that he had been distressed to hear about M. Budd's plane accident and hoped soon to hear of his recovery. That didn't surprise Lanny, for the Budd family was well known in Juan-les-Pins and near-by Cannes, and Raoul had many friends in the neighborhood who could tell him what members of that family were doing.

There was only one letter from Bernhardt Monck, and that was six months old. He had discovered a fine work by the Swiss painter Hodler, and since this painter had done most of his work and attained most of his fame in Germany, Lanny could guess what that meant. Monck wanted only five thousand Swiss francs, but each of these was worth more than ten of the depreciated francs of Vichy. Lanny had no way to reach Monck by mail; he would have to go to Geneva, on chance that the old-time Social Democrat would still be doing research work in the public library there.

Raoul's last letter said: "I am still employed by the bookstore." So Lanny wrote a note to "M. Bruges" in care of the Armand Mercier bookstore, Toulon, saying: "I am home again, and much interested in what you tell about having come upon a Meissonier painting. The price is reasonable, if you are sure of its genuineness. Let me know at once if it is available, and I will come." He added: "I don't want to take any chance of finding that it has already been sold, as happened in the case of the Daumier drawings." That was asking Raoul whether there was any chance of Lanny's getting into trouble, as had happened to him on his last visit to Toulon.

According to Beauty's expectation, Lanny came to her, saying: "I have to go into town to attend to some matters at the bank. If you don't mind, I'd like to take the buggy, because I'll buy some presents for our friends whom I have been neglecting." The generous-hearted Lanny, so the friends would all think; but he didn't fool his keen-minded mother, who had been Robbie Budd's side-partner in munitions deals for a couple of decades and knew all there was to know about intrigue. She had observed this business of giving presents to people who needed them and to others who didn't, and she had managed to figure out what it meant. Lanny must be needing money in small denominations which could not be traced through the bank, and this was his way of getting large bills changed. She had even noticed that his pockets were bulging when he came home! Now she said: "All right," and didn't offer him the pleasure of her company on the expedition. She knew that when he had got the money, he would be leaving shortly.

4

We Cannot Escape History

I

LIFE at Bienvenu went on comfortably in spite of war. Foods were rationed, and that was supposed to apply to everybody, but of course it didn't. Beauty had American money, large sums of it because of the sales of her late husband's paintings. Also, she had many friends, and not merely among the fashionable folk. In one of the valleys which ran back from this rocky coast lived Leese, who for thirty years or so had been Beauty's cook and major-domo; she had purchased a farm out of her savings, and while she herself was crippled with rheumatism, she had a swarm of grandchildren and grandnephews, and the war had not got them all. They would load up a one-horse cart with produce, and in the middle of the night drive to the village of Juan-les-Pins; not to the markets, but to Bienvenu, and at the back door of the Villa they would be met by the lame butler whom Lanny had brought from Spain. They would have a price written on a scrap of paper, and José would take that to Madame, who would make a wry face, for the amount grew steadily larger; but no matter, it was in francs, and they were worth less than a cent apiece.

So the cellar and pantry and icebox of Bienvenu were kept full. And then would come Lanny's old friend and ex-tutor, Jerry Pendleton, whose travel bureau had very few patrons these days. Jerry liked to go fishing, and his wife had a *pension* with hungry boarders. When Jerry had a good day he would appear at Bienvenu with, say, a ten-pound *mérou*, or perhaps a basket of *langoustes*. There would be an argument as to whether they should be paid for, and Beauty would insist that if he refused payment she wouldn't let him come again. Sometimes they settled it one way and sometimes the other; in any case there would be a seafood dinner, and then a cold supper, and next day a *bouillabaisse*, something resembling a chowder. Beauty, a generous soul, couldn't bear to think of anybody being hungry, at least not anybody she knew; so she would send baskets of food to the various refugees she had stowed away on the estate and whom she was rapidly pauperizing—without too much resistance on their part.

She had announced her determination to stay in her home regardless of hostilities. But the recent imperative from the State Department had caused many of her friends to depart, and she was uneasy in her mind and asked what Lanny thought about it. He couldn't give any hint of what he knew, but he could say that he didn't consider the French Riviera a likely landing place for an army, at least not for some time to come. The Germans had done some fortifying, but in a halfhearted sort of way, and it would seem that they agreed with Lanny. He pointed out that there was danger in sea travel also, and surely in the air, as he had proved. If the worst came, Beauty could hitch up her bony horse and drive into the hills and stay with Leese until the issue was decided.

II

One evening she said to him: "Come for a stroll with me." She took him out behind the garage, where there was a storeroom, and near one corner of it a little oleander was growing. "I planted that myself one night," she said. "It is a yellow oleander, and we have no other on the place, so it will be easy to remember."

She was speaking in a low tone, and they did not stop. "I took the precaution to bury some money there, and in case anything should happen to me, I want you to know about it. I noted the fact that when the Italians came into Menton they blocked all accounts at the bank, and I thought it might happen here at any time."

"You are right about that," he answered. "You would be in enemy territory, whether Italian or German. You couldn't draw money from New York, and neither Robbie nor I could send you any."

"That was my thought. I have been getting cash from the bank at intervals and hiding it in the house; but I thought the house might be burned, so I wrapped all the money in oilcloth and put it in an aluminum box which won't rust. The oleander grows slowly, as you know, so you won't have trouble digging it up. I thought it wise to plant something, because that explained the ground being freshly dug. I buried it on Saturday night, and told the gardener the plant was a gift and I had put it into the ground at once to make sure it would live."

"Very clever," said Lanny. "How much is there?"

"I didn't count it, but it must be over a couple of million francs."

"*Whew!*" he exclaimed. "Pirate's treasure!"

"I put my jewels in, too. There's no use having them nowadays because I don't go anywhere. I haven't told anybody else about it; it'll be yours if I go. You will remember the place. Yellow stands for gold."

Lanny, amused, recited:

> Bright and yellow, hard and cold,
> Molten, graven, hammer'd, and roll'd;
> Heavy to get, and light to hold;
> Hoarded, barter'd, bought, and sold,
> Stolen, borrow'd, squander'd, doled:
> Spurn'd by the young, but hugg'd by the old
> To the very verge of the churchyard mould;
> Price of many a crime untold:
> Gold! Gold! Gold! Gold!

His mother said: "Wait until you get to be as old as I am!"

III

While Baby Marcel chased the butterflies in the court and in turn was chased by the dogs, the two learned elders sat in canvas chairs in the sunshine, discussing the profoundest problems which engage the mind of man. What are we, really, and how do we come to be, and for what purpose are we placed here, and what becomes of us when we depart? Above all, what is the origin of that strange faculty in us which we call conscience? Why do we have a sense of duty, and what is the basis of its validity, and of our assurance concerning it? If we are as the beasts of the field that perish, why do we owe any obligation to the world, or to our fellow men, or to ourselves? Even the Communists, who spurn the idea of God, owe loyalty to their Party! Even the Nazis, who despise the mass of mankind, are slaves to their own racial ideal!

A retired real estate man from Iowa had found his retreat across half a continent and a wide ocean, and had instituted a monastery with one monk, a psychical research society with one member and one medium. Parsifal Dingle asserted that there was a Spirit in the universe, and that it created and maintained those illusions which we know as the material world. He asserted that it was possible to maintain communion with this Spirit, and he did so, day and night. "God is all and God is love," he would say. "God is alive and God is real." He would prove it by healing the sick and by setting to all men an example of a harmless life. He asserted that everything that ever existed exists always, and he proved this by exchanging daily communications with persons who claimed to have lived long ago.

For years Parsifal had been getting messages from the old-time monks of a monastery in Ceylon known as Dodanduwa, and he had accumulated a mass of notes concerning their ideas and way of life. Now he informed Lanny that these monks had given place to a representative of a rival sect, the Jains, who claimed to be even more ancient than the Hindus, and who worshiped their *tirthankaras*, or saints, as gods. Parsifal Dingle declared that he had never known anything about the Jains and couldn't say whether they were Hindu, Persian, or Arab; but here was this "spirit," a grave and dignified personality, avowing that he had been a holy man of the Jain shrine of Chitaral—the "Rock Temple," it was called—in South Travancore; it had been founded in the ninth century, and he had been present at the ceremonies. Stranger yet, this ancient one declared himself to be a previous incarnation of Parsifal and spoke as if in soliloquy—"we" have done this and "we" have done that. It was fascinating, but at the same time a bit uncanny.

Lanny read the notes which his stepfather had carefully written out. It appeared that the Jains, heretics themselves, had spawned numerous other varieties of heresy. The holy man, whose name was Chandragupta, belonged to the sect called Digambaras, and warned his later self concerning the rival Swetambaras, explaining in detail what was wrong with their beliefs. The Jains all held the strictest ascetic views and disputed over such questions as to whether women could attain *Nirvana,* and whether it was permissible to wear white costumes or no costumes at all. Chandragupta brought various authorities to converse with his latest reincarnation; one of them was introduced as Siddharaja, King of Guzerat, who had been the first monarch to be converted to the Jain religion, an event something like the conversion of the Emperor Constantine to Christianity. Parsifal Dingle, ex-realtor from Iowa, had never conversed with a monarch before and had striven to keep his democratic balance.

He had learned much about the Rock Temple and the life there. The original structure on top of the rock was in ruins, but the sculptures on the rock itself were intact. There were thirty figures, all formal and rigid, each representing a saint absorbed in contemplation which would continue to the end of time; each saint was bald-headed, smooth-shaven, narrow-waisted, and wore no garments, not even "holy threads," and each had three tiers of umbrellas carved over his head. Parsifal wondered, he said, what "holy threads" might be; he had been afraid to interrupt with questions, and he did not have access to a large library. Chandragupta was distressed because, some three hundred years after his departure from this life, the temple had been converted into a Hindu shrine, and an image of the goddess Sree Bagavathi had been installed. He scorned this interloper and would talk only about the Jain saints and the inscriptions in the language called Vattezuthu which he had spoken in those days. He had no way of reproducing the script, but had spoken some of the words, and Parsifal had written down the way they sounded to him. All very curious, and some day it might be possible to check on the details.

What did these communications mean? To Lanny's stepfather they could mean only one thing, which was what they claimed to mean. Parsifal was positive that he had never read anything about the Jains; but Lanny wondered if he could not have done this long ago and forgotten. Parsifal read everything he could get hold of about religions, old and new; and what could be more likely than that he might have read a few paragraphs about the Rock Temple? The subconscious mind never forgets, and apparently it has the same impulse toward imaginative creation that has filled the libraries of the world with works of fiction. Of course that left unexplained the problem of how these matters had got into the mind of Madame Zyszynski. The phenomena made it certain that at some level her mind and Parsifal's mind were one, or had some way of becoming one for a time; and that seemed a startling discovery, enough to keep the professors of psychology busy for a long time.

Lanny tried experiments with Madame, as he always did. There came "Tecumseh," the Amerindian control, but he seemed an old and tired Tecumseh, not full of "ginger" as in the old days. He produced "spirits" whom Lanny didn't know, also the same old stock figures, who had nothing new to say. Lanny had been hoping that he might get Laurel Creston's grandmother, or possibly some member of the Holdenhurst family; but no such luck. He had to tell Madame that it had been a good session, otherwise she would have been greatly depressed. He went away wondering why Parsifal continued to have success, while for himself the phenomena seemed to be fading? Was it because of his skepticism, his continued dalliance with what Tecumseh called "that old telepathy"? Did that deprive Madame's subconscious mind of its impulse? Lanny could imagine a child who began to invent stories or to make drawings; if the child's parents said they were good, the child would go on working with delight, but if the parents said that it was all foolishness and a waste of time, what talent the child had might die of inanition.

IV

Lanny awaited a letter from Toulon, and in due course it arrived. "Bruges" said that the painting was still available, but that on account of the decrease in the value of the franc it might be well to bring a little more money. He said that he, Bruges, would be at the usual place, but not to let anybody there know about the painting, as this might cause an increase in the price. "Do not talk about it to anybody but me," said the letter, and Lanny understood that this was a warning of danger. He hardly needed it.

He went into Cannes and withdrew more money in small-denomination bills; and he told his friend Jerry that he wanted a train ticket to Toulon, and a seat, if such a miracle were possible. Jerry, who also knew about *pourboires*, said that it would be possible to anyone who had dollars. A wonderful land was America, and more and more French men and women were wishing they could get to it.

The P.A. came back and told his mother that he was going to take a run to Toulon, he had word of a promising painting. There was nothing she could do but believe him, for he might actually show up with a painting, and she could hardly believe that he had done it just to impress her. She had to be content with his promise: "I'll be back soon."

Beauty drove him into town next morning, and on the road they met the postman. There was a letter for Beauty from a village not far from Berlin. That was Marceline, and the mother, driving, handed it to Lanny, who read it aloud. The daughter wrote that she had left Berlin to get away from the bombs; she had been taking care of Oskar, who had been wounded. Soon he would be well enough to return to the front, and then Marceline was going to try to get permission to visit Juan. "I cannot stand to be away from my baby any longer," she wrote. "Kiss him many times for me, and tell him every day that he has a mother."

That was all. Doubtless Marceline knew that a letter to Unoccupied France would be censored, and perhaps she thought that a brief one would stand a better chance. "She doesn't write often," complained Beauty. "You know that she is not a demonstrative person, and she does not tell me much about her affairs."

"Is she happy with Oskar?" the half-brother inquired.

"If she were not, she would be too proud to say so. She has made her own bed. You know what a quietly self-willed person she is, Lanny. She would listen to what I had to say, and give me some vague answer, and then go ahead and do what she pleased."

"I didn't think she would like the attitude of the Nazis to their women, any more than she liked the attitude of the Italians to theirs."

"Oskar von Herzenberg is hardly a typical Nazi, I should think; he is a Prussian aristocrat."

"His father has been hiring his services to the Nazis, and I never saw any signs of disapproval on the part of the son. If she is happy with him, I'll be surprised."

"It makes quite a problem for me," said Beauty. "That my daughter should become the mistress of a Wehrmacht officer and should take to dancing in a Berlin night club won't leave me many friends among the English or the Americans when they return here. But I can't refuse my home to my daughter, and it would break my heart if she were to take the baby away."

"I think your true friends will forgive you, old darling; and you don't have to worry about the rest." He spoke more cheerfully than he felt, for he had warned Marceline that she would have a hard time with the Allies if she committed herself to the Germans. But there was no use worrying Beauty in advance. He added: "She has not troubled to give me her address. If you write, tell her that I wrote to her the last time I was here. Give her my love and tell her that I hope we can meet." He had not seen his half-sister for three years, and he had been out of sympathy with her for longer than that. But he would never get over his old fondness for her; and he was not forgetting the fact that she might have information about Naziland which would be of use to a P.A.

<h1 style="text-align:center">V</h1>

The train to Toulon was in need of paint, and possibly also of coal; it took three hours to cover about seventy-five miles along the coast. Lanny got himself a room at a small, obscure hotel, and then presented himself at the police station. He reported his business as art expert and exhibited the permit to "circulate" with which his Vichy friends had favored him. Those formalities attended to, he strolled to the Mercier bookstore where, a year ago, he had tried in vain to find his friend Raoul. This time he hoped for better luck, and surely meant to do his best to avoid the troubles into which he had then stumbled.

After the French fashion, the store had stands out in front, loaded with secondhand books, and Lanny stopped in front of these and began looking over the titles. He didn't even raise his eyes to the interior of the place; he just picked up one book after another. After a few minutes a man came out from the store, a man several years younger than Lanny, a slender figure, with black hair and finely chiseled, sensitive features, rather pale; the face of an idealist, perhaps an ascetic. When he smiled, you saw that he had even white teeth, and that his dark eyes were alert and attentive. He asked politely: "Can I help you, Monsieur?"

Lanny looked up, but gave no sign of recognition; he looked at the books again, and Raoul Palma's quick eyes glanced one way and the other to be sure there was no one near enough to hear. Then, in a low voice: "In front of the Hôtel de Ville, eight o'clock this evening."

"Right," murmured Lanny, and that was all. The clerk went into the store again, and the book browser moved on down the street.

It was getting late in the afternoon, closing time for dockyards and shops of the arsenal. The streets were thronged with workers carrying their dinner pails, women shoppers with baskets and bundles, and bluejackets from the Fleet with their little round flat hats with a red pompon on top. Lanny, his pockets stuffed with money, stayed in the well-frequented streets, keeping his distance from all comers. He was taking every precaution; when it was time for dinner he resisted the impulse to go to some workingmen's café, where he could enter into conversation and find out what they were thinking; he chose the Grand Hotel, where he would have a table to himself and never be spoken to.

So he reckoned, but, as the saying goes, without his host. Entering by the main doorway, he almost ran into a lady, and there resulted one of those incidents in which both step to the same side and then to the other side. Suddenly he stopped and stared at the lady, who was rather tall and slender, a brunette in her twenties, simply but tastefully clad. "Mademoiselle Richard!" he exclaimed. And the lady, almost speechless, managed to whisper: "Monsieur Budd!"

Lanny, man of the world who had been in many embarrassing situations in his life, was the first to recover his savoir-faire. "*Enchanté, Mademoiselle!*" he said. "I have been wondering if I should ever have the pleasure of seeing your collection of paintings."

Amusement spread over his face, and confusion over hers. He had her at a hopeless disadvantage, and it pleased him to make the most of it. It was in the lobby of this same hotel that he had encountered her, something like a year and a half ago, when she had lured him into her car and driven him up into the hills, where the partisans, the enemies of the Vichy government, had stepped out in the guise of bandits and taken possession of a supposed *collaborateur* and the funds he was carrying. Now he had another load of funds, but he was surely not going for any more drives with strange ladies, no matter how refined in appearance and gracious in manner. Here he had caught her in a situation where he was safe and she was far from safe; it was what is known as a "social situation," and more than that, a political situation. It appealed to his sense of humor, and he could see no harm in having a little fun with her, here in the lobby of a luxury hotel where *tout le monde* surrounded them, and everything was proper and expensive.

The "bandits" up in the hills had gone through a little farce comedy with the lady driver, pretending to frighten her; they had turned her car around and ordered her to drive away and keep silent, upon penalty of death for herself and her family. That hadn't fooled Lanny for very long; he was clear in his mind that "Marie Jeanne Richard" was herself a member of the rebel group. This meant that she was a friend of the cause Lanny was serving, and a very brave and determined person. But he wasn't in a position to tell her so—not yet.

"I trust no harm came to you, Mademoiselle," he said. "I have been intending to look you up and ask about the paintings."

Relief dawned upon her features. Incredible as it must seem, he had really believed her story! She had described herself as the secretary of a wealthy, eccentric "Madame Latour," who owned a collection of fine paintings and kept them up in the wild country behind Toulon, and who had sent her secretary to inform him that some of these paintings were for sale. All right, if Americans were that naïve, Mlle. Richard would play the game with one of them. "A dreadful night, M. Budd! I have never ceased to worry about it. I had no way of finding out what happened to you."

"You did not report the matter to the police?"

"I did not dare to. I thought that if you survived, you would do it."

"I decided that it was not an ordinary crime, that it had a political aspect, and I was afraid it might cause unpleasant publicity for yourself and your employer."

"That was certainly considerate of you, Monsieur. How can I thank you?"

"Very easily, *chère Mademoiselle*. I was about to dine alone, and that is a waste of opportunity. Will you favor me with your company, and tell me a little about life in a great French naval base?"

"Really, Monsieur Budd—" she began.

He saw that she was groping for an excuse. "If," argued he, "I was unconventional enough to go for a motor ride with a strange lady, surely you can risk sitting in the dining-room of a respectable hotel with a strange gentleman. I have an engagement immediately after dinner, so you will be free."

Was it a command? She couldn't be sure. He was a strange gentleman in more than one sense of the word; and she must have reflected that he had only to go to the telephone and call the police to land her in jail upon a charge that would involve the penalty of death for her and her friends. She was completely in his hands. If he had smiled politely and invited her to go up to his room with him, she would have had to obey. But he only wanted her to eat a meal with him!

"*Enchantée, Monsieur*," she replied, returning both his compliment and his smile. She allowed him to escort her into an ornate *salle à manger*, for which she was not properly dressed, and to seat her at a table with ceremony, and to press upon her food which would cost several hundred francs. She knew that he was a rich man—fabulously rich, she doubtless thought, knowing that his father was Budd-Erling, and it was known to all the world that America was pouring out billions of dollars for swift and deadly fighter planes. Well, this was how American multimillionaires treated ladies who caught their fancy; and she could only wonder what was coming next.

VI

It was a rather devilish thing to do to a woman. He treated her as if she were a duchess—he had treated a number of duchesses and knew all about it. He smiled charmingly and asked if she liked the taste of this and that which was put on her plate. Meanwhile he plied her with questions about the paintings in Madame Latour's collection. She did her best, but her confusion grew, and at last she had to tell him that she really didn't know much about paintings and had been kept too busy to study them. He asked about the rich lady, and from what her fortune had been derived; he only let up on his victim when he saw that she was blushing furiously and that the food was threatening to choke her. All the time that smile—or was it a grin? Was he telling her that he was deliberately teasing her, and that it didn't matter much what she answered?

"*Chère Mademoiselle*," he said, with what had suddenly become grave kindness, "it is perhaps difficult for you to realize, in times of stress like the present, that a man can have an abiding faith in the permanence of art, and that he should take it as his duty to assemble a collection which will have enduring value, and which the people of his homeland, groping for culture, may have opportunity to study and imitate. To help in setting a standard of technique and expression for a new nation of a hundred and thirty million people—that is an undertaking for which it should surely be possible to have respect."

"*Vraiment, Monsieur*," she replied. She was studying his face and trying desperately to read his mind. She must have been told by her comrades in this revolutionary *coup de crime* that they had cross-questioned him closely in their mountain hideout and revealed to him that he was suspected of being a Nazi-Fascist agent. Was he now trying to tell her that he was innocent of this charge, and that he really was what he pretended to be, an art expert acting as purchasing agent for American collectors? He had been robbed of fifty thousand francs and had not troubled to mention the matter to the police; he had escaped by bribing one of the band, and that must have cost him still more; yet, apparently, he hadn't told a soul about it—certainly, at any rate, not in the Var. That didn't look like the behavior of a Nazi-Fascist spy; and was he now spending money on a dinner for her in order to say: "I am not what you have thought me"?

Yes, that must be the case. It was hardly likely that he was putting up this meal because he was lonely, or just for the pleasure of teasing her. He was asking for protection. You let me alone and I'll let you alone! And he was doing it in a very clever and altogether charming way. He must have thought of it in a flash, running into her in a hotel doorway. Or could he have somehow found out that she was employed in this hotel, and that this was her time for leaving work? She couldn't ask him that, or hint at it, for she had to go on stoutly pretending that she was the secretary of a wholly imaginary Madame Latour who hid up in mountains with imaginary old masters!

VII

Immediately after dinner Lanny excused himself and left the building. After making certain that he was not being followed, he walked to the headquarters of the city's government, the Hôtel de Ville. In front is a large statue entitled "The Genius of Navigation," and in its shadow Lanny saw his old friend and protégé waiting. When the American approached, Raoul strolled away, and Lanny followed at a distance; two experienced conspirators, they did not join each other until they had made certain they were not being followed, and until they were on a quiet street. This wasn't easy, for it was a balmy night, and most of the population of Toulon lived in the streets. The city was completely "blacked out," but a full moon was shining with dangerous brightness, and it appeared that every nook and shaded spot was occupied by a loving couple; children were under foot everywhere; in short, it was a Mediterranean port.

Raoul's first question was: "Are you all right for a walk?" When Lanny said he was, the other added: "I will take you out to Cap Cépet, and we can talk quietly in the gardens of the *Hôpital*."

First of all, Lanny wanted to know if his friend had heard the story of what had gone wrong when they tried to meet last time. Raoul, speaking English so as to be less apt to be understood if overheard, answered that Julie, his wife, was in Toulon, and had told him everything that Lanny had told to her. "A wretched *contretemps!*" he exclaimed. Lanny smiled and said it would be a story to tell to his grandchildren.

"Have you told anybody about me?" he next inquired.

"Not a soul," the younger man replied. "I am not supposed to know anything about the matter myself. They sent me off on an errand to get me out of the way. They knew that you and I were old friends and that you had helped to support the school."

"I had an idea that the leader of that crowd was a former pupil, but

I couldn't bring him to mind. He was masked, and I had only his voice to guess from."

That might have been a hint for the former school director to talk, but he said: "You know, Lanny, I am under oath."

"That is quite all right," responded the P.A. "I prefer not to know, for if something should happen to him, I might be held responsible." After a moment he added: "Here is something I ought to tell you without delay. An hour ago I was having dinner with Mlle. Richard."

"Richard?" said the Spaniard inquiringly.

"Marie Jeanne Richard is the name she gave me."

"I do not know her."

"She is a good-looking brunette, in her mid-twenties, I should guess; rather tall for a French woman, cultivated, and very good company. She is the person who met me in the hotel last time and told me that she was private secretary to a wealthy lady who had a collection of paintings; so I let her drive me up into the hills—perhaps the silliest thing I ever did in my life. But I thought I knew a lady when I saw one."

"I think I know who she is," said Raoul. "How on earth did you come to dine with her?"

"I ran into her in the entrance to the Grand Hotel. I saw that she knew me, and I thought it would be the part of wisdom to make friends with her and persuade her that I believed what she wanted me to believe—that she was an innocent party in that episode. I think I succeded in that, and perhaps in persuading her that I, too, am innocent."

"That is not possible, Lanny," exclaimed Raoul quickly. "You are in danger. You ought not stay in Toulon tonight!"

VIII

The man of the underground lost all interest in taking his friend to the beautiful gardens on Cap Cépet; he wanted to find some place to hide. But Lanny refused to be worried. Said he: "I have been thinking it over and have things to tell you that may change the situation entirely. You must understand that America's coming into the war has made a great difference in my job. I can no longer go into Germany or German-occupied territory. Even if I wanted to take the risk, my orders are otherwise. I have just been to Vichy and collected a lot of information, but I doubt if I shall wish to go there again, for the reason that those intriguers are getting to be of less importance, and it won't be long before they are of no importance at all. The Americans are coming, Raoul."

"*Sapristi!*" exclaimed the former school director. "You really know that?"

"I do."

"When?"

"That I have not been told, nor the place. But I know they are coming, and in real force."

"That is the point everybody will ask about, Lanny. They all remember St. Nazaire. The people rose to help the British, and then it turned out to be nothing but a commando raid; the British took to their boats again and the Nazis came back and slaughtered the French."

"I know all about it, Raoul. I am authorized to give the assurance that when the Americans come, it will be to stay."

"*Naturellement* that is the most important news in the world to me and my friends. But how can I convince them of it?"

"That's what I'm coming to. I am authorized, at my discretion, to meet some of the underground leaders and put them in touch with our Intelligence service."

"But, Lanny, they are convinced that you are a Fascist agent. It won't be easy to persuade them otherwise."

"It won't be enough if you vouch for me?"

"I am afraid not. It might work the other way and lead them to distrust me. I must tell you, the leader you tried to recognize is a Communist, and you know how it is between the Communists and the Socialists. We have a truce for the struggle against the Nazis and try to keep the agreement loyally, but it is very hard for a Communist to recognize any loyalty or faith except to his own Party. This man is suspicious of me and inclined to oppose any proposition I put before our group. Probably in his heart he suspects me of trying to take the leadership away from him."

"Just like the old rows that used to be fought out in our workers' schools. You saw them in Cannes, and Freddi Robin saw them in Berlin, and I saw them everywhere I went."

"Exactly so, Lanny. I will tell you something horrible that is in my mind—that some day there may be another world war, fought between the Communists and the Socialists."

"Let's not talk about that now, Raoul; we have a war against the Nazi-Fascists, and that is plenty. Tell me this: will your leader respect credentials from President Roosevelt?"

"*Ah, mon Dieu, Lanny!* If you have that, we can knock him cold!"

"O.K., that is what I will show him. I can tell you now that for the past five years I have been what in inside circles is known as a 'presidential agent'—'P.A.' for short. I report directly to the President, and only one other friend—the man who introduced me to the President—knows what I am. Less than a month ago Roosevelt told me what I was to say to you and others who can be trusted: that the Americans are coming, and not too long a time from now, and coming to stay. I have money which I am authorized to pay to leaders of the underground who can use it effectively."

"Lanny, I would like to sing!" exclaimed the younger man; but instead of that, he whispered: "I'd like to have an hour to get two or three people together and tell them this news. I have an idea they'll be meeting to hear what your Mlle. Richard has to tell them. You ought to keep out of sight. But where?"

"One of the safest places would be a cinema. That will be dark, and nobody is apt to notice me in the short time it takes to enter."

"*Bien*," said Raoul, "I will take you to the nearest."

"One thing more," added the P.A. "You know you asked me to bring you something, and I have it."

"All right, I'll take it. Wait until we see a chance."

They continued their walk and presently came to a dark alley, into which they stepped. Lanny transferred his bundles of banknotes to his friend's hands, and Raoul stuffed them into his pockets. They strolled farther, until they came to a motion-picture theater, dark, of course. "Come out exactly one hour from now," said the younger man.

IX

The American purchased a ticket and went into the darkened cave, to see a crime-of-passion story, manufactured in Paris—the Germans didn't care how degraded the French became, provided only that their films contained no ideas of liberty or democracy, or the glory of France past or present. They had tried offering newsreels showing Nazis troopers marching and Nazi propagandists speaking bad French, but the audiences had booed and rioted, and after a few experiments the Nazis had given up and just let the Vichyites feed themselves on their own native garbage.

The two conspirators had compared watches, and promptly on the minute Lanny strolled out of the theater. He saw his friend a short way down the street and presently caught up with him. Raoul said:

"I have talked with my friends, and they want to meet you; but they won't reveal themselves to you until they are satisfied."

"Of course not," Lanny replied. "I am quite willing to take a chance on convincing them. Did you tell them how long you have known me?"

"They knew all about that. What makes them suspicious is that you deserted the school and turned into a Fascist so long ago."

"But that was the way I managed to get information. Did you tell them how I brought it to you, and how you fed it to the Socialist press?"

"I told them all that, and that it was on your money they have been operating most of the time. But it's the old trouble—the Reds don't want to have to believe anything good about the Pinks. They'd have a hard time not being pleased if it should turn out that I am a Fascist agent, spying upon them all."

Lanny chuckled. "If that were the case, they'd hardly have much time to be pleased about anything!"

Their walk took them into the "Old Town," near the docks. They went into an alley and came to an ancient arched doorway of stone; it led into a sort of court, and they entered at an unlocked door, turned through an irregular passageway—very old buildings are like that, for reasons long since forgotten. Raoul gave three quick taps upon a door, and when it was opened he led his friend into a room that was completely dark. A voice said: "*Asseyez-vous*," and Lanny, reaching about him, found an empty chair and took it. He did not have to hear another word in order to know that voice; it was the leader of the band that had abducted him, the masked man who had questioned him for an hour or two up in the low mountains, or the high hills, that lie back of this French naval base. Lanny had been sure that his life depended upon that matching of wits, and he was never going to forget the tones of the voice.

"Monsieur Budd," said the man, speaking educated French, "our friend Bruges wishes us to believe that you are a friend of the anti-Nazi cause and a confidential agent of President Roosevelt."

"That is true, Monsieur."

"You will understand that this is a serious matter to us, *une affaire très grave.* All the machinery of government is in the hands of our enemies, and we are being hunted like rats. If we are betrayed, it will mean torture of the worst cruelty our foes can devise."

"I understand that perfectly," Lanny said.

"Therefore you will not take it amiss if we question you closely, and refuse to accept your story until every possible doubt has been removed."

"That is quite reasonable. In such matters it has to be everything or nothing, and you could be of no use to me unless you were prepared to trust me."

"*Très bien. Alors*, let us hear your story."

"First, a question from me. How many persons besides Bruges and myself are in this room?"

"Two men and a woman."

"You know who these persons are, Bruges?" Lanny asked. And the voice of Raoul answered that he did.

X

"*Messieurs et Madame*," Lanny began. "At the age of seventeen I became interested in the labor cause, and very soon I was calling myself a Socialist. After the war, when I came to Juan, I met Bruges, who was then a clerk in a shoestore. We got together a small group and discussed the idea of a school for workers. I helped to raise the money, and later, when I began earning large sums as an art expert, I was able to carry a good part of the burden. I did this as long as the school existed, paying the money secretly to Bruges. After Hitler seized power, I realized that we were in for a long fight, and that I was in a special position to get information because I had met Hitler and had come to know the Nazis."

"Tell us how you came to know Hitler, for that is the crux of the whole matter."

"At the age of thirteen I spent a summer at the Dalcroze School of what is called Eurythmics, a kind of dancing; that was at Hellerau, a village near Dresden, and there I met a German boy named Kurt Meissner. I went to spend the following Christmas with him at Schloss Stubendorf, in Upper Silesia. Kurt grew up to become a famous pianist and composer. My mother was a widow—her husband, the painter Marcel Detaze, was killed in the second battle of the Marne. She took Kurt Meissner as her lover, and he lived at our home in Juan for a matter of eight years. That led to my meeting many Germans and to visiting that country. My friends were the rich and powerful, persons who despised the Nazis, but later, when the Nazis seized power, they did what we in America call 'climbing on the band wagon'—*montant sur le wagon de la musique*."

"We have observed the same thing in France, Monsieur Budd."

"At Schloss Stubendorf I had met a son of the head forester, named Heinrich Jung, and he became a follower of Hitler in the very early days, and visited him in prison. In the course of the years he converted Kurt, and he labored hard to convert me. That was how I came to meet Hitler. I listened to him politely and then told him that I was a non-political person, an art expert. But as the years passed I realized that I had a valuable asset in that ability to go into Germany and meet its leader; and as Hitler's power increased, I began telling Bruges what he was doing and planning. I did the same for a Socialist friend whom I have in England, the playwright Eric Vivian Pomeroy-Neilson. These two men used to put the information into articles for the Socialist and labor press, and I hoped that I was being of some help in awakening the workers to the threat which Nazism meant to them. Am I going into too much detail?"

"Pas du tout, Monsieur. Continuez."

"I had another boyhood friend, Freddi Robin, son of the Jewish financier Johannes Robin. He became a Socialist and founded a workers' school in Berlin. I helped him and went frequently to that school, and there I met a couple of artists, Ludi and Trudi Schultz. When Hitler took power the Nazis grabbed Ludi and killed him—at least he was never heard of again. Trudi became an underground worker, under the same conditions that you face here. For several years I gave her money, just as I have done in the case of Bruges. Then the Gestapo got onto her trail and I helped her to escape to Paris. To finish that story, they seized her in Paris, smuggled her back to Germany, and tortured her to death in Dachau. In the meantime she had become my wife— that was after my divorce from Irma Barnes—and so you can see that there is not much about your present position that I do not understand. I mean the underground life and the danger."

"You are telling us something new, Monsieur Budd. We have had reports on many events in your life, but not about that marriage."

"I am glad to hear that, because it was a secret known only to persons whom I trusted in my effort to rescue Trudi. Not even my father and mother knew about it. The reason was that by that time I had come to realize that the greatest service I could render to my friends of the Left was to use my acquaintances among the ruling classes as a means of finding out their plans. I took to telling these people, including my own families, that I had become disgusted with political developments and had retired to an ivory tower. I became the art expert, interested only in furthering great collections for the American wealthy, and incidentally in earning large commissions. The rich all understand that you desire to become richer; that is what the game of life means to them."

"Is that what you tell Hitler, Monsieur Budd?"

"I always shade my story according to the company I am in. I told Hitler that I was a complete convert to his cause; for years I addressed him as '*Mein Führer.*' I told him about the many sympathizers he had in Britain and America, and I brought him messages from them—all this, of course, before America came into the war. In return, he confided to me a great deal about his plans."

"You did not feel that you were giving him encouragement and perhaps information?"

"That was a problem about which I used to worry. But when I put it up to President Roosevelt, he assured me that what I brought him was worth any price it cost. That settled it for me, because I have complete confidence in his judgment. For five years I have been what is called a presidential agent, and have done exactly what he told me."

X I

That was the matter about which the three judges were waiting to hear. The leader said: "We have great confidence in the President of your country, Monsieur Budd, even though it is a capitalist country. Will you tell us how you came to enter his service?"

"I was sent to him by a member of his 'brain trust,' Professor Charles T. Alston, who had been one of President Wilson's advisers at the Paris Peace Conference, and whom I had served as secretary-translator at that time. President Roosevelt invited me to his home, heard the story I have just told to you, and said that I could be of help to him. Of course I could not refuse his request. I have a confidential way of getting reports to him, and I have sent him more than fifty so far. He has several times offered to pay me, but I told him I made plenty of money, and so I am what is called in Washington a 'dollar-a-year-man.' I did not even collect from him the sums I have paid to Bruges and other contacts which I have. The last time I talked with the President, which was less than a month ago at his home in Hyde Park, he told me that our Intelligence service was supporting the underground movements where our armies were likely to come, and indeed wherever we could hinder and hurt the Germans. He put money into my bank account in New York, and I have just paid some of it to Bruges. I am prepared to pay more if you can show me ways you can make use of it."

"Just what does the President wish us to do?"

"You understand, we have to make a distinction between the two parts of France. In the occupied portion the Germans rule; we are at war with them, and we furnish our friends with arms, explosives, and all means of sabotage. But with Vichy France we are not at war, and it is not according to our code to encourage sabotage in a country with which we maintain diplomatic relations. Naturally, any harm you can do to German agents here is all right with us, though we do not ask for it or direct it. What we particularly want is to keep the French Fleet out of Hitler's hands, and no doubt Bruges has told you that it was I who urged his coming to Toulon in order to make contacts with the sailors and the arsenal workers."

"He has told us that."

"There is nothing more important to the Allied cause, and nothing for which we would be more glad to make expenditures. If you could manage to start the publication of a clandestine paper, or the printing and circulating of leaflets—"

"We are already doing both those things, Monsieur Budd."

"That is good news, and I shall mention it to the President, with your permission."

"Is it your plan to stay in this neighborhood?"

"That has never been my way. I go from place to place, under the pretense of inspecting works of art. I talk with the people I know and listen to the gossip in the salons, and now and then I send in a report."

"You have recently been in Vichy?"

"I was flown there by way of Lisbon and Madrid. I was a guest in Laval's home and I had a long talk with Admiral Darlan, whom my parents have known since World War I. I picked up a lot of information among the collaborators, and that information should by now be in the President's hands. It goes by air."

"Will you tell us how you expect to work with us?"

"The President's instructions were that I should get into touch with the underground wherever I had a contact I could trust; that I should ask permission to send the leader's name to the President, so that he may give it to the new Intelligence service headed by Colonel William J. Donovan in New York. A properly accredited agent will come to you and presumably maintain continuous contact with you."

"We should be glad to co-operate with President Roosevelt, Monsieur Budd; but we must point out that any letter mailed to any place, whether inside or outside of Vichy France, is very likely to be opened and read."

"Quite so, and you have my word that I will never take such a risk. If you decide to trust me with a name and address, I will memorize it, and not put it on paper until I am in a position to be certain that it will be flown in a diplomatic pouch, and will be seen by no eye until it reaches the President's. Give me a code word, and in due course someone will appear who will repeat it."

"Bruges tells us that you have credentials from the President himself."

"The last thing he did before I left his study was to take one of his engraved visiting cards and write with his fountain pen the sentence: 'My friend Lanny Budd is worthy of all trust.' He instructed me to sew that in the lining of my coat and use it in case of need. I am wearing that coat, and will show you the card; but it must be with the understanding that it is precious to me, and I must have your word of honor that, regardless of what your decision about me may be, you will return the card to me. If it were lost or destroyed, I should have to travel back to America to get another."

"You have our word on that, Monsieur Budd."

There came into the P.A.'s voice a little of that humor which on many occasions had been the means of making friends and influencing people. "I will put the coat into your hands, Monsieur Incognito, but perhaps you will leave the cutting of the threads to the lady who is present. It is necessary that there should be no damage to the lining, and the opening should be no larger than necessary. It would look very suspicious if a fashionable gentleman were wearing a coat which showed signs of repairs."

"We will do our best," said the leader of the band. "Bruges, will you take Monsieur Budd into the next room?"

XII

Patiently the P.A. waited, sitting coatless and in darkness for five or ten minutes while the secret group debated his story. When the door was opened again, there was a light in the other room; only a kerosene lamp, but even so it made Lanny blink when he entered. He saw that all four of the persons in the room were smiling. "*Soyez le bienvenu, camarade!*" said the leader. "Here is your coat and here is your card. We have agreed to accept your word, and you are one of us." He added quickly: "My name is Zed. If you think you remember any other name from past times, please understand that it is not to be spoken."

For a year and a half Lanny had been worrying his brain, trying to identify the voice of the masked man whom he had seen only by the light of a flickering campfire. Lanny had tried to recall the voices he had heard and the faces he had seen in the workers' school—hundreds of them in course of the years. Now, at the first glance it came to him, like a flash of lightning on a dark night: Jean Catroux! Sallow, sharp-featured, eager, and contentious Jean! His father had owned a cigar-store, and the son had been a clerk in the daytime and an incessant troublemaker at the school in the evenings. A partisan of the extreme Left, he was one of a small group who kept the place in turmoil and almost brought Raoul to despair. The pupil had been older than the teacher by several years and considered that he knew much more.

The Reds in those unhappy days had joined the *front populaire* and had helped to vote Léon Blum into power. But they sabotaged him by propaganda and waged relentless ideological war upon him. In truth, Blum had given them plenty of cause, for in the dreadful crisis of the Spanish civil war he had given way to the class enemies and shown himself a broken reed. All this came to Lanny in a rush of memories, and it was like a puzzle to which you cannot guess the answer, but when you have heard the answer, you cannot imagine how you failed to guess it.

"I remember, Comrade Zed," he replied at last.

How much had happened in the world in five or six years, and what did it mean for the future? This man had come out on top because he had energy and fervor, because he knew exactly what he wanted and had the courage to take it. Was this an augury, a portent? Were the Socialists going to fail everywhere because they hesitated and fumbled? Were the Reds going to win because the holders of privilege throughout the world wouldn't permit any social change without violence? Anyhow, that was the way it had been here in the Var. Lanny has heard that Jean Catroux had gone to Spain to fight the Fascists; now he was back, hunted as an outlaw by the Vichyites, and helping to prepare the French workers for renewed war upon the Nazi enemy. In that war the Reds would come forward as leaders precisely because they knew what they wanted and had the courage and the fervor.

XIII

The other man was a dockworker, solid and weatherbeaten, with a horny hand and a devastating grip. Lanny, who played tennis and the piano, was able to survive it. The man's name was Soulay, and Lanny had never seen him before. As he expected, the woman proved to be Mlle. Richard. He was told now that her name was Mlle. Bléret, but of course he couldn't know whether that was a real name or another *nom de guerre*. She blushed as he shook hands with her, and her voice was unsteady as she said: "Comrade Budd, we are dreadfully ashamed of what happened on your last visit here."

He answered, with his agreeable smile: "Don't worry about it. The mistake was a natural one, and it taught me a useful lesson." He was thinking what he had thought the first time he had spoken to this young woman, that she was intelligent and attractive, and that he would like to know more about her. There was a difference, however, between this time and last: he was now a married man.

"This we have to assure you," put in Catroux, alias "Zed." "Every franc of the money taken from you was used for the cause."

"I took that for granted," Lanny said. "It appealed to my sense of humor that you expended so much effort to get what Comrade Bruges would have brought to you more quickly."

Possibly this line of conversation did not appeal to Zed; it was one of his exploits for which he would never be awarded a medal of honor. In a businesslike tone he remarked: "Comrade Budd, it will be necessary that we assign you a code name. Obviously we should never speak your real name from now on. Will it be all right if you become *'Monsieur Zhone'?*"

"O.K.," Lanny said, and restrained an impulse to smile. He was familiar with the forms that English names take to a Frenchman. This one would be written "Jones."

"You will continue to communicate through Bruges, and you will give his name and only his to the American Intelligence service. There will be no need for you to mention the rest of this group, even to President Roosevelt. We will decide who is to meet the Intelligence man when he comes."

Again Lanny said "O.K.," and again he was amused to see Comrade Catroux taking charge of the former patron of his school. The bourgeoisie giving place to the proletariat! "Arise, ye prisoners of starvation! Arise, ye wretched of the earth!"

XIV

With these four anti-Nazis Lanny sat in consultation. He told them as much as he was allowed to, enough to give them courage in a time of seemingly endless defeat. He described the prodigious war works now under way in the New World, especially the Budd-Erling effort which he had seen with his own eyes. In return they told him what they desired from the American government, pending the arrival of an army on any one of the shores of *la belle France*. They repeated what Bruges had said already: "Don't send us commandos. Don't come until you mean to stay!"

Without direct questions the visitor gathered a few items concerning these new comrades. Soulay was an old-time labor man and a Catholic. Mlle. Bléret had no special label; she came of a doctor's family in the northeast, and was earning her living here because she had to; she was helping in the fight against the Germans because her mother had been killed in the wanton bombing of refugees on the highways. An odd fact that came out in the course of conversation was that Catroux had met Raoul Palma during the fighting in Spain, and had asked about Lanny Budd and been told that he had lost interest in the workers and gone back to his own class. That was what Lanny had told his friend to say, and it had caused the Red leader's mind to become centered upon this renegade. It might easily have cost Lanny his life.

"Don't worry about anything you may hear about me," he cautioned them. "Remember, not even the Intelligence people who come to you will know about '*Camarade Zhone*,' and you are not to mention me to them. It is my job to travel and to take any role that will help me get information. If you hear of me in the enemy's camp, shake your heads sadly and say that it was to be expected and that no help can be expected from the *haute bourgeoisie*."

He impressed upon them that the main thing was to keep the Fleet out of Nazi hands. He came back to this a second and a third time, assuring them that a crisis was bound to come soon, and advising with them as to how to meet it. One of the crimes of the Laval regime, they told him, was forcing French sailors to teach Germans how to handle these ships; the Germans were learning fast. Lanny said: "That is our President's greatest concern. With your Fleet they might get control of the Mediterranean, and we might lose the war, or, at any rate, have it prolonged for several years."

The answer of these people of the underground was: "Tell your great friend that it will not happen. The French sailors—not the officers but the *marins*—will sink the ships even if they have to go down with them. *Les boches ne les auront. Jamais, jamais!*"

5

Testament of Bleeding War

L ANNY stayed in Toulon long enough to ask questions about paintings. He once more inspected the collection of the wealthy D'Avrienne family, and gave them another chance to put a reasonable price upon a Nattier which they possessed—a portrait more of costumes than of human features, he told them. Since their views still did not meet, he gave them more time and took the crowded train back to Cannes. He could feel certain that he had done good work in that base of the French Fleet, and that the authorities of the town could have no grounds for suspicion.

His mother was prepared to be told that he was planning next to visit Switzerland. She could not restrain the impulse to protest: "You're not going into Germany, Lanny!" He answered her: "Good heavens! That would be trading with the enemy."

It was all right to trade with the Swiss; they were neutral and were getting rich on the war. To be sure, they had to spend a good part of it on their army, standing guard at all their passes, day and night. Even so, many of them were worried about the future, and some might be glad to have money put to their accounts in one of the great New York banks. On those terms they would part with a painting or two. So Lanny explained, and it made a story—good enough to fool the Swiss, perhaps, but it did not fool Mrs. Beauty Budd Detaze Dingle, who had been in the world a long time.

Lanny's reason for coming back, he said, was to have his clothes pressed and his laundry done; but really he was hoping there might be another letter from Bernhardt Monck. Finding none, he decided to take a chance anyhow. He got his railroad ticket and his Swiss visa, and took the train eastward to the broad rich valley of the River Rhône, familiar to him since childhood, and to invading armies as far back as history records. At the silk-weaving city of Lyon the road divides into three forks, one westward to Vichy, one northward to

87

Paris, and one eastward to Geneva—three cities which had come to be centers of attention and activity for a secret agent.

The Rhône flows down from Geneva, and the railroad follows its valley. Near the Swiss border is the French town of Annemasse, where the Swiss customs and security agents come aboard to inspect papers and baggage. Lanny's papers were in order; his card from President Roosevelt had been neatly sewed back into the lining of his coat, which the polite Swiss did not examine. He sat looking out of the windows at the rushing green waters of the river, which comes out of Lac Leman, or, to be exact, of which the lake constitutes a forty-five-mile stretch. At the foot of the lake, near the dam over which the water flows, is a small island. On it, slightly less than two centuries ago, there had resided a revolutionary writer, much dreaded and maligned by the powers that then were; but the whirligig of time had brought him revenge, and now the island was known as Rousseau's, and tourists came to see his statue.

On both shores of the lake's outlet there had been a town in ancient Roman days, and before that a settlement of lake-dwellers, whose piles could still be seen at various places. Now there was a fine city in which the old and the new were combined, and in which the American art expert had made a few friends. The League of Nations had had its headquarters here, in a grand building paid for by the Rockefeller family; now it had shut up shop, and too late the Genevans were realizing that it had been an important real-estate asset.

II

Lanny had never had the address of Bernhardt Monck, alias Capitán Herzog, alias Branting, alias Braun; the man of the underground could not afford to be known as receiving letters or visits from foreigners. The Swiss were holding rigidly to their neutrality and were trying to restrict the activities of the secret agents who swarmed into the country. This applied particularly to the Reds and the Pinks, for the government of the country was conservative and, like all such governments, found it easier to get along with well-heeled and well-dressed Fascists than with ex-labor leaders and agitators, refugees who generally were destitute and frequently had jail records. This is something which applies to nearly all governments; F.D.R. had complained to Lanny that he was powerless to prevent it, even in his own State Department.

Lanny put up at the Hotel Beau Rivage, as was his custom. His first duty was to type out a report to his Chief, covering the situation at Toulon and giving the name and address of Bruges as a contact with the underground there. This he double-sealed, as usual, and mailed it to the American Ambassador in Bern. Then he permitted himself the luxury of reading a newspaper—one which really deserved the name. The Swiss papers were no longer permitted in Vichy France, for it had been discovered that nobody wanted to read any others. Lanny learned that Corregidor had fallen to the Japs, and that the Germans had taken Kerch, in the Crimea. Always defeats!

The visiting art expert proceeded to make his presence known to the dealers and the possessors of private collections with whom he had done business in the past. Through one of these he had met an editor of the *Journal de Genève*, and he now invited this gentleman to lunch and to chat about art development during the war. The result was an interview in the paper, for not many Americans appeared nowadays in a land which had depended to a great extent upon tourists for its prosperity. The *Journal* sent a photographer and published a picture of the distinguished art authority, so no reader of the news could fail to know that he was in town.

That was the way Lanny had planned it. In the afternoon he strolled into the library of Geneva's much honored university and possessed himself of an American magazine, something difficult to get on the Riviera. But he found it hard to keep his mind on the pages; every minute or two he would lift his eyes and turn them here and there. He couldn't be sure whether his friend Monck was still in town, or even if he was still alive. This afternoon would tell.

His heart gave a leap when he saw the familiar sturdy figure coming down the aisle. Lanny dived into his magazine again; he knew that Monck would see him and, as usual, would pretend to have some business in the reading-room. Presently he would stroll out, and Lanny would follow after an interval. They had to use extreme care, for this ex-sailor, Social Democrat, and *capitán* in the International Brigade in Spain was a man marked by the Gestapo, and by the security police of Switzerland as well. To be seen with him would be damaging to the reputation of a respectable *connaisseur d'art*.

At a safe distance Lanny followed him out of the building and across the park. Monck stopped in front of an art dealer's window—that being a proper place for Lanny. Making sure they were alone, the German whispered: "Reformation Monument, twenty hours this evening." That was their usual place of assignation, and all Lanny had to answer was: "O.K." The German moved on, and the American went inside to inquire whether there was any new talent appearing in this Alpine land, which, as a rule, was interested more in facts than in fancy, more in morality than in genius.

III

This pair's last meeting had been in the month of March; snow had been falling, and they had had to stamp their feet while talking. Now, more than a year later, it was spring, and happened to be a mild night. Lanny's first words were: "We ought to have a good long talk, *Genosse*." It was the Socialist Party's word for "comrade." "Can we not find some place to sit down?" It was a fact that they had never dared have a real meeting since the old days in Paris. "Have you any reason to think you are being watched at present?" Lanny asked.

"It can happen any time," replied the other. "The Gestapo never sleeps. But perhaps we can get out of town and find a quiet corner."

They walked toward the north, following obscure and poorly lighted streets, conversing in low tones, in the German language, as usual. Monck said: "You have been a long time coming. I had given you up."

"I nearly gave myself up, *Genosse*. I set out for England last September, and was in a plane wreck and had both legs broken. I was invited on a yachting trip while recuperating, and I very nearly got caught by the Japs in Hongkong." He did not mention Russia; this pair of secret agents set each other an example in reticence.

"I had important news for you," said the German, "but most of it is out of date now. I learned that the Nazis intended to attack Russia on the southern front and drive for Caucasus oil. Hitler has been saving up all his resources and is expecting to put Russia out of the war in the next two or three months. The attack should be beginning any day now."

"Presumably the move in the Crimea is a preliminary," Lanny agreed. "You have been able to restore your contacts in Germany?"

"To some extent; but it is all so uncertain, I am brought nearly to despair. You cannot imagine the persistence with which our comrades are hunted, of the cold ferocity with which they are exterminated. A messenger comes at intervals, and then I never hear from him or about him again. A new one comes, and I have the problem all over again. Is he the real thing, or an agent of the enemy?"

"I bring you reinforcements, *Genosse*. I have just left America, and

it is unbelievable what is happening there. The country is united at last,
and it is really going to win this war."

"Which war? The one in the Far East or the one here?"

"Both of them in the end. This one first."

"That means conquering practically the whole of Europe. You
really believe that America has the resources and the will for such a
bloody task?"

"I know that it sounds unlikely. I had spells of pessimism myself
until I got back home. I saw with my own eyes what was going on at
my father's plant; and it is the same all over the land. The whole industrial energy of America is being turned to war work. Huge new
factories are going up all through the Middle West, where before was
nothing but prairie. There has never been such a tornado of activity
in all history."

"But the shipping, *Genosse*—"

"We are going to turn out the ships by mass-production methods.
A cargo vessel that used to take a year will now take a month, or perhaps two weeks."

"And the U-boats?"

"We are licking that problem. My father knows about it, but he
gave me only a few hints. We are perfecting devices to reveal the
presence of submarines; they will not be able to move without our
knowing it. Then we shall get them with airplanes from small carriers.
This spring the situation is bad, I know, but soon it will be better. And
we are going to have an army of eight or ten million men."

"You Americans toss figures like that around. But an army takes
years to train—surely a German knows about that!"

"I am not permitted to say anything about the time or the place,
Genosse; but you may be sure that an army is coming, and it will be
much sooner than you think. Take courage and start over again."

"I am a German, but you know that I am a true revolutionist and
am not seduced by any touch of pride in what the Nazi armies have
achieved. But I have firsthand knowledge of their efficiency, and my
mind is not equal to the task of imagining an army brought from overseas being powerful enough to drive the Nazis out of the strongholds
they have taken, all the way from Kharkov to Bordeaux, and from
Narvik to Tobruk."

"You must not forget the air, *Genosse*. The victories so far have
been won by air power, and it has been shown that no army can stand
up very long without air cover. We are going to build an air force

greater than that of all the rest of the world put together. The construction is under way, and the training; the bases are being built, the techniques are being worked out, and the job is going to be done. Believe me, I am fresh from seeing it and hearing about it from people who know."

I V

They had come up the lake shore to the magnificent building of the League of Nations, now silent and dead except for caretakers. It stood upon a rise of ground overlooking the lake, a vast structure, like three sides of an oblong, and with tall square pillars in front. Wide flights of steps led up to it, and at the foot of these steps was an excellent place for a secret conference, because no one could come near without being seen. The stars afforded light enough so that no one could creep up, but not enough for a passer-by to recognize the conferees.

To Lanny it was one of the most melancholy places in the world; the dead shell of what had been his brightest hope, his most cherished dream. In the old days he had had friends here, and had followed the proceedings, giving mankind credit for more collective intelligence than it possessed. He had hoped and prayed, first that Japan would be forced to retire from Manchuria, then that the insolent Mussolini would be driven back from Albania and Abyssinia. The murder of Spain had ended all those hopes and shattered the cherished dream.

"The world has to learn by blundering," declared Monck, as if he had divined his friend's thoughts. "The only question is whether the blunders will be so great as to destroy the pupil."

"One thing we can count on," his friend replied. "This war will put an end to isolationism in America. Whatever happens from now on, we shall have a part in it."

"Yes, but what sort of part, *Genosse?* What will this military effort do to your democracy? And what has any capitalist land to contribute to mankind except a new set of exploiters?"

"Listen," said the P.A. "I am able to talk more frankly than has been previously permitted. I can tell you that I was in Roosevelt's home less than a month ago and spent a couple of hours going over the situation. I have his word for it that the purpose for which our armies are coming to Europe is to see that the people of each country have a chance to decide their own destiny in a democratic election. Surely we Socialists have nothing to fear from that, and we have no right to ask more."

"If he stands by it, and if he is able to have his way."

"Who will be able to stop him? Churchill has pledged his acceptance of the Atlantic Charter, and Stalin has ratified it."

"Those generalizations are wonderful vote-getters in your country," remarked the sad ex-*capitán;* "but we Europeans have learned that when the diplomats sit down to interpret them, they turn out to mean the opposite of what we had thought."

"Let us win the war first," said Lanny, and added with a smile: "That will be task enough for tonight. What I want to convey to you is that I am working under the President's orders and reporting to him by a confidential route. All the news that you have given me since our days in Paris has gone directly to him, and I can assure you that it has been useful."

"That is indeed of interest to me, *Genosse.*"

"It may make a difference in your own affairs. I told Roosevelt about you, but did not give him your name nor even mention Geneva. He wants your consent to put our Intelligence service in touch with you, so that your reports will no longer be subject to delay. You understand, I have an assignment elsewhere, and coming here at long intervals is far from satisfactory."

"That would be a serious decision for me, *Genosse.* When you deal with a government organization you run risks of broken codes and betrayals. The Americans have a number of agents here, and I know who several of them are. Their point of view is different from mine."

"There is only one point of view now, old man: and that is, to beat Hitler. The arrangement I am suggesting would be of a special kind. There would be some picked man who would come to maintain contact with you; he would be trained and would have some occupation or camouflage that would be completely protective. He would provide you with funds; that is something the President mentioned explicitly. We are prepared to spend money without limit—anything that will get results."

"I don't need money for myself, *Genosse.* I have invested the sums which you turned over to me in Paris. My wife and children managed to get out of Vichy France and are here, and are getting along all right. What I have to think about is the group I am serving."

"As you know, I have never asked questions about that; but this is certain, *Genosse:* no group can have any purpose but to aid in winning this war, and there is no way that you or they can do more than by making this contact. There are certain specific things we need to know, and if you can get the information for us, you will have done as much as any Socialist in the world."

The German sat for a while in thought. Then he said: "I ought to put the matter up to my comrades."

"Why take that risk?" argued the other. "You have admitted that you can never be safe against the possibility of betrayal. You did not have to tell them about me, at least I assume that you have not done so."

"Never."

"Well, then, why tell them about some other Roosevelt agent? They know that you are putting the information to use, and you are the one to judge the best use. If I had been killed in that airplane accident, you would have had no contact whatever. As it was, for fourteen months your work has been wasted."

"I am doing other work for the cause, *Genosse*."

"Very well; but I am talking about this particular kind of work. You have admitted that if the war is to be won, we Americans have to win it; and what can you do more important than to get us information? You might be the means of winning a whole campaign and saving thousands of lives."

Monck thought again for a while. Then he said: "All right, I'll take my chances with you."

V

Living close to the border of Naziland, this labor man had many sources of information, and he reported on the situation as it now stood. The food-rationing system there was working—all systems worked with the Germans; the Führer was making good his promise that his people would be the last in Europe to suffer hunger. But Göring was not doing so well with his promise that no bombs would fall on German cities; they were falling faster and faster and doing great damage. But this had not suggested any idea of defeat to the population, so far as a former Social Democratic official had been able to learn; it merely made them rage at their enemies, calling them *Barbaren* and *Mörder;* they discovered that the bombing of cities was a dastardly and wicked practice. Said Monck: "You would think they had never heard of Guernica and Barcelona and Madrid, to say nothing of Warsaw and Rotterdam, Coventry and London."

Lanny said the Germans had seen only the beginning; the American flyers were already in Britain, learning to use British planes; soon their own would be coming over. Not even the British believed the Americans could make a success of their precision bombing by day; the

British, too, would be shown, predicted the son of Budd-Erling. He said it was important to know the details of damage done to targets of the raids, and Monck undertook to get what information he could. Lanny was amused to note his phrase: "I will endeavor to establish a system."

The most important of all targets was German science. Lanny inquired: "Do you have any contacts with the scientific world?"

"You know how it was with Socialists in the old days," his friend replied. "We had contacts everywhere, with all sorts of people. But the greater number are now in concentration camps, or else they are dead—we cannot always find out which. Some have fallen for the lure of Hitler's phrases; some have had their wills broken by torture, and they are—what is it you Americans say?—stooges. We have had to rebuild our organization on the basis of tiny cells, only two or three persons; one is the leader, and he knows one person to whom he reports. I know only two persons who come to me, and if I say to them: 'Can you establish a contact with, say, an authority on explosives, there will be a long wait, and I may never hear any more about the matter, because the Gestapo has got some man or woman somewhere along the chain."

"A slow and painful way of working," commented the American. "Let us hope that more bombings and a few defeats will weaken the hold of the Nazis upon your people. Meantime I will tell you what we especially want. Did you ever hear of heavy water?"

"I have heard the name, but that is about all."

"In it the hydrogen is what the physicists call an isotope of ordinary hydrogen. All you have to do is to remember the name, *schweres Wasser*, for any physicist will know about it. We have reason to believe that the Nazis have set up a plant for its manufacture on a large scale. That may give an important clue to their plans, and we should like very much to know where that plant is situated and how far its work has progressed. You will be helped by the fact that it is apt to be at some place where hydroelectric power is available."

"O.K.," said Monck. "I have a mental note of it."

"Next, we understand the Nazis are working on a jet-propelled bomb which will carry great distances, perhaps one or two hundred miles."

"I have heard rumors of that, *Genosse*."

"Such bombs might do great damage in a city like London which covers an immense area. We want every possible kind of information about them: the structure of the bomb, where it is manufactured, the location of the launching sites. They will be camouflaged, of course, and difficult to get at. We have heard reports that the Nazis are putting some of their more important manufacturing plants under the ground, or in caves."

"We have many caves in our country. I am told that some of them have been turned into comfortable working places."

"We have saboteurs who are training to go into Germany, and no doubt we shall soon be dropping them from parachutes. Get us every scrap of information you can about war industries and their products, about military plans, about transportation, about German connections here in Switzerland—"

"This is quite a task you are setting me," said this Socialist Party member. He said it with no trace of a smile.

"Get what you can," said Lanny. "No one will ask more. Give me the name you are using here and where a note can reach you. That will be in President Roosevelt's hands in three or four days. How soon there will be a man to contact you, I cannot say, but it should not be long. And above all, put anxieties out of your mind; you will have a new and fresh organization behind you, more powerful than anything the Hitlerites have ever dreamed. We Americans may be too confident, and we may get more than one bloody nose in this war; but it has never occurred to us as a people that we can fail, and I promise you that we won't forget those who have helped us."

Backing up these confident words, Lanny transferred to his friend's pockets a lot of Swiss banknotes of various denominations—he had established his bank credit here long ago for his purposes of picture purchasing. "I took the liberty of buying a diamond ring for your wife," he added. "She will probably not wish to wear it under present circumstances, but it is a convenient thing to have hidden away in case of emergency." He told Monck about his own marriage, and received his congratulations.

VI

Next morning the P.A. took the train to Bern, a lovely old city nestled in a U-bend of the young river Aar. He got himself a room in the Bernerhof, with a fine view of all the Bernese Alps, still covered with snow. However, he didn't see them, because he was absorbed in typing out a report, somewhat longer than usual. He double-sealed it in the usual way, addressed it to the Honorable Leland Harrison, and caused it to be handed in at the door of the American Embassy. Then, his mind at peace, he paid visits to the art dealers, to impress them with his agreeable manner and discriminating taste. He spent part of a day in the Art Museum, and another part inspecting a private collection to which he had no trouble in gaining access. Then he returned to Geneva and took the night train back to Cannes, quite certain that he had re-established himself as a respectable member of society, and that he would have no trouble in getting another visa should he wish to return and inspect other works of art in the Helvetian Republic.

He had promised his mother to telegraph her of his coming, and he did so. One could never be sure whether a telegram would arrive, but this one did, and when he stepped from the train, could you believe your eyes? Marceline! "For crying out loud!" he said, in the slang of his youth, and caught her in his arms and gave her a good substantial kiss. She was an *artiste*, a *danseuse*, used to public appearances, and not bound by stiff bourgeois notions of propriety. She was twenty-five, but to him she would always be "Little Sister," whom he had first greeted when she was two years old, and to whom he had taught dancing steps, just as he had recently been teaching them to her son. She hadn't turned out exactly the way he would have preferred, but she could say that she had never done harm to anybody but herself, and certainly none to him.

They had two stories to tell on that drive behind the ambling family nag. Ladies first, and she chose to ask questions: What sort of wife had he got himself, and for God's sake, why had he come away and left her? Couldn't he make enough money selling the Detaze paintings in America? She had a one-third interest in the proceeds of such sales, so it wasn't precisely disinterested advice—he had learned that her advice seldom was. He had put a lot of money to her credit in a New York bank, and she thanked him for this, but then wanted to know what were the chances of her being cut off from it. Did he think that Beauty was wise in defying the State Department's instructions, and what did he think that she, Marceline, ought to do?

"I am not going back into Germany," she declared, and there her questioning of Lanny halted and his questioning of her began. Had she ceased to love Oskar? She made a sort of *moue* and said that she loved him as much as she was willing to love any man, but she couldn't stand the Germans, especially since America had entered the war. Graf von Herzenberg, Oskar's father, had used his influence to make it possible for her to go on dancing and to enjoy complete freedom, but he couldn't keep the German women from making snide remarks whenever she came near them, and asking her how her countrymen dared to bomb the most beautiful cities in the world and to kill the most cultured people in the world.

"You know, Lanny, I never had the least idea of being patriotic. I'm only half an American, and that by accident; nationalities meant nothing to me, and I hardly bothered to know where the countries were. This war has been horrid, I just didn't want to know about it. But now some Germans have cut me dead, and Oskar can't bring himself to blame them, and I'm not supposed to blame him, and I don't—only I do." This wasn't exactly clear, but it was feminine, and Lanny understood. Many years ago he had read a translation of some Latin verses which had come down from old times, and he remembered a part of them:

> The Germans in Greek are sadly to seek . . .
> All save only Hermann, and Hermann's a German.

In short, Marceline had got tired of her young Prussian aristocrat. He was brave and had killed many Russians, and she didn't mind that, but it was a messy business, and none of hers; quite the contrary, she said, for the Russians loved the dance, and up to a year ago she had rather fancied the idea of going to Moscow. Now, of course, all that was *fini;* all Europe was *fini,* it seemed to her. What sort of reception did Lanny think the daughter of Marcel Detaze would get in New York? Was she an American citizen, or what? And would they give her a passport? What a mess this world was!

VII

"Social life" had come pretty nearly to a stop on the Riviera. It was so much trouble to get to any place, and only the very rich could get the food and wine for entertainment. The Americans were nearly all gone, and the English who hadn't gone were interned. In spite of the best efforts of the government, Frenchmen and Germans did not mix very well; those French who tried it were expecting to get something out of it and were looked upon with suspicion by the rest of the population. The fortunate people were those who could be happy with a book, a violin, a garden, a child.

Parsifal Dingle was one of these, and Beauty was learning to be another. Lanny watched to see what his impatient half-sister would do with the problem. Marceline had a raging appetite for pleasure, and to be in what she called the "social whirl." She hated the war, not because it was killing millions of men and reducing other millions to destitution, but because it was destroying that brightly shining world in which she had won a place by much effort of body and brain. To be an artist did not mean to the daughter of Marcel Detaze what it had meant to her father, to express the deep longings of the human soul for beauty and understanding; it meant to be "somebody," to have a place in the world of wealth and fashion, to be talked about, and to have eyes turn to follow her when she entered a public place. Now the public places were mostly dark because fuel was so scarce, and a dancer at the height of her career was expected to be content with sitting at home and making up a bridge four with people who had formerly been elegant but now were dependent upon her mother for a place to lay their heads.

Marceline was enraptured with her lovely little boy and found the role of an adored mother most intriguing; but she soon tired of answering his questions and decided that this duty was more appropriate to a grandmother. She was pleased to talk with Lanny, so long as he would tell her about people of the fashionable world. She would question him for hours about Robbie's family in Newcastle, the Holdenhursts in Baltimore, and the other important Americans for whom he collected paintings; about Lord and Lady Wickthorpe in London, and Rosemary, Countess of Sandhaven, who had been Lanny's old flame; about Baron Schneider and Mme. de Broussailles and other smart friends in Paris; about the Laval family and the ladies of the Vichy government—anybody, so long as they had "succeeded."

Marceline's attitude was not consciously Fascist; she truly didn't want to have anything to do with politics. She was like so many other people Lanny had known, who were Fascists by instinct, or as you might say, *a priori*. They didn't call themselves Fascists, in many cases they didn't have any idea of being that; the basis of their thinking was the axiom that the Reds must be held down. Three great men had shown how to do it—*Der Führer, Il Duce*, and *El Caudillo*. Who else?

Lanny's much indulged "Little Sister" had had her way and had married an Italian army officer, a Fascist devotee. Lanny had warned her that she wouldn't be pleased with this husband's attitude to women, and indeed she hadn't been. She had decided at last that he was a rotter, but she hadn't discovered any connection between his conduct and the political system under which he had been trained. Then she had tried an elegant and haughty Junker, with a dueling scar on his left cheek; this time Lanny hadn't been free to warn her, for he was supposed to have changed his own ideology and couldn't trust Marceline with his secret. She had to make her own mistakes and learn from them if she could.

The idea had occurred to him that she might be an excellent person to go into Germany and collect secrets among the military and governmental classes. She would be paid well for it, and she would like that; but after watching her, he decided that he couldn't trust her. Whether she went to Germany or stayed here on the Riviera she would meet some new man, and whatever his political coloration, she would adopt it, as the way to please him. Doubtless it would be some man of wealth; for after her experience with Vittorio di San Girolamo she had vowed that she would "make them pay." If she broke with Oskar von Herzenberg she would surely decide that two "romances" were enough, and that next time it must be business.

VIII

As always, Lanny would have liked to stay at Bienvenu; but the "hound of heaven" bayed in his soul, and he had to be off again. He told the members of his family about the art commission which obliged him to travel in Algeria and Morocco. A land which he had not seen since boyhood, it shone in his memory with a glory of sunlight because Marcel had painted it. Lanny had been fourteen then, and no boy on earth could have been happier. He had visited all the Mediterranean lands on board the yacht *Bluebird*, made entirely of kitchen soap, or so its owner, Ezra Hackabury, had been wont to declare.

Marcel had made it not merely a pleasure cruise, but a culture cruise, a floating university. He had opened the sensitive lad's mind to the mysteries of human existence on this planet, to awe as well as beauty. For Lanny's then stepfather had been not merely a painter, but a student and thinker. When he painted the ancient ruins of Greece and Rome he tried to make you feel the sorrow of great things vanished forever. When he painted a Greek shepherd in his rags or a Biskra water carrier in his gray burnoose, Marcel was not just getting something exotic and unusual; he had a heart full of pity for lonely men who lived hard lives and did not understand the forces which dominated them.

Lanny took the night train to Marseille, and from there a steamer to Algiers. The latter trip took a little more than a day and a night, and was supposed to be safe. The Allies permitted a supervised trade between Vichy France and its African colonies because they didn't want to have to fight the French Fleet; the Germans permitted this trade because they were secretly getting a part of the goods. However, you could never be sure that a submarine might not make a mistake; so

Lanny spent the night in a steamer chair on deck with a life preserver strapped to one wrist to make sure that nobody else carried it off. The weather was warm in mid-May, and when he was not asleep he could look at the stars and realize the infinite unimportance of the human insect; or he could think about the various North African insects to whom he bore letters of introduction, and how he was going to approach them, and what he expected to get out of them. Thus a philosopher lives upon various planes, and his theories and his practices are frequently not in accord.

In midmorning the mountains of the "Dark Continent" loomed up blue-gray on the horizon, and presently the traveler saw the well-remembered white city spread out on rapidly rising hills. Most Mediterranean cities are like that, for the sea was formed by the dropping of the land in some geologic convulsion. That is the reason real estate in Mediterranean harbors is high in both altitude and price. It is one of the reasons that the workers live in closely packed tenements of anywhere from four to six stories, many of them centuries old, and which have been repaired about once in a century. The harbor seemed smaller than Lanny remembered it, but that was because Lanny had changed, not the harbor. The city had spread along the shore for miles in both directions. There had been a building boom after World War I, and there was now a modern residential district, with villas and hotels for tourists who came to enjoy the winter climate. The population of the city had been doubled by refugees from France.

IX

Lanny put up at the St. George Hotel, high up on the hillside, overlooking the sea; it was old, English, and very respectable, with beautiful gardens where Marcel had once made sketches. Lanny presented letters of introduction and established his credit at one of the city's banks. He knew how to make himself agreeable, and it wasn't many days before he was in the châteaux and elaborate villas which the plutocracy of Algiers maintained in private parks on the hill slopes surrounding the city. He was not surprised to find these people pro-Fascist in sentiment. It had been his observation that all colonial peoples are conservative, even reactionary. In Hongkong he had found the English more Tory than all but a small handful of diehards in London, and now he found the businessmen of French North Africa asking nothing but to be let alone. They were doing a brisk trade with the Germans; everything they could lay hands on was in demand at the highest prices ever known. It didn't take a P.A. many days to realize that these merchants were not going to hold out welcoming arms to an invading army of democracy.

But they were pleased to welcome a visiting art expert whose pockets were well lined, who had lived in the great capitals of the Old World and the New, and who seemed to know everybody you could mention. He presented himself to the director of the Museum of Antiquities, which is in Mustapha Supérieur, a pleasant garden near the Governor's summer palace; he gave attention to Algerian antiquities and Arab art, such as it was, and charmed the director by the knowledge he had acquired in the New York Public Library. He made inquiry as to private collections, and when he inspected these he tactfully intimated that he might find American purchasers for worth-while items. He displayed no special interest in political affairs, but when such subjects were brought up he knew what a proper gentleman was expected to say. As a result he gained the confidence of important persons, and it took him only a short while to form a clear picture of the situation.

In the days when the propaganda of *Le Couple France-Allemagne* had been at its height, the son of Budd-Erling had been guest of honor at a dinner party in the Paris mansion of Baron Schneider-Creusot. This "armaments king of Europe" had been a greatly worried monarch, fearing not merely for his crown but for his head, and he had invited a dozen or so of the leading entrepreneurs to meet an American who knew Adolf Hitler and might be able to explain this new portent risen to the east. Among the guests had been M. Jacques Lemaigre-Dubreuil, an ardent collaborationist and one of the most active businessmen of the country. He was a director of the Banque de France, he published the reactionary newspaper *Le Jour*, and his wife was the heiress of Huiles Lesieur, the great vegetable-oil trust. More important yet, he was organizer and head of the most powerful pressure group in France, the League of Taxpayers, which was something like the National Association of Manufacturers in the United States, at once a propaganda and a "slush-fund" group for turning the heat on politicians and legislators to make sure that they did what the "two hundred families" wanted.

Now, at a social gathering, Lanny encountered this gentleman and was remembered and greeted with cordiality. M. Lemaigre-Dubreuil was a stocky, solidly built man with an odd husky voice and an aggressive, direct manner, like that of an American "go-getter." When he learned that Lanny had recently been in New York and Washington he saw another opportunity to get information. He invited the visitor to lunch at the ultra-smart Golf Club and treated him with great distinction—how charming a Frenchman can be when he takes the trouble! The pair sat on a shaded piazza overlooking a splendid view, and chatted about common friends and the parlous state of the world. M. Lemaigre-Dubreuil found nothing peculiar in the fact that an art expert should be here for the purchasing of Roman and Moorish mosaics. Lanny, on the other hand, didn't have to be surprised by his host's presence in Algiers, for he knew that the principal raw material from which Huiles Lesieur derived its products was the peanut crop of French West Africa. The firm had a great refining plant in Dunkerque, and the Germans had permitted the machinery to be moved to the south, so that it might produce edible oils for the people of France, and not entirely forgetting the firm's German friends.

Lanny asked about Schneider and learned that this owner of several hundred munitions plants was still in Paris; he was feeling his years, which were over seventy. He was ill-content with the kind of gratitude the Germans had shown him; he was distressed as to the fate of France, and, in short, Lanny's informant considered that he was worrying himself into his grave. This was still more true of poor Denis de Bruyne, who was over eighty and in no position to cope with events such as were now overwhelming his country. He was in his château in Seine-et-Oise, near Paris, with his two daughters-in-law and their children. Lemaigre-Dubreuil knew him intimately, and Lanny knew from Denis's lips that some five years ago, when the Cagoulards had been planning to overthrow the French Republic, Lemaigre had been one who knew what was going on.

"I met Charlot in Vichy just recently," Lanny told the vegetable-oil man. "He is active in organizing the Légion Tricolore and seems very hopeful about it. He told me that Denis, *fils*, is in Algeria, and I have been meaning to look for him."

"He is here in the city," volunteered the other, "but I have not seen him. It is rumored that he is a Gaullist."

"*Mon Dieu!*" exclaimed the American. "What a sorrow for the old man! How do you account for such a thing?"

"De Gaulle is a fanatic, but he is also an exceedingly shrewd intriguer, and the broadcasts he is sending from Britain are well contrived to affect French youth. I fear they have done so even more than we realize. It is a calamity, because it can have no result other than a dreadful civil war."

"I will make it a point to see young Denis and try to influence him," Lanny said. "I have known him since he was a boy, you know; his mother was my very dear friend."

The word *amie* can mean two kinds of friendship, and therefore offers a way of carrying delicate intimations; it left Lanny in the position of saying something and yet not quite saying it. When M. Lemaigre-Dubreuil replied: "So I have been told," he, too, had said something and yet not quite said it.

X

In this conversation Lanny followed his practice of giving information in the hope of getting more. He knew that this able Frenchman would be watching every word that both of them spoke; he was not the one to give without getting, and he would not spend a couple of hours and the price of a lunch because of an American's *beaux yeux,* nor yet because of his *beaux arts.* He wanted to know about that young giant of a country and what it was doing and planning. Lanny told him that this giant, who had so much more muscle than brain, was waking up and wiping the sleep from his eyes, but as yet hardly knew what he saw. There was much opposition to the war throughout America, but Lanny feared that this opposition would not be able to do much. He explained the unhappy position of his father, who was forced to turn out warplanes regardless of his own convictions. He had many friends in Germany and had done good business with General Göring; but now the government didn't ask what he thought, they just ordered him to make fast fighters to kill German pilots, and if he should refuse to do it they would take his plant away from him.

It had been the same way in France for many years, the host remarked; businessmen were the prey of military men and politicians, and the dream of M. Lemaigre-Dubreuil's life was that there might some day be a government that was run by and for businessmen; indeed, that was why he had organized his Ligue des Contribuables—of which the last word means, literally, those who contribute. M. Huiles Lesieur said that all the contributing that was ever done anywhere in the world was done by the property owners, the taxpayers, and he and they were tired of it, and surely there must be many in the United States of America who were in the same frame of mind.

Lanny was so sympathetic to this point of view and quoted his father so effectively that his host became confidential and said that the businessmen of both parts of France, fearing disturbances, were trans-

ferring funds to North African banks. Lanny said he had heard this in
Vichy and wondered why the Germans allowed it. The reply was that
there were many Germans, and their ideas and interests were not all
the same. There, as in France, politicians wanted one thing and businessmen wanted another, and the latter had to pay, but they managed
to get back still more. Businessmen knew that wars came and went, but
business continued, and its interests were permanent. There were various kinds of business that were ·half-French, half-German, and the
two halves found no pleasure in fighting each other.

Lanny was here confronting that old situation which his father had
explained to him as a small boy. The great cartels, in America called
"trusts," were international in ownership and operation, and so were
the banks which co-operated with them. The Comité des Forges, a
union of the steel and munitions makers of France, used ore from Lor-
raine, which was French, and coal from the Ruhr, which was German.
. The French and Germans who owned these vast interests wanted nothing but to make goods and sell them at prices which they fixed in
secret with the steel makers of Britain and America. They didn't want
to fight each other, they wanted to save their own property from the
general wreck. So the French chiefs of the Comité des Forges had got
their German colleagues and associates to help them with the Nazi
officials. They had let these officials into their companies, and thus
obtained permission to ship their wealth to their banks in North
Africa. Lanny heard about it from one source after another, and some
said that ten billion francs had come to Algiers, and others said twenty
billion, and all agreed that it was still coming.

XI

Why should a man of money like Jacques Lemaigre-Dubreuil have
become confidential on a subject so delicate as this? Lanny could
guess; and before the talk came to an end it was made plain to him.
The vegetable-oil man was doing the same thing that Lanny did—telling secrets in the hope of getting more secrets. He had somehow got
wind of the fact that the American Army might choose French North
Africa as a safe *pied-à-terre* for its attack upon the soft underbelly of
Europe, and it had occurred to him that the President of Budd-Erling
Aircraft would be apt to know about this and might have dropped
hints to his mysteriously traveling son. In short, M. Lemaigre-Dubreuil
was "fishing," and Lanny let him jiggle the bait for a long time before
he approached it.

Suddenly the Frenchman asked: "Do you know Mr. Robert Murphy?"

This was not the first time the question had been asked of Lanny. The American diplomatic representative, whose title was "Counselor to the Embassy at Vichy stationed in Algiers," was a much-sought-after person, and it would have been natural for an art expert to ask his advice. But Lanny had avoided doing so, because he wanted to feel out the situation for himself and without incurring obligation to any American. Now he answered cautiously that he thought he had met Mr. Murphy in Paris, where the latter had been Counselor to the Embassy before the war broke out; but he doubted if Mr. Murphy would remember him.

"I, too, have known him from the Paris days," said the man of great affairs. "Now he has become my very good friend. He is a charming person."

"So I have been told," replied the P.A. "I gather that he has a rather thankless task with you."

"Oh, we get along perfectly. He is most considerate in the carrying out of his duties."

The special duty of the Counselor and his twelve vice-consuls was to see that the precious supplies which America allotted to French North Africa—such as oil and gasoline without which modern industry comes to a dead stop—were apportioned to the needs of the community and that none of these went to Germany. That would bring Mr. Murphy into conflict with just about everything that M. Lemaigre-Dubreuil wanted in North Africa or anywhere else. If they had become "very good friends," that didn't necessarily mean anything sinister, for a tactful Frenchman would say that in any case and try to pretend that it was so even though it was otherwise. In the same way it might be the Counselor's role to pretend that it was so, even though it was otherwise. The State Department career man would be doing what Lanny was doing, trying to get as much as he could out of the vegetable-oil man at as low a price as possible. And he would be using the same means—that is, being "charming"!

XII

The time came when the host asked the direct question: "Do you think there is much chance of this province becoming a battleground?" A natural question, of course, and entirely innocent. If Lemaigre and his friends of the Comité des Forges were bringing their money into

French North Africa, they would be concerned to know if it would be safe.

Lanny's smile had been prepared in advance. "If I had any idea that Algiers was going to be a battleground very soon, I surely wouldn't be here looking for mosaics." Then, lest this might seem like teasing, he added: "My own opinion would have no value, Monsieur; but my father meets people who are in a position to know, and he tells me that the decision has not yet been taken. There are some who want to risk the chance of a landing in Normandy at once; there are others who think it will be at least a year before we are ready for such a venture. As you know, the Allies are under heavy pressure from the Russians to do something to draw the enemy away from the east."

"We hear much about that so-called 'second front.' "

"That clamor may compel the Americans to make some move this year. My father tells me he has heard the suggestion of Marseille and Toulon, of Genoa and Naples, of Salonika and the Dardanelles. There is a wide range of choice."

"Yes, M. Budd. But I have also heard mention of our own ports, all the way from this city to Dakar."

"It is easy to pick out places on a map," commented the art expert, "but not so easy to estimate the military factors. One, I should guess, would be what resistance was to be expected, here and elsewhere."

It was the most delicate of hints, and a capitalist concerned with the manufacture of vegetable oils was free to take it or leave it. If you have ever watched ants, you have seen them rushing along an ant highway, and when one encounters another coming in the opposite direction they stop for a small fraction of a second and touch each other ever so lightly with their sensitive feelers; when they have made certain that it is a friendly ant and not an enemy, they both hurry on about their affairs, so urgently important to ants. This vegetable-oil ant appeared to be satisfied with what his feelers reported, for he chose to answer: "My friends and I discuss that subject frequently, as you can guess. Opinions differ as to what our policy should be; but this much is certain, the decision would depend in great part upon the nature of the force which attempted a landing. I have heard one of our generals say, and not entirely in jest: 'If they come with one division, we should fire on them; if they come with twenty divisions, we should embrace them.' "

Said Lanny: "On that point, Monsieur, my father's informants are most positive. Wherever the Army comes, it will come with the full intention of staying. You should make your plans upon that basis."

6

A Tangled Web We Weave

I

THE vegetable-oil magnate recommended an assistant to the art expert: an educated Arab, middle-aged and substantial, who had served as steward to a wealthy French lady recently deceased. His name was Hajek, and he spoke reasonably good French. Lanny could suppose that M. Lemaigre-Dubreuil had dropped him a hint that he might watch this plausible American and report on what he was up to; but Lanny didn't mind that, for he was really going to find some mosaics and have them shipped, and if this white-robed and black-bearded half-servant, half-scholar was any good at all, Lanny would keep him busy. The visitor was careful never to talk politics, but he acquired a mass of information on such subjects as the practice of the Mohammedan religion, the various tribes which inhabited North Africa, and their ways of life and history.

All subject races have their underground means of communication, and word spread with surprising rapidity that there was an eccentric American desiring to buy mosaics, wall fountains, and possibly a doorway or two, for transportation across the sea. It was Hajek's duty to interview all callers, and if what they had sounded promising, to make an inspection and report. Should the report sound good, the American lord—so they were calling him in Arabic, as not long ago they had been calling him in Chinese—would hire a conveyance and be driven through the streets of Algiers, which climb the hills in zigzag ramps, and sometimes have a step every few feet, so that only a donkey can make it.

Visiting the Casbah, the vile and filthy native quarter, Lanny was led to an old house which had once been the home of a merchant and now served as lodgings for a score of squalid families. There he found an inner courtyard with a fountain, now used to store junk. On all four sides of the fountain were floors, and when they were cleared of trash and scrubbed, Lanny discovered beautiful iridescent tiles. He had

studied enough designs to know what was representative, and he had
known good coloring most of his life.

Hajek undertook to find out the price at which these items could be
bought. The owner, an Arab, of course decided that he had the world's
greatest art treasure, and his price was a quarter of a million francs.
Lanny knew about Mediterranean bargaining and took it as a safe rule
that the asking price was six times the real price, and for an American
even higher. He left the matter to Hajek, who took delight in it, and
in the coffee drinking which was part of the ceremony. In the final
settlement he would get a rake-off, called *dasturi;* it was the custom,
and worth while to an American lord whose time was precious and
would not let the sordid details of business interfere too greatly with
his pleasures.

The one essential to the bargaining process is that there must be no
hurrying. Arabs have a great sense of dignity and are extraordinary
conversationalists. They take the same interest in a financial deal that
Americans take in a baseball game, and if it is a really big deal, it is
like the World Series. The wretched tenants in this decayed mansion
knew what was going on and asked eagerly for the score; every gain
for their side, the Arab side, was received with pleasure, and every loss
with sorrow. All sympathized with the landlord, who lay awake at
night in an agony of fear lest the American lord should make some
other purchase and depart. The lord encouraged this idea by finding
other mosaics which were as good or better.

The news about the battle spread through the bazaars, and it became
a betting game—the natives are great gamblers. These negotiations and
others went on for two or three weeks, and Lanny carried a notebook
with memoranda containing names and addresses, details about the
works offered, and the prices with the date of offering; the last was
important, for you must know how long to wait before a reduced
offer is to be expected. All this must have been convincing to anyone
having suspicions as to the good faith of a visiting art expert. Lanny
wanted it that way and helped to spread the news by telling his French
and American acquaintances funny stories about the difficulties he was
having. They all assured him that it was quite in order.

II

There came word of treasures to be uncovered in the old city of
Constantine, three or four hundred miles to the east; so Lanny engaged
accommodations for himself and his assistant on the fearfully over-

crowded and always late French railroad. He took the day train because he wanted to observe the scenery and the people in the interior
of the country, which he had never visited. The road ascends along
the slopes of the snow-covered Djurdjura Mountains, which form a
distant background to the landscape of Algiers. The mountains are
brown or gray against a deep blue sky; big trees line the roads, and on
isolated points here and there are perched tiny villages of the Kabyles.
Everything in this country tells of centuries of invasion and plunder,
and the peoples sought safety in the most inaccessible places.

It is this which had determined the building of the city, one of the
strangest a world traveler had seen. It stands on a rocky plateau, surrounded by a chasm of something like a thousand feet, through which
flows a roaring river; the plateau is four-sided, something more than
half a mile on each side, and there is only a narrow isthmus connecting it with the surrounding land. The rocks are red. Maupassant had
compared the river and its gorge to a dream of Dante. A city with
only one gate, it is said to have withstood eighty sieges. Hajek, proud
of himself as an historian, assured his employer that during the first
thirty years of the preceding century no fewer than twenty Beys, or
rulers of the city, had died by poison, the bowstring, or the sword.

In this small space, less than half a square mile, are crowded a European, an Arab, and a Jewish quarter. Marble of the ancient Roman city
had been used for modern buildings, and the white city on red rocks
appeared most impressive, until you were inside and investigated its
narrow stone-lined alleys filled with men, donkeys, camels, and the
filth of all three. The Arabs wore their dirty white robes, as everywhere, and when nature called they just squatted in the street. The
Jewish women dressed in bright colors and wore tiny red felt hats, and
heavy jewelry, broad bracelets of gold and silver and heavy rings in
the lobes of their ears. The war had brought prosperity to all lands to
which it had not yet come; and around Constantine were the broad
plains which had been wheatfields for at least two thousand years. This
part of North Africa had been one of the granaries of the ancient
Roman Empire.

Ruins were everywhere in this countryside. Through the centuries
they had been plundered to build peasant huts and storehouses. Lanny
was shown a few stones which marked where a villa had once stood.
He took a chance and offered the peasant owner of the land ten thousand francs for the privilege of digging and taking away whatever he
might find. Hajek brought workmen from the city, a donkey train of
them, one of the most comical spectacles the art expert had ever be-

held. The donkeys were the smallest ever, and each had apparently been conditioned to traveling only in response to a tattoo of strokes from the rider's slipper-clad heels. Each rider sat on the rump of his beast, and in front were strapped saddlebags or baskets. Lanny discovered what these were for—when the work was done the worker would use his wages to buy produce and carry it to town.

A couple of days' digging sufficed to uncover a tessellated floor with a fine representation of the huntress Diana. Lanny stayed right there and saw it taken up piece by piece. With a borrowed camera he took pictures at the start, so it wasn't necessary to mark each piece; but each had to be wrapped in cloth, and the packing boxes had to be small, and then half a dozen of them packed in larger boxes. This was a lot of work, and his commission would hardly pay for the time; but it was a novelty, and he learned a lot about Arabs which would be useful to him later on. Always he had in mind that the American Army was coming and would want every scrap of information. Here, as everywhere in wartime, goods were more precious than money, and G.I.'s exchanging trinkets for fresh eggs would owe thanks to the son of Budd-Erling without having any idea of it.

III

The shipment properly labeled and sent off to Algiers, Lanny wanted to see Timgad. He wouldn't be able to buy antiquities there, but he mustn't miss inspecting the site. He succeeded in finding a motorcar that ran on gas from burning charcoal, and was driven through a land which in many ways reminded him of the American Far West—the combination of wild scenery and a fine road. He passed through the town of Tébessa, a name which he was to hear often before that year 1942 had come to an end, but not having the gift of prevision he did not pay any special attention.

On the slopes of the Aurès Mountains, three thousand feet above the Mediterranean, lies what is left of the outpost town of Thamagudi, built by the Emperor Trajan a hundred years after Christ, and now known as Timgad. The Arabs had conquered and destroyed it, and for more than a thousand years the place had been left to the jackals. Recently the French had restored it as far as possible, clearing away the driven sand and setting up the broken columns. So there are long streets, with paving worn by the feet of the Roman legions; and there are a great gate, a forum, and many arches; everything solid and magnificent, for this had been no haphazard growth, but a planned city, covering a whole mountain slope and occupied by some fifty thousand people.

Lanny was used to Roman ruins, from his childhood on the Cap d'Antibes, and later in England and Spain, but he had never seen anything like this. He inspected the remains of a noble public library—the Roman equivalent of what the Americans call a "Carnegie" library. It had been built at a cost of four hundred thousand sesterces, bequeathed to his native town by the senator Marcus Julius Quintianus Flavus Rogatianus—a gentleman known to the modern world solely because of the inscription found in these ruins.

In his youth Lanny's heart had been touched by a tablet found in Antibes, telling about a "little Septentrion child" who had "danced and pleased in the theater." Here in the forum of this ancient city of the Emperor Trajan he read an inscription from those same ancient days and in that same spirit: "To hunt, to bathe, to play, to laugh, that is to live." How he would have enjoyed being able to do those same things!

IV

Among Lanny's purposes in North Africa was to meet the younger Denis de Bruyne. The Army had been in great part demobilized under the terms of the armistice, and both officers and men were required to wear civilian clothing. Lanny might have found his friend by inquiring among military people, but he could not take the chance of knowing a reputed Gaullist. He employed a device which had worked on previous occasions, bringing it about that his presence in the city was mentioned in the newspapers. So, when he returned to Algiers, he found at his hotel a note in the familiar handwriting of his near-godson. Denis was living in one of the suburbs of the capital and said that he would call wherever Lanny asked. The P.A. wrote, appointing an hour and signing the name "Bienvenu."

It was a pleasant afternoon, and when Denis came they strolled into the extensive gardens of the hotel and found themselves a quiet seat in the shade of a great bougainvillaea vine. They weren't exactly hiding, they were avoiding making themselves conspicuous in this spy-ridden town.

Denis was only a year or two older than his brother, but he looked ten years older; there were lines of care in his face and traces of gray in his hair. He was of medium size, slender but strong. His dark eyes were melancholy and his manner grave, with none of Charlot's humor and *élan*. He had been twice wounded in the course of desperate fighting near Maubeuge, and after he had recovered his health at home, he had had the devil's own time escaping from the Germans and getting into Southern France. He had been hidden for a time on the Côte d'Azur and had come near seeking refuge in Bienvenu, but had decided that it wouldn't be fair to Lanny's mother.

Now the young *capitaine's* position was sad. He had made no open breach with his family, but the difference between his ideas and those of his father and brother made it impossible for them to co-operate, or, on account of the censorship, even to discuss the subject. Mail between Occupied and Unoccupied France was restricted by the Germans to a postcard with various printed statements, of which you crossed out those which did not apply. It was a criminal offense to use any sort of code—it might even carry the death penalty if you conveyed political or military information. So Denis, *fils*, could tell his father and his wife and children that he was well, and he could get the same news from them, but he could not tell them what he was thinking or ask what they were thinking.

The brothers had been inseparable; and now, when Denis learned that Lanny had talked with Charlot in Vichy, it was pathetic to see his excitement. He wanted to hear every word that Charlot had spoken, and when he learned that his brother was helping to organize the Légion Tricolore in the service of Pierre Laval, his despair was pitiful to see. Nor was he comforted when Lanny hinted: "All those factional disputes are going to be wiped out, Denis. The American Army will be coming." Denis didn't ask when or where or how. He was thinking only about his brother and exclaimed: "They will shoot him!"

"No," declared Lanny, "the Americans won't be like that. They will shoot only Germans."

"The French will shoot him, Lanny. They will call him a traitor, and he *is* a traitor! What defense can there be for a man who betrays *la patrie* into the hands of a *fripon* like Laval or for his *apaches* who seize French patriots and turn them over to the Nazis to be tortured and shot?"

Lanny looked about him hastily. "Be careful," he said, moving a little closer. "Remember, I am a foreigner, and I'm supposed to be here buying art works."

V

Lanny had had weeks to think this problem over in advance. He knew that this young officer was the soul of honor. There was no one

Lanny knew better or would trust more completely. The only question was, what his ideas were now, and whether they were such that he could fit in with American policies. If so, a presidential agent would have another contact, and one whose value might prove to be great.

"Denis," he began cautiously, "as you know, I have had nothing to do with political questions for many years. I have told myself that my work as an art expert justified me in keeping aloof, so that I could travel in all countries and meet all sorts of people. Now the fact that my country has been attacked makes that attitude more difficult."

"*Vraiment, cher ami!* I have been wondering how you could expect to keep it. I don't see how any man can keep it in these times."

"I have been doing a lot of worrying over the question. Give me your advice about France. What do you think is going to happen, and what could I do to help?"

"You ask me—and I have been looking forward to asking *you!* I am clear in my mind that De Gaulle is the man to whom France must look for salvation. What troubles me is my own course, whether to try to get to Britain and join him, or to stick it out here and do what I can to influence my friends and others. When I heard that you were here I was greatly pleased because I thought you would be able to tell me about America and what we have to expect from her."

"First, tell me about De Gaulle. You are in a position to hear his broadcasts?"

"This is something secret, of course, for it is considered treason for an officer to listen to them. Vichy has reason to fear his words, for he thrills the soul of every true Frenchman who hears him. To me he has become a symbol of *la France libérée*. What do they think of him in America?"

"One hears many different opinions, and people ask me to find out. Some are troubled because, so they say, he has Communists active in his London committee."

"But what can he do, Lanny? In war you have to accept what allies come to your standard. The Russians are fighting on our side, and even Churchill has had to welcome them. So has Roosevelt, unless I am misinformed."

"We know those men, and we can understand their maneuvers. But nobody that I know seems to have met De Gaulle, and so we find it harder to decide what is maneuver and what is his real belief."

"I do not know him, Lanny, but I have read his book, *Au Fil de l'Épée,* and anybody who has studied it will know that he is a French patriot, *pur sang.* He is the last man in France who would be influenced by Red ideas; he stands for the rights of property, for order and discipline, for the defense of *la patrie* against foes inside and out."

"If Roosevelt can have his way in this war," suggested Lanny mildly, "the slogan is to be democracy."

"I know, and we all use the word, but we give it our own meaning. To the Reds it means confiscation and dictatorship in the name of the proletariat; but Roosevelt means nothing like that, I am sure, and the order-loving people of France will not mean it either. If De Gaulle can have his way, there will be no more venal politicians stirring up the mob as a means of lining their own pockets."

Lanny let his friend talk and weighed his words carefully. Lanny had never seen the book of the new French Jeanne d'Arc—so De Gaulle had described himself—but he had seen extracts quoted. The very title, meaning "to the edge of the sword," repelled the American, who couldn't conceive a man using that title unless he meant to convey a threat. The quotations had had a decidedly Fascist color and indicated that the Colonel de Gaulle—so he had been when the book was published—was calling for something resembling what General Franco had done in Spain: the Fascist temper and technique, without the label, adapted to a Catholic culture and the purposes of the Church hierarchy.

Right now Lanny's attention was on his near-godson and what this London-sponsored crusade meant to him. Lanny was interested to discover that the defeat and enslavement of Marianne hadn't changed the young *capitaine's* social ideas a particle. He still believed in the right of the De Bruyne family, in co-operation with the other hundred and ninety-nine great families, to control French industry and finance, and, through the Army, control the government. He still wanted what Pétain wanted, a Catholic France, benevolently kept in order by the general staff. He would have endorsed the old Marshal's slogan of fatherland, labor, and family. Lanny reflected that it shouldn't be hard for the two brothers to get together after the war was over; they both wanted the same thing, the difference lay only in how they expected to get it.

VI

This realization would modify somewhat the extent to which Lanny could confide in his younger friend, but it didn't change the basic fact that he had here a man of honor who could be of great use to the American Army, if and when it was ready to establish its *pied-à-terre* on French North African soil. If it was proper for General de Gaulle to use Reds, it would be equally proper for a P.A. to use a Catholic. So presently he said: "Denis, I am going to entrust you with a secret, and you must understand that it is the most confidential thing I have ever told you. You are not free to mention it to anybody else without first getting my approval and consent."

"Certainly, Lanny. I hope you are going to tell me that you have decided to be on the side of France in this dark hour."

"That is a part of it," Lanny said and dropped his voice to a whisper. "The rest is that not long ago I had the good fortune to meet President Roosevelt and to gain his confidence. The reason I am here now is to sound out the situation and learn what the Americans have to expect if they should come to this shore."

"You mean that they are coming, Lanny?" This in a tone of excitement. "*When?*"

"If I knew that, I could not say it. But the truth is, the decision has not yet been taken. This much is sure, however; before this war is over, our armies will come here. So no effort that is spent in inquiry and preparation will be wasted. If you accept that, and act upon it, you will surely not be disappointed."

A military man, who knew what secrecy was, could not ask more. Denis laid his hand on Lanny's arm, and Lanny could feel it trembling. "That is the most wonderful news I have ever heard, and you may count upon me to the very death. I had about made up my mind to make a run for it and try to get to Brazzaville; but now I will stay, and you may consider me as under your orders."

"That is more than I would ask, *cher ami*," replied Lanny with a smile. "I am not used to giving orders and am far too uncertain as to my own judgments. Let us say that we shall consult together. You give me the benefit of your knowledge of the local situation, and I will pass it on to the government without naming you or giving any indication of how I got it; that is, of course, unless you wish me to act otherwise."

"What I wish," declared Denis fervently, "is to drive the Nazi *doryphores* out of France, and indeed off the earth."

"*Très bien!*" agreed the American. "But tell me, what is a *doryphore?*"

"Oh, you haven't heard that? A *doryphore* is a potato bug, and we apply it to the Germans because they demand and get nearly all of the French potato crop. In our food-saving campaigns we send the school-children out to pick the bugs off the plants, and they have had the bright idea of carrying signs reading '*Mort aux doryphores!*' The Ger-

mans can do nothing about that, so it gives delight to our people, who
have not yet been entirely deprived of their sense of mischief."

VII

They skipped their dinner, not wishing to appear together in any
café, and continued their conference into the night. Lanny told about
his talks with Lemaigre and with others of the ruling group in this
colonial capital. (Nominally it was a part of "Metropolitan France,"
and proud of that fact, but in most ways it resembled a colony.) Lanny
was interested to observe the reactions of his old-time friend to the
various cliques which were pulling and hauling the community's political affairs. Denis, *fils*, despised the vegetable-oil man as a collaborator, but at the same time he respected him as a man of great affairs and
as a friend of Denis, *père*. It was a worthy work that he had done, trying to save the taxpayers of France from being plundered by the mobsters; also, it was the most natural thing in the world that his friends of
the Comité des Forges should be trying to save their funds by bringing them to North Africa. In fact, Denis, *fils*, took it for granted that
his father would be in on such arrangements.

Once more it was that powerful thing called "social position." The
scion of the De Bruynes enjoyed it, in spite of being one of the wicked
Gaullists. He went about in the salons and was able to reveal to a P.A.
many details of what was going on. The same thing had been true even
in the Army; Denis had never said it, for that would have been bad
taste, but Lanny had understood that he had been no mere *capitaine*,
but a prospective heir to fortune and power, a man who might some
day be able to offer social advantages to his major, his colonel, even his
general.

What was going to be the attitude of demobilized Army officers to
an American landing? Denis reported that to a man they hated the
Germans, and "collaboration" was not in their vocabulary. Many of
them also disliked the British, but few objected to the Americans, and
they would find it easier to tolerate an invasion by them. What stood
in the way was their loyalty to the old Marshal. Denis himself despised
the "old fraud," as he called Pétain, saying that his piety was "political"—he was a freethinker, and married to a divorced woman. But
to most of Denis's brother officers the Marshal was still the hero of
Verdun. "You know," explained the *capitaine*, "we French have a notion of what we call 'legitimacy'; our monarchy was based upon it, and
the idea survived all the storms of the Revolution. The old Marshal is

the legitimate head of our state, and especially of our Army; that authority has been properly handed on to him, and it is hard for us not to recognize it."

"Like the apostolic succession in the Church," commented the American. With anyone else he would have smiled as he said it, but he knew that Denis was one of the faithful and would see nothing humorous in the idea that St. Peter had received power by the laying on of hands of the Lord, and that he had passed on that power to the bishops, and so it had come down, even through the blood-smeared hands of the Borgias. "The apostolic succession in grace conferred by ordination," was the formula.

Lanny inquired as to the attitude of the Navy, and Denis replied that the situation would be far more delicate there. The officers of the Fleet were even more "legitimist" than those of the Army, and their hatred of the British was far more intense because of the pounding they had taken at Mers-el-Kébir. Any expeditionary force would have to be convoyed by the British, and the French would be strongly tempted to resist it. Propaganda was difficult to spread on board the ships, but Denis said he had whispered his ideas among such officers as he could trust. "Navies are always ultra-conservative," he explained, and Lanny said that was true in America, even under the New Deal.

VIII

The time came when Denis asked the inevitable question: "Have you met Mr. Robert Murphy?" Lanny explained that he was working independently, observing the situation from all angles, and this diplomat was one of the objects of his attention. Denis had met him several times and reported that he was a good man for the post; he was gracious and genial and tried to understand all points of view. Denis had attempted to explain to him the position of the Gaullists, and Mr. Murphy had thanked him but had avoided committing himself.

"Apparently," said the *capitaine*, "your government has a prejudice against General de Gaulle which we, his admirers, do not understand and which no one will explain to us. Mr. Murphy would not admit it, and apparently he wanted me to believe that it was the policy of his government to maintain strict neutrality among the different factions of the French. But I happened to know from other sources that elaborate negotiations were carried on with ex-Premier Herriot, at his home in Lyon, urging him to come to North Africa and assume leadership of the Free French. When this plan did not succeed, they approached

General Giraud, who just recently made his escape from the German fortress of Königstein. My understanding is that he is to come to Algiers for that purpose."

"I have heard such a rumor," responded the P.A. "Tell me what you think of him."

"He is a soldier and a man of honor. He will fight for *la patrie* to the best of his ability. But I do not see how he can have any success as a leader of the movement. What claim to legitimacy could he have?"

"I am trying to understand your point of view, Denis. What claim of that sort can General de Gaulle have? When I mention him to Frenchmen here, the response is: 'A mere brigadier-general, self-proclaimed as head of our government.'"

"I know that it is difficult to explain, Lanny. De Gaulle was first in the field and he has managed to get the ear of the people. He seems to us an inspired leader, one of the deliverers whom God has always sent to our nation when the need became extreme."

Lanny would have liked to say that legitimacy and inspiration were different things, and frequently opposite; but he didn't want to hurt his friend's feelings, he merely wanted the "lowdown" on the followers of De Gaulle so as to know how to deal with them, and to report them to the Boss—one who seemed to Lanny to possess both legitimacy and inspiration. The secret agent wanted also to understand Mr. Robert Murphy, and what he was telling members of the "two hundred French families" about the intentions of the American government toward *them*. Lanny could understand why a kindly and trusting career man of the State Department seemed such an excellent choice to Denis de Bruyne; he was a gentleman, and knew how to talk to other gentlemen; he was Catholic, and knew how to deal with Frenchmen of that conservative sort.

Lanny learned from Denis that the Counselor had made M. Lemaigre-Dubreuil his confidential adviser and practically his righthand Frenchman. It had been Lemaigre who had suggested Herriot and had sent agents to that statesman, who called himself a "Radical Socialist"—in much the same way that Southern defenders of property rights in the United States call themselves "Democrats." It had been Lemaigre who had suggested General Giraud, and even, so it was whispered, had persuaded the Germans to let him escape. When Lanny expressed incredulity at this idea, the scion of the De Bruynes explained: "You know how it was before the war, Lanny. Many of our leading men of affairs were intimate with the Germans; they did not wait for *Le Couple France-Allemagne* to be realized officially, but went ahead and introduced it on their own. Now, of course, they have influence among Germans, and if they ask a favor, and pay for it, they may get it. Who can tell what secret pledges General Giraud may have given before he slid down that rope from the fortress window?"

"Now, now, Denis! That is a Gaullist voicing his prejudice!" is what Lanny wanted to say, but he bit off his tongue. His purpose wasn't to educate his near-godson, but only to use him, as he would use everybody he met, at home and abroad, for the safety of the American Army. Every time Lanny walked or drove along the esplanade of Algiers he saw with his mind's eye that Army coming in under the fire of machine guns and cannon. How many guns there were, and how straight they were shooting, might depend upon what Lanny was doing now, and what Mr. Robert Murphy was doing, and all his twelve young vice-consuls, whose trail Lanny kept crossing now and then.

IX

What more could a P.A. do? What questions should he ask, what people should he meet? He racked his brains and those of his old friend. Denis said there was a small group living like the early Christians, not literally in catacombs, but meeting in secret places and arranging to print and distribute leaflets and otherwise wage ideological war upon the Vichyites. There were several of these people with whom President Roosevelt's friend ought to consult, so the *capitaine* insisted. When Lanny objected that he couldn't afford to identify himself with the Gaullists, Denis replied: "They are not Gaullists; that is just a bad name used by the enemies of *la France libérée*. These friends are patriots. There is a Communist among them, and a Catholic priest; there are several small business people, there are students and teachers and some workingmen."

Lanny asked: "What are the chances of there being a spy among them?"

"Who can ever be sure about that? All I can say is that I cannot imagine which of our twelve would be the Judas. If you cannot risk meeting a large group, let me choose three or four of whom I can be absolutely certain."

"That sounds better, Denis. I cannot be sure of coming back to Algiers, and what I must do is to put trusted friends in touch with our Intelligence service. If you give your consent, a specially trained man will be sent here to contact you and arrange to furnish you with money and supplies."

"That would be a serious proposal for an officer of the French Army to accept, even a demobilized officer. I would prefer that you put it before the group I will bring together. You know how it is when you have pledged yourself and accepted a leader."

The other replied: "It will be much better for me to be dealing with a group, and with someone of whom I am not personally quite so fond. Let me meet not more than four other persons and tell them my story—but not all of it. Let me be the judge of that. You say nothing, except to vouch for me personally."

"It's a deal," said the young officer, speaking American. "I will send you a note to this hotel. It will be signed, let us say 'Annette,' for code." That was the name of Denis's devoted young wife, whom he had not seen for a year and a half. "It will be better to use a woman's name," he explained; "for then, if a spy should read it, he will assume that it is an assignation."

"O.K.," said Lanny, and went back to his hotel room. He spent half an hour typing a report. He double-sealed it and addressed it to Mr. Robert Murphy, Counselor of the United States Embassy. Next morning he went walking. On the street he picked up an intelligent-looking Arab lad and offered him twenty francs to deliver the letter to the Consulate, just across the street from the Admiralty. Ten francs when he started, and the other ten afterward, Lanny said. He went up in the *ascenseur* of an office building and saw the letter handed in at the door. He smiled to himself, considering it something of a joke on the genial career man mentioned in the report. Lanny could be quite sure that as an honorable official he wouldn't open the inside letter; but suppose he happened to be psychic!

X

A note from "Annette" made an appointment for the following evening. The spot agreed upon was in the Place Bugeau, near the harbor, and there happened to be a military band concert. After one of those dreadful moist and sticky hot days for which the climate of Algiers is notorious, the night was cool, and a great crowd had come out for fresh air and free entertainment. Lanny had to do some searching before he found his friend. They did not give any sign, but Denis started to walk and Lanny followed at a discreet distance.

He was prepared to be taken into some dark alley and to dive into a cellar of underground conspirators. He didn't relish the prospect; the alleys swarmed with Arab refugees who had no other place to sleep, and the filth was such that you hated to set foot in it. But Denis led the way along the main street, the Rue Michelet, past throngs of people on their way to the movies. He entered number 26, a modern apartment house, and waited in the entrance for his friend. Their goal was the home of Professor Henri Aboulker, a Jewish physician.

In a drawing-room furnished in the demoded French bourgeois style, with heavy fumed oak furniture, the thickest carpets, draperies, and tapestries possible, and gilt on everything that could carry it, the P.A. was introduced to four men: first, the professor himself, nearly seventy, and crippled from World War I; he was a professor at the university medical school. Second, to the professor's son, José by name, a medical student of twenty-two, eager, intelligent, and determined. Third, to M. d'Astier de la Vigerie, middle-aged, very French, slender and dapper, good-looking and aware of the fact, Lanny decided. The fourth man was younger and wore the garb of the Jesuit order; he was the Abbé Cordier, and it soon became evident that he regarded D'Astier as his leader.

The *capitaine* had complied with Lanny's request to say nothing except that here was an old friend and the bearer of important news. Lanny revealed to them that he was an agent of the American government, sent to gather data and report on the prospects in the event of an American landing in French North Africa; he desired to be informed concerning every aspect of the situation, and would arrange for Intelligence agents to get in touch with the most dependable persons. He requested that these friends of his old and very dear friend tell him as much as they were willing about themselves, their organizations, their plans, and their hopes.

They did this freely. The doctor was president of the Algerian Jewish Federation. He reported that the large population of his people were chafing under the shameful restrictions which the local government had imposed upon them—compelled, of course, by the Vichyites, compelled, in turn, by the Nazis. José declared that the Jewish youth were ready to rise to the last one; but they could do nothing until they had arms. If they acted prematurely they would bring on only a frightful pogrom. Lanny replied that all American and British broadcasts to France were warning the population to do nothing until they received orders; and this applied to Jews more than to any others of the population.

D'Astier de la Vigerie was one of the organizers of the "Chantiers de la Jeunesse," an Algerian youth organization with all the Fascist trimmings. He now assured Lanny that this was mostly camouflage, that secret propaganda had been carried on, and that his four thousand young people—their ages up to twenty—despised the *collaborateurs* and would put themselves at the service of the Americans to do whatever was desired. Denis de Bruyne put in the remark that the youngsters adored M. d'Astier and called him "Chief." The Abbé Cordier added that these facts were well known to Mr. Robert Murphy, who was counting upon them in his plans.

All this, of course, was good news and a source of satisfaction to an itinerant investigator. He spent several hours questioning these gentlemen and storing their replies in his mind. The intricacies of French politics presented few mysteries to the son of Budd-Erling, for he had watched them for a long time, and on this African shore he found everything reproduced in miniature. He was somewhat startled to learn that the youth leader and the abbé were royalists, that is to say, followers of the Comte de Paris, the pretender to the throne of a monarchy which had been dead for more than a century. This meant that they were the most fanatical of all French reactionaries, devotees of Roman Catholicism in its unreconstructed medieval form. The group in Paris had been headed by Charles Maurras and Léon Daudet, publishers of ferociously abusive newspapers and tireless conspirators against the Third Republic.

Lanny wondered, had Denis come out of the war a "subject" of this Comte, who was at present a refugee in Spanish Morocco, under the protection of a Catholic-Fascist Caudillo? The American reminded himself that all three of the De Bruynes, father and two sons, had been supporters of the Cagoule, a sort of Ku Klux Klan of France, but far more violent and deadly. Lanny listened to these two conspirators and saw the light of fanaticism in their eyes. He realized that he was keeping dangerous company; but that was a part of the game he was playing, and if the readers of *L'Action Française* were willing to help save the lives of American soldiers, they must surely be allowed to do it. Five years ago F.D.R. had explained to his new agent that there were millions of Catholics who were not French royalists but loyal American citizens, and who controlled a mass of votes without which there could be no Democratic Party. So he had sent his friend Admiral Leahy to pray with the old Maréchal in Vichy, and the Catholic Mr. Murphy to Algiers to line up a Jesuit abbé and the leader of an imitation Fascist youth group against the old Maréchal's supporters in the colony which was the richest jewel in his crown.

Lanny went away from that secret meeting whispering to himself: "Good Lord, we are going to take Algiers with the boy scouts!"

XI

While Lanny was engaged with these activities, he read the miserable newspapers which the censors plus the paper shortage permitted to the people of Algiers. Everything was treated from the propaganda point of view, the German successes played up and the Allied played down. General Rommel had begun a fierce attack against the British line, which had seesawed back and forth over a distance of some five hundred miles and had been established west of Tobruk. After a week or two of fierce fighting, the British were beginning to show signs of weakening, and this made a deep impression upon the rest of North Africa, both the Europeans and the natives. Lanny could see doubt and fear in the eyes of his friends, and exultation in the eyes of the near-Fascists whom he had to pretend to hold as friends.

At the same time the Germans on the eastern front launched the tremendous attack in the Ukraine which they had been preparing for many months. They, too, made gains, and the pro-Vichy newspapers hailed these as the beginning of the end. When the British chose this time to make a twenty-year military alliance with the Soviet Union, this seemed to complete the Vichy case. "You see," said their newspapers and radios, "just as we told you, the British Empire is the devil's ally, and this is a war for the salvation of the Christian world." When the elegant ladies of the colonial plutocracy echoed this in Lanny's presence, he expressed regret that his recently shattered legs made it impossible for him to play a soldier's role in this conflict. These ladies, as a rule, distrusted Americans as socially dubious, but they had learned that the son of Budd-Erling had been honored with the friendship of Admiral Darlan and had even been received by *le vieux lui-même*.

There were successes to counterbalance the Allied defeats, but these the Algiers newspapers did not mention, or if they did, it was only to cast doubt upon them. London issued the claim that eleven hundred bombers had attacked Cologne, and in the short time of an hour and a half had destroyed a great part of the city's industries. Vichy said that claim was absurd on the face of it; there weren't enough airfields in Britain to launch such a number of big planes at one time, and they would have bumped into one another in the sky. It was the same when the American Navy claimed to have destroyed a great part of a Japanese Fleet by air attack near Midway. Nobody from Vichy had been there to see it; nobody but Americans had been there, and it was obvious that they were making up stories to keep their public satisfied.

There was an "Armistice Commission" of the Germans and Italians in Algiers, for the purpose of seeing that the French obeyed the orders of their conquerors. That meant hundreds of Nazis, both military and civilian, and Lanny might have met some of them and sought to trade on his old-time friendship. But he didn't think he could get anything out of any Nazi now, and it seemed to him the part of wisdom to meet as few as he could and to be the ivory-tower art lover, wholly aloof from a cruel war into which his country had been dragged by forces beyond any art lover's control. The Germans would have their doubts about such an attitude, but their spies would be unable to disprove it.

XII

Lanny's various art purchases had been properly packed, and arrangements had been made for shipment, no easy matter, requiring influence and many *pourboires*. In these days of food shortages and black markets, everybody's palm was held out, and you couldn't blame him, poor devil. Robbie Budd's son had been taught from childhood that the way to get along in the world was to have plenty of money and to distribute it freely; this attitude had been confirmed, as a war measure, by no less an authority than the Commander-in-Chief of his country's Armed Forces. Lanny spent; and while he dared not keep any written records, he kept in mind a rough estimate of what he had expended as a P.A., and when he got back to New York he would withdraw that amount from the account which F.D.R. had established for him.

He was going to French Morocco, partly because Casablanca was a convenient place from which to jump off, and partly because he had been told that Moroccan mosaics were even finer than those in Algiers. Also, he reflected that if any of the collaborators had become suspicious of his activities, it would be better that he should manifest interest in more than one part of the African coast. From the Mediterranean port to the Atlantic port was some twelve hundred miles as the planes flew, and he would keep the enemy's mind jumping from one to the other.

The evening before his departure Lanny spent in the home of the Jewish doctor, along with Denis and the other three conspirators. They had gone to work with renewed ardor as a result of his assurances and they had much to report. Later they turned on the long-distance radio set and heard the voice of an announcer: "*Ici Londres.*" He introduced the hero of the Free French, General de Gaulle, and the five conspirators listened to that fervid oratory which had so thrilled French refugees all over the world. It wasn't so good this time, because the orator devoted most of his talk to scolding the American government for continuing in its refusal to recognize his government as the one and only representative of France. It was made quite evident that this Jeanne d'Arc in striped military trousers had little love in his heart for Americans; and this was embarrassing to the four Frenchmen who had agreed that America was the only power in the world that might be able to help the French to freedom.

They talked about the problem, and Lanny explained the position of his government, that to recognize De Gaulle as the sole French authority would mean a formal break with Vichy and would have the effect of closing a window into the Axis world. Lisbon and Stockholm were other such windows, but not to be compared with Vichy. "There are millions of Frenchmen who are loyal to the old Marshal, but who hate the Germans, and these people help us and we can help them," Lanny argued. "But if we should break with Vichy, or force Vichy to break with us, all that would come to an end. I personally am here because of that contact, and the same thing applies to Murphy and his vice-consuls. We don't want to fight you, and surely it's important that we have a chance to come here and tell you so!"

Nobody among the rebels in Algiers could deny the soundness of that argument. Lanny said nothing personal about their hero, but he came away from the broadcast with the conviction that however courageous a soldier the General might be, he was a very poor statesman and no sort of diplomat. When the P.A. put into the hands of Denis de Bruyne the large bundle of medium-sized French banknotes which he had been accumulating for this purpose, he felt obliged to say: "This money is not mine, it is the United States government's; and I have to put upon you the restriction that it is to be used to further the policy of that government, which is that we are not favoring any faction or group of the French, but are appealing to the whole French people to help us in ousting the Nazis, and setting you free to choose your own government in a democratic election."

Denis replied: "That is all we have a right to ask."

XIII

The flight to Casablanca took some five hours, part of it through bumpy air. Soon after the plane left the fertile Algerian plateau the landscape changed, and in place of wheatfields and vineyards on the

terraced mountain slopes the country became lonely and in parts desert. Morocco was a country whose wild tribes had been conquered by
the French and the Spanish only with the greatest difficulty. The rains
were uncertain; when they fell the great land companies made money;
and when they failed, the poor peasants starved or took to wandering
as their forefathers did. Forests were few, and from the plane you
could see herds of cattle, goats, and sheep, tended by solitary white-
clad men. Great gullies had been cut in the land by stormy waters.
Here and there were clusters of mud huts, and on the hilltops little
cubical Moslem shrines with white domes.

In Casablanca, Lanny found a fine modern port, made by a break-
water of which the French were proud. In its business district were
office buildings of whitestone with many balconies, a concession to
the climate; its native quarter was a place of vice and danger. The
shops were known as *souks,* and most of them were the size of a booth,
made of American oil cans cut and flattened. Whining beggars followed Lanny everywhere, calling for *baksheesh,* and he had to learn
to say *"Imshi!"* which, he was told, means " 'Tis naught!" It seemed to
do the business.

Lanny had brought letters of introduction and quickly found out
who had mosaics to show him. He was surprised to learn that the native grapevine worked even at a distance of a thousand miles; the people
knew who he was and what he wanted. While waiting for the in-
dispensable Hajek to arrive, he had a pleasant time inspecting various
art treasures. "Infidels" were not permitted inside the mosques, but
they could stand outside and admire the details of fine buildings,
erected in a far-off age of glory. Mosaics were everywhere, and some
could be bought. It was only a question of time to bargain.

Meanwhile, in the evenings, Lanny visited the homes of the *haute
bourgeoisie* of "Casa," as fashionable and as French as in Paris. They
were pleased to be exclusive, but circumstances forced them to be
curious about Americans, and they all wanted to ask questions of a
son of Budd-Erling. Lanny found them somewhat more free-spoken
than those of their class in Algiers. They were a thousand miles nearer
to America, and perhaps the winds from the broad Atlantic had swept
their heads clear. The wife of a wealthy exporter of wines and olive
oil said to him at her dinner table, in the presence of several guests:
"When are you Americans coming, and will you come with enough?"
The guest smiled enigmatically and asked: "Do you want us to come?"
The reply was: "We'll be polite to you. *Mais pas d'Anglais, s'il vous
plaît!*" No English!

He was still more surprised when he presented a letter that Denis had given him to a certain Lieutenant-General Émile-Marie Béthouart, who, Denis said, was a cousin of his mother's family. Denis wrote: "Lanny Budd was a dear friend of my mother's, and you may talk to him as you would to me." The cautious officer arranged the conference in the home of a friend, and took the guest out to a summer house in the garden, where they could be safe from intruders. There the stiffly corseted officer unbent enough to ask the customary questions: "When?" and "Where?" and "How many?" Lanny had to make his usual reply: "The decision has not yet been taken, but it will be as soon as we can assemble the force."

"This is the absolute essential," declared Béthouart. "It must be enough. You must not fail, and you must not change your minds after you have started."

"That I am authorized to promise," replied the P.A. "I am told that one of your high officers has declared that if we come with one division he will fire on us, and if we come with twenty he will embrace us."

"That was General Weygand, and it explains why he is no longer in command in North Africa. You understand that courage must be combined with discretion."

"*Oui, très bien, mon Général.* Let me inform you that I expect to fly to America in a few days, and what you say will be reported to President Roosevelt personally, and to no one else except under his orders."

"Explain to your great President that the French armies here have not been demobilized as in Algiers; the Germans did not wish the task of controlling the Moors. I command a division, and if your forces land near Rabat they will find my forces lined up on the beaches, but withholding their fire. You must come ashore fast, because otherwise I may be court-martialed and shot. Our commander, General Noguès, does not agree with my point of view, and I doubt if he will let himself be persuaded."

Lanny promised, and when the time came he did his best to keep that promise; but the General came within an inch of seeing himself proved a prophet—too late to do him any good!

XIV

Lanny got word of art treasures in Marrakech, and decided to throw a scare into the negotiators in "Casa." (Everybody demanded a fortune from an American millionaire, and they didn't give way normally.) So Lanny hired a venerable car equipped to run on charcoal, and with a little trailer to carry the fuel for a round trip of three or four hundred miles. The route lay toward the south, through wheatfields alternating with barren stretches, with aloes such as stood by the gates of Bienvenu and giant cactus such as he had seen in the California deserts. The little Mohammedan shrines called *marabouts* were everywhere.

All this scenery was dominated by the Atlas Mountains to the southeast—taller than the Alps, and covered with perpetual snow. As it melted, streams cut great chasms through the land, and the life of the ancient civilizations through the centuries had depended upon catching this water at high levels and spreading it over the land or bringing it to the cities. Aqueducts were everywhere, built out of the stones of the earlier ones. Those in Marrakech were low and appeared like swift-moving brooks. Approaching the city you passed over a bridge a thousand feet long, with twenty-seven graceful stone arches built by the Almohades, rulers of this country some eight hundred years previously.

Marrakech is a vast city, an oasis of palm trees, spread out so that it seems bigger than it is. It has immense estates with high walls, and the owners were living in comfort untroubled by war. It has a mosque and minaret, the Koutoubiya, built of rose-colored stone, and when Lanny stood and watched it at the hour of prayer he marveled at the power of the human spirit, for these beautiful things had come out of the soul of a humble and untutored camel driver of the seventh century. There is plenty of fault to be found with the Koran as a guide to conduct in the modern world, but no one could doubt that it had been superior to the forms of idol worship it replaced.

Lanny had a letter to a Moorish dignitary who lived not many miles from this ancient city. He owned an oasis and had groves of oranges, and palm trees loaded with great clusters of dates; there were herds of camels, goats, and sheep, and at the same time many appurtenances of civilization, including a radio set and a motor truck of Detroit manufacture. The master of this household, who spoke a little French and understood still more, showed the guest about his estate. Near one of the sheep pens Lanny noticed an ancient drinking fountain, and behind it a large plaque with one of the most beautiful mosaics he had yet come upon. He expressed his admiration and asked tactfully if it might be purchased and taken to show Americans what Moorish taste at its best could be. He was told to wait until the morrow, and the matter would be discussed.

X V

He was to spend the evening in this household, and it proved to be interesting. He did not meet any of the women, but he guessed that they were listening behind portieres. He met about a dozen men, tall, dark, and handsome, dressed in ceremonial white for a distinguished guest. There were two lads, grandsons of the master, slender youths who reminded Lanny of himself in the days when he had danced all over the lawns of Bienvenu and the beaches of Juan. There was a banquet, the like of which the world traveler had never seen; ten courses, and he had to eat them all from a low table, sitting with his heels tucked under his thighs: chicken broth with rice; lamb roasted whole on a spit—you tore off chunks with the thumb and two fingers, and it was hot; pigeon pie, sweetened; chicken roasted, with a custard gravy; rice fritters in oil; pigeon stuffed with sweetened vermicelli; *koos-koos*, made of grains chopped up with mutton or chicken and highly seasoned; olives baked in a bowl and covered with poached eggs; caramel custard; and last of all oranges. Before and after each course Negro slaves, wearing large silver earrings, brought you a basin, soap, and towel to wash your hands. Each course was washed down with scented mint or jasmine tea.

Later in the evening Negro slaves played the flageolet, the flute, and the drum, the melody in thirds and sixths; then a troop of graceful youths showed the dancing they had learned in a school maintained by the Giaour, the native governor of this district. Lanny told them about the "eurythmics" he had learned as a boy at the Dalcroze School in Germany, and it turned into quite a lecture on the dance arts of the West. It was impossible for these men to imagine themselves dancing with a lady in their arms, but they knew that it was a custom, to them much more barbarous than eating with your fingers.

Far into the night these Moorish gentlemen conversed with their cultivated guest. They told him that the sooner the Americans came to French Morocco the better it would please the Mohammedan population. They were so pleased with his compliments and interest in their culture that in the morning the master of the family insisted upon presenting him with the mosaic. Lanny protested, and ceased only when he saw that he was committing a discourtesy. The host would have his workmen chisel out the tiles and they would be packed with care and delivered by that wonderful Detroit truck. Lanny took photographs of the fountain, and of the one-story red stone mansion with all the men of the family standing in front of it. He promised to come again and to send some Detaze sketches of North Africa in remembrance of his visit.

He drove back to "Casa" in the rattly tin Lizzie. From there he sent a cablegram to his father: "Am ready to return." It had been agreed that Robbie was to notify Baker, who would see to providing transportation from wherever in the world a P.A. might show up. Lanny made arrangements for the packing and shipping of the various art treasures; he paid off his faithful translator and guide; and two days after the filing of his cablegram he received notice that a place had been reserved for him on a plane flying from Tangier to Lisbon. The Army had charge of everything now, and whenever the President's confidential man asked for something he got it quickly. A passenger was just a different kind of package—but one that had to have food and drink on the way, and a bed to sleep in, and magazines, a checkerboard, writing paper, anything he might fancy, including an aluminum can if he got airsick, and a "Mae West" and rubber boat if he had to land in the middle of the Atlantic Ocean!

BOOK THREE

A Mad World, My Masters

7

Love Is Love Forevermore

I

LANNY BUDD, three times a husband, had learned a lot about women. One of these things was that the chosen one is never to be taken for granted. The three simple words, "I love you," which have been spoken so many millions of times since the human race began, have never once been found monotonous—save only in sad instances where the sentiment is not shared. When a woman has given herself to a man, and especially when she is carrying his child, she wants to know that this enterprise is to be co-operative, and that she has made no mistake in a commitment which, once made, is hard to withdraw from.

Lanny wished his chosen one to be in no slightest doubt on this subject. Therefore, when he was in her presence, he spoke the magical words on every occasion, together with the smiles and gestures which accompany and confirm them. When duty took him away from her, he never failed to write her once a week, using the time which other people took to attend church. This letter had to be written with one eye on the censor, a suspicious anonymous person who kept watch for unusual expressions, names, numbers, anything which might be code. Fortunately the censor had no objection to "man and woman stuff"; you were free to say "I love you," but beware of repeating it too often, for that might be code, and if you made some "x" marks you would surely damn your letter to the furnace fires, even though you might add the explanation: "These are kisses."

All this Lanny had explained in advance. He would never express any political opinion or refer to any military event; he would never say where he was or whom he had met, unless it was some commonplace name, like Emily or Sophie. He would say "I have bought a fine painting," but never "I have bought a fine Meissonier," for the censor might think that was the name of an airplane or a tank. He would sign his own name and address the letter to "Miss Laurel Creston," because

134

she was keeping her maiden name as a writer, and also because sweethearts might be more intriguing to European censors than wives. He would add something of a complimentary nature for the severe functionary's benefit: "The French are kind to me; they never lose their interest in art"; or, "You would be surprised to know how many of the people here, in spite of all their troubles, labor to preserve the flame of their culture."

Now, when the plane deposited him at the Washington airport, the traveler delayed only long enough to get Baker on the telephone and ask for his appointment; then he put in a call to New York, and when he heard Laurel's voice he said: "Darling, here I am, safe and well."

"Oh, Lanny!" she cried. "Such a relief! I have been holding my breath."

"Be careful," he cautioned, with a smile in his voice; "you are breathing for two."

"Where are you?"

"In Washington. I have to make a report, and then I'll take the first plane. I'm not sure how long it will be, but I'll keep in touch with you. I am well, and have some interesting adventures to tell you. Incidentally, I love you."

"*Truly?*" It was an invitation to repeat, and he no longer had to worry about the censor.

"Truly, truly, with understanding."

"Understanding of what?" came the greedy query.

"Of the treasure you are, and of my need of such treasure."

II

It had been possible for a P.A. to be taken quietly into the "summer White House" because the reporters stayed in Poughkeepsie and were furnished with a list of the day's guests—from which Lanny's name had been omitted. But it would have been another matter for him to come openly into the real White House, where reporters swarmed all day and most of the night, watching for stories as hawks watch for field mice and baby chickens. He followed his well-established procedure of walking to an appointed street corner at night and stepping into Baker's car when it stopped. A few minutes later he was in that familiar bedroom on the second floor of the President's home, with the big mahogany bed, the chintz curtains drawn back for the night breeze, and the prints of old sailing ships on the walls.

In that bed, half lying and half sitting, with pillows propped behind him, was the large bundle of intelligence, kindness, and fun which was a gift of Providence to the people of the United States—a gift much better than they deserved, for they would never have chosen him if they had known in advance what he was going to do. Or so, at any rate, the worshipful Lanny thought. He had come to center all his hopes for social justice and world order on "That Man in the White House."

Here the man was, clad in a blue-and-white-striped pajama coat, and with a sheet over his crippled legs, as it was a hot night in June. He was a big man with a big head, and with powerful shoulders and arms which he had developed by swimming, and by the necessary labor of lifting himself into whatever positions he took. Always he greeted his visitors with a hearty smile, and none more so than his Number 103, for he knew that he was going to hear a good story, and he was prepared to enjoy every word of it. "Welcome to our city!" was his call. "Our hot and muggy city! Take off your coat and turn the fan on you. Would you like some iced tea, or something with a stick in it?"

"No, thanks," Lanny said. "Anybody who has come from Algiers will not mind Washington." He wanted to get down to business and not take the great man's time. Always there was what he took for a warning—a stack of documents and correspondence on the reading table, and some on the bed where this cruelly burdened man worked until far into the night. "You received my reports, Governor?"

"All in numbered order, received and contents noted. Thanks, as always, old man. Your data have been invaluable."

"That's all I need to hear. Here is a statement of the money I spent. I prepared that on the plane coming here, the best I could from memory. I did not dare to make notes of any sort on my trip. I never have a scrap of writing that the enemy is not free to inspect. I think it would be correct to say that my baggage was gone through once a week at every hotel in Europe and North Africa where I stopped."

"Err in your own favor in these accounts, Lanny. As I have told you before, you ought to be paid."

"I bought a couple of paintings in Vichy and a lot of stuff in North Africa, and my commissions will amount to three or four thousand dollars, which will more than cover my expenses. What I have listed here are the sums I paid to members of the underground. I couldn't tell you exactly how much, because I don't dare to draw money at a bank and hand it over to them. I have to change the large bills by making small purchases, and when I have a lot of small bills I tie them into a bundle and slip them into pockets. So when I go to a rendezvous I look like a badly stuffed sausage. I have made several valuable contacts, but didn't dare say much about them in my reports. I'll tell you, or Colonel Donovan, whichever you say."

"Tell *me!*" exclaimed F.D.R. and grinned like a schoolboy. "Sometimes I read a 'whodunit' to put myself to sleep."

Lanny began with Raoul Palma and his underground group. When he came to Mlle. Richard and his two meetings with her, in the Grand Hotel and then in the unlighted den in the Old Town of Toulon, the auditor remarked: "That is really operatic. To complete the libretto you should go back and fall in love with her." Lanny grinned in his turn and said that the libretto would be ruined by the fact that he had a wife in New York. To this F.D.R. remarked: "By the way, my wife met her, and spoke very highly of her. It is better that a secret agent should have a proper wife—he is not so apt to fall for any of the Gestapo ladies."

"I think my record is clear on that score," said Lanny. "I have had several passes made at me, I suspect."

III

Next the story of Monck, then of Denis de Bruyne, and then of General Béthouart; F.D.R. said for Lanny to stop in at Colonel Donovan's office and give him a detailed report on these persons. What the President wanted especially was to ply the traveler with questions about the political situation in all these various places, how well or ill his declared policies were being carried out, and what Lanny thought the effect of them was likely to be. It was a "blue" time, for the Germans were driving hard into the Ukraine and the British were in what appeared to be a rout in Tunisia; but if this responsible man felt any doubts or fears he did not let his agent and friend get the slightest hint of them. He said: "We are getting ready, Lanny, and we are going to do this job. Don't let anybody tell you anything different."

He put the P.A. through a grilling on the subject of the Vichy leaders. What faith, if any, did they have, and what was going to be their conduct in a showdown? Lanny said: "If you could drop an army into Vichy from the sky, they would all be on your side. As it is, they are prisoners of the Nazis, and they have to force themselves to believe that they are right. Laval said to me, in exactly these words: 'I desire a German victory.' I didn't see any signs of his shaking in his boots, but that will be happening some day, no doubt."

And then the problem of Charles André Joseph Marie de Gaulle, author of *Au Fil de l'Épee* and favorite orator of the British Broadcasting Corporation. There was a clamor in circles in America known as "Liberal" that the State Department should recognize this man of both the sword and the pen for what he so loudly claimed to be, the sole head of the government of France. How shocking of us to trade with those hucksters of Vichy, who had sold the honor and the very life of their country to the Nazi tyrants! This agitation was a thorn in the flesh of F.D.R., it appeared; for he, too, had called himself a "Liberal" through his public career and had fought men of the Laval and Darlan type wherever he had met them in American public life—which was frequently. He seemed to be pleading with Lanny to tell him that he was right in the course he had chosen; Lanny, fresh from the scene, was able to do this.

"I was unable to find that General de Gaulle has any following of consequence in North Africa. I have no doubt there are a great many who listen to his broadcasts and cherish affection for him in their hearts; but I am speaking of organized support, anything that you can count on when it comes to action."

"That is what I have to be concerned with, Lanny."

"I bore your instructions in mind and kept before me the image of an army coming ashore. I found that of the people who exercise power of any sort, the greater number hate and fear De Gaulle and call him a puppet of Britain. Most of that, no doubt, is due to the fact that they have compromised, while he has stood out and is attacking them with bitterness. But allowing for that, there seems to be another factor: those who know him say that he is egotistical to the point of fantasy, that he is building himself into a cult, and will have nothing to do with anybody who does not make obeisance at the shrine. They say: 'He makes a fine propagandist, but he would make a wretched administrator.' "

"That is exactly the impression we have of him, Lanny. He is a stickler for punctilio, and does not know how to distinguish between things that are fundamental and those that are petty. He persists in acting as if France were the victor; as if he were doing us favors instead of asking them. He talks about liberty and democracy, but I get the impression that what he is really thinking about is *la gloire,* and that his point of view is fundamentally authoritarian and reactionary."

"Concerning that there is not the slightest doubt," said the P.A. "He was Pétain's Chief of Staff, and his point of view is that of St. Cyr plus the Catholic hierarchy. You do not like me to refer to the religious aspects of the matter, but it seems to me a fact of our world, which nobody can escape, that when you have a Church insisting that it has immutable law and authority handed down from on high, you have a force which cannot be excluded from politics. Whenever it is a question of fundamental social change, you will have the priests preaching against you from every pulpit in the land."

F.D.R. grinned. "I am never going to have them preaching against *me*, Lanny! Believe you me, I keep the Encyclicals of Leo XIII right handy on my desk, and when one of the archbishops starts pounding my desk, objecting to one of my New Deal measures, I read him the marked passages and make him listen."

Lanny would have liked to retort: "I said 'fundamental,' Governor," but he knew that would start an argument and take a lot of a busy man's time. At present there was only one thing fundamental in the world, and that was to unhorse the Axis dictators.

I V

Of the greatest importance to the Commander-in-Chief of an Army soon to land on foreign soil was to know how his agents were working and what success they were having. Lanny did not wait to be questioned, but said: "I avoided Robert Murphy, because I didn't want to attract his attention to myself, and I didn't want to be influenced by personal feelings. I gather that he is an easy fellow to like, and he has made many friends. I came on the trail of his agents in various places, and it is evident that they are doing a job of getting data of all sorts. I suppose that material is coming to the Army, and not to you personally."

"It is important for me to have your confirmation. Have you any suggestions to offer?"

"There is one thing I could not get out of my mind, and that is the question of what commitments Murphy is making with those *collaborateurs* who have already jumped onto his bandwagon, or are preparing to do so. I don't know whether you care to talk to me about that—"

"You have a right to know everything on the subject; you could not work intelligently otherwise."

"Well, I met a great number of Murphy's friends—a dozen at least. He seems to have picked out the big business people, the financial and social oligarchy. I don't know whether that is deliberate policy, or whether it is because he finds it easier to make headway with that sort. Certainly he has managed to please them. But I am wondering whether he is taking them into camp, or whether they are taking *him* into camp."

"It might be a bit of both, and still be of advantage to our cause when the showdown comes."

"These men, you understand, are the last in the world to yield to impulses of good fellowship, or to give something for nothing. They know what they want, and it isn't to be fed taffy."

"But they might want a lot of things and find that they aren't going to get them, Lanny."

"That is what I am wondering about—what commitments are being made."

"Nobody is authorized to make any commitments, except as regards the personal safety of these individuals, of course. Those who help us will escape with their necks—if we are able to arrange it."

"That's fair enough. But what is their political and financial position going to be?"

"The answer to that will be given by the people of France, who will determine the future of their country in a democratic election. That is our public commitment, and nobody is authorized to make any other."

"Let me give you a case, Governor. Does the name of Jacques Lemaigre-Dubreuil mean anything to you?"

"I have heard it, but I'm not sure if I can sort him out from Jacques Benoi-something."

"Benoist-Méchin is a journalist who has become a member of the Laval Cabinet. He is a small potato. But Lemaigre-Dubreuil is one of the most important of the big moneymakers of France. To give his American equivalent, let us say that he is Frank Gannett or Joe Patterson, or some such reactionary publisher; at the same time he is a member of the Federal Reserve Board, and his wife owns General Foods and he runs it; also he is president, or whoever it is behind the scenes who directs the propaganda, of the National Association of Manufacturers and directs its lobby in Washington."

"Quite a Frenchman, indeed!"

"I had a couple of long talks with him and I met him socially on several other occasions. He is in Algiers ostensibly to run his vegetable-oil business, but in reality to protect the interests of his associates of the Comité des Forges, both French and German, who are bringing their money to safety in North African banks and are preparing to follow the cat whichever way it jumps. As I told you before, I don't know what is in Murphy's mind, but I know that in Lemaigre's mind there is a clear conviction that he has got matters fixed up so that when our armies land he and his friends will have the inside track; that, in substance, they will be the government of North Africa, just as in the old days they used to be the government of France—operating, of course, behind a screen."

The President of the United States thought that over for a while before he spoke. "Put yourself in my place, Lanny. I lie here on a comfortable bed with an electric fan to cool me, and anything I choose to ask for is brought to me at the pressing of a button; and I have to speak the words that will send ten or twelve millions of our best young men overseas into jungle heat and arctic cold to fight and bleed and die. I want to save every life that I can, and every pang of agony that I can spare to any and every one of those boys. If I can save a million, or even a thousand, do you think I ought to worry about the fact that a few economic royalists of France will discover that they haven't got everything they thought they were going to get?"

"No, Governor, but that's not my point. What I don't want is for the economic royalists to fool *us.*"

"Do you really think they can fool *me*, Lanny? I know them here, and I'm sure they are exactly the same in all other countries. If I have the power, I shall help to tame them there, just as I have tried to do in this country."

"If they are allowed to entrench themselves—"

"Listen, Lanny. You have been to that country, whereas I know it only from the map. I measured it with my pencil today. From the east corner of Algeria to the west corner of Morocco is about as far as from New York to Kansas City."

"If you travel by the coast it's almost as far as to San Francisco."

"A vast country, with poor communications. Somebody has to govern and police it. If we have to do this with our armies, it will take one or two hundred thousand men, and all the ships to supply them. If we can find Frenchmen who will do it for us—any sort of Frenchmen, so long as they know the job—we can save all those Americans and all those ships and supplies. What we want is to drive the Germans out, from North Africa, and from Italy, and from France. That's our job, and yours is to trust your country and trust me, and believe that when the war is won we shall know how to find out what the French people want, in the same way that we find out what the American people want, by letting them go to the polls and vote."

Lanny took it as a rebuke and said humbly: "Yes, Governor, I get the point. But you have to be forewarned that you're going to take an awful shellacking if you let men like Lemaigre-Dubreuil take charge of French North Africa."

"Don't worry about that either, Lanny. I've been in public life a long time and I've grown a tough hide. I'm going to win this war and pay what it costs—but no more than I have to! And anybody that doesn't like that program can lump it, as we used to say when we were boys."

V

F.D.R. paused to put a cigarette into that long thin holder which he liked to stick up in a jaunty manner, and which had become a symbol dear to the hearts of cartoonists along with "Winnie's" big dark cigar and "Uncle Joe's" pipe. (Hitler did not smoke, so all they had for him was a Charlie Chaplin mustache and a swastika.) F.D.R. lighted his cigarette and took a couple of puffs, then said: "The question of where the first landing is to be is still being argued, and with a great deal of heat. I am expecting Churchill here in a couple of days, and we shall go to it. You understand, of course, that this is strictly *entre nous.*"

"You may be sure that I never speak about your affairs, Governor. I haven't told even my father or my wife that I am working for you."

"Winston, as I believe I told you, is hot for the Balkans. He insists that we can land there practically unopposed and have a clear road up the Vardar valley."

"I suspect that he has reasons in addition to military ones for that suggestion."

"Of course. He makes no secret of that. His 'Empah,' as he calls it, expects to be in that part of the world for a long time to come; whereas we cherish the hope that we can finish up the job and bring our boys back home. It may be a fond hope, but I'd hate to have to tell our mothers and wives and sweethearts that their boys will have to stay over there. What Winston wants, of course, is to get our armies into that part of the world so that we shall block off the Russians from the Balkans and the Dardanelles. That would be the best possible ending of a war from his point of view."

"Stalin is not so keen for the idea, I gathered."

"What Stalin wants is for us to come straight across the Channel and head for Berlin. From the military point of view that seems to me the only way to be considered. That is where we shall meet the bulk of the German armies, and they are what we have to beat."

"You can't do it without command of the air, Governor."

"That I know. And I think the British should be bombing German communications from now on, to prevent their moving reinforcements and supplies to the Channel. I've just been going over some of the data supplied by our General Staff. There's going to be a hot time in the old town when Winston arrives."

"It's a pretty hard strain on you," ventured the P.A. He had been watching this great man's face and noting the lines of care increasing and deepening. It had been only five years ago that Lanny had met him, but he seemed to have aged ten or more.

"Strictly between you and me, Winston as a guest is something of a trial. He has the habits of an owl, or perhaps a half-owl. He will come ambling into this room about midnight, full of ideas and conversation just when I am tired out and ready for sleep; he can sleep until late in the morning, while I have a schedule to keep." The tired man spoke as if it were a relief to have somebody's sympathy; but then in a moment the schoolboy grin came back to the mobile face. "Wouldn't you like to come and take him off my hands part of the time? You could listen, say, from midnight till three or four, and then go to your hotel room and hang out a 'Do not disturb' sign."

Lanny wasn't sure whether this was all jest or part serious. He grinned in return and said: "*Zu Befehl, Herr Kommandant,* as the German soldiers say."

"Joking aside," continued the President, "I think Winston would like to hear your report on North Africa. I could give him what you have sent me, but he'd probably put the papers aside and never find time to read them. If he talks to you, he'll have questions to ask. Can you stay a few days?"

"If you have nothing else in mind, I'd rather go up to New York and wait until you call me. I'll come at any hour of the day or night that you say. I'll motor or fly, according to how much time you allow me."

"Very good then. Give your address and telephone number to Baker and we'll arrange it."

"If I come to the White House openly, won't the reporters get hold of it?"

"I'll see that your name is not listed to the press; and for the White House staff we might change it a bit. Your middle name is Prescott? Then suppose you be Mr. Lanning Prescott? I'll give Winston your real name and explain matters to him."

"O.K. by me," said the P.A. "Let me remind you that you were going to fix it with him to have me taken off the British blacklist. It's important, because I can't fly through Bermuda. Also, I'd like to be able to stop off in England because I have important friends there, and a little daughter whom I haven't seen for more than a year."

"I'll make a note of it," said Roosevelt. "Remind me if I don't speak of it."

VI

Lanny spent the night in a hotel. Next morning he took a taxi to the old houses which had been converted into offices for the Co-ordinator of Information and his rapidly growing staff. They were down by the Potomac River, amid coal yards, behind an old brick brewery, and almost under the shadow of the gasworks; nobody objected, because office room was so scarce that you were lucky to get any sort of roof over your head. Armed guards kept watch, but the all-powerful Mr. Baker had telephoned, and Lanny was ushered in as soon as he had identified himself.

Colonel William J. Donovan was a short, somewhat plump Irishman who had commanded the famous 69th New York Regiment in World War I. He had earned all the decorations there were, and the sobriquet of "Wild Bill." He certainly gave no such impression in his office, for his voice was gentle and rather slow, and his manner lazy and easy-going. Sometime early in his life he must have kissed the Blarney stone, for in the first half hour he made Lanny think that they were old friends, and that the story Lanny had to tell was the most interesting the Colonel had ever heard. He seemed to have unlimited time, and it was only after he had heard Lanny all the way through that he thought to call in his confidential stenographer and a couple of department heads, to hear it again and take down the essential facts—names and addresses of Raoul Palma and Bernhardt Monck and Denis de Bruyne and General Béthouart, and what each of them wanted and what sort of person would be best to send them. Lanny got the impression that this amiable officer's organization was going to be somewhat loosely run; but, then, so was F.D.R.'s, and still we were going to lick the Nazis!

The Colonel gave his caller a pat on the shoulder, called him by his first name, thanked him with all the warmth of his Irish heart, and assured him that his secret would be kept and also those of his friends. He wound up by asking the son of Budd-Erling if he wouldn't like to come in and start another department and run it. Apparently there was room for an unlimited number of departments, and when the chiefs and directors and chairmen and what-nots began treading on one another's toes, the Colonel would pat them on their backs and give them a new title and some more assistants and secretaries to make them happy. That was apparently what it meant to be a "Co-ordinator" with a capital C.

Lanny spent most of that day and part of the evening in conference with various groups of the Colonel's administrators, telling them all he could about the old Continent which he knew so well and which most of them knew only from the newspapers; about Hitler and Göring and Hess and their subordinates, and the enormous military and governmental and propaganda machines they had built up; about their ideas and ways of life; how they had achieved power and how they were keeping it; about Pétain, Laval, Darlan and the rest of the French collaborators, and the underground which was opposing them, what sort of people they were, and how to reach them and win their trust; about the conditions they would find in Algeria and Morocco, and who would be their friends and who their enemies in those ancient, half-barbarous lands.

All these men of the C.O.I. agreed that this experienced man ought to join them, and he couldn't tell them frankly why he didn't. He just said: "I have been working independently for a long time, and I have some contacts that I am not free to reveal to anybody else. But I'll keep in touch with you, and maybe I'll meet some of you in the field." They all promised to keep his secret; they were going to send thousands of men and women into the enemy lands, and would keep the secrets of all of them. Very soon the name of their organization would be changed to the Office of Strategic Services, and the cocktail-party wits of Washington and New York would say that O.S.S. meant: "Oh, so secret!" But you could be sure that the men and women in the field didn't object to that secrecy nor to the armed guards keeping watch over the offices and the files at home.

VII

There is a midnight train to New York, and Lanny had asked Baker to make a reservation for him. He had just time to phone Laurel that he was coming; then he found himself in a compartment with two other men—for train space was beyond price. Washington had suddenly become the capital of the world, and New York had become a suburb, with big businessmen commuting, and sometimes sleeping, in limousines between the two cities at night.

It had been some time since Lanny had had a home of his own—indeed, had he ever had one? His father's home, his mother's home, his *amie's* home, his wife's home! When he had been Mister Irma

Barnes he had lived in Irma's palace on Long Island, and in one that she had rented in Paris, and it had all been the way Irma wanted it. When he had been married to Trudi Schultz he had visited her in a tenement room in Paris where she was hiding, carrying on her anti-Nazi activities; that had been her home, and only a stern sense of duty had made it tolerable to a reformed playboy.

He had said to Laurel: "Get a larger apartment so that you can have a room to work in and I can have one and Agnes can have one." She had told him that she wanted to pay her own way, even as a wife; she was a feminist. But now he pleaded: "Let me pay for it, please, *please!* It will be the first time in my life that I ever supplied a home for the woman I loved!"

That sounded strange, but he proved it to her concerning all the five love affairs which he had had, and about which he had told her truly. One of his wives had died, and another had left him to become a countess; oddly enough, the same thing had happened to two of his sweethearts—one had died and one had left him to become a countess. The third of this unlegitimized group had left him for a stage career, and that surely hadn't been the young Lanny's fault. "I never left a woman in my life," he insisted to his present one, and added: "And believe me, I never mean to."

The point was that all five of these ladies had had a home of one sort or another, and the only times when the grandson of Budd Gunmakers and son of Budd-Erling had been able to pay their bills had been when he had taken them traveling. So now Laurel had let him have his way, and the two women were established in an apartment house in the East Sixties, with three bedrooms and two baths. Servants were hard to obtain, but they had a woman who came in and cleaned up twice a week, and they had a kitchenette where light meals could be prepared when they did not feel like going out. It seemed to the economical Laurel a terribly expensive way to live, but New Yorkers took it for granted that you had to spend money in order to make it. Lanny had to have a room in which to type his mysterious reports, and certainly a woman who was carrying a baby and a novel at the same time had a right to comfort and convenience.

There she was when a taxi delivered him from the Pennsylvania Station at about seven-thirty in the morning. She had his orange juice cold and his toast hot, and Agnes Drury had gone to work early in order to take herself out of the way. Laurel was lovely in one of those dressing gowns with a big floral pattern. He could see at a glance that she was well, and her happiness was written on every feature and in every gesture and word. He caught her in his arms; time didn't matter—the orange juice would stay cold in the refrigerator and the toast could be reheated. He could say "I love you" as often as he pleased, and could make x-marks for kisses, and with no censor to question whether they were code. Parting might or might not be sweet sorrow, but certainly and without question coming home was sweet joy.

VIII

Meeting after two months' absence, they both had a lot of news. Because ladies like to talk and listening seems more polite, Lanny learned first what had happened to his wife. She had written two articles, one about their trip through China and one about what they had found at Yenan; both had been accepted and were soon to appear; he would read the manuscripts that day. Laurel was working on her novel about an American girl at a German university in the days of the Nazis, and there was a chunk of that awaiting his judgment. Her pregnancy had made no special difference in her work, she told him; she had kept her promise and not let herself get tired. Agnes had been lovely to her; she was a sensible, settled woman, who had great admiration for the art of writing and took many burdens from her friend's shoulders.

Then began a questioning of Lanny. How was Beauty, how was Parsifal, and the dear little boy? Lanny recounted what they had said and done and gave her the messages they had sent. He told about the refugees at Bienvenu and how they were getting along; the relationship of benefactor and beneficiary is seldom entirely satisfactory, and poor Beauty was finding this out. Lanny hadn't considered it his duty to take a hand; she had her own money, a thousand dollars a month that Robbie sent her, plus the large sums from the Detaze sales. He told about Marceline, whom Laurel had never met; a curious nature, quietly cold, pleasure-bent in a silent, incessant, almost vegetative way. Some day Laurel would meet her and probe her secret soul and put it into a story.

Then the other ladies. Sophie Timmons had obeyed her government and come back to her large hardware family in Cincinnati. Emily Chattersworth wasn't well enough to move, in fact she was all but bedridden. Lanny had been to call on her twice, and they had talked about the problems of their time. The chatelaine of Sept Chênes had lived too long, she thought; the world had taken on an aspect which she did not understand, and it terrified her; she could not imagine how social life could continue on such terms. Lanny had tried to tell her the basis of his faith, that they were in the midst of the birth pangs of a new social order. A birth is a messy thing, and if you had never seen one before, it would alarm you greatly; but when it is over, it is discovered to be a natural phenomenon.

Lanny told his wife what Emily had said, that she was going to leave part of her considerable fortune to her near-godson. Lanny had protested that he didn't want her to do that, that he had no need of more money; but she had answered that she had no special interest in her surviving relatives and thought that Lanny might find some way to put money to good use. He had asked what she wanted done with it, and she had said something to stop these cruel and dreadful wars. Lanny had decided that she was not long for this world and thought he ought to give her some hint that he was not just an ivory-tower dweller but was rendering service of importance to his government. She had told him: "I guessed that years ago. I have known you since you were a babe-in-arms, and I perceived that you were drawing out our near-Fascist friends. Don't worry, I have never spoken of it."

IX

It was Lanny's turn to ask questions of his wife. She had been down to visit the widow of Reverdy Holdenhurst, her aunt by marriage, to condole with her and tell her how it had happened that two passengers of the *Oriole* had been left behind in Hongkong and how the yacht had sailed away to its doom. "Poor soul!" Laurel said. "She was never able to forgive Uncle Reverdy's offense against her, but now she remembers only his good qualities and is a prey to remorse. She cannot make up her mind that he and Lizbeth are really gone. She studies the maps and speculates about what may happen to people on jungle islands, and whenever she reads in the papers a story about a sailor or a flyer who has come back to civilization, she starts hoping all over again."

"Did you tell her about your psychic experience?" Lanny asked.

"I told her, and it disturbed her greatly. You know, she is a devout Episcopalian, but she was educated in a Catholic convent, and I think she has the Catholic attitude deeply buried in her mind—the notion that there is something dangerous and even immoral in dabbling with 'spirits.' She came back to the subject again and again and cross-questioned me. I had brought the notes you had taken down and I read them to her. You remember, the spirit of Lizbeth, or whatever it was, said that her childhood rag doll in the old gray trunk in the attic had been used as a nest by mice. We went and found it was so, and I thought that Aunt Millicent was going to faint. An extraordinary thing, Lanny, and I don't know how to account for it."

"Let's give Lizbeth another chance to tell us," Lanny said, "if it isn't a strain on you."

"Not at all," she replied. "That is one of the things that surprise me; it seems to be a natural process, like falling asleep. I am puzzled as to how I manage to distinguish between going to sleep and going into a trance."

"I take it that you give an order to your subconscious mind. It is like what you do in breathing and swallowing food; you are using the same apparatus, and it is a question of which of two valves you close. Sometimes you make a mistake, and then you have a disagreeable choking spell."

"I must have made a mistake that day on the plane, flying to Ulan-Bator; I thought I was falling asleep, and instead I went into a trance."

"Possibly you do it often and never realize it. I shall have to practice listening while you are asleep." It reminded him of a story he had heard as a lad and had almost forgotten. It was told by a visitor at St. Thomas's Academy in Connecticut, which he had attended during World War I. It had been introduced playfully, as "a story that nobody can understand." A woman came into a grocery store and ordered a dozen boxes of matches. The grocer said: "But Mrs. Smith, you bought a dozen boxes of matches last week." The woman answered: "Yes, but you see, my husband is deaf and dumb and he talks in his sleep!"

X

They tried a séance that evening. A curious procedure, which would keep Lanny wondering as long as he lived on this earth. It disappointed him frequently, for these manifestations of the subconscious mind are vagarious and undependable, and the psychic prospector is like that other kind who goes wandering out into the desert with pick and shovel, blanket, food, and water, all loaded upon a patient burro; he may search for years and even for a lifetime and find no gold, but if he does find it—well, it is gold. Any chemist knows what gold is, but where is the soul chemist who can tell you where trance phenomena come from?—fragments of mentality that seem to be floating around loose in an infinite universe, and sometimes put themselves together in a fashion beyond the power of any conscious mind to explain.

Laurel's "control" was a personality whom she had met long ago, but only casually, and if she had been especially interested in him she had entirely forgotten it. The idea that he would some day decide to move in upon her subconscious mind and take his residence there would have sounded utterly crazy to her. But now, whenever she dropped into a trance, which she had discovered by accident, here he was, seemingly always at hand. She herself did not hear his voice, but whoever sat by and listened heard him speaking through her lips—or claiming that he did so, and what were you to make of the claim?

This "spirit" Otto Kahn chatted with urbanity, just as he would have done in life. He took it as a queer sort of joke, exactly as he would have taken it if anybody had presented him with such a proposition while he was alive. He was good company, and at the same time dignified, accustomed to be treated as a person of distinction. How he would have behaved if he had been treated otherwise Lanny had no means of knowing, for he had never tried it.

On this occasion Otto was in his best drawing-room mood. He responded to any playful remark about what was going on in the world, and especially in the great metropolis which had been his home. When asked if he had any messages for his family, he said No, they seemed to be getting along very well. When asked if he had any message for a certain operatic soprano, he said No with emphasis; she was married now, and he wouldn't take any chance of disturbing her tranquillity. When asked if there was any way he could find Reverdy Holdenhurst or his daughter Lizbeth, he replied that he was keeping away from the spirits, they bored him, and besides, he couldn't make up his mind that he believed in them. Then, somewhat incongruously, he added: "That old bore Zaharoff is here as usual. I don't suppose you are interested in him, Lanny?"

"Not especially," was the reply. "At least not until he can figure out some way for me to get that money he wants me to pay out for him."

Then—one of those unforeseeable developments—there came suddenly from Laurel's lips a different voice, surprisingly like that of the aged Sir Basil, Knight Commander of the Bath and Grand Officer of the Legion of Honor. "Go and see my niece in London, and she will give you the money."

"I'd be afraid to, Sir Basil," said the son of Budd-Erling, smiling. "She might have me arrested for attempted fraud."

"Tell her to consult a medium, and I will talk to her," commanded the voice of the Knight Commander.

"That would only make it a more elaborate fraud, Sir Basil. And besides, such things cannot be arranged nowadays. Don't you know there's a war on?" This was a stock formula of the time; it caused the former partner of Kuhn, Loeb and Company to break into laughter, and it brought the séance to a sudden end. There was a long silence.

"Did something go wrong?" asked Laurel when she opened her eyes. "I have a strange sort of feeling about it." When he told her, she said: "You offended the old man, and he took it out on me."

XI

Laurel told how she had been to call upon Mrs. Roosevelt, and what they had talked about. A truly great woman, she said, and one whose impress upon the country would not soon be erased. For the first time in our history there was in the White House a woman who was not merely a housekeeper or an ornament, but a democratic force. She was that in her own right, by the power of her own mind and heart. "She and her husband make a team," Laurel said. "He might not have the same steadfastness if he stood alone."

Lanny would have liked to say: "I was with him in Washington," but he didn't. It might seem strange that he had revealed his secret to friends such as Raoul and Monck, and would not reveal it to the woman of his heart. But those people in Europe needed the facts for the work they were doing; Laurel did not need them. She understood that and never asked. What she guessed was her own affair, of course.

He told her the details of his trip: the aspects of Vichy, the elderly roués being taken to the baths in wheel chairs, the half-starved poor standing patiently in front of half-empty foodshops. And then the Riviera, where the contrasts between the conditions of rich and poor were even greater; and then Switzerland, standing on guard day and night, making money, but having to spend most of it on defense preparations. He told about the paintings he had inspected and those he had bought; about North Africa and the mosaics, and the amusing process of bargaining; about the ruins of Timgad, the mosques and minarets and *marabouts* of Morocco, and the ten-course banquet he had tried so valiantly to eat. But nothing about the underground, nothing about the *collaborateurs* or the American vice-consuls. "Everybody is expecting something to happen, and everybody tries to guess what." That was as far as he would go.

Robbie sent a car down as usual, and Lanny took his wife driving and showed her the country in the luxurious robes of early summer. The first hot spell had come, and he worried about leaving her to be sometimes parboiled and sometimes baked in a vast stone oven—so impolitely did he describe Manhattan Island. But she assured him that it could be turned into an excellent summer resort for a writer who wanted to be let alone. She had a refrigerator well stocked with fruit juices and a room with an electric fan. In extreme cases she would work in the summer costume which nature had provided for her, and find it most comfortable. In the evenings she and Agnes would stroll on the edge of the park or go to an air-conditioned movie house if there was anything that wouldn't bore them too greatly. War pictures were dreadful, but Laurel said: "I want to face the facts of my time."

They drove out together to see the Budds of Newcastle. They were a philoprogenitive tribe and paid all honor to a bride as a guardian of their tribal future. They found it hard to understand that a woman left alone should refuse shelter and protection in Robbie's commodious villa on a hilltop overlooking the river and the distant Sound. But they had "queer" ones among them, and they accepted the fact that a literary lady might be another; some of them had read her stories and were a bit afraid of her, lest she some day make use of them as "copy." In this they had good reason.

Lanny hired a stenographer and dictated letters to his various clients. He prepared an elaborate dossier on the subject of the mosaics and the gateway he had purchased, with detail photographs of each and the history so far as he knew it. He drove out and presented these to the delighted Mr. Vernon, and told him the story of his travels, the sights he had seen, and the people he had met. When this wealthy gentleman realized how much trouble Lanny had taken and the expenses he had incurred, he said that ten per cent commission was not enough and insisted upon doubling it. He could not understand how a man had been able to travel to all these places in wartime, and Lanny attributed it to his father's influence, intimating that he had picked up a little information for his father on the side. It pleased a patron of the arts, of course, to have an expert who was not merely an employee, but a man of means, a social equal. That made it easier to believe what he said, and Mr. Vernon was pleased to put in an order for more art treasures which he could boast of being able to get from two continents at war. His fortune came out of a flour-milling empire, and the money poured in automatically, day and night, like the grain into storage bins and the flour into sacks.

XII

Lanny told his wife that he was expecting a call to Washington and might have to take off on another errand very soon. She did not utter a word of complaint, or even of sorrow; she knew now that men by the millions were going off to war. She was much in love with her man, and frank in showing it, but she would not add her grief to whatever burdens he was carrying. She set her teeth and said: "The job has to be done." She hated the Nazis almost as much as she loved her husband, and that made it easier for her.

She wanted to be with him every minute of this precious time, so she would dress and go out with him, in spite of being in a condition rather difficult to conceal. He took her to dinner in a chophouse in the theater district, where he knew that good cooking was to be had. It was his duty to feed her, so he ordered a green salad, which the dieticians recommend for her condition, and then she was going to have two freshly broiled lamb chops on buttered toast with green peas, and after that he would try to persuade her to find room for fresh strawberries and ice cream. He was watching over her, entertaining her, doing everything he knew to make her happy. He was going to leave her with the best possible memories, and the same sort of hopes for the future.

He meant to give her a peaceful evening, taking her up Riverside Drive where there would be a pleasant breeze, or at least there would be a breeze while driving. But this was wartime, and things didn't always happen according to schedule. A man came into the restaurant and took a seat at a table near by, not facing Lanny, but so that they were both facing in the same direction. It was by accident that Lanny happened to turn his head and see him: a well-dressed man in middle years, wearing a palm-beach suit. He had a light-colored mustache and a beard trimmed to a point, not usual in New York. The face was thin and rather dissipated looking, and something about it caught Lanny's attention in the first flash. He began looking out of the corner of his eye and presently said to Laurel in a low tone: "Don't turn to look. There's a man I think I know, and if so it's important. Go on talking, anything you please, but don't expect me to listen."

Laurel discussed the war news she had heard on the radio, while Lanny kept looking out of the corner of one eye while the man ordered his dinner. Once the man's eyes turned in Lanny's direction, and Lanny turned his head quickly. Presently he said: "I am pretty sure this man is an Englishman in the pay of the Nazis. I want to get a look at him from the front. Go on eating and don't pay any attention to him or to me."

He got up and went to the restroom. Through the partly open door he took a good look at the man, and when he came out he went down the other side of the room and passed behind the man, some distance away. Rejoining Laurel, he kept his head averted from his quarry and whispered: "Listen, darling, this is very, very urgent. I have to get the government agents to trail this man, and you have to help me."

"*I*, Lanny? How?"

"Don't look at him. Listen carefully. This won't be pleasant for you, but it may be the most important thing you've ever had to do. You have to keep him in this place until I give you a signal that I have him covered. I want you to strike up an acquaintance with him."

"Good gracious, Lanny! *How?*"

"After I'm gone, tell the waiter to bring you pencil and paper and write a note to the man. Ask him if you can have the pleasure of his company. Tell him you are in trouble. Offer to pay for his help—anything at all. Fold it up and tell the waiter to take it to him. Give the waiter a five-dollar bill at the same time and he won't find it too strange. When the man reads the note, give him your most heavenly smile. Don't be afraid, he can't carry you off."

"Does my figure look heavenly, Lanny?"

"He won't notice it, certainly not so long as you sit at the table. Once you have him here, keep him listening, entertained. Make up a story—your husband has just left you, he's no gentleman, you want to teach him a lesson. If I'm any judge of character, he's proud of his conquests and won't object to making another. Anything so long as you keep him busy."

"And then what?"

"When I've arranged for him to be trailed, I'll come back and stand in the door of the restroom until you see me. Then I'll step back out of sight, and you turn the whole thing into a joke—tell the man your nerve fails you, you're afraid your husband might be violent, arrange to meet him later in a park. When he's gone, you go to the women's room for a while and wait. Give me time to make sure the coast is clear. Then I'll tip the waiter again and he can take us out through the back door of the restaurant."

"Suppose the man doesn't accept my company."

"Keep after him. Use your wits and your sense of humor. At any cost, don't let him get away. If necessary, take his arm and go along with him. I'll be on watch outside, and I'll follow you at a distance. Don't let him take you in a cab, of course."

"Are you planning to have him arrested?"

"Only as a last resort. What I want is to have him followed and find out where he lives and what his connections are. For all we can know, he might be planning to have all the bridges around New York blown up tonight."

"I'll do my best," she said. She was a game person.

"You have what it takes," he answered gallantly. He got up quietly and slipped out, in the direction away from the bearded Englishman.

XIII

Outside the restaurant Lanny hurried to a near-by telephone booth and put in a call to the F.B.I. To the agent in charge he said: "My name is Lanning Prescott Budd. My father is Robert Budd, president of Budd-Erling Aircraft. I have been doing confidential work for the government, and am speaking on the basis of knowledge so acquired. Tonight, dining in Brown's Chophouse, I recognized a man whom I know to be a German agent. I can't go into details over the phone; he was connected with the flight of Rudolf Hess to Britain, and he is either a top man, or he deals with such. In London he was going by the name of Branscome. My wife is trying to hold him until your men come. Don't arrest him, but trail him and find out where he lives and what he is doing. It may lead to something of first-rate importance."

"O.K., Mr. Budd. We have a station in that neighborhood and should be able to get a couple of men there in a few minutes."

"This Branscome knows me, and I have to keep out of his sight. I will wait outside the restaurant, a little west of the entrance. I am wearing a panama hat with a black band. I will set it back on my head a little."

"Very good, Mr. Budd. Thanks a million. Will you drop in and see us in the morning?"

Lanny promised, and then hung up and hurried back to the restaurant. He was wise to the ways of the world and knew that establishments which aim at respectability do not relish having ladies "pick up" gentlemen at their meals; they might well invite such a lady to leave. Lanny put a dollar into the doorman's hand and instructed him to inform the head waiter that a gentleman outside wanted to speak to him about an urgent matter. To the head waiter Lanny quickly explained the situation and added: "It is possible that the F.B.I. may lose this man, so take a good look at him, and if you see him again, call the F.B.I. at once. He may be the most dangerous of enemies."

Lanny took up his post at one side, watching the restaurant door, prepared to turn away quickly if the suspect should emerge. After what seemed a long time but was less than a quarter of an hour, a young man who looked as if he had just come out of college approached him and said: "My name is Tulliver." Lanny replied: "Mine is Budd." The man flashed his badge, and Lanny described Branscome, also his wife, and told of the arrangements he had made. "I have told the head waiter the situation, and if you give him the high sign he will place you so that you can study this man."

"Very good, sir. There should be another man here any minute. Tell him how this man looks and tell him to wait here. Five minutes should be time enough for me to get the man fixed in mind; then you can come in and signal to your wife."

Lanny waited. Presently another man arrived, slightly older but equally dapper. Lanny told the story again, and after another while went into the restaurant. His wife was engaged in a vivacious conversation with the blond-bearded Englishman. Keeping as far away from them as he could, Lanny made his way to the men's room and stood in the doorway until Laurel's eyes met his; then he drew back into the room and stayed there for a considerable interval. When he took another peek he saw that Laurel was gone, Mr. Branscome was gone, and Mr. Tulliver was gone.

In a minute or two Laurel emerged from the women's room. She was flushed and excited, and didn't want any more dinner. She wanted to get out into the fresh air and away from a place where she had been making herself conspicuous, something most painful to ladies of her upbringing. She went outside to make sure the coast was clear. Meanwhile Lanny paid his bill and thanked the head waiter, warning him not to talk about the matter. The man said: "That party has been here several times before. I'll know him if he comes again."

XIV

Outside, there was nothing to be seen of either the man or his "shadows." Lanny took his wife to his car, and when they were under way she could at last relax. "I never did anything like that in all my life before!" she exclaimed; and Lanny had to stop his chuckling and assure her with all seriousness that he accepted her word on the point.

"Tell me all that happened," he said; "it may give us some clue."

She told him that Branscome was a man of education, and what she would have considered a gentleman if she had met him under normal circumstances. He had moved over to her table at once and showed himself ready to play the gallant. Laurel had exercised upon him those arts of pleasing which every lady in Baltimore acquires as second nature. He had ordered a bottle of wine and had pressed her to drink; he had asked her name and address and other questions about herself. She had stated that she was an actress out of employment at the moment, giving the names of a couple of plays in which she had had minor roles. "I don't know whether he believed me or not. He told me he was here with a mission from the British government. Do you suppose that could be true?"

"It might be, of course. A traitor may be deceiving his own government; he could hardly get here otherwise in wartime. I promised the F.B.I. man to come down in the morning and tell them what I know about him. They may never tell me what they learn--they don't do any superfluous talking. I'm not supposed to talk either, but I will tell you this much: when I met that man in London he had received a message from Rudolf Hess concerning Hess's intention to fly to Britain, and he was sending an answer back."

"Are you sure he's the right man, Lanny?"

"I only had a brief talk with him, but I made note of him for future reference. He has grown whiskers, but his eyes haven't changed. He was extremely nervous when he met me, and I suspected that he had been drinking, perhaps to keep his courage up. I suppose that with you he was at ease."

"He was greatly disappointed when I told him that I had made a mistake, that he was not the gentleman I had met. He said: 'You have met me now, so it's all right.' I had a hard time extricating myself. I told him that I had become frightened; that my husband might come back and that he was a very violent man."

"You did all right," the husband assured her. "If you weren't so worth-while a writer, I would introduce you to Colonel Donovan and let you take up a career with his organization."

"God forbid!" exclaimed the lady from Baltimore. "I am so exhausted from the strain of it, I believe I'd rather serve in the infantry!"

8

Much Depends on Dinner

I

IN THE morning Lanny went down to the offices of the Federal Bureau of Investigation and told them what he knew about the Englishman called Branscome. They revealed to him that they had followed the man to his apartment, and would keep after him and do a thorough job. They said also that they would get in touch with the British; so Lanny knew that they would learn that he himself had been blacklisted by the British because of his dealings with the Nazis. He told them to call the President's man, Baker, who would give him an O.K. They assured him that they were not unfamiliar with complications of this sort.

When the P.A. got back to his home there was a call for him from Washington, and when he called back he was told that he was invited to dinner at the White House that evening: "Seven-thirty, black tie." He answered that he would be on hand. His white evening jacket was hanging in his closet, freshly laundered, and now it was taken down and laid in a suitcase, all by itself. While he ate his lunch he told Laurel what the F.B.I. men had said; then he packed his bags, kissed her good-by, and went down to his car. Laurel herself would doubtless have been invited, but she had told the "First Lady" that she did not care to attend evening affairs in her present condition.

Across the park to the highway that runs alongside the Hudson, then by the tunnel which runs under the great river, then by the Skyway to Newark—that is the fast route out of the crowded metropolis. Highway Number 1 was crowded with wartime traffic; great heavy trucks loaded with oil, with pipe, with lumber, or mysterious crated boxes, were bringing supplies to the factories and taking finished products to the ports. Newark and Trenton and Philadelphia and Baltimore—Lanny was familiar with these cities and their fast-growing suburbs. He was a careful driver and enjoyed few things more. He

158

watched the speedometer and the clock on his dashboard, and knew where he was and how long it would take him.

A room had been engaged, and he had time to bathe and put on his light-weight black trousers and cool white jacket. He took a taxi to the White House, so as not to be bothered with the problem of parking his car. When he told the driver "Pennsylvania entrance," he reflected that it was the first time that he had approached by that customary door. Since taxis were not admitted to the grounds in wartime, he got out by the curb. Soldiers with fixed bayonets were walking post in front of the fence that encircles the grounds. Inside the gate was a wooden sentry box, and in front of it stood a young Navy officer with a tommy gun over his arm. A second officer appeared as the visitor approached the gate.

"Good evening," said the visitor. "My name is Lanning Prescott. I am invited for dinner." They gave him a long look, then one of them said: "Proceed."

He walked up the curving drive to the portico of the mansion, where two Secret Service men stepped out from behind the tall columns and closed together in front of him. They were burly, tough-looking customers, with straw hats pulled low over their eyes. Lanny felt a bit uncomfortable, but said "Good evening" again. He could guess they had telephone connection with the gate, so he kept on coming and they kept on looking him over. Only when he was almost close enough to touch them did they step aside, and one signed for him to enter. Lanny knew that protecting the President's life was a Secret Service job both in war and peace, and he wished them success. He didn't think they were strict enough in his case.

II

The door was opened by a uniformed elderly Negro. He bowed slightly and said: "Good evening, sir," in a low, liquid voice. Lanny found himself in a spacious and brilliantly lighted hall, with many doors, a staircase, and several irregular rows of portraits and historical scenes on the walls. Another uniformed servant took his hat. Then came a slender man in formal attire, who announced himself as the chief usher. "Mr. Prescott" gave his name, and this official consulted a cardboard which he carried under his arm. "You will sit at Mrs. Adamic's right," he said. Lanny, who was used to these formal affairs, replied: "Thank you. I will remember."

He was escorted to a reception room and introduced to other guests:

a Mr. Robinson, tall and sunburned, a cousin of the "First Lady," as he learned later; two pretty girls of eighteen or twenty whose names he didn't get—they were English by their accent; finally a couple, Mr. and Mrs. Louis Adamic. Lanny recognized the name and knew the man as a writer, of Yugoslav descent, much interested in the problems of the foreign-born in his adopted country. He was about Lanny's age, and as tall, with thinning hair, gentle features, and a quiet voice. Lanny would have liked to talk to him, but circumstances did not permit. The two girls were worried because they were not wearing long dresses—they had been invited at the last moment and told to come as they were. Mr. Robinson was worried because the Allies were doing so badly in the war; he had just arrived from Peru and had got the full impact from the papers. How could it be that the Germans were able to have their way in the Crimea and North Africa, and the Japs all over the eastern world?

The usher appeared again and led them to a small elevator which took them to the second floor. Just as they emerged, Mrs. Roosevelt appeared from a door in the corridor. She wore a light blue gown in which Lanny thought she looked especially impressive; the upswept hairdress and long gown made her appear even taller than she was. She looked well and strong, but sad and harassed when her face was in repose. Now she was smiling, and stretched out her two hands to her women guests.

The English girls, having been the last to enter the elevator, were the first to emerge. She greeted them as friends of the family and motioned them to enter the Lincoln room. Then came her cousin; she revealed her affection for him and commented upon his sunburn acquired in high altitudes. Then came the Adamics—Lanny having lagged behind out of politeness. Mrs. Adamic, a tiny person, was enfolded in one of the First Lady's arms; the author's wife had just been told that she was to sit at the President's right hand, which could be expected to scare her. Then it was Lanny's turn, and the hostess shook hands with him warmly. "How do you do, Mr. Prescott?" she said distinctly, to let him know that she had been told and was not going to forget.

III

The Lincoln room contains fine old period pieces and chintz-covered armchairs; there are cheerful green-and-yellow drapes, and too many pictures and prints crowded onto its walls. Lanny had heard the tradition that sometimes late at night the residents of this mansion hear footsteps and see a very tall man clad in a long black frock coat. Certainly they could not be the steps of the present master of the household, who was taken everywhere about the building in a wheel chair. At present he was discovered seated at a desk halfway down the long wall of the room, amusing himself with a cocktail shaker, a bowl of crushed ice, and several bottles with fancy labels. If he had any worry about the state of the world, he wasn't going to let his wife's cousin see it. "Hello, Monroe," he called, and held out a firm strong hand. His face was ruddy and his close-set gray eyes flashed with a zest of living that infected everybody who came near him. When anything was going on he watched with his head cocked, ready for a bit of fun or a chance to start it ahead of the next fellow. He wore a well-fitted dinner jacket, soft white shirt, and natty black bow tie; his long broad-shouldered torso and powerful arms were so active that you lost all thought of his disability.

Mrs. Roosevelt brought up the other guests and introduced them, and he shook hands with each and had a friendly word. To Lanny he said: "Glad to see you, Prescott," putting emphasis on the name and grinning at the same time, a sort of half wink in his eyes. At this moment the President's little black Scottie appeared from somewhere and began sniffing at the visitor's shoes and the cuffs of his trousers; then, seeming satisfied, he sat back on his haunches. "You pass," said Roosevelt, laughing. "Do you have a dog?"

"My mother has too many at her home on the Riviera," Lanny replied. "You cannot give them away in wartime."

"For fear that someone might eat them?" And then, addressing the circle of guests: "Fala has been getting a very good press—much better than I. But nearly everybody misspells his name."

"It is an unusual name," remarked Mrs. Adamic.

The President reached down to pat the little dog's head. "One of my Scottish ancestors, away back, was Murray, the Outlaw of Fala Hill. No doubt he had a dog who thought his master was a great man."

Lanny thought: This is how he keeps sane in an insane world; calm in the dead center of a tornado. Even Cousin Monroe would have to put aside his worries and at least pretend to enjoy social life. It was as if the head of the state were saying: "I know things that you don't know. Trust me, as Fala does."

The President passed out the cocktails, one by one, then lifted his glass as a salutation to his guests and took a sip. "Orange Blossom," he said, and savored it. Mrs. Roosevelt set her glass down and went about with a tray of *hors d'oeuvres*. Lanny, knowing the customs of Europe, reflected that there a liveried servant, not the hostess, would have performed such a duty. The guests began drawing up chairs in a semicircle in front of the host. There was a large armchair, and Lanny moved that, intending it for Mrs. Roosevelt; but when she saw his gesture, she said: "We will save that for the Prime Minister."

Lanny had been wondering if Churchill was coming to this affair. There hadn't been a line in the newspapers about his presence in Washington; it was a war secret. All the reporters must have known it, and the burden must have weighed heavily upon them. Later in the evening F.D.R. repeated, with one of his infectious grins, the remark which one of his secretaries had made at a press conference that day: "I am carrying two battleships around, one in each of my side pockets." He meant, of course, the President and the Prime Minister.

Roosevelt started talking and all the others listened. He wanted to know how Adamic's latest book had sold. Lanny hadn't read it, but gathered now that it was a proposal that immigrants and sons of immigrants in America should be used to help restore or set up democratic institutions in each of the Nazi-conquered lands; that a carefully selected and trained commission should be sent to each of these lands to give them material aid and political guidance. The President didn't say what he thought of the idea.

Said Mrs. Roosevelt: "It will interest you to know that the Prime Minister has had the book in his room four or five days."

The author's sunburned cheeks were flushed with pleasure. "I'd give anything to hear his reaction," he said.

"So would we," replied the First Lady with a laugh. "The President told Mr. Churchill he might not like the last part; so, no doubt, he read the last part first." For the benefit of the other guests she explained that the book concluded with an imaginary discussion between John Bull and Uncle Sam on board an American cruiser anchored in the fog off Iceland on a midsummer's day of the previous year. To Churchill that would mean himself and the President of the United States at the time they had agreed upon the Atlantic Charter; and naturally Adamic, an American liberal, not to say radical, had given the British Tory the worst of the discussion. "I am afraid he won't like it," said the author, in the tone of a man who has committed a faux pas. His hostess lifted her hands in a gesture which was equivalent to: "What can we do about that?"

IV

The company was seated; the President was tossing popcorn into his mouth; Fala was snoozing. Lanny was taking note of the technique whereby a shrewd and determined woman exercised influence upon public affairs. She had read a book which presented a program for democratizing Europe; she had had the same idea that her husband had expressed to his P.A., that the powerful and busy gentleman who governed the British Empire wouldn't read a book but could be made to listen to conversation; so she had invited the author and his wife to Washington and had added a couple of pretty English girls to "balance the table."

Lanny understood that this was no time for him to show off any of his social gifts; he was there to listen and learn how his country was being governed in this time of world crisis. He had been promised a talk with the Duke of Marlborough's descendant later in the evening—while the President of the United States was trying to get his beauty sleep!

Mrs. Roosevelt arose suddenly from her chair and hastened to the door. Here came John Bull himself, and she held out her hand and greeted him formally, respectfully: "Good evening, Mr. Prime Minister." The answer came in a close-lipped voice: "Good evening, Mrs. Roosevelt." The speaker held a fat, freshly lighted cigar in front of him, as if he were making sure that no evil should befall it.

Five years had passed since Lanny had met the Right Honourable Winston Spencer Churchill, who had grown even stouter in those years. He had a rotund dumpy figure with short, slight arms and legs, rather narrow in the shoulders; mostly girth, chest, and head; no neck. He had a pink-and-white baby face and light blue eyes. He advanced into the room with what seemed a semi-scowl on his face; he moved as though he were without joints, all of a piece; solid, unhurried, impervious to obstacles, like a tank or a bulldozer. Behind him came his personal secretary, a slight pale young man named Martin.

"Hello, Winston!" cried F.D.R., and extended his hand dramatically. The reply came through barely moving lips: "Good evening, Mr. President." It was the first time Lanny had heard them address each other—and what a world of information was in those greetings! Two civilizations meeting and establishing their agreements, but also their disagreements, once and for always! Lanny could imagine that at their first meeting the American had spoken first and had said in effect: "I

call you by your first name because that is the American custom." To
that the Englishman had replied in effect: "I address you by your title,
because that is the English custom." Having begun that way, neither
could yield with good grace. Having once said "Winston," F.D.R.
couldn't very well take to saying "Prime Minister." On the other hand,
for the Prime Minister to have said "Franklin" would have been a ca-
pitulation, and that was not his nature. So, in spite of all temptations to
belong to other nations, he remained an Englishman!

For a longish moment these two gazed at each other, at once knowingly and quizzically. The President's expression mixed amusement and
concern; the Prime Minister's large round phiz was perfectly smooth,
and oh, so innocent!—except for the eyes which were shrewd and the
mouth which was determined. The newspapers were making much of
the fact that these men were friends; but they were not merely two
human beings, they were two parties, two nations, and there were
tensions between them.

No one knew this better than Lanny Budd, alias Prescott. Winston
Churchill had adjusted himself to democracy in his own country, but
he didn't want any of it in international affairs; he certainly wouldn't
consider it a substitute for the divide-and-rule policy of the British
Empire, politely known as the "Balance of Power" on the Continent
of Europe. And here was a woman, as determined as he, scheming to
force him to read a book and meet an author who was some sort of
Pink and perhaps a Red—the Almighty alone could tell the difference.
Had he and Roosevelt been arguing that day about it? Had they been
at a deadlock over it ever since the two "battleships" had met? Was
the democrat presuming to remind the imperialist who it was that had
the money and was dispensing the lend-lease?

The democratic man put on one of those smiles which were at once
sincere and an act. "Had a good nap, Winston?" he inquired. And at
this perhaps undignified revelation the Prime Minister appeared to
pout. He stuck his cigar into his mouth and mumbled something which
Lanny couldn't catch although there was dead silence in the room except for that one sound.

V

The V.I.P.—Very Important Person—received his cocktail from the
hand of his host; then he sat down in the armchair. Lanny was amused
to notice that it had been contrived for the author of *Two-Way Pas-*

sage to be next to him. "Mr. Prime Minister," said the contriver, "Mr. Adamic is the author of the book I gave you."

"Yes, yes," was the reply, rather abruptly given. "I am reading it." But he didn't say what he thought of it. He deliberately dodged the subject by pulling from his pocket a letter from his wife. "She thanks you for your gift," he said to Mrs. Roosevelt, and put on his spectacles and read a paragraph. Then he added: "I have no words to express my appreciation of all the gifts that were sent to me the last time I was here. Someone sent me a corncob pipe!" He put the cigar in his mouth and made it glow.

"I get several every year," declared F.D.R.

"Are yours worm-eaten, too?" inquired Churchill.

The President grinned and offered him another "Orange Blossom," but Churchill declined. Meantime Mrs. Roosevelt took a tiny sausage impaled on a toothpick and held it up before Fala, who eagerly did his stunt of rolling over, and then sat up to get his reward. "Good boy, Fala!" said the President, and the little dog came and plopped down at his feet.

A butler appeared in the doorway, and the hostess rose. The others all followed suit, and in the momentary diversion the President quickly slid himself from his chair to his wheel chair. His wife wheeled him out to the hall and to the elevator, the ladies following her and the men following the ladies. Churchill and Adamic were last, and Lanny ventured to linger with them, for he was curious about the little drama.

Adamic said very politely: "It is a privilege to meet you, Mr. Prime Minister."

The reply was: "I am readin' your book. I find it int'restin' "—a strong accent on the first syllable of that word.

"Thank you, sir. How far have you got into it?"

"About halfway. Do you really think there is a problem there?"

"I do, sir. Unless we succeed in mustering our American idealism and putting it to work. . . ."

That was as far as this discourse got. They had come to the elevator, and the President, inside, was waiting. "Come on in, Winston," he called. "The rest of you boys walk down." On the way Lanny said to the author: "It looks as if he's not going to be drawn out." Adamic replied: "I am afraid so."

When they arrived at the lower floor a uniformed servant was wheeling the President into the dining-room. The First Lady paused and called the attention of the guests to a painting, and so, when they entered the room, the President had already been transferred to his high-backed chair at the large oval table. Lanny observed these deft proceedings; it was important that guests should be spared reminders of his physical handicaps, for the preservation both of his own dignity and the cheerfulness of the guests.

The table had as its centerpiece a silver bowl filled with roses, shining directly under the chandelier. The service began at once: a consommé, broiled fish, roast chicken, a salad, an English trifle, and a demitasse served at the table. Lanny had been placed between Mrs. Adamic and Mrs. Roosevelt's secretary; he understood that it was better for him to be inconspicuous, and he was glad to listen to what the great and famous had to say.

VI

The President of the United States rubbed his hands, grinned, and, looking over the centerpiece at his wife, remarked: "Well, we had a good day today."

"Indeed, Franklin?"

"I had a fine press conference. Our newsmen are pleased because I have combined all our information and publicity services into one organization and put Elmer Davis at the head."

Lanny was familiar with the voice of Elmer Davis, but it hadn't reached Cousin Monroe in Peru. He asked who this person was, and the President explained that he was a radio commentator so highly respected by his colleagues and by newspapermen that he would be able to put a stop to the bickering that had been going on among the various unco-ordinated bureaus. Having said this, F.D.R. beamed and took a spoonful of his consommé. Lanny thought: How much like Robbie, coming home in the evening and telling the family and guests what he had done that day, and what excellent judgment he had displayed!

"I hope you are not too optimistic," said the wife. "I am afraid he will find he has taken a very hot seat." Lanny said to himself: That might be Esther!

"Of course, the old crowd will fight him," replied the husband. "There are many who are afraid of having the government acquire any means of getting news to the public—and especially any ideas." Then, looking across the table: "Don't you find the same thing, Winston?"

"You forget," growled the Prime Minister, "that our government owns the B.B.C. and has from the beginning. We are far from being as reactionary as some people imagine." He went back to scooping up his consommé. Behind him was the concentrated knowledge which a statesman of Britain had acquired through a lifetime of observation and experience. He knew his half of the planet; and at present it was keeping him so busy that he had no time to bother with the other half. He sat calmly sure that he was wiser and more mature than anybody else in this room.

Perhaps the host felt the need of livening up the party; or perhaps he was tired and wanted to keep himself entertained. "Our enemies have got a new one on us," he announced. "They delight to keep track of the proliferating of our bureaucracy. At the press conference I was asked if it is true that we have a 'Biscuit, Cracker, and Pretzel Subcommittee of the Baking Industry of the Division of Industrial Operations of the War Production Board.' "

Everybody laughed, and someone asked: "What did you say, Mr. President?"

"I said I didn't know, but I hoped so, because I was very fond of biscuits, crackers, and pretzels."

"You get a lot of fun out of your job, Mr. President," remarked the author's bright little wife, having evidently made up her mind not to be scared.

"I take the fun as it comes. One of our O.P.A. men told me a good story this afternoon. It seems that somebody prepared a nine-page typewritten order on the subject of cotton duck, and it was passed around among the officials who had to do with it, prior to its being mimeographed and sent out to the industry. Each official had to sign it, and eight or ten did so before the discovery was made that it wasn't all about cotton duck—somebody had inserted a paragraph about Donald Duck!"

They all had another good laugh; and then the President, enjoying himself hugely, looked across the table at John Bull and said: "By the way, before I forget. Someone has sent me a painting of you. It's on my desk in the office; don't let me forget to show it to you. The man is a Canadian; Vancouver, I believe. He admits that he has never seen you, but I think he's got a pretty good likeness—except that he's given you a little more hair than you actually have."

The Prime Minister of Great Britain rubbed a gentle hand over his sparsely covered pate and grinned a little ruefully at his lack of immunity to the ravages of time. "Perhaps I have lost some since the painter started."

"There's a new portrait of me, too. Have you had a chance to take a look at it?"

"Which one, Mr. President?"

"Now see here, Winston! There are not so many portraits of me. There's a curious story about the one I refer to. The painter has a considerable reputation in his own country, which is not one of the lesser parts of the Western hemisphere. His country's ambassador requested three sittings, and I gave two of them, but then the Secret Service forbade me to sit any more for him. It turned out that the man was a two-time spy, working for a faction of his country's government and for the Germans at the same time!"

Everybody gasped; and F.D.R., waiting for the next course of his dinner, lighted a cigarette and waved it in the long holder, as if to say that he was still alive and it was all in a presidential day's work.

"What did the man do then?" inquired the Prime Minister.

"He finished the portrait without me, and it's quite good. I'm supposed to be making a fireside chat. The fireside is not shown, but one side of my face is flaming red. I thought I'd entitle the picture 'Roosevelt in Hell,' and offer it to somebody who might like to have me that way."

"Until recently the Wall Street boys would have been delighted to have it," remarked Churchill, and there was a gust of laughter.

VII

The situation which these statesmen confronted at this hour was perhaps the worst in the history of their countries. There had been a veritable deluge of bad news in the last few days. General Rommel had taken Tobruk, with more than twenty-five thousand British prisoners; his forces had advanced a hundred miles into Egypt, and the peril to Alexandria and the Suez Canal was extreme. The outer defenses of Sevastopol had been pierced. The submarines were sinking ships all up and down the Atlantic coast, a situation which could not be hidden by the strictest censors. At the same time the Japanese had taken nearly all of Burma and were threatening Calcutta and Ceylon; they had taken Kiska in the Aleutians and had shelled Vancouver and a point on the Oregon coast.

The President's cousin by marriage was worried about all these things and brought them up in the midst of a dinner party. F.D.R. refused to abate his cheerfulness, but said that measures were being taken and preparations being made. "We can't expect to make much of a showing as yet; but our boys in the air have shown the Japs what is in store for them. You perhaps don't realize the full significance of the victories we have won in the Coral Sea and at Midway."

"It has been hard for me to realize anything from so far away, Franklin."

"Well, we have shown the definite superiority of our carrier forces; and be sure that we are going to have plenty of them. The enemy is taking territory which he will not be able to hold."

The watchful hostess intervened. "Tell Franklin what you have observed of democracy in South America."

"I have heard much talk about it," was the dry reply.

The President took up the conversation: "I was down there and visited Vargas in Brazil. Wonderful people—they gave me a grand reception. In this country, when we make a to-do over a visitor, we throw confetti and ticker tape and torn telephone books. In South America they throw flowers, tons of them; roses, carnations, even orchids. Vargas met me at the quay in Rio and we got into an open car and drove through the city. For miles the streets were lined with people, and the windows and balconies were full—everybody throwing flowers and shouting '*Viva la democracia! Viva Roosevelt!*' as though the two were synonymous."

"Friend of the underdog!" rumbled Churchill.

Laughing, the other continued: "As we rode along, Vargas leaned over to me and said: 'Perhaps you have heard that I am a dictator.' I leaned over to him and said: 'Perhaps you have heard that *I* am one, too.'" Everybody laughed again, and then F.D.R. continued: "Vargas said to me: 'But I really *am.*'" There was another laugh, in which the narrator joined.

Said Adamic: "I recall that in your last re-election campaign you used that phrase '*Viva la democracia!*'"

"Yes," replied the President. "Those are about the only Spanish words I know. In Rio, of course, they were supposed to be Portuguese."

"In your Columbus Day speech," put in the author, "they were supposed to be Italian."

"I hope I did not mispronounce them," remarked the President, again joining in the laughter.

VIII

Did the First Lady make up her mind that this dinner party had given enough time to wisecracks and anecdotes? The main course had been served, which meant that the affair was half over; suddenly she remarked to her husband: "You know, Franklin, I am taking our guests to a concert, so we won't have time for a chat with you ' want you not to fail to talk to Mr. Adamic."

Never did the President fail to follow a lead from his wife. "By all means," he responded cordially. "I think it is important that people from overseas should understand that America is an amalgam of a great number of races and nations. Because we speak English and have so many Anglo-Saxon features in our culture, our British friends are apt to forget how many non-British people we have, and what an important part they play in our political and international decisions." The President was looking across the table as he spoke, and everyone at the table was listening to him. "It is a painful fact that distrust and dislike of the British Empire have been in our national tradition since the Revolution and the War of 1812; later there has been the Boer War, and India. Despite our intense admiration for a great statesman personally, these feelings remain, and anyone in our public life must reckon with them."

It was a little sermon, directed at the Right Honourable Winston Spencer Churchill, who sat as silent as a sphinx, holding a big cigar and looking at the long ash at the end.

"You, Mr. Adamic," continued the preacher, "remind us in your books that these foreign peoples, too, have their traditions, whether they are Yugoslavs or Irish, Germans or Italians, or Jews unhappy about what is happening to their fellows. The feelings of these people and of many old-time Americans about the British Empire may not seem very intelligent to the British, but they are natural enough, and justified from our different angles. The fact that they exist makes for all sorts of difficulties—all sorts—all sorts of—"

Had the President intended to go into details, and then thought better of it? He smiled suddenly and said: "I am English myself, but also I am Scotch and Dutch. That combination makes for a good bargainer." He was looking directly at his house guest. "I remember well," continued F.D.R., "when I was a boy of seven or so my mother took me to England, and I saw Queen Victoria being driven down the street, and I was quite sure that I disliked her greatly."

That was rather rubbing it in, and Lanny could only wonder what arguments had been going on and what tensions developing in the conferences between these two strong-willed men. Certain it was that the First Lady knew about them and was supporting her husband by bringing to Washington a writer who had put emphasis upon the non-Anglo-Saxon elements of the American community. She had tried to get the head of the Conservative party of Great Britain to read a book

which said in substance that the peoples of Central Europe wanted
democracy and not any kings; but Churchill, in the slang of his own
land, "wasn't having any"! What a difference, Lanny thought, between
him and the genial, overflowing conversationalist of five years ago!
Also, Lanny wasn't forgetting that he was the man who had saved England and the world in 1940–41. Give him full credit.

IX

Mrs. Roosevelt spoke a few words to the butler, and the dessert and
coffee were served quickly. "We must not be late for the concert,"
she said. "I dislike that because it makes people stare so." When she
rose the others followed suit, and they went out into the hall, leaving
the President to be transferred to his wheel chair. While they were ·
saying their farewells, Lanny stood near Churchill, listening, while
Adamic attempted to say a few words about Yugoslav affairs. The
Prime Minister still wouldn't have it; he hadn't relished this dinner, and
his disdain for a "Pinko" author was apparent in his face and in his
grumbled words. To be sure, he was a guest in this household and had
no right to be rude to any other guest; but he didn't have to talk unless
he felt like it, and he played the role of his ancestor, the haughty
duke.

As Adamic turned away, Lanny followed, and caught a glimpse of
the President being wheeled to the elevator. It was as if a different
man had been put into the chair. Gone was all the bonhomie, the
laughter; his face was drawn and lined with care, perhaps with grief
for the ten or twelve million boys whom he was getting ready to send
into the inferno of war. Lanny remembered some history and knew
that it was just so the tender-hearted Lincoln had grieved in these same
rooms eighty years ago. That had been another black time for the
Union; and the tall ungainly railsplitter from the West had done just
what the Squire of Krum Elbow was doing—trying to keep himself
cheerful by hearing and repeating funny stories.

Now the President's wife and her guests were going off to enjoy
fine music, but there would be no such respite for the Chief. He was
going up to his room to engage in a wrestling match with a stubborn
British Tory, a match which might decide the future of the world for
a long time to come. Lanny knew enough about the situation to be able
to guess what the topics would be: Palestine and Egypt, India and
Hongkong, the Ruhr and the Dardanelles, and what kind of govern-

ment should be had by Yugoslavia and Rumania and Hungary and Bulgaria and Greece and Italy and Spain.

The guests and secretaries were to be driven to the concert in two limousines. In the first of these Mrs. Roosevelt sat in the back seat with Mrs. Adamic, while the author and the cousin sat in the two movable seats, facing the ladies. The obscure Mr. Prescott sat beside the chauffeur, and that suited him, because he didn't want to talk but to listen. Doing so, he discovered that his guesses about the evening's events had been correct.

Said Mrs. Roosevelt to the Adamics: "I can't tell you how grateful we are that you two came tonight. The President has been having considerable difficulty in getting the Prime Minister to grasp what kind of country we are. I've tried to help out. I talked with Mr. Churchill yesterday and again this afternoon. I explained that many of our Americans have strong ties with the countries from which they came, or from which their parents came. The Prime Minister was somewhat impatient, as I am afraid I was with him. He said he understood, but I don't think he does. Not *really*."

X

When they were getting out of the car the hostess said to Lanny: "You understand that I am taking you back to the White House after the concert." He thanked her and followed the rest of the party into the hall. It was a hot night, so although the hall was not very large, it was only partly filled. Lanny saw by the program that there were several performers, and he could guess what had happened—this kind-hearted lady had been persuaded to further the careers of a group of aspiring young musicians. The first, a violinist, played the Mendelssohn concerto, and that is always pleasant to hear, even though it was not as well played as Lanny was accustomed to hear it from his brother-in-law Hansi Robin. The second artist, a young lady, played a Chopin étude, and Lanny thought that he could have done almost as well himself; so he took the liberty of losing himself in thought about what he was going to say to the Prime Minister of Great Britain.

Very certainly he wasn't going to take up the task of turning a rock-ribbed Tory into any sort of "friend of the underdog." No, indeed; it would be better to go back to his ivory-tower attitude and give the Duke of Marlborough's descendant to understand that the son of Budd-Erling was helping Roosevelt as an American patriot and not as any sort of New Dealer. Churchill would approve that, and Lanny would get what he wanted on that basis. He was invited, not as an adviser on policies, but as an expert on France and Germany, and especially, at this moment, on North Africa.

After the concert the other guests were delivered to their hotels, and then Lanny and the First Lady were taken back to the White House. With them rode a well-known columnist whom they had just met in the lobby; he was going in the same direction, and while they were driving he told a story which was going the rounds of Washington. It had to do with Churchill's previous visit. The President had then brought up the subject of Hongkong and the necessity of returning it to the Chinese. John Bull had declared: "You have nothing to do with Hongkong! I won't talk about Hongkong!" He wouldn't talk, but he had to listen, and the President had climaxed his efforts by saying: "Very well then, if you won't take my advice, I'm going to have to go over your head and appeal to the King."

That of course was a most horrible thing. The Prime Minister fairly shouted: "The King has nothing to say about the matter!"

"Maybe not, Winston," the tormentor continued, "but I am going to take a chance on it. I shall write him a letter, something like this: 'Dear King: Your Prime Minister is so stubborn that he will not listen to reason, so I am venturing to point out to you personally that we must have the continued help of our valiant and long-suffering allies, the Chinese people, and that they are in danger of falling into despair and giving up to their Japanese conquerors. I suggest that the way to hearten them is to make clear that in the peace settlement they will have all their territories returned to them, no matter by whom the territories are held.' Don't you think the King might be interested to read such a letter?"

"He would know that it would be unconstitutional for him to do so."

"At the same time I would write to Chiang Kai-shek, saying: 'I enclose a copy of the letter I am sending to the King of England, and I suggest that you might write him in return, assuring him that if Hongkong is returned to the Chinese people, their government will show its gratitude by guaranteeing to the British all trade rights and privileges which they have enjoyed in the past.'"

Such was the story. It was received with laughter, and then the columnist revealed why he had told it. Turning to the First Lady, he inquired: "Can you tell me if that really happened, Mrs. Roosevelt?"

Lanny, listening attentively, made note of social training in operation. With her most friendly smile the First Lady replied: "I was not there."

Inside the White House, Lanny had a few minutes with his hostess. All that evening he had been listening, saying very little, and now, with her customary graciousness, she asked his reaction to the principal topic of discussion. He told her: "I have an interest in Central Europe and its problems because I have visited Silesia, Poland, and Austria. The Germans, by a carefully thought-out policy, have integrated the whole industrial system of that region with their own, making it impossible for anyone to replace conditions as they were before the war. It seems to me that it would be folly to try. The thing to do is to turn the system into one public-service corporation under international control, and put it to work to restore the ruined cities and serve the welfare of all the people in that region."

"But what about the national boundaries, Mr. Budd?"

"The great cartels of Europe have shown us that boundaries need not interfere with the production and exchange of goods. The French and the German steel masters got along together before Hitler, and will do so again. Why cannot the consuming public do the same?"

Late as the hour was, the First Lady sat down to ask questions about that idea; and when she excused herself she said: "I will talk to the President about that. It is a service I am able to render—to bring him ideas which seem likely to be helpful."

XI

Left to his own devices, Lanny wandered about the ground-floor rooms, examining the many portraits which hung upon the walls. They were more interesting to him as a student of history than as an art expert. Having taken government by popular consent as his religion, he was concerned to see what sort of men the people of his fatherland had chosen as their guides and counselors. He stood in front of each, trying to recall what he had read about that statesman, and asking him mentally what advice he now had to give to the Republic, standing at bay against its foes on all the continents and all the seas of the world.

Well after midnight an usher came and escorted the patient guest to the second floor of the mansion, to the Prime Minister's room. He tapped, then opened the door, and found himself in the presence of the pale young secretary, Mr. Martin. "The Prime Minister is having a shower," said that functionary. "He will be out very soon."

Lanny had started looking at more portraits when the door of the bathroom was thrown open and there emerged what he found an extraordinary spectacle—the governing head of the British Empire, clad in the costume he had worn at the moment of his emergence upon earth and nothing else, not even a towel. Lanny had thought he looked like a large cherub in evening dress, and assuredly he looked still more like it when stark naked. His skin was white, slightly tinged with pink, and his flesh formed immense folds.

He didn't show any sign of embarrassment, but said a casual "Hello," and then to his secretary: "You may go to bed, Martin." The young man said: "Good night, sir," and departed, and Churchill addressed his visitor: "Take off your coat and make yourself as comfortable as you can in this damnable climate. Will you have a drink?"

"No, thanks," said Lanny. He took off his coat gladly.

"Make yourself at home," said the host. He had his own way of saying the last words—"a–tome." "I suppose a man can get used to this muggy weather, but I thank God I don't have to."

"You forget that I have recently come from Algiers."

"Oh, yes. I suppose that is worse. Well, Budd, I trust we don't have to go on with the 'Prescott' business while we are alone."

"I doubt that there are any dictaphones, Mr. Prime Minister."

The great man let his globular form down into a soft chair and remarked: "Let me see, how long since we had our talks at Maxine Elliott's house?"

"Five years and several months. You may not remember, but you were quite positive that you had been laid on the political shelf to stay."

"Yes, yes, to be sure! We seldom foresee what life is going to do with us. Did you?"

"Oh, God! Surely not!"

"The President tells me you have been doing very fine work for him. I congratulate you. Do you mind if I bother you with a lot of questions?"

"Not at all, Mr. Churchill." With Englishmen, you use the title once, and, if you are a social equal, once only.

XII

So began a merciless inquisition which lasted two hours. Churchill knew exactly what he wanted to ask, and it was everything concerning the enemies he was facing. Pétain, Laval, Darlan, Benoist-Méchin, Pierre Pucheu, Fernand de Brinon, Paul Marion, Joseph Barthélemy—he had met them just before the Franco-German armistice, when he had been trying to persuade them to hold out. What were they doing now and what was the state of their minds? And the people in North Africa—Lemaigre-Dubreuil and General Noguès and the rest of the Army crowd. And whether or not those who were in sympathy with the Allies dared reveal it. Lanny was free to tell about the vegetable-oil magnate and about General Béthouart and his group, and what the Arabs had said, and the Jews, and others he had met. He reported, without naming names, that he had friends from the old days who had whispered to him of the spread of the underground movements.

"Surely you don't think they can do anything against the German milit'ry power!" exclaimed the Prime Minister.

"Not at present. But if ever you put an army on those shores, you will find the partisans of great help in cutting communication lines and handicapping the enemy. The job at present is to get them organized and trained; to get the tools to them and teach them the know-how. Our own Army is doing that, and I suppose yours is also."

"Of a certainty; but that is some time in the future." He said it "few-chah," and went on to add that milit'ry hist'ry showed that a hostyle population could inflict much damage upon an invader.

Then he wanted to hear about Hitler and Göring and Hess. Lanny's knowledge was a year old, but even so it might be important, and he had to tell in detail how he had managed to keep the friendship and confidence of these Nazis. The Prime Minister called them "Nah-zies," and didn't care if they didn't like it. Lanny told how he and Hess had experimented with spiritualist mediums and astrologers, and how he had managed to persuade the Number Three Nazi that there was a large group of Englishmen sympathetic to the *Neue Ordnung* and making plans to oust Churchill and put in a Prime Minister willing to work out terms of peace. "Apparently," said the American, "your B4 was playing the same game with Hess."

"Quite so," said the cherub in the overstuffed chair. He had reached for one of his cigars and lighted it, and if there was any spectacle in the world more comical than an immense naked cherub puffing a big dark cigar, the son of Budd-Erling had never beheld it.

"I am told," continued Lanny, "that your B4 wrote letters in the name of Ivone Kirkpatrick and the Duke of Hamilton and others, and that Rudi fell for them completely. The Governor—I mean the President—told me that you gave them a good wigging for it."

There was a gleam in those bright blue eyes. "It was an outrageous violation of the rights of Englishmen."

"But it worked," said Lanny with a grin. "I rather guessed that B4 was paying the Germans off for those two agents of yours who were lured to the Dutch border and kidnaped just after the outbreak of the war. No doubt the Nazis would be glad to swap them for Hess."

The Prime Minister gave a grunt expressive of agreement. "The President tells me you got into a jam with our people over that episode. I'll be glad to straighten it out for you."

"Thank you, sir. You understand, I was under a pledge not to mention my connection with the President; so when your agents questioned me about my dealings with the enemy, I was helpless. They were perfectly right in their judgment that I knew too much."

"Or that you knew too many," chuckled the enemy of all collaborators.

"There is another detail about this Hess matter which may interest you, Mr. Churchill. The man who brought me a message from Hess just a few days before his flight to Scotland came to my London hotel and gave me the name Branscome. I suppose he made that name up for the occasion. Naturally I was interested in him and took a good look so that I'd know him the next time. And it happened. I saw him last night in a restaurant in New York."

"The devil you say! Did you speak to him?"

"I very carefully kept out of his sight and phoned the F.B.I. to get on his trail. This morning I went to see them and told them about the fellow. They've found out where he is staying and are keeping after him."

"Good for you! Your F.B.I. has been extraordinarily successful in preventing sabotage so far. Very capable men, and we give them all the help we can."

XIII

They talked about spies and saboteurs for a while, and then Lanny thought it a good occasion to bring up a subject he had thought of while motoring to Washington. Said he: "There is something I should like to suggest in connection with Hess, Mr. Churchill—if it's not too late in the night."

"By no means. What is it?"

"May I ask, did you get any important information out of him?"

"Not very much. He is a fanatic, and nothing could make him weaken. But we had already got together a pretty good dossier on all those blighters."

"This is what occurred to me: that it might be worth while to let me have a talk with him and see what I could get."

"You really think he would talk to you?"

"He made me his confidant in several important matters; and now he has been a prisoner for more than a year and must be pretty lonely. I can't doubt that he'd be glad to see an old friend."

"But he would know that we would never let you see him unless we were certain that you were against him."

"It would be my idea to frame up a little drama. Let me be taken to him in the middle of the night, in pretended secrecy. I'll tell him that I have bribed the jailer. I think I could get away with that. He knows that my father is a rich man, and he doubtless thinks I am, too."

"By Jove! That might get us something! What would you give as your purpose in seeing him?"

"I could tell him that I have a message from the Führer. Bear in mind that I have a code that I use with these men. Hitler gave me the name 'Siegfried' to use if I wished to send him a secret message; and I gave Hess the name 'Kurvenal'—you may remember the character in *Tristan* who is called 'the truest of the true.' Imagine that I should have the jailer smuggle in to Hess a bit of tissue paper with the name 'Kurvenal' written on it, rolled, let us say, into a pellet and hidden in a slice of bread. Rudi would be thrown into a state of great excitement and would be ready for a frank talk when I came into his cell, or whatever he sleeps in."

"What would you expect to get from him? All his information is more than a year out of date."

"Even so there might be secrets that have not yet come to light. I have one idea that may sound fantastic, but I keep thinking about it in spite of myself—that I might get some message from Rudi to be delivered to the Führer, and by this device I might have another go in Germany."

"Would you dare try that?"

"The President thinks I should not. He has the idea that because I had an interview with Stalin the Nazis must surely have decided that I am a phony. I agreed with that for a time, but now I'm not so sure. Hitler's Intelligence service is by no means perfect. I have proved that more than once. And if I found that he had learned of my passing through Russia, I believe I could convince him that I had gone there in his interest, to pump Stalin and bring back a report on the possibility of a deal. Hitler made one in 1939, and why might he not consider another in 1942?"

"He'd jolly well be glad to in his present fix!"

"Exactly. Hitler gave me messages to take to the collaborators in Britain and France and America; and what more natural than that I should have been looking for some of the same stripe in Moscow? The Nazis must know of some, and I might find out from Hess who they are. Wouldn't that be worth while?"

"Good God, yes!"

"And that's only one of many possibilities. I am fascinated by the idea of coming to my old friend the Führer with a message from his *fidus Achates.*"

"My information is that Hitler raged at Hess for his folly in taking the flight—plain idiocy."

"I don't doubt that. But he must know perfectly well that no matter how misguided it was, Rudi had no thought but to serve his adored master and protect him from having to fight a war on two fronts. And now if I should come to him with a message from the friend's heart—and possibly with a talisman, or some password that Rudi would give me, something that would convince Hitler I had actually talked with him—wouldn't the Führer's heart be touched? It might even be possible for you to cause a rumor to start, after I had left England, that it had been discovered that I had bribed a jailer and had got in to talk with Hess. I wouldn't want it in the press, but you could find a way to let it become known in one of your prison camps for German officers. You may be sure that the Nazis have some spy lurking on the outside of such camps to pick up stories, and they wouldn't miss that one."

"Look here, Budd," said the Prime Minister. "Is this the scenario of a cinema you are telling me?"

The P.A. replied: "The whole war is the scenario of a cinema, Mr. Churchill. My guess is that it will furnish plots for many thousands of them before mankind loses interest in these events. And be sure that you will be in them."

"Get out!" exclaimed the pink-and-white cherub. "None of your treacle!" Then, as Lanny took the advice seriously and got up, he held out his hand and said cordially: "Come and see me when you find yourself in London. I'll think all this over in the meantime."

9

Treasons, Stratagems, and Spoils

I

FOR the first time Lanny exercised the privilege of calling his Chief on the telephone. He called the White House at eight in the morning, when he judged that F.D.R. would be having his breakfast in bed. He said to the operator: "I would like to speak to the President; the name is Traveler." He wondered what would happen next, and was taken by surprise when, a few seconds later, he heard the voice of his friend. "Hello, Presidential Substitute!"

"Did you have a good sleep?" ventured the caller.

"The best in some time. I wish you could keep it up."

"I will if you say the word."

"No, I'm afraid somebody might have his feelings hurt."

"What do you want me to do next, Governor?"

"Can you come back in a week or ten days?"

"With pleasure."

"It's a date. And by the way, Alston should be in New York in a day or two—he's been out West. Have a talk with him. He may have suggestions."

"I'll do it."

"So long, Traveler."

That was that; and Lanny, who was still in bed himself, had his bath and ate his breakfast, and then dressed and went down to his car. Such a pleasant thing to be a married man again, and to have somebody to come home to and to tell about your adventures, if only part of them! On that six-hour drive—heavy traffic slowed him up—Lanny thought about what he was going to say to Laurel, and then about what he was going to say to Rudolf Hess if he should meet him, and then, a truly serious question, what he would say to Adolf Hitler if he should meet *him*.

Lanny had phoned, and Laurel was awaiting him with happiness she did not try to hide. He was free to tell her about the dinner at the

White House, for there were no war secrets in that. Also he could tell about Churchill in the "altogether," though not about the topics they had discussed. He persuaded her to dress and have dinner out with him. He would take her to a roof garden and hope they wouldn't run into any more German spies. She protested that she looked too awful, and you couldn't hide anything in summer. But he insisted that women were getting bolder about such matters, and she, who called herself emancipated, could help to set the fashion.

II

Next morning he went down to the F.B.I. office and listened to a report on the mysterious Mr. Branscome, who was now bearing the name of Hartley. He had been watched closely and appeared to be just enjoying New York night life; he had only a few personal acquaintances, harmless persons so far as the watchers were able to learn. He had a three-room apartment and stayed in it most of the day, and what he was doing there was something the F.B.I. wanted very much to know. They were trying to find a plan to get him out of the way for a couple of hours so that they could enter the place and investigate. The agent, quiet in manner, but determined, fixed a pair of gray eyes upon his caller and said: "We are hoping, Mr. Budd, that you may be willing to give us a bit of help in this matter."

"What do you have in mind, Mr. Post?"

"We should like you to run into this man again—by accident, as you will pretend—and recognize him and renew the acquaintance and see if he will give you his confidence. At the least you could take him for a drive or something and keep him out of the way for a while."

Lanny did not answer at once; he was thinking what to say. The agent went on to point out that Branscome alias Hartley had every reason to assume that Lanny was a German agent or sympathizer, and he might be glad of someone to talk to. If he declined to renew the acquaintance, he might give some reason, and that might be a clue. If he showed fear or embarrassment, a desire to get away, it might indicate that he had dropped his treasonable activities; on the other hand, it might indicate that he was up to something especially dangerous.

Lanny said: "Your request embarrasses me, Mr. Post. I am not free to do what you ask, and I am not free to explain why. I can only tell you that when I met this German agent in England I was not just amusing myself. I was under orders, and I am still under them."

"Could you possibly get permission to do this?"

"I don't think I ought to ask permission, for it would indicate a lack of appreciation of the importance of my own work. I have connections which I am not at liberty to jeopardize. If I were to meet a German agent, and soon afterward he were to be arrested, I should be drawing suspicion upon myself. In certain contingencies that might cost me my life; and while a soldier is prepared to sacrifice his life in wartime, there are others who are ordered to stay alive."

"I can understand, Mr. Budd. Your position and your father's position make it possible for me to guess something about your work. But suppose I could pledge that under no circumstances will we arrest this Englishman?"

"But what good could it do you to find out about him if your hands were tied by such a promise?"

"One thing leads to another, and there might be many advantages we could gain. If the man is doing anything important, he will have associates, and we might be able to find out who these persons are. We might uncover a whole chain of activities so far away from the original clue that not even Hartley would suspect that he was involved. Another thing, we might make it possible for Hartley to make good money, so that he would be very well content with the results of his friendship with you."

"You mean trying to buy him?"

"No, that might give everything away. I mean that you might introduce him to certain persons of wealth who sympathize with his peculiar ideas, and he would know how to get money out of them without any more than a hint from you."

"How do you happen to know that I know such persons?" inquired the P.A.

The other smiled a quiet slow smile—he was from somewhere in the South, as his accent revealed. "You know this game very well, Mr. Budd, and you must not take offense that we made sure what sort of person we were dealing with."

Lanny smiled the quick smile which was characteristic of him. "Some day when the war is over, you must let me see that dossier. It would give me an amusing half hour."

III

The two of them spent the rest of the morning working out a program. When Mr. Hartley went out to dine, the agents would note where he went and then phone Lanny, who would be dressed for the occasion and who would stroll into the place and recognize the messenger of Rudolf Hess and greet him. He would try to soothe him down if he was scared, assure him of his high esteem, chat with him amiably, and take him for a drive. During that drive Lanny would assure him of his own devotion to the Nazi cause and would offer to introduce him to others of that way of thinking—first among them being Miss Cornelia van Zandt.

"You know this lady?" asked the P.A. The answer was: "We know her well, and all her friends. We even know the dates when you dined there with Forrest Quadratt, and again with Senator Reynolds and Mr. Harrison Dengue."

"I see you move in the best near-Fascist circles, Mr. Post. I trust you do not let yourselves be awed by big names."

"Not in the least, Mr. Budd. We don't arrest senators and congressmen, but naturally we know who their friends are."

"Let me ask you something especially confidential. Has your attention ever been called to the existence of a conspiracy to kidnap the President of the United States and hold him under the orders of a group of active and aggressive anti-New Dealers?"

"Indeed, yes, Mr. Budd, and I can assure you that the dossiers on those gentry fill a large cabinet."

"You wouldn't be surprised to hear that the name of the very wealthy and important Mr. Dengue is among them?"

"Not in the least, Mr. Budd."

"Nor that the names include several high officers in the United States Army?"

"Not the highest, we hope, Mr. Budd!"

"Not the highest, but still dangerously high."

"Some of them have been retired, and some, we are assured, are soon to be."

"Well, then, we understand each other, Mr. Post, and can talk as friends. I won't drop any hint to Hartley concerning this conspiracy, but I'll take him to dinner in Miss van Zandt's rather dingy old mansion, and maybe some day she will reveal the plot to him. What I will tell Hartley is that this is a slightly daffy old cow who gives the richest cream ever known, and whom all of us friends of Hitler and Mussolini have been milking for the last ten years or more."

"Twenty," said the F.B.I. man. "And one thing more. I hope it won't seem too risky if, while you are entertaining him, we take the chance to find out what is in his apartment."

"That is a pretty dangerous thing for my work, Mr. Post."

"I assure you it won't be. We have experts who know their business. They do not damage doors or locks and do not leave the smallest trace in the room. We can photostat documents at the rate of a few seconds each, and everything will be replaced exactly as it was. We rub out all fingerprints and dust that might tell tales."

"And how about the other people in the apartment house?"

"Everything has been taken care of. We have an apartment on the same floor, we have taken an impression of the lock and have a key to fit it. An hour will be the utmost that we need."

"You are tempting me unduly," said the P.A. "I ought to say no, but I don't!"

IV

Lanny went home and told his wife what he had learned and what he had promised to do. This was an adventure in which she could take no part, but she was an excellent adviser, and they discussed the psychology of an English Nazi and whether he was apt to be a fanatic or a crook or both, and how it might be possible to gain and keep his confidence. They agreed that he was certain to be a snob, and that Lanny's best bet would be his intimacy with Lord and Lady Wickthorpe. He would pose as a rich man's impecunious son and would suggest that Branscome might be introduced to the overpecunious Miss van Zandt, and the two men would divide whatever they could get from her.

At six in the evening Lanny was dressed in his elegant white jacket, soft white shirt, and black tie, and sat reading the evening paper, but rather inattentively. Before he had finished the phone rang. It was the F.B.I. man informing him that their quarry was settled in the Oak Room of the St. Regis Hotel, a place frequented by the richest refugees and therefore good for spies. Lanny's car was at the door and he hopped into it. Crowded traffic slowed him down, and it must have been fifteen minutes before he found a place to park his car near his destination. However, when he entered the room he was the picture of carefree grace. To the head waiter he said: "I am looking for a friend," and so he was left to stroll. When he saw the neat-whiskered Englishman he stopped in front of him, with a smile of pleasure on his face. "Well, well! What a happy coincidence!"—but no name, of course.

The victim looked up. He could not keep dismay from his features. Lanny made things easy for him, as any well-bred person does when he knows that he may not be remembered. "I am Lanny Budd," he said, "and we met in London." Then in a lower tone: "Kurvenal." That didn't relieve the tension, and Lanny realized that the man was greatly worried. It was the P.A.'s role to take the aggressive and keep it, so he continued: "I have been wishing very much that I might meet you again. May I join you?"

Branscome made a feeble attempt to get out of his predicament: "I am afraid you have me at a disadvantage, sir. I don't remember—"

"That's all right," said Lanny soothingly as he took the seat opposite—it was a table for two. "Let us wait until we are alone. I have something important to tell you; and be sure that I understand the situation."

The man was trapped. The waiter came, and Lanny ordered a small salad and a glass of iced tea; he wanted to be free to leave when his victim did, and without seeming hurried or importunate. His victim had a half-eaten mutton chop before him. "Beastly hot weather for June," Lanny remarked. "One doesn't feel like eating." And when the waiter had departed: "Don't be uneasy, my friend. You may count upon my discretion and good faith." Then, in the manner of casual conversation: "How long since you left London? I haven't been there for a year. Did you by any chance hear the funny story of my leaving?"

"I haven't heard anything," said the Englishman, not relaxing his un-cordial manner. He was obviously in distress, and his eyes shifted from one part of the room to another, avoiding the other's steady gaze. His eyelids were red and the eyes slightly bleared, and Lanny thought: "He drinks." The man was somewhat stouter than he had been in London, and that was to be expected, since food wasn't so scarce in New York and rationing didn't seem to apply to restaurants.

The P.A. began making himself agreeable, an art which he had been practicing since early childhood. He must manage to interest this man, gain his confidence, or at the least awaken his curiosity, before that mutton chop was finished! "I have just come back from Unoccupied France and French North Africa. You know, my profession of art expert puts me in an especially fortunate position. I am able to travel, and people talk to me frankly because they assume that I am nonpolitical. In Vichy I had the pleasure of meeting Premier Laval and Admiral Darlan. I found they were getting along very well, far better than the newspapers had given me to expect."

Lanny paused for a moment to give the Englishman a chance to say how bad he thought American newspapers, but the Englishman did not take the chance. So Lanny went on to tell about his mother's home on the Riviera, and how he had found conditions there, especially how well the Italians were behaving in the tiny strip of France they had taken, and how little the armistice commissions were interfering with the daily lives of the French. "So different from what we hear!" said the art expert. Again he paused for a comment, and again the Englishman cut off another chunk of mutton chop.

Then to North Africa. The interior of that country is not often visited, and Lanny could tell interesting stories about ancient Roman ruins and mosaics and mosques and *marabouts* and Moorish banquets and veiled ladies in the casbahs. He told them; and in between times, when the waiter was gone and nobody near, he would say: "You may trust me, my dear sir; I am an entirely discreet person and I have something really worth while to tell you. I can show you a way to make quite a good sum of money."

When the waiter returned, or when others were passing, Lanny would talk about the great prosperity he had found in all North Africa, and how well affairs were being conducted; the French still had an army in Morocco, and General Noguès got along perfectly with the Germans. Having said this, Lanny would take another cautious glance about him, and add: "I have a car outside, and I hope that you will take a drive with me and give me an opportunity to put a business proposition before you. I have thought of you several times, and had the idea of looking you up the next time I was in London. I have friends there, you know, and I had the idea that I might find you through them."

That was a "lead," and took the conversation to a territory familiar to Branscome alias Hartley. He didn't have much to say about it, but Lanny had enough for two. He told how he had a little daughter there, and how his former wife was now the Countess of Wickthorpe, and they had remained friends in spite of a divorce. "Ceddy" Wickthorpe had been Lanny's friend from boyhood, and Lanny had been at the Castle at the time that a certain unnamed friend had made his surprise landing by parachute. "Some time I'll tell you a funny story about what happened at the Castle on that occasion," said the art expert.

With that hint, just enough to awaken curiosity, he passed on to Lord Londonderry and Lord Redesdale, whom he had known as ardent appeasers in the old days. Lord Redesdale was the father of Unity Mitford, and Lanny had met her in the mountain retreat of a Very Important Person who had to be nameless in a New York restaurant. That poor girl had apparently shot herself because of disappointment in her personal expectations. Did Mr. Branscome know what had happened? Mr. Branscome said he didn't, and Lanny went on to talk about the love life of the unnamable great one, saying only polite things, of course, and speaking with contempt of the slanders which were circulated by the kind of press, "well, you know the kind I refer to, both here and in England."

V

All this time Lanny was feeling somewhat queasy, thinking of what the F.B.I. men were doing. But he gave no outward sign, and by the time the meal had been eaten he had made himself so agreeable that his victim consented to walk to the car with him and be taken for a drive in Central Park. After the engine had been started and they were in the stream of traffic, Lanny said: "Now we can talk, and not be afraid to name names, Mr. Branscome."

"I am going by the name of Hartley in this country," replied the other. "As a matter of fact, that is my real name."

Lanny guessed that the fact was otherwise, but he wouldn't say so. "Thank you, Hartley. I don't want to ask any improper questions; but before I go into the details of my plan, tell me as much as you care to about who you are and what you are doing."

"To put it bluntly," said the Englishman, "I am keeping alive. I don't like the bombs."

"I can understand," replied Lanny. "I have been under them, too. You remember the Abbé Sieyès who was asked what he had done during the French Revolution, and he said: 'I survived.'"

"I want to tell you," continued Hartley, "I have dropped the sort of activity I was carrying on in London. I decided that it was inadvisable."

Lanny had expected just that and had planned in advance how to deal with it. "Surely, Hartley, you are not reconciled to turning the world over to the Reds!"

"No, but this war has become too big for anybody to control, and certainly for a man in my obscure position. I can't see how anybody can win it—except General Chaos."

Had the scamp lost his nerve or was it just that he wanted Lanny to think he had? It was up to the host, driving in the twilight of a warm evening near the end of June, to find cheerful things to say, cheerful from the point of view of Nazi-Fascism. Lanny expatiated upon the strong position of both Germany and Japan; many years would be required to drive them out of this position, and both Britain and America would be bankrupt before it could happen. Moreover, as one who had access to secret information, Lanny could say that the Nazis were working on new weapons which would make it impossible for Britain to stay in the war for another year. "You'll be even more glad to be out of London when those rocket bombs begin to fall, Mr. Hartley."

Thus discoursing, they drove through the park and over to Riverside Drive. The farther they went, the longer it would take to get back, and the more time the Federal agents would have to complete their work. Lanny didn't think that Branscome alias Hartley—or Hartley alias Branscome—really needed any reconversion to the Fascist cause; but the longer Lanny talked along that line, the more apparent he would make it that he was a genuine friend of this cause. He told so many inside facts and talked so freely about Berchtesgaden and Karinhall and the other shrines of Nazi glory that the Englishman could only conclude that this was a remarkable man, one of the insiders who were shaping the destiny of the world.

"Tell me frankly, Hartley," this insider opened up suddenly, "do you know Rudi personally?"

"Rudi?" replied the other. "What Rudi?"

"Rudolf Hess."

"Why should you think that I know him?"

"That message you brought me in London was from him. Didn't you know it?"

"I didn't know anything about it. I was told to give the password 'Kurvenal,' and take any message you might have."

Lanny was prepared for this answer; like all the others, it might or might not be true. He could see that Hartley was playing his cards close to his chest, and Lanny had to go on wooing him with facts and fancies, all having to do with the New Order of Adolf Hitler, the successes it had won so far and the fresh ones which were sure to follow. Lanny told about his friendship with the Führer's Number Three, his home, his wife and friends, and especially his interest in psychic phenomena, and how he and Lanny had consulted mediums and astrologers, and some of the curious things which had happened. Did Mr. Hartley know anything about this subject? Mr. Hartley replied that he had always supposed it was a lot of rubbish, and mostly fraud. Lanny said there was plenty of fraud in it, and unfortunately his friend Rudi wasn't very discriminating and had let himself be played for a sucker more than once.

VI

When you chat like that for hours you become friends, and when these two were far up through Yonkers and the villages beyond, Lanny decided that it was time to get down to business. "Listen, Hartley," he said. "I told you I had an idea of how you and I might make some easy money. Let me explain that I'm in a jam, because my father is making planes for the government, and I think it's a hellish thing to do, and I've told him so. The result is I can't expect money from him, and I can't make much at my profession in wartime, so I'm up against it. I have an idea, but it can't be worked by one man. I need a partner, somebody of the same way of thinking. I thought several times of you; and now I have the luck to run into you in the very place where I wanted to try out my idea."

"Tell me what it is," said the other.

"I don't know how much you know about America, and how easy it is to collect money here. There are so many people who are lousy with money and don't know what to do with it; they take up all sorts of 'causes' and put up sums that would startle you. I know an old lady who thinks nothing of writing a check for five or ten thousand dollars, just for the trouble of going to a dinner at her home and telling her what she wants to hear and offering her a new way to promote it."

"What is it she wants to promote?"

"I won't say that she has brains enough to understand the theories of National Socialism as it would be applied in America, or even that she would like it if she saw it applied; but she knows enough to be in terror of Bolshevism, and that's what you have to put up to her. You are an Englishman, so you have a new angle of approach. You tell her about the Labour Party and how it is riddled with Communism, how it is really nothing but a secret plot of the Reds to take over the country and align it with Russia. When this war is over, the Reds will be on top, and there will be no stopping them."

"That's really true, Budd."

"Of course it's true, and you know how to tell it with conviction, and to get her stirred up so that she won't be able to sleep at night. Tell her that you want to devote your life to putting these facts before the American public; you want to start a paper, put out leaflets, and get speeches into the *Congressional Record* and distribute them over the country, whatever we decide will be most effective. We'd have to do some of it, of course; the thing mustn't be a racket. We'd open an office and do real work, but the point is, we'd be able to pay ourselves good salaries, and we could travel and have expense accounts. We'd make it all perfectly respectable, and the money would keep pouring in. I've seen it done several times, and it can't fail if you have the brains to keep it on the right track."

"But I can't do things like that in America, Budd. I am a British subject, and the government would put me out."

"It wouldn't have to be done in your name. We'd find some Americans to serve as a front and carry the responsibility. I think I know one such man, a close friend, Forrest Quadratt, and Miss van Zandt knows him well. Perhaps you've heard of him."

"I have, of course. But he's been convicted of some war offense!"

"He's quite certain that his conviction will be reversed by a higher court. Meantime he's out on bail, and he's going right on with his work."

"But I couldn't afford to have anything to do with a man like that. He's bound to be watched by government spies, and a foreigner can't be put in that position."

"All right then, forget him. I might ask Miss van Zandt to suggest a man. That would help to give her confidence."

"You mean that she would put up money for a complete stranger, and an alien?"

"I would take you there and vouch for you. I know her well, and she knows I'm a rich man's son, so she thinks I'm above suspicion. She'll invite us to dinner, and all you have to do is to get ready your spiel, and make it good and hot, for there's nothing she won't swallow. She has a right to spend her money as she pleases, and, thank God, it's not yet against the law to tell the American people about the dangers of Red Communism. She owns an old brownstone mansion on lower Fifth Avenue, and she bears an old and honored name, so she's above suspicion and safe from any attack. If you're under her protection you'll be absolutely safe. You must understand, I can't do this alone, because I can't afford to let Miss van Zandt or any of my other rich friends know that I am broke; that would destroy my prestige. But here comes an Englishman with a load of new ideas, and I'll introduce you to one person after another and the money will come rolling in. You can insist that you need my guidance, and that I ought to have a salary, and I can reluctantly consent, and Miss van Zandt will agree, and maybe write another check."

Hartley alias Branscome hesitated for a while. He had other duties, he said, which he was afraid of jeopardizing. Lanny asked tactfully, might it be that these were dangerous? This plan had the advantage of being perfectly legal, and even honorific. "Don't forget that you'll meet tremendously important people who can be of use to you all the rest of your life. I can give you a string of names out of the Social Register, to say nothing of Dun and Bradstreet. And if it's a question of your time, this plan wouldn't take very much. All that you and I would have to do is the money-raising; for all the other work—the writing, printing, office management, and so on—we can hire. We don't have to worry about any of it. Let the others do that."

It just wasn't possible to turn down such an offer. After more hesitation the man of mystery said that he would go at least as far as to dine with the eccentric old lady and tell her his story and see how she reacted. Thereupon Lanny turned the car back to the city, and they arrived late in the evening. All the way he was shivering at the thought: Suppose the F.B.I. had run into trouble and hadn't finished yet! Or suppose they had left some clue and that Hartley alias Branscome discovered it and told his Nazi associates that the too plausible son of Budd-Erling had played this dirty trick upon him!

VII

Next morning Lanny wrote a note to the "angel" of the pro-Nazis, telling her about the remarkable Englishman he desired to introduce. He laid it on thick, for he didn't in the least mind if Hartley got some of her money—he told himself that if one rascal didn't get it, another would. He sent the note by messenger and then he went down to the F.B.I. office.

"I got what I wanted. Did you get yours?" he asked the competent Mr. Post.

"Indeed, yes," answered the agent. "If I tell you about it, you'll keep extra quiet?"

"I can't keep any quieter than I am," Lanny said. "I was learning to keep my father's secrets when I was four or five years old."

"Well, the man's room is lousy with diamonds. He has them hidden in at least half a dozen places."

"What on earth is he doing with diamonds?"

"He is part of a ring that is shipping them to Sweden, to be smuggled into Germany, we assume."

"That would be rather important, wouldn't it?"

"The German machine-tool industry depends upon them."

"Well, we've been lucky. Are you sure you left the place in order?"

"I went along myself to watch everything, and I was glad I did. We finished in less than the hour you allowed us."

Said Lanny: "I'm surprised that the fellow would come in on a scheme like mine if he has such an important matter already in hand."

"One thing you learn, no crook ever gets enough money. This one may be playing a minor role, the others getting a larger cut."

"I got the impression that he has a bad case of the jitters. So I put my proposition up to him as something within the law, and it may be he'll be glad to get out of the more dangerous racket. I hope you didn't take any of those diamonds, Mr. Post."

"Surely not. But we ought to get them before they disappear. That is going to be really difficult, because diamonds are so easy to move. We have to find a way to keep track of them without involving you."

"I have tried to make things easier," explained Lanny. "I suggested to Hartley that we might have to find another man, someone to carry the responsibility of our proposed organization. He had no objection, and he won't have any objection to a business manager and other people to do the work. You can surround him with your agents, both men and women, if you wish."

"If you don't mind," said Post, "let me introduce you to a chap who is working on this case, and if you approve you might tell your old lady about him and let him put up some of the money."

The agent pressed a button and told the secretary to send in "Cartier." A young man, slightly built, entered the room—Lanny learned later that he was twenty-one, but he might have been taken for a boy. He had a thin, eager face, bright blue eyes, and an expression of alertness, as if he were playing some game which required him to be on his toes every moment. "Mr. Budd," said the agent, "this is Tom Cartier. He has left the University of Virginia to help us out in this emergency. His conscience is troubled because he isn't in the Army, so we'll have to give him something dangerous to do."

Lanny shook hands with the youngster and promised to do his best. Cartier had evidently been told about the son of Budd-Erling and had conceived a great awe of him. The youngster knew German and had been "boning up" day and night on the subject of Nazi doctrines and practice. He had been working among the "Christian Mobilizers," the "Crusader Whiteshirts," and other fanatics who were trying to introduce the New Order into the sweet land of liberty. It amused Lanny vastly to hear the Nazi language with a Virginia accent.

He took a great shine to the youngster, and Post sent them off into a room where they could talk about the details of their scheme. Lanny was to tell both Hartley and Miss van Zandt about a capable young man who had some money and was eager to put it into the anti-Bolshevik cause. "I expect to find a note from the old lady when I get home," Lanny said. "She is always in a hurry, because she has visions of the Reds coming round the corner from Union Square and seizing her mansion."

"They would if they could," said the F.B.I. man, with a grin. "Some day she'll be asking us for help, and we'll have to give it to her."

VIII

Returning to the apartment, Lanny found the letter, as he had predicted. "Miss van Zandt requests the pleasure of Mr. Lanny Budd's company at dinner this evening. Seven o'clock. Black tie." There was a similar note which Lanny was supposed to deliver to Mr. Trescott Hartley, but he had no way to do that, for Mr. Hartley had not entrusted him with an address. He had said that he would telephone Lanny at four in the afternoon, so all Lanny could do was wait.

Meantime he went to call on his old friend and employer, Professor Alston, who had just arrived in New York from the Middle West. The presidential "fixer" had been trying to resolve what he called "an interdepartmental jurisdictional dispute." He didn't name names, or even departments, for he was the most discreet of counselors; but he was also a tired and overstrained old gentleman, who was glad to have a friendly ear into which to pour the story of human inadequacy in the giant crisis which was threatening the nation's existence.

Lanny drove him so that they could be alone, and took him to a roadside café where a "headliner" wasn't apt to meet a reporter and be asked for the name of his luncheon companion. So this ex-professor of geography with the little white beard and the gold pince-nez set forth his idea that the development of man's mechanical devices and economic organizations had outrun that of his moral codes. You could find men who were "big" enough to build colossal enterprises, but it was hard indeed to find those who were "big" enough not to quarrel with their associates and let personal antagonisms paralyze their usefulness in the public service.

"Here I am," said Charles T. Alston, "close to seventy and by no means a Hercules, and I have to spend my time being flown about the country and sitting in hotel rooms in stifling hot weather, administering paternal scoldings to schoolboys of anywhere between forty and eighty years. I have to get them together and plead and pray with them, threaten them with the Nazis, find slogans to inspire them, make them swear oaths of loyalty to their duty which they ought to have learned in school. I have to make them kiss and make up—"

"Actually kiss?" inquired Lanny, ready for a good laugh.

"No, that would be in France. Here they shake hands and get a soulful look in the eyes, or at any rate they refrain from punching each other in the nose. That may last for the duration, or it may not last till I get out of town."

"You should write a book called *The Memoirs of a Bureaucrat,* Professor."

"Don't fool yourself, my boy. Power is power, whether it is political or financial. It goes to men's heads and you see them swell up like bullfrogs, and it's just the same whether they are heads of alphabetical departments in the government or of coal or oil or steel combines. I go through the same ritual in Wall Street as in Washington, or out in the field, wherever jealousy and greed and self-will have taken root in the hearts of men."

"And women?" inquired the other.

"Women don't *do* so much, but they talk more, and oh, it's dreadful! Women take my suggestions more readily, I suppose, because I am a man. Sometimes when I'm dealing with the men I wish I could be a woman."

"A young one, perhaps?"

"Better a motherly one. I once had to call in the mother of one of our great big masterful men and tell her the situation. She gave her son a scolding that he wouldn't take from anybody else; and afterward he told me I had taken an unfair advantage of him! I said in his palatial office: 'Listen, man, you think that I enjoy giving you orders, as you call it? Let me try to set you straight. I am a geographer, and right now at my little place in the country I have on my table half a dozen books on exploration, and I'm counting the days till this damned war will be over and I can go home and lie in a hammock and read.' "

"And what did he say to that?"

"He said: 'I've got a trout stream on my place, Alston, and when it's over, come and we'll go fishing.' "

IX

Lanny underwent a thorough interrogation as to his recent trip. Vichy, Toulon, the Riviera, Switzerland, Algeria, and Morocco—Alston wanted to know about them all: what were the living conditions, what the people were saying about the war and about the Allies and the Germans. He explained: "The decision has not yet been taken where the first landing is to be made; and, of course, it makes a lot of difference whether we shall find ourselves among a friendly or an indifferent population."

"I should think," ventured the other, "that a decision will have to be taken soon if anything is to be done this year." When his friend nodded, Lanny went on: "Not meaning to fish, but just to guess, the longer they put it off, the more likely it is that it will be the Mediterranean rather than the Channel."

"It is hardly likely that the Germans will fail to make the same guess," smiled Alston. "Between you and me, the decision is to be taken at a conference of the military men in London very shortly. The President has indicated that he wishes me to attend."

"We may meet there, Professor. Churchill has promised to fix matters so that I can return to England. That is important to me because I haven't seen my little daughter for more than a year."

Lanny told of the interview in the White House, incidentally mentioning the odd detail of having met the Prime Minister of Great Britain freshly out of his bath. The ex-geographer remarked: "I had the same experience. He said to me: 'You see, Dr. Alston, I have absolutely nothing to conceal.'" They chuckled over this, and the older man added: "Has anybody told you what the Prime Minister's wife calls him? Her term of endearment is 'Porky'!"

Such are the delights of being among the "insiders"; you pick up amusing items of gossip and pass them on and feel proud of your privileged position—while hundreds of your fellow men are dying in agony and your civilization totters on the edge of an abyss. When Lanny's smile had died the ex-geographer remarked: "War makes strange bedfellows. If, while I was a humble instructor at a freshwater college, someone had told me that I should some day be hobnobbing with the Duke of Marlborough's seventh lineal descendant, I should have considered it extremely unlikely."

"He is good company," commented the younger man, "and a good ally in battle. But I'm afraid you'll have a hard time with him when it comes to setting up new governments in Europe."

"It is the people who are going to do that, Lanny. The British people will decide the destiny of Britain; and Churchill will submit to their will, I hope."

They talked about Lanny's plans, and he explained his idea of paying a visit to Rudolf Hess in pretended secrecy and getting from him a message to be delivered to Hitler. Alston shook his head. "I don't believe the Governor will want you to go into Germany again. He told me definitely that he considered it too dangerous."

"What does he want me to do?"

"To go back to Vichy France and North Africa, especially if the London conference decides upon an invasion there. We shall need every scrap of information we can get, and the Governor counts on you because you can meet the top people."

"If that's what he wants," Lanny said, "of course that's what I'll do. Do you know the line of Dante, '*In la sua volontade è nostra pace*'?" When Alston said that he didn't know Italian, Lanny translated: "In his will is our peace." It was a good wartime motto.

X

The "fixer" had two matters of especial urgency on his mind and proceeded to reveal them to his one-time secretary-translator. The first was the problem of the rocket bomb, the jet-propelled missile reported as capable of traveling as far as one or two hundred miles. If the Germans should use this, they might be able to destroy London and make it impossible for the British to be of any further use in the war. "We know definitely that they have it," said Alston, "and we have hints as to where and how they are working. The trouble is, we have too many hints, and we strongly suspect that they are being 'planted' for the purpose of confusing us. We have become convinced that the Germans have one principal center of activity, and that is where their best and most trusted scientists are to be found. We'd like to get that place, and if possible the scientists, in one of our thousand-plane surprise raids. There is nothing more important in the whole war."

"I talked with my man in Geneva about it," reported the P.A. "He promised to do his best. The arrangement was that Colonel Donovan's office was to send a man to him, and I do not know what has come out of that."

"I talked with the Colonel's office this morning over the phone—we have a code name for the project, of course. They report that nothing satisfactory has come in so far."

"I don't know what more I could do, Professor, unless it is to go into Germany myself."

"Are you free to tell me more about this man of yours?"

"I think I am free to tell you everything. He has given me permission to trust our Intelligence organization, and you are surely a part of that. His name is Bernhardt Monck, and he is an old-time German labor man and Social Democratic Party leader, one of those who did not turn patriotic in either the first World War or the second, so I suppose he should be classed as an Independent, though he sticks to the thesis that the party will arise out of the ashes of this calamity and lead the German people into Socialism. He went under the name of Capitán Herzog in the International Brigade in Spain, and now he calls himself Braun, or Brun when he writes to me in France."

"You are certain that he is trustworthy?"

"I trust him as I would trust you in the same circumstances. He was recommended to me by the woman who became my second wife. I told you about that marriage and its tragic end. She was in Paris, and the Nazis kidnaped her; I tried to save her and Monck helped me. He risked his life, and no man can do more; he didn't even want to let me pay him, although he knew I was what he would call a rich man. Now he is living the life of a student, pretending to be doing some historical work, and keeping his contacts with the anti-Nazi underground. Of course he has never told me what these are; but several times he has given me information as to German plans, which I have sent to the President, who has told me that it was useful."

"We cannot ask more than that. I think you should see this man again and impress upon him the urgency of the rocket-bomb matter. Give him whatever money he can use."

"I did that, and I assume that the new contact man will do the same. It may be that he will have some new lead that I can follow up. I'll ask him, of course."

"And now for the other matter, which is the problem of atomic fission and what progress the Germans have been making. Did you talk to your man about that?"

"No, because you didn't authorize me to. I asked him to find out where the Germans are making heavy water, that is all."

"I am quite sure they know we are working on atomic fission, so I don't see what harm it can do for you to mention the subject to your man. You should be guided by circumstances; if you find he has no contacts with that part of the scientific world, then there's no use telling him anything. But if he has a contact, tell him, not what we know, but only what we need to know."

"You forget, Professor, I am ten months behind the times on that subject, and that may mean ten years of ordinary times."

"That is true. Would you like to stop by and see Professor Einstein again?"

"Could anybody say no to that?"

"You remember his assistant, Dr. Braunschweig? He is kept up to date on the details and will tell you to what extent we are still in the dark about the Germans and their progress on the subject."

"You forget, Professor, a man doesn't just drop in and say to an atomic physicist: 'Tell me the most precious secrets of this war!' "

"I'm not forgetting. I'll make arrangements for you, and you phone and make a date before you go. It needn't be until you are ready to return to Europe. The old formula is reversed now, and a day may be as a thousand years. Good luck to you, Lanny, and see you in London!"

XI

Hartley phoned at the agreed hour, and Lanny made an appointment to meet him at once and brief him for the evening. They kept the car in movement while they laid out their plan of campaign. Lanny went into details about this old Knickerbocker lady who made no concessions to modern customs but lived as she had lived since girlhood, hating all the forces of change.

"Don't forget your glad rags," said the son of Budd-Erling, and the other said he had them. When Hartley showed up in front of the old mansion which remained stubbornly in a district of tall office buildings, he was in every way *en règle*.

Lanny had often wondered, did Miss van Zandt have one long black silk dress, carefully preserved through the decades, or did she have rows of them, and upon what system did she choose one each time? The cords in her thin neck were partly hidden by an old-fashioned "dog-collar" studded with diamonds; in addition she wore one string of pearls and a small tiara in her white hair. Her features were severe and pale—she scorned the use of rouge. She received her guests with stately courtesy. She served no cocktails, only a variety of wines at dinner. Hartley, forewarned, had got himself a drink or two in advance.

Whatever he was, he played the English gentleman acceptably. Lanny could understand Laurel's saying that she might have found him plausible if she had met him under normal circumstances. Hartley fully convinced his hostess that he was a person of conservative tastes, who had lived among the old "county families" and shared their ideas. When he turned loose upon the "Red peril" he became really eloquent and displayed a fund of knowledge which surprised his sponsor.

Yes, indeed, the world was in a desperate way, and unless it was going entirely to pot at the end of this war, America must be prepared to take a firm stand against the Reds both at home and abroad. The public must be awakened to the peril in advance, and Hartley was the Englishman who knew how to do it. Before he was through, he had the Jewish clothing workers, who walked up and down in front of Miss van Zandt's mansion every weekday noon, exchanging their cheese sandwiches and pickles for revolvers and hand grenades; and there was Hartley himself, standing on the steps in shining armor, holding aloft the banner of the American Christian Union and sweeping back the floods of blood and terror. The mixed metaphors were Hartley's own, and no more confused than the state of mind of an economic-royalist spinster born half a century too late. The outcome of the dinner party was that she wrote a check for five thousand dollars to promote this righteous cause, but she wrote it to the order of Lanning P. Budd and said in her royally firm way: "I am doing so because I have known Mr. Budd longer and wish him to have the handling of the money. I am sure that you, Mr. Hartley, will understand this decision."

"Certainly, certainly, Miss van Zandt," said the Englishman cordially. "Mr. Budd is my friend, and we are entirely in unison. I am impressed by your clear insight and splendid courage in this matter." Lanny wondered if the old lady's reason was that she had noted the promptness with which Hartley had emptied his wine glass.

When they were outside, Lanny said: "I hope you understand, I didn't have any idea the old bird would drop this thing into my lap."

"I take your word," replied the other. "But we don't have to take her orders seriously, do we?"

"I promise to see that you get the better of every deal," was Lanny's response. Which wasn't quite the same as saying: "I'll turn the money over to you."

XII

It was late, and Lanny suggested that they should meet in the morning and work out the details of their plan. But Hartley wanted to know if they couldn't take a drive now and settle the question of money. He was obviously uneasy, having every reason to assume that Lanny might be another such as himself. So they motored up to Central Park and along its winding drives, all the way around, since Lanny had to keep the man satisfied. He would surely not give him the money, knowing that he might bolt with both it and the diamonds.

"You must understand, Hartley," said the P.A., "the last thing I was looking for was to get a business on my hands. But until we have raised more money I carry the responsibility for this check. Will it be satisfactory to you if I allow you three hundred a month out of it?"

"And how much will you take?"

"I'll be satisfied with two hundred at the start," Lanny said. He had to take something, because he was supposed to be hard up. "You should have more, Hartley, because you will be doing more work than I. You know more about the subject, and besides, I have to do some traveling to keep my art business going."

"That sounds fair," admitted the other, showing his relief.

"We shall have to pay office rent, and we must find an office with a telephone, because, as you know, new phones are practically unobtainable. Also, we must have a secretary, and I should think a business manager, since I don't suppose you want to bother with the details of getting literature printed and distributed."

"It seems to me," objected Hartley, "you'll be getting rid of the money in a very short time and leaving us on the rocks."

"We're only getting started, man. I'm going to introduce you to other people, and you'll raise a quarter of a million before you finish. Moreover, I have in mind a man who will work without salary, at least until we get going. It's quite likely that he'll put in a hunk of money when he sees what fine work we're doing."

Lanny told the wonderful story of his friend Tom Cartier, who hated this stupid war and had used his family influence to keep out of it. He was looking round for something to do that would satisfy his conscience, and he was ready to take Lanny's word for it that the American Christian Union represented the most worthy cause. Hartley, well fortified with wine, swallowed every word of it and exclaimed: "Righto! If you can produce a piece of magic like that, O.K."

Lanny said he could produce that magic the first thing in the morning. The agreeable young Virginian had a grandmother who owned the better part of a county down there, and she was much the same sort of person as Miss van Zandt; they might visit her before long and get another check. Also, Cartier had an uncle who owned a lot of real estate in New York and might be persuaded to rent them an office with a telephone, a treasure almost beyond price at the present moment. In short, Aladdin's lamp was at work and Lanny said: "Notice that everything has happened as I promised you!"

XIII

Next morning the pair met by appointment, and they picked up Cartier and drove into the park again. They stopped at a quiet place by the side of a drive, where they could talk for hours without interruption. Cartier surprised Lanny in much the same way that Hartley had done on the previous evening. Cartier had been studying the Communists; he had attended their meetings and even one of their conventions, and he said that they were planning the after-the-war conquest of the world. He had read a volume of Lenin and could quote verbatim what the master Bolshevik had said on the subject of revolutionary versus bourgeois morality: how the Communists must always think of themselves as soldiers in a war, using all the devices which soldiers use against enemies. "When there is need of it, we must know how to employ trickery, deceit, lawbreaking, withholding and concealing truths."

In short, the lively young Virginian was a perfect model of a crusader on behalf of the American system of private enterprise, slanderously called "capitalism" by the "Commies." He was as ready for a fight as they were, and wasn't going to be fooled by any of their camouflage. Hartley, who might or might not have believed what he said to Miss van Zandt, could hardly refuse to believe what Cartier said to him, and his rosy English complexion shone with pleasure when Cartier announced that he had already talked with his uncle, who would let them have a suite of three office rooms at the ceiling price and with no secret rake-off because of the two telephones.

Later on they went to inspect the place, which was everything the most fastidious propagandist could have desired. One of the rooms was to be Hartley's private office, and Lanny wondered, could it really be, as Post had told him, that the disk of the dictaphone was so hidden in the desk that nobody could find it without taking the desk apart, and the wires so wound in with the telephone wires that only an expert could have detected them, and then only by cutting into the wires. The dictaphone was legal, while telephone tapping was not. However, this was wartime, and against the enemies of the nation the F.B.I. would probably do what it pleased. Whether Branscome alias Hartley would be so indiscreet as to make appointments with his diamond smugglers over that phone, or to invite them into that office, were questions which only time could answer. Cartier felt quite certain that the blondined young lady whom he introduced as stenographer and secretary would be able to keep the susceptible Englishman busy at dinnertime whenever the government men desired to make another search of his apartment.

10

Man Is Born to Trouble

I

THERE came a call from Washington, and when Lanny called back it was Baker, telling him that an engagement had been made for him to meet Dr. Braunschweig in Princeton early the following afternoon. The day after that he would drive to the small town of Thurmont in the western part of Maryland, where he would find Baker and be taken to another appointment. "Both are for Mr. Prescott," said the President's man, and Lanny didn't have to ask for an explanation.

The much-traveled P.A. packed his bags again and said to his forewarned wife: "It's a Number One matter, darling, so forgive me." She answered that she had a Number One matter, too, and he teased her, pretending not to know whether it was the baby or the book. She thought she was a feminist, but after all she was a woman in love. Millions of women were sending their men off to war, but they weren't enjoying it.

He had told her about developments in the Hartley matter, because that might fairly be considered hers; but he wasn't free to mention the awful subject of atom splitting, nor the town in the Catoctin Mountains, which he guessed contained the President's hideout. F.D.R. had dropped a hint that he had such a place, since the Secret Service and the Navy combined had refused to let him enjoy his former recreation of yachting. Not even Chesapeake Bay could be considered safe in these days of triumphant submarines.

Lanny took a bite of lunch early and set out. His route was the same as he had taken to Washington, and he had learned that you couldn't count upon making speed on Highway Number 1. He had been told to go to the Institute of Advanced Study, and just a few minutes before the hour specified he parked his car down the street from this new Gothic building. He announced himself as Mr. Prescott to see Dr. Braunschweig, and in a minute or two he was seated in the modest study of the learned scientist. He was perhaps ten years younger than Lanny, but what he knew about the universe was appalling to a mere art expert. Over a period of two months in the previous summer he had tutored Lanny for an hour or two every day, and most of the time Lanny had had to learn words and formulas like a parrot, without being able to understand at all what they meant. He had come away with the feeling that this dark-eyed, rather frail, and extremely serious young physicist possessed a brain of a type wholly beyond the imagining of the ordinary man. Sir James Jeans had written that "the universe appears to have been designed by a mathematician," and that sentence had stayed in Lanny's mind.

This time the tutoring wouldn't take so long, because Lanny would be free to make notes and carry them away with him. Alston had said that would be all right, provided he kept them pinned up in an inside pocket and destroyed them before he left the country. Dr. Braunschweig had a list of data which had come in during the past ten months concerning German progress in atomic research, and what particular details might be useful to the Americans. It was pleasant to hear him say that they believed the Germans were far behind, mainly because the Führer didn't believe in the possibility of atomic fission and had put his top physicists at other tasks. Lanny might have said: "He is concentrating on jet propulsion," but he didn't.

He listened with all the faculties he possessed, and when he did not understand he asked questions. He was embarrassed because he had forgotten so much of what he had previously learned. The physicist comforted him by saying that it was not to be expected that a man should remember so many details wholly outside the range of his own interests. Lanny had it all to do over again, but he didn't mind because he could tell himself that it was the most important subject in the world at this time. If he could gather the smallest mite of knowledge and have it passed on to the men who were working day and night in his country's laboratories—that might be the best contribution he had ever made to the cause of freedom.

I I

This "advanced study" continued without interruption for a matter of four hours. Then the teacher said: "We will resume at eight o'clock, if that is agreeable." Lanny went out and telephoned his friend Alonzo Curtice, who had fed and sheltered him during the previous sojourn here. The art expert—so he was known here—explained that he was passing through and had a couple of hours. It meant inviting himself to dinner, but they had fed him something like a hundred and eighty times, and he was sure they wouldn't mind once more. He drove to the estate of this Wall Street investment banker and was welcomed by the owner and his wife. The story of his trip around the world was enough for anybody's dinnertime, and the couple could feel repaid for their hospitality.

Back to the advanced study, and time passed quickly, as it does when one is too busy to think about it. At about half-past ten there came a gentle tap on the study door, and there entered what to Lanny was a vision of delight—although entirely different from the one to which the poet Wordsworth had referred. It was a gentleman in his middle sixties, short and well filled out, with a rounded cherubic face, a small gray mustache, and a floating mist of uncontrollable white hair. He came in with that mischievous smile and two hands outstretched, and then appeared to change his mind and put his arms around the visitor and patted him on the back with both hands. "*Willkommen, Herr Budd!* It is good to see you still alive!"—which showed that somebody had told him about the accident. Then he turned to Dr. Braunschweig. "You are cheating me! You promised me time enough for three sonatas!"

The young assistant, who lacked a sense of humor, appeared flustered. "I am sorry, Dr. Einstein."

"I forgive you, but no more tonight! You must not cram this easygoing gentleman!" Then to the visitor: "You have a little time in the morning, *nicht wahr?* You can spend the night at my house, and we can play."

"That suits me fine," said Lanny, for he loved this warmhearted great man, one of the simplest and most genuine people he had ever met. Albert Einstein was comically out of place in this elegant university town, whose freedom and informality were of a conventional English sort. The wives of the faculty members must have had a hard time deciding how to deal with a German-Jewish scientist who forgot to keep his hair cut and went about the streets clad in a white shirt open at the throat, a pair of baggy pants, sandals, and no hat. In cold weather, when he had to be more warmly clad, he put on a celluloid collar, just about the most plebeian article of apparel that an academic hostess could imagine.

The two friends strolled over in the moonlight to the old and entirely unpretentious frame house which sheltered the discoverer of formulas which had changed the thinking and destiny of the human race. A wistaria vine, now loaded with blossoms, covered the front porch and filled the night air with scent. Apparently the door wasn't locked; the master just walked in and turned into the parlor, which had a piano and a good music stand, also a table and several chairs. "Any room will do to think in," he had told Lanny, and apparently any room would do to play the music of Mozart and Bach. The professor picked out the violin and piano scores of Mozart's sonatas and set the former on the music stand and the latter on the piano rack. He got out his fiddle, tuned it, and said: "*Also!* We played the first three. Shall we start with four?"

Lanny thought to himself: "My God! The greatest mathematician in the world has room in his head for the numbers we played nearly a year ago!"

They played Number Four, which is delightful, and then they played Number Five, which is also delightful. The old gentleman apparently knew the scores by heart, for he played with his eyes cast upward most of the time and an expression of heavenly bliss on the rounded, cherubic face. He played well, for this had been his form of recreation since early childhood. He had been very poor and had had a hard struggle to get along in the world and to win an education; he had been slaving for seven years as a clerk in the Swiss patent office when he had evolved the physical formulas which had revised the Newtonian conception of the universe.

They played the proper allowance of three sonatas; more would have been a dissipation—so the learned professor had said the first time and he repeated it. They sat for a while and talked about the bad state of the world, and then the Professor raided his pantry and made two cheese sandwiches, which they washed down with a pint bottle of beer divided between them. "Friendship is a delightful sentiment, and lends a glow to the most ordinary actions of life," thus spoke the author of *The General and the Special Theory of Relativity* as he escorted his friend upstairs to a modest chamber. In the morning, or rather, later the same morning, he fed the guest a light breakfast and then said: "It will be better if you walk alone to the office, for it happens, unfortunately, that I am an object of some curiosity. It is as if people came to see the giant panda"—this with his shy twinkle.

Lanny made his way back to the Gothic building and spent another three hours of the hardest kind of mental work. The lesson over, he said his thanks to the solemn young physicist. "You have taken a lot of trouble with me," he remarked. A shadow seemed to cross the teacher's dark eyes. "Mr. Budd," he replied, "I have a very special interest in what you are doing. The Nazi gangsters are every man's enemy. They are doubly mine. I am a Jew."

They both knew that they were playing with the fantastic notion of an atomic bomb, and the issue at stake was whether a missile of such destructive power should land on Berlin before it landed on New York or Washington.

.The Professor wished to say good-by, so Lanny was taken into his office, or perhaps it was the seminar room, Lanny couldn't be sure. It had a large table in the center and several leather-seated chairs. As any room would do to think in, so any pencil would do to jot down a formula, and any piece of paper to receive it. Lanny knew that Einstein was now searching in the recesses of his unfathomable mind for the formula of what he called his Unified Field Theory, which would reconcile his Special Theory of Relativity with his extension of Max Planck's Quantum Theory, thus bringing all natural phenomena under one universal law. Recently he had thought that he had it, but it hadn't worked out, so he had told Lanny sadly.

Now he bade farewell to this agreeable guest. *"Glück auf, Herr Budd!* I know that what you are doing is dangerous, and I wish I had as much courage."

"Didn't it take courage to upset the entire scientific world?" inquired the P.A. mildly.

"Oh, that!" replied the Professor. "That is not so much. I have a mathematical mind and it will not rest. It goes its own way into the far reaches of this mysterious universe and I cannot hold it back. It finds harmony where chaos once seemed to reign." The great physicist said that, and then a shadow darkened his face. "It is a dreadful thing that we are doing now, trying to unlock the secrets of atomic power for purposes of war. The future will hold us responsible for the use we make of that knowledge if we get it! *Viel Glück, Herr Budd, und leben Sie recht wohl!*"

III

Lanny followed the highway as far as he could and then struck off to the west through the rolling farm country of Maryland. Fields and orchards and woodlots and farmhouses were rolling by, but he withheld the attention he ordinarily gave to such a panorama; his mind was absorbed with the subject of atomic fission and the means of producing it, and, more important yet, of controlling the process. It was something new and terrible in the world, and he never tired of speculating about the changes it might bring in human affairs.

Gradually the land rose, and there came into sight the beautiful Blue Ridge mountains. Here, so Alston had told the P.A., an area in one of the National Parks had been set aside for the use of a Chief Executive who could not walk and had been deprived of his recreations of fishing and swimming. Oddly enough it was the Navy which had taken charge of this forest preserve; the crew of the presidential yacht *Potomac* and its auxiliary tender and fishing boat had set to work, with the help of local mountain labor, and put in a paved road and a group of buildings for use as a rest camp. Now they guarded and ran it, and the President motored each week end from the capital, bringing officials and others with whom he desired to have conferences. Churchill had been here twice, and various generals and admirals, to consult with him; but not a line about it had appeared in any newspaper.

Lanny did not enter the little town of Thurmont, but telephoned from outside. He was told to be in front of the post office at eight o'clock that evening and he would be picked up in the usual way. Meantime he parked his car in a grove of chestnut trees alongside a little stream and sat and studied his atomic notes. Later he found a roadside inn and had a bit of supper, and then studied some more until it was time to drive into the town. Precisely on the minute he stepped into Baker's car and was driven up the new road, which climbed a couple of thousand feet to the camp. It was ten or twenty degrees cooler here than in the sweltering city of Washington; a gentle night breeze murmured through the trees, and fireflies showed their mysterious tiny lights. Lanny, who was worried about his great leader's health under the terrifying strain of war, thought this hideout the pleasantest discovery he had made in some time.

He felt free to ask questions on the three- or four-mile drive. Baker told him there was a massive lodge built of local timber, a number of smaller cabins, a swimming pool, and fine trout streams running through the area. One of these emptied into an abandoned quarry near the lodge, and this made a unique fishing place, well stocked with rainbow trout from the government's hatcheries. A feature of the main building was that one wall was on heavy hinges so that it could be let down like a drawbridge, making a ramp on which the President could be wheeled out in case of fire. Also, in the rear, there was a smaller lodge for the adoring Fala.

Lanny had seen mountain camps all the way from the Adirondacks to Bavaria, and many of them had cost more than the twenty-five thousand dollars this one represented. Also he was used to having flashlights turned upon his face, to make sure that he was the person expected. Baker had the right to bring anybody in, and no questions were asked. In the entrance hall, while they waited to be announced, Lanny surveyed a map of "Shangri-La," as this place was called. He noted that here, as everywhere, Americans had to have their fun. This building, the President's home, was labeled "The Bear's Den"; the laundry was "The Soap Dish"; the building set aside for the Filipino stewards was "Little Luzon." There was a row of cabins marked "Baker Street Urchins" on the map, and Lanny asked whether these were named after his escort. The reply was: "The Secret Service men get their names from Sherlock Holmes, not from me."

IV

A door was opened before Lanny, and he entered the President's room. Roosevelt was resting on a couch by an open window, wearing tan-colored linen trousers and a soft white shirt; he gave a welcoming hail, as always. Seated beside him was a man in his fifties whose features were familiar to all readers of newspapers. He was tall and thin, with deep-set, keen brown eyes, a sallow skin, hollow cheeks, and a prominent lower jaw. He was loosely put together, slouchy in his way of sitting, and informal in manner. He was a harnessmaker's son from Iowa who had gone through college in the American fashion, by working his way. He had devoted most of his life to social service, first for the Red Cross, then for the Tuberculosis and Health Association in New York, then as chairman of the New York State Temporary Emergency Relief Administration. When the newly elected President had been faced with the worst financial collapse in the world's history, he had given this man the enormous job of finding work for fifteen million unemployed. He was trusted by the President above all other men, and hated by the President's enemies to the same extent. In this war crisis he was working himself literally to death—he had had a perforated ulcer and now had a rare intestinal disease, and he looked rather ghastly as he lifted himself out of his chair to greet the new arrival.

"Lanny Budd, this is Harry Hopkins," said the President. And Lanny said: "I have never had the pleasure before, but I had plenty of time to look at you, something over a year ago, when we crossed on the same Clipper."

"I remember your face well," said "Harry the Hop," as his genial Boss called him.

"I didn't suppose you were seeing anything on board, Mr. Hopkins, except the papers in your portfolio. I took the liberty of guessing that they contained the lend-lease figures."

"You were correct, of course."

"Later on," added the ex-playboy with a grin, "I was told that you had landed with only one shirt and no hat, and that you had had to go to work without having time to shave."

"I see that you move in the best circles," was the dry reply.

"My father used to complain that you were spending more money than any one man in the world ever did before. That was in the old W.P.A. days. Now, doubtless, you are spending ten or twenty times as much, but my father doesn't seem to mind it at all."

"He is getting so much of it himself," put in the President, and all three of them enjoyed a laugh.

V

They got down to business quickly, there being little time for joking these days. "I want you to know Harry," said "the Boss," as Harry called him. "He will be in London while you are there, and I should like you to report to him anything interesting that you may come upon. The same goes for Alston, of course."

"Fine!" said Lanny.

"Churchill has told me about your idea of having a talk with Hess. That is interesting, and all right with me; but I don't want you to go into Germany. There are others we can send, and I can't spare *you*."

"All right, Governor. My wife will call that good news."

"There will be danger enough where you are going. I want you in Vichy France and North Africa. It may seem like treading in your old footsteps, but events are moving fast, and we need every item of information about the attitude of the big people there. Some of them are bound to be worried, and more so as the summer passes. Some will be ready to desert a sinking ship, and we want to know who they are and how we can use them. It's going to be a dirty business, and you may have your faith in human nature greatly tried. But keep your nerve, and never forget the one purpose we have in mind, which is to save the lives of American boys and win this war at the lowest price in blood."

"Yes, Governor," replied the P.A. meekly. He took it as an answer to the objections he had been raising, as to the wisdom of dealing with the rats deserting the Vichy ship.

"Remember our clear intention—the French people will decide the future of France, and we have no wish to do it for them. Our job is to put down the Nazis, and after that to see a free and fair election in every country we have entered."

"I get you, Governor." It was the nearest to an order the son of Budd-Erling had ever received, and it pleased him because it relieved him of responsibility. He added: "Professor Alston wants me to go to Switzerland and meet my old-time labor and Socialist friend there."

"That's all right; Switzerland, Spain, Portugal, wherever you think there is information to be had, but not into any German-held territory. It is possible you might get some of your Nazi friends to meet you in Switzerland. What is the name of that musician?"

"Kurt Meissner. He would come if I asked him, but I'd have to have something important to tell him, and something he could believe. It would be a dangerous game, because I'd be attracting attention to myself again, and they might comb the world to find out about me. It would be pretty hard for me then to continue as an art expert."

"Does anybody really accept that since we've entered the war?" It was Harry Hopkins, his questions always direct and to the point.

"I can never be entirely certain," replied Lanny. "I suppose it varies with different persons. The French are polite, and they pretend to believe it. Nobody has accused me to my face, except some of my friends of the underground, where I got into a jam. I suppose the *collaborateurs* whisper about me behind my back and speculate. I spend money freely, and that helps."

The thin-faced chief of lend-lease nodded his head slightly. "That helps!" he echoed. "I know!"

Lanny took the opportunity to bring in a subject that lay close to his heart. "The last time I saw Kurt Meissner I told him about a plot of some of our high-up business tycoons and Army people to kidnap the President and make him obey their orders. That made a tremendous hit with Kurt, and later on with Hitler when I saw him. I think I could still use that story, but I'd have to report progress, and I might need to have some hint leak out here. But the Governor doesn't seem to want that to happen."

Lanny was speaking to Hopkins, as if answering his question. He took it for granted that F.D.R.'s best friend must know all about this affair, and Lanny wanted to know what the friend's attitude was. This was not difficult, for Hopkins was an outspoken person who said what he thought on any subject—unless it was a subject about which he didn't want to talk, and then nobody could get a word out of him. Now he said: "So far those bastards haven't done anything but talk, and it's one of the requirements of democracy that every bastard shall be free to shoot off his mouth."

"Even in wartime, Mr. Hopkins?"

"Even in wartime, Mr. Budd. The Nazis can liquidate people for talking, and so can the Communists; but if we do it, we have lost the war before we fight it."

"And more than that, Lanny," put in F.D.R., "you must admit that it wouldn't help morale either at home or abroad to let people know that such a junta exists in this country."

"You are the boss," replied Lanny. "I am just pointing out that this is the one way I can get any Nazi to warm up and talk to me as a friend. They would greatly like to get the Jewish-Democratic Herr Rosenfeld out of their path."

"You don't tell me!" responded Herr Rosenfeld with one of his infectious grins. "Do this, Lanny. Tell them anything that will help to loosen them up, and when you come back report to me about it, and I may figure out some way to give you a bit of support." Then, suddenly serious, he pointed to papers on a table beside him. "Here is a stack of orders that I must sign tonight; so you two fellows go into the next room and get acquainted."

VI

Lanny had read much about this chief boondoggler and leaf raker who now made his home in the White House; a greatly abused man, but he didn't seem to mind it—he had chosen his enemies carefully. He didn't believe in the system of monopoly capitalism any more than Lanny did, and he didn't care if his system of relief by public spending brought the profiteers nearer to their doom. He had been quoted as saying about the program of the New Deal: "We shall spend and spend, and tax and tax, and elect and elect." He had carried out this program to such good effect that his great friend and hero had become the first man ever to be elected President for a third term, and by all the political signs he might have a fourth term if he wanted it.

Now the harnessmaker's son had set out to put the Nazi-Fascists out of business by the same method of unlimited spending. Oddly enough, he had most of the big businessmen behind him in this, but that didn't either worry him or please him especially; he had only two-thirds of a stomach left, and no time or strength for a superfluous emotion. He had reports to study, orders to give, quarrels to abate. He had to fly to England with the President's instructions and guide the controversies of high-ranking British and American staff officers, bringing them to an agreement as near as possible to what the President desired. He needed all the help he could get, and when he had sunk into a chair in the next room, sliding down into it until he was sitting pretty nearly on the back of his neck, he opened up. "The Boss said to me: 'Lanny Budd is one of us.' And that is enough. I want to talk to you frankly. May I call you Lanny?"

"Indeed yes."

"Call me Harry; it comes easier. There's going to be what the English call a good show in London this month. We have to settle definitely upon the plan of campaign. The Boss wants very much to invade across the Channel this summer, but Churchill won't hear of it; he insists that we haven't the air power for anything but a defensive attitude, and he won't have anything to do with an invasion. But meantime the Russians are clamoring and, strictly between us, threatening to quit if we don't come to their help with a second front. So we have to do something. Churchill wants us to go up through the Balkans. I assume you understand what he has in his mind."

"Of course. He wants us to be in possession of that territory when the war ends, and to keep the Russians away from the Dardanelles."

"And of course our military men are not going to tie us up in any balance-of-power game between Britain and Russia. We want to beat the Nazis in the quickest way we can, and the cheapest with regard to the lives of our boys. So I think the decision will be for some action in North Africa this fall. That would cut Rommel off and be a minor disaster for the Germans. It would settle the control of the Mediterranean and save us the tonnage we waste carrying stuff around Africa. Also, it would enable us to take Sicily and Southern Italy."

"And have airfields from which to bomb the munitions plants of Austria and southern Germany," ventured the amateur strategist.

"I see that you have the picture in mind. I'm not saying that will be the final decision, but that's the way matters appear to be shaping up. If you are in London when the decision is taken, I'll tell you about it. You won't be free to tell anybody else, but it will guide you in your work."

"That suits me fine," replied the P.A. "I have a little daughter in England whom I'd like to see."

"I know about her. I met Irma Barnes once or twice in night clubs before you married her. I did a little playing round with the smart crowd in those days. I wanted to understand their minds. It helps me now."

"The same for me," replied Lanny with a smile. "But I liked some of them a bit too well."

They talked for a few minutes about people they knew; but the burdens of the time pressed upon them, and presently they were talking about the bleak outlook before the country. The Germans had taken Sevastopol, and their plunge into the Ukraine had reached the Don River. The British were making a stand at a place in the deserts of Egypt called El Alamein, but it was uncertain if their line would hold. Hopkins said: "If the enemy gets to Suez, it may set us back for a long time. But don't ever doubt it, Lanny, we are going to get the troops and the weapons and win this war!"

He wanted to question the son of Budd-Erling and proceeded to put him through the same sort of grilling as Alston had done. He desired to know everything there was to know about conditions in Unoccupied France and French North Africa. Not merely did he have to consider what materials must be allotted for a campaign there, but he had to start guessing what foodstuffs and other supplies might be required later. Lanny told him that the natives, who wore nothing but cotton sheeting, were pretty nearly in rags now, and what they would look like after the havoc of an invasion was beyond any P.A.'s power to guess. A curious whim of destiny, that a harnessmaker's son from a town of the corn-and-hog country should have the job of deciding what food should be eaten and what clothing worn by the people of Morocco and Dahomey and Iceland and Trinidad and China and the Solomon Islands and pretty nearly every other strange part of the world you could think of!

VII

The competent Baker came and took Lanny back to the town. On the way he said that he had been instructed to provide Mr. Budd with a properly visaed passport, and when would he want it? Lanny said in about a week, and Baker said he would have to be in New York before that and would deliver the document personally. Also he would provide a ticket for him on the Clipper. Lanny gave Baker his phone number, and that was that.

The sensible thing would have been to stop at a hotel for the night; but the breeze was cool, and the moonlight on this foothill country so lovely, that he decided he would rather drive and think out some of his problems on the way. How many things he had to think about! He had been born into a time of strain and suffering, but at least nobody could say that it lacked variety, nobody had a right to be bored! Lanny had identified himself with a cause, and he lived in that and for that, and it kept him busy most of the time. Only rarely did the thought occur to him that the cause might fail; and those were indeed uncomfortable moments. In that case, he reflected, he wouldn't want to survive—and probably would not be allowed to.

Back by the same road he had come, a dog's journey, as the saying goes. West of Wilmington he picked up Highway Number 1 again, and it wasn't so crowded at one o'clock in the morning. The great trucks were moving slowly; the factories were blacked out—but all of them full of activity. Night or day was the same in wartime, and Lanny knew that was the case all over this vast land. America was going into action, preparing to show the world what a free people could do in the machine age. The P.A. had been that night in the brain center where the whole project had been conceived and from which it was directed. His whole being was afire with the sense of living in a great period of history, of seeing the world's future in the making. With Tennyson's Ulysses he could say:

> Much have I seen and known; cities of men
> And manners, climates, councils, governments,
> Myself not least, but honor'd of them all.

It was after three o'clock when he arrived at the apartment. He had a key and let himself in quietly. He undressed in his own room, and the first awareness Laurel had of his presence was when he slid into bed beside her. He said: "Go to sleep again. I am tired." She complied, and when later on she opened her eyes at the normal hour she lay still so as not to disturb him. That was easy for one who had not made herself a slave of the coffee habit and who found this hour of fresh awakening a good time to plan the story she was going to write that day.

Later they prepared the combination meal known as "brunch," and afterward he told her the news that he was scheduled to leave in a week or so. She could not hide the look of distress which crossed her sensitive features, and he hastened to say: "I am one of the lucky ones, darling. I'm not going to be in any danger. I am only going where I have been before; first to London, where the bombing now amounts to almost nothing; then to Vichy France and Algiers, where there is no bombing at all."

"And when am I to expect you back, Lanny?"

"I can't be sure about that. It is usually two or three months. It will surely be before your confinement—if you take care of yourself and don't overwork."

She made the promise, but he wasn't sure that she would keep it. She, too, had a stern master, who went by the name of Art, and sometimes she couldn't be sure whether it was more important to produce a baby or a minor masterpiece. She was modest about her talents but quietly determined to make the most of them, and she was rebellious against the vegetative state her condition called for.

"Listen, dear," he said, to spare her feelings; "there are interesting things that I would give anything to be able to tell you; but I am under explicit orders. It appears that the military forces are especially afraid of wives."

This brought a sparkle of mischief into her brown eyes. "I grant you, I have known a few who would not be good keepers of secrets; but I have also known men of the same sort."

He answered: "Professor Alston tells me that in one single project with which I am concerned there are thousands of wives who have no slightest idea what their husbands are working on."

"Misery loves company," she said. "But, as a matter of fact, I have been putting two and two together—a good many twos. Be sure I'm not saying a word to Agnes or anybody else, and I'm not having my feelings hurt. Some day you will tell me all about it, and I promise to be interested." It was the sort of wife for a P.A. to have, and he put his arms about her and made plain with many kisses that he knew what a prize he had drawn in the marriage lottery.

VIII

Downtown there was the efficient Mr. Post, an executive with many problems on his mind, and just now a smile on his face after the fashion of the cat which has swallowed the canary. "Hartley has talked over the telephone," he said, "and has made appointments which he must have thought sounded innocent. We have picked up the people and I am awaiting more reports today. I think they are the men we are looking for."

Lanny said: "I have orders to leave for abroad in about a week; so anything you get from me will have to be within that limit."

"I think we have everything already, Mr. Budd. If you don't mind, it will be better if you don't say anything to Hartley until the day before you are going. No use to unsettle his mind."

"Quite so. I have a handy excuse—an important client who has given me a commission. I suppose it will be all right if I leave the propaganda business in charge of Cartier?"

"He is prepared to carry it on as long as necessary. Hartley won't like it, of course, but you can give him a raise in salary to salve his feelings."

"What troubles me, Mr. Post, is the fear that Hartley will get his mind fixed on me as being responsible for his betrayal. I don't see how that can fail to happen. And sooner or later he or his associates will make their suspicions known to the enemy world."

"We mean to take the greatest pains to avoid that, Mr. Budd. We shall not arrest any of these men until we are sure we have them all; then we shall carefully prepare a story of how we came to detect them, and it will be a story which has nothing to do with you."

"It will be bound to get into the papers, will it not?"

"Unfortunately we cannot avoid arraigning them in court, nor keep them from getting lawyers to represent them. But the account we give of the affair will reveal some clue which put us on their trail, one which will convince them and leave no reason for suspecting you."

"But if Cartier testifies against them, and I introduced Cartier to Hartley—"

"Cartier will never testify. He will be arrested with them and arraigned with them. He will be in a cell with Hartley and will pretend to be furious with Hartley for getting him into this jam. In the course of their arguments Hartley may reveal details of importance. If later on Cartier is released, it will seem natural to Hartley and his gang, for they know perfectly well that Cartier was not in the secret of the diamonds and that his propaganda efforts were no crime."

"All that sounds plausible enough. But can Cartier afford to have his family name dragged into such a mess?"

"Cartier is not his real name, Mr. Budd. I apologize for not telling you that, but you know how it is, the less a man knows, the less chance there is that he may let something slip by accident. Cartier is a name for the occasion; when he comes out of jail, he will be a martyr in the eyes of Miss van Zandt and people of her sort, and will be in an excellent position to keep contact with them and report on what they are doing."

"That sounds all right to me," declared Lanny. "I hope that among those who will appreciate his martyrdom will be Mr. Harrison Dengue and the rest of the group who think so ill of President Roosevelt."

"We are surely not forgetting them," declared the F.B.I. man with emphasis.

IX

Lanny went up to the newly established office of the American Christian League, which so far consisted of three men and a secretary, unless you counted one elderly spinster on Fifth Avenue and her secretary and companion. Things at the office were peaceful, but promised activity. Hartley had been to call on the spinster—without consulting Lanny—and had brought back with him a manuscript which had been composed by a member of the numerous retinue which surrounded this old lady and plied her with compliments day and night. It was entitled *The Red Nightmare*, and Hartley said that he had listened carefully to what Miss van Zandt thought of it, and then repeated it all to her in more vigorous words, thus confirming her opinion that he was a man of excellent judgment. He had asked if she did not think it would make a good opening shot for the new League, and she had assented.

Lanny read the article and found it a collection of all the most uncomplimentary things which had been said about the Soviet Union. It was old stuff, and he commented: "We could do better; but if this is what Queen Hortensia wants, it is a command performance." So they had something to do right away, and the efficient Tom Cartier had collected samples of other such propaganda literature and was in process of getting estimates for a first edition of ten thousand copies. Lanny said: "Let's go easy on this one, because it's really not very good, and if we send it to Miss van Zandt's mailing list and put it on sale at a few meetings, that is all she will ever hear about and it will satisfy her."

"But we ought to be doing something at the office to make things look right," said the Englishman.

"I'll make out a list of names and addresses of the right sort of people, and you and Cartier can get up a letter telling them about our work."

Lanny went back to the apartment where he had such a list, compiled during the years that he had been watching the Nazi-Fascist agents and their dupes. He didn't in the least care how much money Hartley might collect, especially since he was hoping that the F.B.I. would scoop it all up in a few days. He told Laurel what he was free to tell her about it, and she helped by typing out the list. He said: "They won't get very far with it, because most of these people have their own movements and won't want any rivals; but it will help to make it look like the real thing."

Next day Baker telephoned and brought the passport and the ticket for the Clipper, five days from date. Lanny took those precious documents and put them in his safety-deposit box at the bank; then he drove out to have lunch with his friend Mr. Vernon, who had just received the shipment of the first mosaic from Algiers and was as happy as a child with a new toy. In truth there could be no jigsaw puzzle so fascinating; all his friends had come in to see it, and it was that rare thing in the lives of the very rich, something entirely new. This country gentleman, who had already paid Lanny's bill in full, was now open to a proposition for a large and really beautiful Moorish fountain, used for ritual ablutions, which Lanny had observed on his last visit, but hadn't quite had the nerve to buy. Mr. Vernon supplied the necessary courage, and the art expert drove back to New York well content with his day. It wasn't that the money was so important, but he had a business letter to carry in his suitcase, to be read by all the spies and secret agents who would rummage through his belongings in the hotels of two continents.

X

To his wife he said: "I think you have a holiday coming to you. Let's have some fun before I leave." So they packed several suitcases and stowed them in the car and drove on a warm summer evening through a thunder shower to the town of Newcastle and had a reunion with the Budd tribe. They were begged to stay, but no, they were for the open road. Next morning they set out along the little Newcastle River and into the Berkshire Hills; from there northward to the foothills of the Green Mountains, and westward into the Adirondacks. Fine roads winding through endless pine forests, and vistas of mountains, tier behind tier, with rushing streams and blue lakes in the valleys—they were reminded continually of southern Bavaria where Hitler had his eyrie, and where they had had their first adventure together. They had been in fear at that time and hadn't been able to give much thought to scenery, but now by agreement they put all cares behind them and enjoyed their lives while still the little lamp shone. *Freut euch des Lebens weil noch das Lämpchen glüht!*

They had lunch at a summer-resort hotel, and Laurel slept for a couple of hours. Then they drove again, and toward evening came to the "camp" belonging to Lanny's old friends the Murchisons. He had telephoned to make sure Adella was there, and on the way he told Laurel about this couple, how Harry had wooed and not won Beauty Budd in the carefree days before World War I, and how he had married his secretary on the rebound, and how Adella had taken Goya for her hobby and purchased several examples with Lanny's advice. They had this comfortable camp on Saranac lake, and Adella was there with three women friends, enough to play bridge, but they were bored and glad to see company. In these days the men were all up to their ears in work in hot and smoky Pittsburgh; so were most of the women, but Adella had overworked and the doctor had ordered her away, and she had brought with her three members of the "younger set" who were "expecting" and therefore had an excuse. Now Lanny had brought a fourth, and they could have a pleasant time sympathizing with one another's symptoms while Lanny went fishing. In the course of his career he had caught a number of big political fish, but he didn't succeed in getting a single nibble from an Adirondack trout.

Laurel and Adella became friends at once, and Laurel was begged to stay and spend the summer in this cool delightful spot. But duty called her back to the sweltering city—she had to be near a library, so she declared. Adella said that Harry would be grieved at having missed them; he might not get here more than once or twice in the whole summer. He had given his plane to the government, and it wasn't considered patriotic to drive a car, and anyhow, you couldn't get the gas. They all wanted to know how Lanny had got it, and he explained that the car belonged to his father, and Lanny was using a couple of months' supply of ration coupons. Robbie, who had half a dozen cars, didn't have time to drive any of them except between his office and his home.

They stayed two days, and then set out again, through Keene valley and past Schroon Lake, and so out of the mountains and down along a little river to Albany. There was their old friend the Hudson River, where Henry had been so disappointed not to find the Northwest Passage. In a couple of hours they were passing Krum Elbow, and Lanny said: "The Squire doesn't have much time to look at his Christmas trees these days." He said nothing about "Shangri-La," and nothing about a P.A.'s duties; but Laurel knew well what he was thinking. Her lovely holiday was over, and she was coming back into the world of suffering and danger.

XI

That night, in their snug little nest, she said: "Let's try one more séance." They had held several, but always with disappointing results. Otto Kahn had talked only idle pleasantries and had reported that the "spirits" who made their appearance were persons of no social distinction, nor yet of intellectual; he kept insisting that he knew nothing about the Holdenhursts and did not have the honor of the acquaintance of Laurel Creston's grandmother. Now the time was growing short, for Lanny was to depart the day after next, and Laurel wouldn't dare to try a séance with anybody else. She had told her friend Agnes that sometimes she talked in her sleep, and not to worry about it if she heard it.

They tried again; and there was the genial banker, always on call. They could imagine him, dapper and elegant in his evening clothes, for surely he would not have appeared otherwise. He was ready to chat, but didn't have anything important to say. When they asked him to produce some of their friends in the spirit world he said that conditions here were difficult; but he didn't explain why. He said there was a spirit named Hodges, who had been one of his—Otto's—stockbrokers, but who wasn't a very talkative man, especially where there was no ticker and no quotation board. There was tiresome old Sir Basil, as always; and there was a lady who claimed that she had a special revelation from God. "You know, how persistent these religious souls can be," said Otto.

"You haven't seen anything of God yourself?" inquired Lanny. And the reply was: "How would I know?" quite in the style of the New York sophisticates. When Lanny asked about Reverdy Holdenhurst and then about Lanny's former wife Trudi, the banker said that he was feeling under the weather that evening, and his voice faded away. It was for all the world like a phonograph running down.

Laurel came out of her trance and was told about all this. She asked, as she had asked before: "What can this fantastic thing mean?" Lanny's reply also had been heard before: "I'd give a good part of what I own to anybody who could find out."

It was difficult even to talk to the average person about these phenomena. You might explain ever so clearly that you didn't pretend to know what these entities really were; they called themselves "spirits," and that was as far as you could get. The person would say "Spirits!" and go off and report that you had "blown your top," and everybody to whom he mentioned the matter would agree. But that wouldn't stop the phenomena from continuing, everywhere, all over the world. There were thousands of persons who had this mediumistic gift, and many who never made money out of it, and gave no signs of being "cracked." The voices spoke and did their best to convince you that they were real, even to having their feelings hurt when they weren't believed.

Laurel said: "The most amazing thing is that my subconscious mind should be full of such fragments of human personality of whom my conscious mind never can get direct knowledge, and that they should use my voice without my ever hearing it. If it is Otto Kahn really, why can he not speak to me when I am awake?"

"Ask him," said Lanny, half seriously.

The wife replied: "All right." Then, after a moment's pause: "Mr. Kahn, won't you kindly use my voice now? I'll keep perfectly still and not interfere."

There followed a long silence; no sound whatever, and Laurel felt no power tugging at her vocal cords. No, she would have to go back into that other kind of sleep, which she knew was different, although she could not say in what the difference consisted or how she managed to turn the switch that brought one kind instead of the other. "I suppose it's a suggestion," she said, "but how I give it I could not say."

"Do you know how you tell your muscles to lift you up from your bed or to let you down again? You don't know that, and the wisest scientist in the world cannot tell you how a desire, or an act of will, can cause one of your muscles to contract."

XII

There was another aspect of this subject pressing upon her mind. "Lanny dear," she began, "there is something we ought to have an understanding about. You are going away, and I might never see you again."

"I am really not going into any danger, darling."

"I know you have to tell me that, but I don't want to fool myself. There isn't any safe place in Europe now, and everything will get worse before it gets better. What I want you to know is that if you should die, I won't be thinking about anything but trying to find you. Psychic research is just a curiosity now, but then it would become my life. Promise me you will try your best to come back to me!"

"Of course, Laurel!"

"I will go into a trance every night. Let us agree, exactly eight o'clock by New York time. You won't forget that?"

"Surely not."

"I will have Agnes sit by and tell me if you come. And if I don't hear from you that way, I'll go to other mediums and try. Don't tell me now, but think of things about yourself that I don't know, and tell them to me in the trance, so that later I can get Robbie or Beauty or others to verify them."

"Be sure that I'll think up plenty of evidence," he assured her, not without a smile. "Apparently I won't have much else to do. I can't find that the 'spirits' ever seem to have any work."

"It's curious; they appear to be wandering about in a void, lost and bewildered. What little they do, they don't seem to know how they do it. Let's promise that, if we ever find ourselves in that world, we shan't rest until we find each other."

"What else could interest us?"

"And when we do, we'll get busy with some medium and devise a way to convince our friends on earth that it really is Lanny and Laurel and not just 'that old telepathy.'"

"It's a bargain!" he said. "But I'm afraid it wouldn't do much good. Whatever the evidence might be, it would be embodied in one of the volumes of the Society for Psychical Research and gather dust on the library shelves." He had become discouraged about trying to interest people in another world. It would have to wait until this world was a more decent place to live in.

XIII

In the morning Lanny went to call at the F.B.I. offices. He found his reticent friend Mr. Post in a state bordering on complacency. "We have four men and one woman inside the trap at this moment and all we have to do is to shut the door. We are waiting for their chief, who is expected in the city tomorrow morning. Then we are ready to go into action."

"Good work!" said the P.A.

"Incidentally we have a story for the newspapers that will completely cover you and lead them off the track."

"I have been thinking that over," Lanny said. "I have a suggestion, if you don't mind."

"Surely not."

"Imagine this for the moment. As soon as you give me the signal tomorrow that everything is ready, 1 rush into the League office very much excited. I tell Hartley I have just learned from the janitor of my apartment building that Federal agents have been there and ransacked the rooms in my absence; that they have had my telephone wires tapped for weeks and have been getting the contents of my trash basket. I tell Hartley that I'm going to bolt, and he had better do the same. I give him half of what is left of the money—or a little more. When he comes out of the building, your men nab him at the street door. Wouldn't that leave me in the clear?"

"The trouble is, Mr. Budd, he wouldn't bolt until he had telephoned at least one of his gang and told that one to warn the others."

"I have thought of that, too. You might have the telephone wires cut, but that would excite suspicion. I am wondering if it might not be possible to have his wire diverted in the exchange, or perhaps on the roof of the office building, and have a woman answer his calls; and when he gives a number, sound the busy signal. That would make him try several different numbers, and it might be important for you, because it might provide fresh clues."

"Let me think about that, Mr. Budd." There was silence in the room for several minutes; then the man said: "I can't see any flaw in that, and, as you say, it might bring us something new. But suppose you didn't find Hartley in the office tomorrow morning?"

"I have promised him a check today, and I can phone him and say that I am very much rushed and will see him the first thing in the morning."

"What hour will suit you?"

"The earlier the better; I am taking the Clipper for England at noon. What time do you expect the man whom you call the chief to arrive?"

"He is not going to arrive in the city; we are going to take him off the train at a near-by stop, for fear that he may be intending to get off before he reaches the city and transfer his valuable baggage to somebody else. We can be ready for action at ten tomorrow, if that is agreeable to you."

"Exactly right," Lanny said. "I'll be packed and have my bags in the car."

"I will phone you at nine if all goes well. I will say your name three times—Budd, Budd, Budd. That will mean that arrangements are complete and that you are to proceed to the League office and carry out your part. If there is a delay, I won't phone; just wait at your place until I do."

"Don't make it too late," Lanny replied. "I have a really important mission and I can't afford to miss that Clipper."

"Don't worry," said the other. "In case of emergency I could call the airport and arrange to have the Clipper wait for you."

Lanny chuckled. "I have thought myself important sometimes, but never that much!"

XIV

The P.A. went home and from there telephoned Hartley. "I have good news for you," he said, "also some money. I've been out of town, and I'm crowded today, but I'll see you at the office in the morning without fail." That was that, and he set about writing letters to his clients and making business arrangements for his trip.

In the evening he took Laurel for a drive and told her what was in the wind. It was a relief to be able to tell her something, and this was an achievement in which she had a part. It seemed to her the height of melodrama—and so indeed was everything connected with this war. She was so excited that she wondered if she could sleep, so he took her to a roof garden and they had supper. They were spending every moment together that they could. When they came home, and she was undressed and ready for bed, she suggested: "Let's try one more séance."

She lay down and closed her eyes, and Lanny sat by the bedside, waiting for any voice that might speak. But there came no voice, only the sound of gentle breathing, and after a while he realized that his tired wife had made the wrong mental connection, had got aboard the wrong train. He lay beside her, speculating over the question of how this had happened and what it meant. Had there been spirits waiting to communicate, and were they now disappointed? Would they wake her up, or would they come to her in her dreams? Here was the thing called sleep, just ordinary sleep, and yet what a strange thing! In it his wife went off into a world of her own, often a completely crazy world of fears and adventures in which she was apart from her husband, in the company of fugitive and fantastic beings, "the fickle pensioners of Morpheus' train." Lanny was possessed by the thought of how little man knows of himself and his own mind.

XV

In the morning the P.A. finished his packing, and sat reading the papers ˙˙˙ ˙f disturbing news which he could not think about consecutively. His wife's nerves were also on edge, for she had had bad dreams, she told him; she was becoming what the world called super-stitious. The phone rang; it was Robbie to say good-by, and Lanny had to excuse himself: "I am expecting a call about an urgent matter. I'll call back before I leave."

Then silence again, and more waiting; until at last came another ring, and the voice of Post, giving the signal: "Budd, Budd, Budd." Lanny answered with "Roger," which was part of the lingo of the war. "Start now," said the voice.

His car was at the door, and he took his bags down. Laurel followed. She was going with him to the airport and would drive the car back to the garage. A girl from Robbie's office would come and get it there. Robbie had offered to leave the car, but Laurel didn't want it; she said that taxis were easier in big-city traffic.

Lanny drove to the neighborhood of the League office and managed to find a parking space on a side street some distance away. He walked to the office quickly, so that he might have color in his cheeks. Once, years ago, when his friend Rick had been writing and staging plays, he had watched an actor behind the scenes working up excitement prepa-ratory to bursting in upon the stage. Now Lanny did the same, and found no great difficulty, for he really was nervous, having thought of so many things that might go wrong.

There was Hartley, waiting, and the little drama was played through convincingly enough. When Lanny told the bad news the Englishman leaped up, exclaiming "Good God!"—this, it appeared, was the stand-ard exclamation for the English gentleman. He wanted to get out of there instantly; but then he thought of his confederates and said: "Wait a moment!" and took up the telephone, just as Post had pre-dicted. He gave a number, and Lanny, standing near, could hear the busy signal. "Oh, hell!" the man exclaimed, and gave another number.

Lanny said: "I can't wait," and planked a roll of bills down on the table. "This will keep you going." And then: "When things have set-tled down you can write me in care of my father. Mark it personal." He turned and bolted out of the room.

And that was all there was to it. Lanny observed a dapper young man standing in the hallway, and two more down at the entrance of the building. He hoped they wouldn't mistake him for Hartley, and they didn't. He hurried to the car and drove to one of the East River bridges, and so to the airport, where the great seaplane was resting in the water basin. On the way he told his wife about what had happened, and when they reached the airport he called up his friend Post and said: "This is the man whose name is pronounced three times." The answer was: "Everything is jake, and we are everlastingly obliged to you." Lanny added: "If ever I want to take up a stage career, I'll come to you for a recommendation."

XVI

There was time to spare, so he showed his wife what a luxurious vehicle he was going to travel in. She did her best to pretend that it comforted her, but she had learned that he was flying north, by much the same route on which he had been wrecked before. Now and then her lips would tremble, but she said very bravely that she didn't want to make it hard for him and would go on and do her work, and learn to pray, after the fashion of his esteemed stepfather. He took her back to the solid concrete, and they strolled up and down until the last call came. Then he gave her a long kiss, and with tears running down her cheeks she said: "Don't forget, if anything goes wrong, I'll still be waiting for you."

"Eight P.M. on the dot," he answered, and forced a smile, because it is embarrassing to a man to have to wipe his eyes in public.

He went aboard, and the great seabird glided out into the Sound and rose into the air and away. It was a warm and quiet July day, and all the prognostications were favorable. Lanny had plenty of things to read, and a good appetite—he told himself that he had helped with an important job and might help with others, and he couldn't do any good to the Allied cause by worrying about it.

No voyage could have been pleasanter. He was flown to Newfoundland, this time to the seaplane base of Botwood on a clear blue sound. From there on to the ancient island of Iceland, with its many glaciers and boiling springs; now many Yanks were there—or "G.I.'s," as they were calling themselves, playing with the idea that they were "government issued," like everything else they touched. The Icelanders hadn't invited them and were making the best of a trying situation. Lanny saw few of them, for the plane paused only to refuel; it sped on through the unbroken daylight, and set its passengers down in the harbor of Prestwick in western Scotland, now a great airport. When he presented his credentials he was concerned lest the P.M.'s secretary might have overlooked the little matter of having a name taken off the blacklist; but evidently it had been done. The official, speaking with a strong Scottish burr, bade him welcome to the United Kingdom.

The first thing Lanny did was to borrow one of those little sheets, made up of four half-size pages, which passed for a newspaper in a nation under siege. There, under a modest headline and a New York dateline, he read a dispatch revealing that the Federal Bureau of Investigation had just arrested a group of five men and one woman charged with purchasing diamonds in America and smuggling them to Sweden, from there to be taken into Germany. Names of the gang were not given, but there was a dramatic story as to how the discovery of this conspiracy had happened to be made.

It was narrated that a man walking on Broadway had been observed to draw his handkerchief from his pocket, and from it had dropped a rough diamond. The man who saw the incident chanced to be himself a "diamond man," and he picked up the stone, intending to return it to the owner; but first it occurred to him to walk ahead and look at the man's face. Diamond men are a small group and rather clannish, and they know one another; but this man was a stranger. Realizing that it was wartime, and that diamonds were among the most important of war materials, the man had followed the stranger to his hotel, observed him get his key and go to his room, and then had called the F.B.I. There had followed a patient and careful job of detective work, continuing for several weeks. Lanny chuckled to himself as he reread the story; he didn't begrudge the hard-working agents the credit they had taken—he surely didn't want any share of it for the son of Budd-Erling. He thought that the story put him "in the clear."

BOOK FOUR

Still Point of the Turning World

11

Mother of the Free

I

LANNY'S first thought in England was of his little daughter. He had cabled Irma, and as soon as he reached London he telephoned the Castle to ask if it would be agreeable for him to call. It always had been, but he never neglected the formality. The relationship of a man to his ex-wife and her new husband is a difficult one at best, and the pair were trying to show what good manners could achieve in that field. Irma said: "Frances has asked about you every day for more than a year." Lanny might have made some joking remark about how trying that must have been; but he knew that a sense of humor was not Lady Wickthorpe's strong point, so he replied: "I appreciate your patience."

Gone were the good old days when Lanny had been able to step into his car and run out to Wickthorpe Castle in less than a couple of hours. Now he had to look up a timetable, and get to Paddington station on time, and be jostled by crowds that never failed to be there in spite of the government's efforts to reduce travel. When he stepped off the train he found that the child had come to meet him, driving her pony-cart, with a groom riding behind. Fourteen months had passed, and he was amazed when he saw her—this tall, long-legged girl! But when she flung her arms about him and kissed him, it was the same Frances, more demonstrative than her mother, more like her father in temperament, and having to be continually repressed. "Oh, Father, why did you take so long?" None of the business of calling her parents by their first names, of which Irma had always disapproved.

The groom touched his hat, and tucked two suitcases under his feet and the typewriter on his lap, and the pony trotted off—a properly trained English pony who knew that the right side of the road was the wrong side and that the left side was the right side. And while the well-trimmed hedges of an English village glided silently past them,

Frances plied this wonderful, rarely seen father with questions about where he had been and what had happened to him. Presently he told her that he would make a bedtime story of it; now she should tell him about herself and what she was studying and how the family was. So the floodgates were opened, and he learned the latest news about a castle which dated back to the time of Shakespeare and Sir Francis Drake, and which was an important factor in the life of this blessed isle, controlling the destinies of something like a thousand people.

The estate couldn't have been kept going if it hadn't been for the money which Irma Barnes had inherited from J. Paramount Barnes of Chicago, a disciple of Sir Francis Drake who had operated in the field of street-railway finance instead of on the high seas. The people of the estate knew all about her ladyship's fortune; the men all touched their hats and the women smiled and bowed to the little girl, and to her father, whom they knew at least by sight, for he had lived in a residence known as the Lodge years ago when he was still Irma's husband. These proper villagers tried their best not to think of this as a scandal, but as something exotic, characteristic of the wild and woolly West, which they took Chicago to be. After all, Britain was an empire, and might receive a visit from the King of Dahomey, or the Akhoond of Swat, bringing not one extra wife but four, the limit permitted to Mohammedans.

II

The Countess of Wickthorpe emerged from the "lift" which was a part of her modernization of the Castle. She wore a white housedress and looked vigorous and handsome with her crown of dark brown hair. Lanny's first thought was that the monster of *embonpoint* had been licked by the war; Irma appeared at least ten pounds lighter, and it became her well. She greeted him cordially, saying: "You have stayed away from us a long time!" Apparently she had never learned that he had been put on the blacklist by B4; he didn't tell her, for the less gossip there was on that subject the better. He told her that he had found travel less easy to arrange.

As on the last occasion, he was going to be put up in the cottage occupied by Mrs. Fanny Barnes, Irma's mother; and, as before, he said that would be perfectly agreeable. So many friends had fled the capital, Irma explained. Some of the refugee children had gone back to London, but they might be coming again any day—there were rumors of deadly new German weapons. Lanny said he had heard such rumors; and so they got to Irma's favorite topic, her hatred of this fratricidal conflict which was wrecking the modern world and could only end in the triumph of the Bolshevik terror. Conversation at Wickthorpe wasn't very entertaining these days, for all roads led to Moscow.

His Lordship came in from making the rounds of the estate. He was playing the role of country gentleman, having taken the increase of food production as the one rational thing a man could do in a mad world. He rode horseback, because petrol was so scarce. His erect figure looked well in a riding suit and his blond hair shone when he took off his hat in the sunshine. He shook hands cordially with his old friend Lanny, asked after his health and that of his father and mother, and then fell to talking casually about the state of his crops. Such was his manner, and whether you had come back after fourteen days or fourteen years wouldn't make much difference. Ceddy took life seriously, but rarely talked about it. The only place where he permitted the expression of emotions was on the stage, and not too much of it there.

He was deeply concerned about politics, both at home and abroad, but circumstances no longer permitted him to expound his ideas publicly. Once in the House of Lords, and then his duty was done; people knew what he thought, and some day he would have the melancholy satisfaction of saying: "You remember what I told you?" When he was among persons who agreed with him, he would speak freely, and few others were invited to the Castle nowadays. Lanny, in his role of near-Fascist, was one of these; and in the evening, seated outside in the cool twilight, the wife, the husband, and the ex-husband enjoyed the luxury of complete agreement.

Lanny, of course, was asked about his trip around the world and about his marriage in Hongkong. He said that his wife was a writer of magazine stories, but he didn't mention the character of her stories nor that her pen name was Mary Morrow. He answered questions about Hongkong and southern and central China, but didn't mention that he had visited "Red" China, and said only that he had been permitted to fly out through Russia, but had had no opportunity to make observations. Much more interesting to the earl and his countess were his more recent experiences in Vichy France and North Africa. Ceddy, until recently a Foreign Office man, knew most of the appeasers in France and had done everything in his power to further their program. Now, apparently, it was too late; Churchill was in the saddle, riding madly, and Britain was approaching a precipice, beyond which was the abyss of Bolshevism.

Lanny tried to be as cheering as he could. He said there was intense anti-Red feeling in America which was bound to produce a sharp reaction immediately after the war, however it ended. "How can it end," asked Ceddy, "save in the ruin of Western Europe? France will be a battlefield, and Germany completely exhausted." When Lanny said that Russia would be exhausted, too, the other answered: "Yes, but she will recover more quickly, because those people breed like rabbits. And she will have all the border states, and China, too, and how long will it take her agents to stir up revolution in India?"

Such were the ideas which Lanny had always heard in this ancient castle. They were the ideas of the privileged in all the countries he visited, the people to whom class was more than country. Lanny hated the ideas, but it was his job to express agreement and listen, and find out what powerful persons were still spending week ends at the Castle and voicing these ideas and the latest schemes for putting pressure on statesmen to bring about a compromise peace. Lanny would go back to London and type out a report and have it delivered to the American Ambassador. No doubt when F.D.R. received it he would tell some of it to Churchill over the transatlantic telephone, and sometimes it would be news to the anti-Nazi Prime Minister and sometimes not.

III

When Lanny returned to London he phoned Rick, who had taken to helping one of the labor papers for the duration. Once a successful playwright, able to entertain even the carriage trade, Eric Vivian Pomeroy-Neilson now couldn't think about anything except countering the intrigues of the Fascists and the near-Fascists all over the world. He despised the Cliveden and Wickthorpe sets and had been blasting them for years. For that reason Lanny no longer went to stay at The Reaches, Rick's home; the two men met in secret in a little hotel they had agreed upon. Lanny booked a room there, and the lame journalist and his sympathetic wife came and spent the day.

What a time they had, catching up with fourteen months of personal history of two families, indeed of several more, for Nina and Rick knew both Robbie and Beauty and had to be told about them, and still more important, about Lanny's marriage, and what sort of partner he had got. He had sent a photograph, and also the stories of Mary Morrow cut out of magazines; but that wasn't enough for Nina; she had to be told how they were getting along, and how Laurel was living, and how she took her husband's long absences.

Lanny had to recite once more the story of his year's adventures; and this time he didn't have to hide anything, save only the name of President Roosevelt. He could tell Rick about China, and especially Yenan; about Ulan-Bator and Kuibyshev and Moscow, and the two-hour interview with Stalin. Rick could make notes and could use this information in his writings, of course omitting anything that might point to Lanny as a source. The same was true for France and North Africa and other lands. For years before the war Lanny had been doing what he could to light the path of the British labor movement by bringing inside stories, forecasts, and warnings to this trusted friend, who would write them up and get them published, sometimes by a secret and indirect route.

In return Rick would tell all that he knew about the course of events; some of it inside stuff, for a baronet's son had access to important people, even to many who did not share his political coloration but who respected him for his integrity and believed that the people had a right to know what was going on behind the scenes. In spite of all the Nazi atrocities, there were still influential persons who wanted to beat Hitler but not too badly, and who were dreaming of an agreement which would prevent the Reds from breaking into the Balkans and gaining control of the Dardanelles. Lanny told what he had heard over the week end at Wickthorpe, and Rick told what his father had heard among his associates in the Athenaeum and the Carlton clubs. Rick said there was going to be a big military powwow of the Allied staffs, beginning in a week or so, and he might be in a position to get some of the inside stuff. Lanny didn't say that Harry Hopkins had promised to tip him off on the same subject; he just said: "Maybe I can learn something too."

IV

Lanny's arrangement with the Prime Minister had been that he was to drop a note, marked personal, to the unobtrusive young secretary, Mr. Martin. He did so, and received no direct answer, but next day was called to the telephone at his hotel, and a voice said: "Mr. Budd, this is Fordyce, whom you may possibly remember having met just before you left for home last year." Lanny replied promptly that he would never forget. When the voice asked if he might have the pleasure of seeing Mr. Budd again, Mr. Budd said yes, and agreed to await the arrival of this representative of B4, the ultra-secret British Intelligence department.

Lanny had acquired a great respect for this organization. They had done a perfect job on him, and as a professional he could appreciate it. When their representative was safely ensconced in his room and had started to present apologies, Lanny said: "Not at all, Mr. Fordyce; you were perfectly correct, on the basis of the evidence you had. You understand, I was not at liberty to reveal to you for whom I was working."

"Certainly, Mr. Budd. I had an uneasy suspicion about it. Also, I could guess that you might be on your way home, anyhow."

Lanny chuckled. "That guess was correct, and you saved me trouble by arranging for my prompt flight. So all is well, and we are friends, I trust."

"Righto! The Prime Minister has sent us a note, saying that you are to have everything you want. May I say, that is an unusual privilege in these times."

"The Prime Minister has his reasons, which some day I may be free to explain to you. Let me say straight off what I have in mind, and that is, to have a private talk with Rudolf Hess."

"I presume that might be arranged. You understand, he is an important prisoner of state, and especially guarded. He is a difficult prisoner and has to be treated to some extent as a mental patient. We use great care not to excite him."

"Knowing him well, I can readily believe that. You must know that he thinks of me as his devoted friend and sympathizer, and I wish to continue in that role. If you were to take me to him, he would know at once that I had gone over to your side, and so he would close his mouth, or possibly even break into bitter reproaches. It is my idea to make him think that I am coming to him clandestinely, and without the knowledge of his captors. I should like to have a jailer smuggle me into his room in the dead of night, and I'll tell Hess that I have paid that jailer, say, a hundred pounds. Hess is used to bribery and corruption himself and would have no difficulty in believing such a story."

"I see what you mean, Mr. Budd, and it seems to me a promising idea."

"You will naturally wish to know what I expect to get from the prisoner. I have no wish to keep matters secret from you, and if you have a dictaphone in his sleeping room it will be all right with me—rather better, in fact, because it will save me the task of having to remember what may be a long conversation. Rudi, who is supposed to be so reticent, is really a talkative fellow among his few intimates, and I don't suppose he has seen any of these in the past year."

"Indeed not; he is kept strictly, but he is fairly well informed as to the outside world, because he is permitted to have a radio set."

"You are indeed treating him well!"

"We are treating him according to his rank in Germany, and of course in strict accord with the Geneva Convention. We could not fail to do this, even if we wished otherwise, because they have many prisoners of ours upon whom they might retaliate. But of course Hess is not satisfied; he argues that he came as an ambassador and should enjoy diplomatic status; we consider him a military prisoner, because he is an officer of the Luftwaffe and came in uniform. Those in charge of him have had many wrangles with him on this subject."

"That I can imagine; no doubt I'll hear about it from him. You must understand that I have been posing as a Nazi sympathizer for many years, and have enjoyed the friendship of Hitler for about fifteen years, and of Hess about five. I cannot guess what I may find out from him, or rather, I could guess a great number of things which might or might not come out in our talk. One thing, I ought to be able to learn whether he has ever had any message from Germany or has been able to send one. That I am sure would be of interest to you."

"Indeed yes, Mr. Budd. And there might be one or two other things which we could suggest that you give him a chance to talk about."

V

The B4 man went on to reveal that the Number Three Nazi had recently been taken to the Maindiff Court Hospital, near the small town of Abergenny. Mr. Fordyce pronounced it so, with the accent on the third syllable; then he explained that it was spelled Abergavenny, with the accent on the fourth syllable. It was in the county of Monmouth, close to the border of Wales, and was an old town; near it was a twelfth-century Norman castle which appeared to exercise a spell upon the imagination of the unhappy prisoner. He was permitted to drive there, accompanied by an officer of the guard, and with other members of the guard following in the rear. He and his mongrel dog, called Hippo, would lie by the double moat of the ruined castle and watch the ducks on the surface of the water and the two golden carp which dwelt below.

"We'll be happy to motor you there," said the agreeable agent; and when Lanny objected that he didn't like to use up any of the nation's precious petrol, the man said that it wouldn't take much, only about fifteen gallons, and what they might get out of it was worth the price.

"You will be the guest of B4," he insisted. When Lanny had talked with this middle-aged gentleman a year ago, Fordyce had given the impression of being well filled out; now he was considerably slimmer, and his cheeks were not so rosy as they had been. That was the case with pretty nearly everybody in besieged London, and some of the people gave the same depressing effect as the ruins of the buildings.

Lanny said: "I hope that you will confine discussion of this project to as few persons as possible, for I am still playing a dangerous role, and you know that there are always possibilities of a leak."

"No one knows about it so far except my superior, who got the order directly from the Prime Minister. The only other person who needs to know is the medical superintendent in charge of the hospital. He carries the responsibility for Hess's welfare, and naturally we could not keep him in ignorance of a matter which will undoubtedly have an effect upon his patient, whether for the better or the worse we cannot be sure."

Lanny assented to that, and added: "Won't you also have to tell one or more of the jailers?"

"I don't see why they need know anything about it. If you are let into Hess's room in the middle of the night, he will not see who lets you in, and will have to accept what you tell him. It had better be the medical superintendent himself, and then none of the men will question what is going on."

"Fine!" exclaimed the P.A. He took out his billfold and from it extracted a folded sheet of paper which he opened. "Here is an idea," he said. "Here are four slips of flimsy. On each I have typed the names 'Kurvenal-Siegfried.' The first of these is the name of a character in Wagner's *Tristan*, who is described as 'the truest of the true.' It is the code name I gave to Hess so that he could communicate with me in England. Siegfried is the code name that Hitler gave me so that if I had anything to communicate to him I could be sure he would know where it came from."

"You have indeed been playing a difficult game, Mr. Budd."

"I have had special advantages, which were prepared a long time before this war. Now it is my idea to roll each of these slips into a little ball, and get it to Hess in his food. Such a pellet could be pressed into a chunk of bread, or into an apple, or a not-too-soft pudding. He might fail to notice one or two and swallow them; that is why I should try several times. It might be that he wouldn't eat that particular chunk of bread, and if so, we could put the pellet into another for the next meal. It wouldn't do any harm if he got several; they would all mean one thing to him and one only, that I was on the outside and planning to help him. He would be greatly excited, but would try to hide his excitement, and if this went on for several days, he would be prepared to have me appear in his room in the night, and to believe that I had really been corrupting his guards. We could talk in whispers and with all the atmosphere of melodrama."

"You Americans read detective stories, too!" was the Englishman's comment.

Lanny replied: "It was Sherlock Holmes who taught us most of what we know on the subject. And let me remind you that I watched the process by which you chaps lured Hess to Britain, and if there was ever a rawer piece of melodrama, I have never come upon it in any of our 'whodunits.' "

An Englishman's natural color came back into the B4 man's cheeks, and he beamed as he remarked: "It was rather good, we do admit." He couldn't refrain from adding: "Is 'whodunit' an American word, Mr. Budd? We are supposed to keep track of them, out of courtesy to your Armed Forces."

"It would pain you to mutilate the language in that fashion," replied the P.A. with his most amiable smile.

Said the Englishman: "I understand that our two armies are now in process of dividing up the burden of learning a new language. They are listing the objects which have different names and are going half-and-half on them. We are to agree that a spanner is a wrench, and you in turn are to agree that gas is petrol. So we hope to operate without confusion—except to the Hun."

VI

The program they agreed upon was that Mr. Fordyce was to drive that afternoon to the town with the abbreviated Welsh name and have a confidential talk with the medical superintendent. If he approved, the pellets would be fed to the patient one each day, and on the evening of the fourth day Lanny would be driven to the place early enough to confer with the superintendent. At midnight he would be escorted to the prisoner's room, and the guard who always slept in the room with him would be instructed to go outside until summoned again. Lanny said that was all O.K., and he would spend part of the interim making up his mind what he wanted to say to the prisoner and what he would try to get from him. If Mr. Fordyce had other suggestions, he might give them to Lanny on the drive.

So it was agreed, and the son of Budd-Erling went back to the job of renewing his acquaintances in London and picking up ideas and information. Rick had given him the address of his elder son, Alfy, who got leave and came to town. Alfy had been taken out of his fighting job and put to training younger flyers; that had come near to breaking his heart, but now that he was used to it, he had to admit that it was a better employment of his experience. The relief to his parents hadn't lasted long, for now his younger brother had been stationed at "Hell's Corner," down at the southeast point of this tight little island. He had got it rather badly a couple of months ago, but now was nearly all right again and ready for another go.

How different appeared the situation of England since Lanny had last talked with this young, old friend! Then it had been touch and go; now Alfy was quietly certain that they had got the Hun down. The new Budd-Erling pursuit plane was tops, as good as even the newest "Spit." That would tickle Robbie Budd, but unfortunately Lanny had no way to get the word to him until he, Lanny, got back home. The only thing that could change the situation now, said Alfy, was something completely new from the enemy. Lanny warned him about jet propulsion, and this slender, high-strung Englishman said maybe so, such bombs might make a bit of trouble, but before they could be produced in quantity the British would have them, too. "We're working on them, day and night, let me tell you."

Alfy revealed other secrets of his dangerous trade, for he had known Lanny from boyhood, and knew that Budd-Erling had a right to know everything. Blueprints and models and formulas of aerodynamics were all of first-rate importance, but nothing could take the place of actual combat experience, the things that men reported day after day as they came in from meetings with the enemy in which one or the other had to die. Alfy had had two full years of it, in addition to what he had learned in trying to help the Spanish Republic. He was only twenty-five, but had lines of care in his thin, sensitive features and a touch of gray in his hair. He slept very badly, but counted himself lucky to be alive and still to have something to give to his "Mother of the Free."

"We're going to hold the fort for you," Alfy declared. And his friend could assure him: "The Yanks are coming! We'll put enough weight on this little island to sink it!"

Said the airman with a smile: "We must get more barrage balloons to hold it up."

VII

The B4 agent had said: "When I call you on the telephone, I'll talk about a golf game." So, next day, he reported: "I have inspected the golf course and it's in good condition. I think we can have our round in three days." Two days later he called again: "Three of the four golf balls have been lost, and I think I know who found them." Lanny chuckled and said that he would be ready to play off the match on the morrow.

At two o'clock the next day Fordyce called for Lanny in one of those smallish Austin cars which were saving much precious petrol for Britain. Lanny, who had long legs, could just get them in. They drove by the road he had always taken to Wickthorpe Castle, and then on, slightly north of west, through Oxford and Gloucester, historic names. The Englishman told about his visit to the hospital and what he had found there. It was a fairly large place, new, and full of wounded men. Hess had a room at the extreme end of the "female wing," opening onto a small lawn with iron railings. He was never alone, day or night. He would stroll about the countryside on parole. Being a wealthy man, with money in several banks in neutral countries, he could indulge his whims and was permitted to do so within limits; he chose to dress himself in a blue sports coat, gray flannel trousers, and flaring yellow boots.

"That isn't like the Rudi I knew," said Lanny. "Then he wore a plain S.A. uniform."

"That was glory in those days," replied the other. "Now he chooses to be an English country squire—but yellow boots rather spoil the effect! The people of the neighborhood refer to him playfully as the Kaiser of Abergavenny. They are used to the sight of him on the roads, or sitting somewhere in the sunshine; he will stay for hours painting or sketching. Time hangs heavy on his hands, we may be sure."

"He is a military student, Mr. Fordyce, and must know that victory for his side is a long way off. No doubt he fights against the realization."

"He fights against everything and everybody. He frightens the nurses with his scowls. He cannot bear to take orders, and while he has never offered physical resistance, he has made it necessary to have a force of thirty men, mostly soldiers of the Welsh regiment, to guard him. I suppose that counts as a military gain for Germany."

They talked for a while about what Lanny might find out. It was of

great importance to know if Hess had any way of communicating with
the outside, and it would be a master stroke if he could be led to name
any confederate or agent in Britain. It was entirely likely that the
Nazis, who had apparently foreseen everything, had established a system for meeting just such contingencies as now confronted their
Nummer Drei. B4 would have paid a small fortune for the information
which Lanny was trying to get for them without charge.

VIII

They were winding through the hills of Monmouthshire, with its
tree-shrouded country lanes and gray stone cottages. In the fields the
old men, the women, and the children worked from dawn to dark,
growing food for the workers and the soldiers.

They came to the town of Ross, and then by the "old road" to the
small town of Abergavenny. "Aber" is Celtic for "mouth of," referring
to a stream; there was an Abertillery and an Abersycha and others in
the neighborhood. They were only a short drive from the great soft-
coal centers of South Wales, where the miners were toiling long hours
to provide fuel for the making of guns and shells. To the south lay
the harbors of Swansea and Bristol, now crowded with war shipping.

They drove to the hospital, a modern building beautifully set among
shade trees. The guards knew the B4 man and passed him and his guest
without questioning. Lanny was taken to the home of the medical
superintendent and whisked inside. This official's name was D. Ellis
Jones; he was in his early forties, rather tall, smooth-shaven, and wore
horn-rimmed glasses. He had the rank of major in the British Army.

Major Jones explained the peculiar responsibility which Rudolf Hess
represented to his custodians. If Hess were to die, the Nazis would be
certain to claim that it was the result of mistreatment, and they might
take the lives of hundreds of the British officers whom they had at
their mercy. Therefore the hospital was scrupulous in welcoming the
Swiss Neutrality Commission which was charged with enforcing the
Geneva Convention. They came whenever they wished and talked with
the prisoner and made sure that he had everything to which he was
entitled. Because of the fear that he might commit suicide in spite of
the utmost watchfulness, the guardians babied him considerably, allowing him harmless little indulgences which were surely not in the convention. "As a rule he doesn't have much appetite, and he has lost
weight in spite of our best efforts."

Said Lanny: "I can understand the extreme humiliation he feels. It is hard for me to imagine that he would want to live if the Nazi cause goes down."

"That is what we fear, Mr. Budd, and why we have to be so careful in handling him. He is liable to fits of depression which may last for weeks."

"You need not fear any result of that sort from my visit, Major. It has always been my role with the Nazis to be optimistic and admiring —that is how I have got them to trust me and to talk. You may be sure that your patient will have hope after our meeting. Of course, he will have disappointments later, but that is inevitable—since I am assuming that his cause will fail."

"It's damn well going to fail," said the medical man. He added that he thought Hess must have received at least one of the code messages, for he had shown signs of restlessness during the past two or three days. Of course he would not speak a word about the matter to any of his captors.

They discussed the program to be followed. There was no need to wait until midnight, for in order to save electricity they all went to bed with the chickens. After ten o'clock everything was as quiet as could be, and the Major would take Mr. Budd to the prisoner's bedroom and slip him inside without a sound. At the same time the guard who sat in the dimly lighted room all night would move out, as he always did when the Major entered.

That was all. The two secret agents drove to an inconspicuous inn and had supper, and then, since there was time to be passed, they paid a visit to the ancient Norman ruin called Whitecastle, of which Hess was so fond. He wasn't there now, so they got out and strolled around, and Lanny saw the ducks, and one of the two golden carp. A woman custodian showed them about. They climbed the well-worn stairs and inspected the defenses of the castle, which included many slits for bow and crossbow fire, planned in such a way as to give the maximum field of vision. "Herr Hess was greatly interested in this," remarked the custodian.

Later they sat by the double moat and watched the twilight settle over the beautiful scene. Fordyce told the inside story of how he and his fellow agents had lured Hess to England by getting up a conspiracy of pretended Nazi sympathizers. Lanny told how puzzled he had been when Hess had revealed this conspiracy to him, and for some time Lanny had been unable to decide whether or not it was real. He told stories about the secretary and disciple of the Nazi Führer who had risen to become a Reichsminister and party chief; about the country

home he had maintained near Berlin, and Klara, the lean and by-no-
means seductive lady he had married. She believed in psychic phenomena even more ardently than her husband, and had discoursed
learnedly to Lanny about the mystical books of ancient India.

IX

Promptly at ten they returned to the hospital grounds. Lanny sat
in the car until Major Jones came out and led him along a tree-shaded
path to the "female wing" where the prisoner lived his strange solitary
life. The medical man carried a small instrument case and requested
Lanny to carry it into the room and out again; the guards were being
told that he was making some observations of the prisoner during his
sleep. The Major apparently had complete authority; he spoke a whispered word to the two soldiers at the door, and to the one who sat
at the door of Hess's bedroom. The Major opened the door—it had no
knob on the inside, so he had told Lanny. The latter stepped quietly
in, and then moved out of the way of the man who had sat on duty
inside, and who rose immediately and came to the open door and out.

Lanny stood in silence, looking about the room, which was plain, as
became a hospital. There was a dim light burning, well shaded. There
was a chest of drawers and a couple of chairs; by the starlight outside
Lanny could see that the windows were not barred. On the bed lay the
figure of a man wearing striped pajamas. Lanny waited until the door
had been closed, then he stepped softly to the bedside and whispered:
"Rudi."

Evidently the man had not been asleep. He sat up instantly. "Is it
really you, Lanny?" he whispered.

"Yes, Rudi. You got my messages?"

"I got one, but could hardly believe it."

There was a chair by the bedside and Lanny slipped into it. The
rest of the conversation was carried on in the lowest audible whispers;
in English, which Hess knew as well as German, having been born in
Alexandria and educated there.

"Lanny," he said in a tone of great stress, "have you turned against
us?"

The P.A. was prepared for the question, and put pain into his reply.
"Can you ask me that, Rudi, after all these years?"

"But how can you be admitted here?"

"That is a long story. The gist of it is a hundred pounds sterling,
paid in cash this night."

"*Herrgott!* They are that venal?"

"A nation of shopkeepers, Rudi."

"Who has taken it?"

"I had to give my word not to tell. Suffice it that the right man got the money. It has taken me three weeks of making friends before I could drop a hint of what I wanted."

"And what do you want from me?"

"First of all, to see you, and to hear your voice. To let you know that you still have friends. How are they treating you?"

"Well enough, so far as food and shelter are concerned. But it is an outrage that I should be a prisoner. I came here in good faith, as a diplomatic representative. I am convinced now that I was trapped."

"I believe the same thing; but I did not find it out until it was too late. Did you get my messages?"

"I got only one, that everything was progressing satisfactorily."

"There it is! We cannot depend upon anybody! I sent you detailed accounts of my talks with the persons you had told me about. There was a man who gave me the name of Branscome, but I could never feel sure which side he was on. It has been very difficult for me to work in England."

"I can't see how you manage to do it!"

"I use my father's influence. I am supposed to be helping him. He used to be on our side, you know, until our government offered him so much money."

"American money is making it very hard for us, Lanny. Everything is going the way I feared and tried my best to prevent."

"You are not getting discouraged, I hope, *lieber* Rudi. Your armies hold all the vital points in Europe, and it would take decades of fighting to expel them."

"Do you really believe that? I try hard to hold to the idea; but it is not territory that will count in the long run, it will be air power, and you are building more of it."

"Don't say *me*, Rudi, say American big business. I have never been their man, not even in my boyhood."

"You are a true friend, Lanny, and I believe what you tell me. Have you been in Germany since you saw me last?"

"No, I have been crippled; I was in a plane wreck and had both legs broken. I have only recently been able to get about freely, and my first thought was of you. Tell me, is there anything I can do for you?"

"I don't know what it could be—unless you could figure out a way for me to escape."

"Believe me, I have been thinking about it day and night. There are many circumstances which might favor the plan. In Newport there is a large camp for German war prisoners. Many are bound to be seeking ways of escape, and I could get into touch with them and tell them where you are and how you are guarded."

"But what could they do in England, Lanny? The whole country-side would be up and after them."

"The action would have to be co-ordinated with what the British call a commando raid, say from Cherbourg. Later, when the nights are longer, there will be time for speedboats to come and go in the darkness. Parachutists might be dropped at this place, and bring you out, and the two forces might meet."

"That is possible, I suppose; but what could keep the British Navy from getting us on the return trip? They swarm in the Channel and claim it as their own."

"That would be a job for your airplanes. Surely they could provide a cover for the three or four hours it would take speedboats to get back to the French coast. Think what a colossal prestige stroke it would be to take you out of the hands of these insolent people! Surely the Führer wouldn't be in any doubt about that!"

"Yes, Lanny, but it would not have much military effect, and I am afraid that is what he is forced to concentrate on at present. I would fear to burden his mind and distract his attention for my benefit."

X

Lanny's eyes, growing used to the faint light, roamed over the features of this man leaning from the bed and not more than two feet away from him. A strange square face, with a stern mouth that made a straight line, and bushy black eyebrows making another. Lanny had known him at the height of his glory, a grim, implacable man in the service of his cause, but genial enough with the few friends he trusted, and oddly credulous when it came to the mysterious underworld of the "spirits." Now he was thinner; the bones stood out in his face, and the black hair was growing sparse. He suffered from gastritis; it might be due to British cooking, but more probably to worry. Lanny could see that his hands trembled when he made a gesture; he was obviously moved by this visitation out of his triumphant past.

"Listen, Rudi," began the solicitous friend. "You aren't by chance worrying over the idea that the Führer may have misunderstood your flight to Britain!"

"No, I am sure he knows me too well for that; he knows that I could never have any thought but to help him. All that troubles me is that I failed. It was an enterprise that had to succeed, or it was nothing."

"We can all fail, *lieber Freund*. Even the Führer has failed more than once. He hasn't been able to invade England, and he wasn't able to take Moscow last autumn."

"Yes, Lanny, but that is a cold sort of comfort. What tortures me is the bombing of our beautiful German cities, and the awful slaughter of our best youth. Day after day I listen to news of it, and while I know that the enemy newspapers and radio lie, I cannot suppose they invent whole campaigns."

"It is dreadful, and I share your heartache. I am troubled by the thought of your loneliness. Do you have no communications from the outside?"

"They permit me to receive letters from Klara, but of course if she said anything about political or military matters they would cut it out. There is not much else to say nowadays."

"You mean that you have not been able to get any communication from the Führer?"

"Not a word. I am far too carefully watched, and I have not the large sums of money that it would require to bribe anybody."

"It is dreadful that you should be so neglected, Rudi! Surely there must be many agents in this country!"

"Yes, but they have more important matters to work on than to bring birthday greetings to a prisoner of war."

"It is worse than I imagined. Would you not like to send a message to the Führer?"

"I would indeed."

"I was able to have Switzerland included in my passport. As you know, my mother lives in Unoccupied France, so that I have a good pretext for a trip. If I were to get word to the Führer that I had a message from you, he would surely send somebody to get it."

"He would do more than that; he would make it possible for you to come to him, if you were willing to take the risk of having the fact leak out."

"I cannot think of anything that would please me more. It might be that I could bring out some message to his friends abroad which would help to terminate this blind and cruel fratricide."

"I am afraid he has few friends in the so-called democracies now, Lanny."

"Many more than you think, take my word for that. But tell me, what message do you wish to send?"

"Tell him first of all of my undying love and devotion. Tell him that I have never wavered for one moment in that, and never shall."

"And what else?"

"I should have to think, Lanny. I am quite overwhelmed by the idea of being able to send word to him. I think of so many things that ought to be done, and that I might suggest to him if we could speak, but none that is important enough to send as a message. Quote him the English saying that the darkest hour is just before the dawn. Remind him of the glorious example of Frederick the Great, who was beaten more than once but refused to recognize it. Tell him that I lie here in the solitude and darkness and try to send him courage and hope by the secret channels of the subconscious."

"He will be deeply touched, Rudi, as I am. You have no concrete news of any sort for him?"

"What can a poor wretch in what is practically solitary confinement have to tell? Not a word! Describe how I exist, and how I wait for him to bring me deliverance. And of course if he can send me help without too great risk of loss to the Fatherland, I will do what I can to fight my way out."

XI

Lanny kept on giving leads and hints until he satisfied himself that he wasn't going to get any information of importance from this Number Three Nazi; either the Nazi didn't have it, or he was no longer trusting his American friend. Lanny had had no part in the scheme of B4 to lure Hess to Britain, but Hess, brooding over the matter in his too abundant leisure, was likely to have hit upon the possibility that Lanny might have been in on the plot. Or he might have decided that all Americans were enemies now. Anyhow, what he wanted was to get information, not to give. He wanted to ask about Lord Wickthorpe and others who were supposed to sympathize with his cause, and after that he wanted to tell his troubles, to repeat the complaints he had put before his jailers and before the Swiss commissioner who had visited him not long ago.

Lanny decided that the once vigorous master of the N.S.D.A.P.— National Socialist German Workers' Party—had become a querulous neurotic and a bore. He said: "Rudi, I am allowed only one hour here, and I promised not to overstay. Tell me frankly, do you want me to see the Führer for you?"

"Of course, Lanny."

"Well then, give me something to prove to the Führer that I was here. I hardly need to point out that he will not trust anyone from my part of the world." Lanny took from his coat pocket a small writing pad and pencil. "Will you write me a few words for him?" When Hess said "Surely," Lanny went on: "Write it as small as you can, in one corner of the paper, so that I can cut it off and conceal it in my clothing. If it were found, I should be turned over to the American Army and pretty certainly shot."

Hess wrote a few words in one corner of the paper. "This won't look much like my handwriting, written so small," he commented.

"Is there some talisman you could give me? Something the Führer would know?"

"I will give you my wedding ring." Hess took from his finger a plain gold band. "The Führer gave me this, and he will remember the inscription. To make it more sure, repeat to him what he told me when he put it into my hand: '*Dies wird das Lästermaul zum Schweigen bringen!*'"

Lanny knew what that referred to. In the old days of political strife the enemies of the Party had accused Adolf Hitler of improper intimacy with his devoted secretary, and they had had a nickname for the secretary, *Das Fräulein*. The story had it that Hitler therefore had ordered Hess to marry his Klara. "This will shut the mouths of the scandalmongers!"

Lanny took the ring. "You are doing me an honor, Rudi, and I appreciate it. I will put it into the Führer's hands, and when the victory has been won, he will return it to you. And now, *Lebewohl!* Take care of yourself, and keep up your courage. Every moment you give to doubt and worry is a moment wasted. Remember what Goethe said: '*Alles in der Welt lässt sich ertragen.*'"

They exchanged a firm handclasp, and Lanny picked up the Major's little bag and went to the door of the room and tapped gently upon it. Almost at once it opened, and Lanny stepped out and a guard stepped in. Lanny left the bungalow and walked to the Major's residence, in front of which Fordyce was waiting with the car; the B4 man offered to take the bag inside, which Lanny understood to mean that he wasn't expected to make any report there. "Tell him that everything went off well," said the P.A., and that was enough.

XII

They decided to drive home that night. On the way Lanny gave an account of the conversation, complete except that he said nothing about the scrap of writing and the ring. If B4 had had a recording device installed in the room there would be no harm done, but otherwise Lanny would keep that secret. He said he was sorry that he hadn't been able to get anything more important out of the prisoner. His guess was that Rudi had been telling the truth, that he didn't have any contacts with the outside world. The agent professed himself well pleased, but in his heart he must have been disappointed, for if he had helped to uncover a conspiracy it would have been a bright feather in his cap.

Churchill had suggested to Lanny that he would be interested to hear the outcome of the talk with Hess. But now Lanny told the agent: "I am guessing that I didn't get enough to make it worth the Prime Minister's while. Will you tell him, or shall I?"

"My senior will report to him," replied Fordyce. "His time is especially taken up at the moment."

"I have no doubt of that," said the other. "I understand that important decisions are being taken." That was as near as either of them would come to mentioning the fact that the top-flight American staff officers, the commanders of the Army, the Navy, and the Air Forces, had been flown to Britain a week or so previously.

When they got to London, Lanny bade good-by to his escort and went to his hotel room. There he took out the pad of paper. He read the fine script: "*Mein Führer: Ich bin es. Rudi.*" Literally translated the sentence means "I am it," but in English the words are reversed, and people say "It is I," or more commonly, "It's me," against which the grammarians fight in vain. Lanny took his nail scissors and cut off the bit of paper, about two square inches; he folded it once, and carefully sewed it into the lining of his coat—on the other side from Roosevelt's card. He put the ring on his finger—he, too, being a married man. It was his idea to go back to America soon and use these magical objects—the Ring and the Tarnhelm!—to persuade F.D.R. to let him go into Germany again.

XIII

The news of the military conference then going on was a closely guarded secret; but the newspapermen knew it, even though they could not give the least hint of it in print. Rick had told Lanny that the party included General Marshall, Chief of Staff, and Admiral King. Already in London was the newly appointed Commanding General of the American forces in the European Theater, whose name was Eisenhower. Lanny had never heard this name until the appointment was announced; he had to take it for granted that F.D.R. and his advisers knew their man.

"General Ike" had set up headquarters in some "flats" in Grosvenor Square, one of the fashionable districts of London, and the playful Americans had taken to calling it "Eisenhowerplatz." It seemed to them a charming stroke of fate that the new "C.G." should be of German ancestry and carry a German name. The words mean "iron hewer," and the word "iron" has been through the centuries a favorite of all military-minded German poets and orators. Now a hewer from the prairie state of Kansas had come to hew the German iron, beginning with the "blood and iron" of Bismarck and including the "iron soul" of Adolf Hitler.

Among the arrivals from Washington was Mr. Harry Hopkins, with the Army physician who labored to keep him alive through the strain of eighteen-hour-a-day conferring. The party had put up at the Dorchester, which was why Lanny hadn't been able to obtain a room there and had gone to the Savoy. After the trip to Abergavenny Lanny got some sleep, and then he called the Dorchester and asked for Mr. Hopkins's secretary. To that functionary he pronounced the magic word "Traveler," which had been given to Hopkins. It had the same effect as at the White House; Hopkins came to the phone.

"Are you going to be in town for the next three or four days?" he inquired, and Lanny answered that he had meant to spend the time with his little daughter at Wickthorpe Castle, but would come to town in response to either a telegram or telephone call. "Fine!" said Hopkins. "You'll hear from me."

Lanny called Rick, and they took a bus out to Hampstead Heath, and strolled by the ponds near the Vale of Health, where John Keats had lived; and then on to the ancient Spaniard's Inn, haunt of many poets. They had dinner in a place where no one knew them, and then sat out on the heath, discussing the future of the world, now being decided in town. Rick had attended a press conference given by the "C.G.," and reported him a straightforward and democratic fellow, a beneficent example to the brass hats of Britain. "The only thing is, I'm afraid he may be a little too kindhearted for a general."

"Don't worry," Lanny assured him. "Our fellows are really going to fight. I am told that our maneuvers in the Louisiana marshes were quite terrific."

"I know," agreed Rick. "They are drilling like all-possessed in North Ireland and practicing landings all round our coast. The Germans send in a tip-and-run plane now and then and get photographs. They can't find them very reassuring."

Lanny couldn't say "Roosevelt told me," but he could say: "I am told that Roosevelt is determined that American forces shall go into action somewhere this year. If it's not to be across the Channel, then it must be the Mediterranean, or we'll change our plans and concentrate first upon the Japanese. I don't suppose your people want that."

"Hardly," said the baronet's son. "But from all I hear Winnie is dead set against any more Channel crossings until we have overwhelming forces. So I suppose it will be the Mediterranean, and the farther east it is the better it will suit our Tory leader. If he could invade through the Balkans he would consider that he was killing two birds with one stone, winning two wars with one expedition."

"The Second World War and the Third," replied Lanny with a smile. They didn't need to say more, for they had both been in Paris early in the year 1919 when the descendant of the Duke of Marlborough had come there and labored mightily to persuade the Allies to undertake a holy crusade to crush the cockatrice of Bolshevism, just emerged from its egg and not yet having had time to develop its poison fangs.

"Winnie hasn't had a new idea in a quarter of a century," said the "Pink" journalist. "He wouldn't get another in the next quarter of a millennium."

Lanny thought that was extreme, and replied, "He was a consistent supporter of the League of Nations, and of collective security."

XIV

Lanny took an evening train to Wickthorpe and enjoyed a peaceful sleep, guarded by the elderly dragon lady who had once been his mother-in-law and now was his co-parent, so to speak—he an ordinary parent and she a grand one. She was a grand lady in her own estimation, also in physical aspect. Lanny had no doubt that in her secret heart she disliked him; how could she have any other attitude to a man who had failed to appreciate the magnificent Irma and the equally magnificent Barnes fortune? But he had over her a terrible power; at any time he might choose to take the little Frances away for a holiday, even to America, and if he chose to keep her there, who could guess what the law might say about it?

The result was that Fanny Barnes the haughty was polite to the point of obsequiousness. Lanny's room in her cottage was kept inviolate, and the place was silent while he slept or read or pecked on his typewriter. Poor old Uncle Horace, ex-manipulator of Wall Street securities, was rudely forbidden to bore him, and Fanny herself didn't even invite him to make a bridge four, but left it for him to confer that favor if he chose.

So Lanny lived a life of ease, roamed the estate, played tennis and bowls with the little one, played the piano for her, and danced with her to the music of radio or phonograph. They lunched with the grandmother, and dined at the Castle with mother and stepfather and whatever guests might be on hand. The child was old enough for that now; she was perfectly behaved; her mother was a strict disciplinarian, and Lanny could find no fault with the upbringing of a future heiress and bride of some British nobleman. He would have liked to teach her some of his ideas, but his role forbade that. He could only hope that events might do it for him.

He lived this elegant and expensive life, in which even the play was formalized, and all the time he was thinking: "The future of the world is being decided!" Not a line about it in the newspapers, not a word over the radio—you couldn't have dreamed that the directing brains of the American Armed Forces were in London. But the Earl of Wickthorpe and his countess knew it, and imparted it to Lanny as a state secret, and he was duly grateful for the favor. The guests speculated as to the probable decisions, and of course they expected to hear what a much-traveled art expert thought. Lanny could make a good guess, and did so, for it was important to him to keep the respect of the "Wickthorpe set." He might have need of it again!

Early on the morning of the twenty-fifth of July there came a telegram reading: "Can see you this afternoon. Urgent. Harry." So Lanny bade farewell to this life of a country gentleman, and to his dear little daughter, who could not be told why her father had to leave so soon and never knew when he would return. Always a new heartache, wherever he was, in Connecticut or New York, in Buckinghamshire or Provence! He was sure that he'd be leaving Britain in a few days, but all he could say was: "I'll write you, darling; and I'll come back as soon as I can."

XV

The President's right-hand man, clad in a pair of shorts on a hot summer afternoon, looked like a very sick man indeed; but apparently he had learned to live with his diseases, and they did not inhibit his cheerful manner. He offered his visitor a drink, and when it was declined, remarked: "I am on a schedule, too." Then: "Excuse me if I stretch out," and let himself down on the bed. He signed Lanny to a chair alongside.

"You won't mind if I come right to the point, Lanny. These have been strenuous days for all of us."

"Indeed, I am surprised that you remembered me."

"The Boss told me to remember you. This is the result of the conference. The British refused positively to go in with us on a cross-Channel invasion this year. They say we couldn't force the Germans to divert anything from Russia, because the Germans have enough forces in France to withstand anything we could put ashore this year. And another defeat would be a catastrophe."

"That's about what you expected, isn't it?"

"Yes, but we had hopes. Now we have to change all our plans. It's to be the Mediterranean. Churchill, of course, wants it to be the Balkans; he fought like a tiger for that. You should have been there—it was quite a drama. The first time he saw me he gave me the devil because I had talked to some of the generals before I talked to him. That's not protocol, it seems. He gave me to understand that he was the master of the British Empire, and that he, not any of the generals, is running the British part of this war. He grabbed the law book in which this is written and read me the passages in the same tone as if he were making a speech in Parliament; when he finished each passage he ripped the page out of the book and threw it on the floor. A good show, as they say."

"I hope you stood up to him, Harry," ventured the P.A.

The harnessmaker's son looked intently at his visitor. "Listen, brother," he said. "You are a plutocrat, I take it, and Churchill is an aristocrat; I'm only a democrat, and with a small 'd.' But I had to learn to stand up to our business tycoons in the old W.P.A. days, and even before that, in Albany. They want the earth with a blue ribbon tied round it, and when they can't have it they roar you down. The Boss told me to talk back to Churchill from the beginning, and I did, and he took it like a good sport."

"There is a thing that he calls 'lease-lend,'" remarked Lanny. "Who pays the piper calls the tune."

"Not in this case. We can't go it alone, or even threaten to. We agreed to compromise. We gave up the Channel and the P.M. gave up the Balkans. We're going to invade through French North Africa and put Rommel into a sack."

"Oh, good! That's been my hope from the beginning."

"You understand, this is top secret, and for your own use only."

"The Governor seemed to mean that I would be free to share it with one or two persons who are working on the spot."

"If he said that, it goes, of course. But be sure they are persons you can trust to the death. You know what it means to be caught spying on the Nazis."

"Indeed I know. I have visited their dungeons; and Göring once put me in one. It was his idea of a joke, but I got all the feelings."

"The name of the operation is Torch. Eisenhower will command; it's to be kept an American show, with the idea of riding easier with the French. The coast is long, as you know, a couple of thousand miles. We may take Dakar or Casablanca on the Atlantic, or Oran or Algiers on the Mediterranean. We leave the enemy to guess. Between you and me, it will be all, or most of, those ports."

"I see. And the time?"

"Nobody knows the time yet. We have to change a million details, and it depends on when we can be ready. But it will be this year—that is the agreement. You will be going there immediately?"

"Vichy is my first goal."

"You have transportation arranged?"

"I have to cable Baker."

"That is not necessary. Let me attend to it for you."

"I don't want to put any burden upon you, Harry, I—"

"I have secretaries. You'll take a Clipper to Lisbon and fly by way of Madrid?"

"That will be fine."

"O.K., I'll see that you get a seat on the first plane. You travel under your own name?"

"Always. I am an art expert, you know. I have commissions to buy paintings in Vichy France, also a very fine fountain for ablutions in Algeria."

"Harry the Hop" broke into a grin. He started to get up, but Lanny saw that it was an effort and said: "Stay where you are. Thanks, as ever."

"I have to get up. Our train is leaving tonight. You may be interested to know that I am flying back to Washington to be married in the White House."

"You don't say! Congratulations!"

"I have found a woman who is willing to take care of these tired bones. I understand that you have recently been married also. Good luck to you and yours, old man."

They exchanged a handclasp and a smile. So men parted in wartime, knowing well that they might never see each other again. Very often they didn't, and then they were not supposed to wreck themselves with grief. As Goethe had said more than a century ago: "Everything on the earth can be endured." Lanny had quoted it to Hess.

1 2

Lull before Storm

I

LISBON was still in its safe berth by the River Tagus, and still pleasanter from the air than from the ground. Portugal was making money out of both sides in the war, and, as always, the rich were adding to their hoards while the poor discovered the meaning of inflation and that wages never kept up with the stealthy increase in the cost of food. The city was so full of spies that they tried to work on one another, and, of course, the arrival of an American art expert via London was not overlooked. Lanny was glad that he had to spend only a few hours telling ladies and gentlemen with assorted foreign accents that he was an esthete, entirely aloof from the hateful intrigues of politics; also, that he never lent money, no matter how sad the story.

In Madrid he had to stay over until the next day, and he didn't mind that, for he could spend the evening at the home of his elderly friend General Aguilar, and be internally drenched with *copitas de manzanilla*—in English, cups of camomile tea. This white-whiskered old aristocrat with the many medals, which he wore even at home, was one of the few Spanish Fascists who were interested in the outside world and made a pretense of culture—meaning, of course, the kind that cost money and was elegant and exclusive. He listened with interest to Lanny's account of the wonderful art collection which Reichsmarschall Göring was assembling in Germany. "A man out of the old times!" he exclaimed admiringly, and went on to reveal the fact that a year or two ago this conquistador had assembled more than three hundred of the largest guns ever made in the world, with the intention of taking Gibraltar. The fact that the elaborate emplacements had been constructed on the soil of Spain, which was supposed to be a neutral country, and that they were aimed at the property of Britain, which was supposed to be a friendly country, troubled the military commander of Madrid so little that he didn't mention it and probably didn't think of it.

"I suppose those guns have been taken to the eastern front now," remarked the art expert casually.

"No, they are still there," said the General, who was in a mellow mood, having listened to much flattery. "They serve a useful purpose in protecting the neutrality of Morocco."

He didn't say Spanish Morocco, but Lanny knew he meant that; he was refusing to acknowledge the existence of French Morocco. "Do you mean," asked the American, "the guns are powerful enough to be effective across the Strait?"

"They might be; but I mean that our ability to take Gibraltar will exercise a restraining influence upon hostile forces that might wish to land on the other side."

"I keep hearing talk of such expeditions," remarked Lanny, "but of course a civilian never knows whether it is something real or just a smoke screen. From what I can gather, the most likely place for a landing appears to be the Vardar valley in Greece."

Said the Spaniard: "It is a never-ending source of wonder to me, how you Americans continue to let yourselves be persuaded to pull chestnuts out of the fire for the British."

"I don't think it is going to go on much longer, my General. There are signs of an awakening. Just before I left New York I had a part in the founding of a new organization called the American Christian League. I was amazed by the extent of the public response." Lanny reached into his pocket and took out one of the leaflets which he had taken off Hartley's desk. *The Red Nightmare*—he translated, *Le Cauchemar Rouge,* for they were speaking French. The document suited the old General's ideology, and he was glad to hear about the sums of money that had been collected and the mass meetings that had been held. In return he talked freely about the "Blue Division," which represented the first installment of El Caudillo's promised million men to help the Führer put down the Red demon. These "Blues" were volunteers, in the same sense that the Germans and Italians who had come to fight in Spain had been—that is, they could volunteer or be shot. They had been meeting with heavy losses in Russia, but now the Axis armies were advancing rapidly toward the oil of the Caucasus, and it looked as if the dawn were breaking at last.

Too bad this victory could not have been won by Christian armies, instead of by the Nazis, who were not exactly cordial to Holy Mother Church! But Marshal Pétain had the word of the Führer that the Church would be restored in France as a bulwark against the Reds. They talked about the old Marshal for a while; Aguilar had come to know him intimately while Pétain had been French Ambassador to Madrid during the period of the *Sitzkrieg*, before the German invasion of France. The fact that Lanny had been received by Pétain here at that time, and had been able to visit him in Vichy, was one of the reasons that the commandant of the Madrid district trusted him completely and talked to him freely. Lanny wasn't a Catholic and couldn't pose as one, but he could cite the names of wealthy Americans who recognized the Hierarchy as the chief means of holding down the labor unions and keeping the Reds and the Pinks out of power. Lanny had discussed this subject with Mr. Hearst and Mr. Henry Ford, and what these great men had said on the subject was heard gladly by generals and admirals as well as cardinals and archbishops throughout Europe.

II

In Vichy a free-spending American was an old friend by now. A landlord would vacate his own room for him, and *maîtres-d'hôtel* would greet him by name. He could look up important ministers of state and tell them what their friends in Washington and London and North Africa were doing, and promise to take them messages in the course of his travels. To M. Benoist-Méchin and others of his set Lanny could explain that the present depreciation of the franc offered unusual opportunities to do business in old masters. American collectors were attracted by the prices which Lanny reported to them; and while this would represent a loss to French culture, the French might consent to look at it from the international point of view and be willing to assist in uplifting the American hinterland. When the matter was put thus tactfully, any statesman could agree, and would tell friends who needed ready cash, and Lanny would be invited to inspect art works in elegant country villas; mostly they were third-rate, but it cost him nothing to say: "Very interesting, and I'll be happy to report it to my clients."

Meantime he invited important persons to lunch or dine, and was invited to soirees where the elite of this miserable government displayed their shoddy splendor. "A banana republic without any bananas," some wit had called it, and yet, the smaller the prizes, the more bitterly men fought for them. Intrigue, jealousy, and hatred appeared to be staple foods at Vichy buffets. Lanny had never been in any place where secrets were so ill kept; you could hear all the crimes of all the world, except of the person who was talking to you, and you might hear about him from any of his associates. Bourgeois France was falling to pieces, and Vichy was the garbage can.

First of all Lanny sought out his friend Charlot de Bruyne. Here was one man who still believed in his creed and was willing to make sacrifices for it. Lanny felt pity for him and would have liked to say: "Wake up, *jeune homme!* You are in the middle of the twentieth century, not the eighteenth." But of course he couldn't speak such words; he had to go on with his role of superspy, which he had not chosen, but which had chosen him.

What he did, the first thing, was to tell Charlot about his older brother. Denis was well, he was doing his duty as an officer, and he had received Charlot's messages of love with the same affection that had prompted them. "But so far as concerns his political opinions, I'm afraid there's nothing to be done, Charlot. I argued with him, but it was useless; he is not to be moved from what he believes."

"What does he believe, Lanny?"

"He believes that General de Gaulle is a great man, a prophet and all that sort of thing. And of course it's a very dangerous opinion for an officer to hold; it won't further his career. All we can do is to recognize the fact that he is sincere, and respect him for it."

But the younger brother couldn't leave it there. The times were too critical, the feelings too intense. Men were killing each other, and not even brothers could be spared. Lanny had to take refuge in his ivory tower, the stairs of which were getting badly worn with his footprints running up and down. "You know, Charlot, you mustn't expect an American to take part in French politics."

"But your President is doing just that, Lanny! He made a radio speech in the French language, denouncing our present government!"

"It was in very crude schoolboy French, Charlot, and can hardly have made any impression on your intelligent public. Don't blame this old friend for anything that any politician does. Let me stay *au-dessus de la mêlée*, and continue to work at my profession."

Lanny asked about Charlot himself and what he was doing. He was working hard at organizing and training his Légion Tricolore, for the purpose of repressing the traitor enemies here in France; they were expecting an Allied landing somewhere and planning to aid it, and Charlot was planning to put them down—yes, even if it proved to be his own brother! There was no keeping away from subject of Denis, and Lanny saw that there couldn't be any peace or reconciliation between them, only a war to the cruel death.

III

The P.A. followed his practice of not seeking out the higher-ups but letting them seek him. This increased his importance and at the same time laid him less open to suspicion. What Lanny did was to tell Monsieur le Ministre Jacques Benoist-Méchin that he had recently come from New York, where he had been instrumental in organizing the American Christian League, and what great encouragement this group would offer to Christian France. Later on, he asked after the health of Admiral Darlan, and expressed his great admiration for that sailor-statesman, knowing that Benoist-Méchin was the Admiral's man, or had been until lately. The next time Lanny met the ex-journalist he was told that the Admiral had expressed the hope of seeing M. Budd before he departed. Lanny telephoned promptly and an appointment was made.

What did this pipe-smoking Commander of the French Fleet want of an American dilettante and playboy grown up? First, to offer him some of his favorite Pernod Fils brandy; then to chat politely, asking about the visitor's mother and father, and where he had been and what he had seen; then to state how deeply he had been hurt by the American attitude toward Unoccupied France since the formation of the Laval government. He wanted Lanny to tell his father and his influential friends how Frenchmen had been compelled to choose between Red anarchy and White law and order. Also, he had felt his personal honor impugned by the suspicion, so generally expressed in America, that he, Commander of the French Fleet, might somehow be persuaded or intimidated into letting that Fleet come into the possession of the Germans. "*Jamais, jamais, jamais!*" exclaimed Jean Louis Xavier

François Darlan, and he said it several times more in his discourse. It just wasn't going to happen. But of course if the Americans should be so misguided as to put troops ashore upon the soil of France, the French would have no choice but to defend their *patrie* and their *honneur*.

Did Lanny think the Americans were preparing to do this? The Frenchman had heard rumors and was greatly worried. Lanny said: "Believe me, *mon Amiral*, if I knew I would tell you. I hear this and hear that, and I wonder, does anybody really know? This I can tell you: My father expects it will be Salonika and the Vardar River. He talks learnedly about reaching the Germans in their unarmored back, and I get the impression that he has got it from some of the military men who come to Newcastle to supervise the fabricating of fighter planes. I can tell you only of my sincere hope that none of those planes will ever be flying over French soil."

"The British have flown over it, as you know. They recently bombed the Renault plant, near Paris, and I think the bitterest experience of my life has been the discovery that there are Frenchmen depraved enough to have rejoiced in that bombing, and to welcome the murder of their fellow citizens."

"I have never met any such, *mon Amiral*, but I have heard that it is so. I am told there are clandestine papers being published and circulated, but I have not come upon one."

That was true at the time, but it didn't remain true. That very evening, strolling to his room after a soiree, Lanny was passed on a dark street by a man wearing the blouse and cap of a workingman. This man put out a hand to him, saying: "*Pour la France!*" Lanny saw that he had a leaflet and took it automatically. He hadn't far to go, so he ventured to keep it till he got to his room, and to read it by the dim light that was permitted. A leaflet, entitled *Le Témoignage Chrétien*— The Christian Witness—it gave the text of a manifesto issued by a group of Catholic priests and Protestant pastors who had come together to protest against Fascism and Nazism in the name of freedom and the dignity of the individual human soul. This discovery warmed Lanny's heart, for he knew that there was another side to Christianity than the defense of capitalist property rights, and he was glad to know that there were humble priests who did not share the political attitudes of the Hierarchy. He mentioned this leaflet in the report to his Chief, which he wrote and sent through the Embassy.

IV

Darlan was important because he commanded the Fleet, and the Fleet might command the Mediterranean. Of second importance was Pierre Laval, who would hardly have dared to interfere with the Admiral. He, the *fripon mongol*, commanded the Army; but if the Allies could keep their hold on the Mediterranean they could deal with whatever army the Germans had allowed to the French in North Africa. With the Premier, Lanny pursued the same waiting tactics; an American art expert went about his business, while the word spread among members of the government that he had been to London and met the "Wickthorpe set," and to New York, where he had founded a powerful new organization in support of the Axis.

Just as he was making his plans to leave, there came to his humble lodgings one of the Premier's undersecretaries, bidding him welcome to Vichy and saying that the Premier would be pleased if he would call at *quinze heures* that day. Such an invitation was a command, and Lanny said it was also a pleasure. He took an ancient horse-drawn cab—taxis being nonexistent—and drove to the Hotel du Parc, where the Mongolian rascal had the royal suite. It was, Lanny thought, the hottest day he had ever known in France, and he found the head of the state in his undershirt amid the best French gilt and rococo. The visitor was invited to take off his coat, and did so, hanging it carefully on the back of his chair and never forgetting it. There were two treasures hidden in it, one of which would have lifted him to glory, and the other of which might have caused him to be hanged.

The son of Budd-Erling wasn't going to be taken out to Châteldon this trip; relations with his country were too bad, and it wouldn't do for the head of the State to exhibit too much intimacy with an American. But in the privacy of his office was another matter, and the butcher's son spoke as if the son of Budd-Erling were an ambassador, able to swing the destiny of nations. Pierre Laval said that he was desolated by the situation between the two countries, and by the blind, unreasoning prejudice which President Roosevelt and Secretary Hull showed to his harmless self. He said that he was firmly resolved never to break relations with America; if that calamity occurred, it would be Washington's act, not his.

Having said this, Pierre proceeded to "fish." What was Lanny's own attitude in the present calamitous situation? Surely he could not have weakened in his abhorrence of the Red Terrorists! When Lanny said that he was the same friend of order and property rights that he had always been, Pierre appealed to him as a personal friend to tell him what he knew about the *méchanceté* which the Allies were preparing to inflict upon Europe. Lanny in reply explained that he was not well informed, for the reason that the ruling people in America knew his sentiments, and the only place where he heard frank talk was in his father's home. There the opinion seemed to be that the Allies were planning an invasion through the Vardar valley. "A safe distance from France," he commented.

"*Vraiment*," said the Premier, "*mais quelle ivresse!* They really imagine they can conquer the whole of Europe? They will make a shambles of it, and what they leave the Reds will finish!"

"Perfectly true, *cher Maître*. The only question is whether our people can be awakened in time."

"Look at the situation, M. Budd! The Germans are almost at the Volga and the Caspian Sea. When they have reached those goals they will have cut Russia in half, and will stop her oil supply and bring all her machinery to a halt. And Rommel is at the gates of Alexandria and Suez, and then of what use will the Mediterranean be to the Allies? They will have to go all the way around Africa, and what means will they have to keep the Panzer forces from penetrating to India and meeting with the Japanese?"

"I agree with you altogether, *cher Maître;* the situation is the most encouraging we have yet seen."

"May I talk to you in confidence, *mon ami?*"

"Indeed so; I shall feel honored."

"As you must know, I have never had any heart for this or any war. I am a man of peace, a lawyer and no killer—even my worst enemies will tell you that. As a French statesman, I am by no means pleased that one nation should be gaining too great power on this old Continent where we all have to live."

"I understand that, and you are right."

"What I desire to know is whether, when Russia has been forced out of this war, Britain and America cannot be persuaded to listen to reason, and to make a settlement with Herr Hitler and myself, whereby a peace can be established in Europe that will last for the lifetimes of our grandchildren. All that any of us want is to keep what we have, and to unite in establishing and maintaining a government in Russia that will respect the rights of private property and will not carry on propaganda of social revolution throughout the rest of the world. I have the personal word of Herr Hitler that that is all he desires, and that he is willing to respect and to guarantee the rights of both the British Empire and of the United States. Surely that is statesmanship, M. Budd!"

"It is, and also it is what I have been urging upon my friends."

"Here is what I have in mind, *mon ami:* would you be willing to take that message to the public men of Britain and America for me?"

"*Hélas, cher Maître,* I do not have access to such persons; nor do I have confidence in my own ability as an envoy."

"That last statement is surely a mistake; you have the ability, and I should be glad to give you a note stating that I have authorized you to speak for me. The time to act is now, before the German victories have become too great, and before their armies have advanced into territory which they might not be so willing to give up."

"Everything you say is wise, *cher Maître;* and I promise you this—I will do my best to make contact with men of influence and present your views to them."

"When do you intend to return?"

"I wish to see my mother on the Riviera, and then I have several art commissions to carry out, one of them in North Africa. I hope to return to New York by way of Britain, where I have a little daughter whom I try to see as often as I can."

"If it is because of business reasons that you do this work, M. Budd, let me make it possible for you to postpone it, and attend to this far more important commission for my government."

"Thank you for the kind offer, but I do not need money, and would not consent to take the money of the people of France in this tragic hour."

"Let me assure you, *cher ami,* there is no service that would be worth so much to the people of France as to get them peace and national unity once more. For that they would authorize the payment of half the contents of our treasury."

The pair had a little debate over this proposal. Pierre Laval simply couldn't believe that any man was actually turning down money; it was contrary to human nature, and to good manners if not good morals. He was sure that the son of Budd-Erling was holding out for a high price, and first he offered half a million francs and then he offered a round million, to be paid in dollars in New York, and strictly on the quiet. "We know how to handle money, M. Budd."

Lanny saw that the matter was serious, and he had to be careful or he might awaken suspicions. He said that he had lived most of his life in France, and that Marianne was his fostermother; he would do everything he could to help her, and some day he might receive a medal for it, but no money. He would be willing to drop everything and go to her aid, but his recent talks with British and Americans of his way of thinking and Laval's convinced him that the time was not yet. Let the Germans get to the Volga and across it, let them actually divert the oil of the Caucasus into the tanks of their Panzers, and then there might be a chance of putting some sense into the heads of Roosevelt and Churchill—or possibly of replacing them. Lanny brought encouragement to the soul of Vichy's Premier by telling of the conspiracy of high-up Americans to do just that, and the pair shook hands warmly and parted on the basis of friendship and trust. Of course the *fripon mongol* wouldn't really trust anybody, but he would tell them that he did, and with the manner which the French call *empressé*.

V

A train which needed repairs and did not run on time conveyed the P.A. to Cannes. At the station he was met by the "Bienvenu local," as he had dubbed the family buggy. The steed was thinner, it seemed to him, and so was the driver; he congratulated her as he kissed her, and she said: "I am getting so that I cannot eat when I know that so many other people are hungry." He assured her that it was the way to live longer, and she answered that it was the way to make wrinkles deeper, and to shudder every time you caught a glimpse of your own throat.

At home everything was peaceful, as much so as was possible with a World War in the newspapers and radio waves, and in the atmosphere, too, for guns were heard out at sea now and then, and military planes large and small passed overhead. Parsifal Dingle refused to let himself be troubled by the war; it was God's plan, otherwise it could not have been. Beauty insisted that whether it was God's plan or Satan's, the lovely little Marcel wasn't allowed to hear anything about it, and that had become one of the rules of the household.

One of the first items of news Lanny got was that his half-sister had gone back to Berlin. "Oskar crooked his finger, and she went," said Beauty. "He wrote her, and she wouldn't even show me the letter."

"Perhaps he neglected to be polite," ventured Lanny. "Or maybe he was a little too frank as to the nature of his interest. The Nazis are that way."

"Love is a terrible thing to a woman, Lanny. Marceline does not trust her man, I don't think she even respects him; and yet she goes to him."

"My guess is that snobbery has much to do with it. Oskar is an aristocrat, and she takes him at his own valuation. The more arrogant he
is, the more she admires him in her secret heart, even when she herself
is the victim. You brought her up wrong, Beauty."

"What can you do?" demanded the mother, making a French gesture with the shoulders. "The world is more powerful than any person
in it, and what the world admires is what a child desires. I must admit
that I have looked at Marceline with surprise most of her life; she is so
self-centered, and so quietly determined."

"Why not start over again with this new one? Let him set out to be
useful at once, and let him understand that all his life he is never going
to get anything without earning it."

"What strange ideas you have, Lanny! I believe you are just as much
a radical in your heart as when you were young!"

"Say that to me, but never to anybody else," replied the son.

He listened to his mother's account of what Marceline had been
doing before her departure. She had got an engagement to dance at
the International Sporting Club in Monte Carlo. A fantastic story. The
Italian Army was respecting the independence of that tiny principality,
and the hotels, *pensions*, and villas were packed with wealthy refugees
from every country in Europe. Gambling at the Casino was going on
from noon till daybreak, and hundreds of millions of francs changed
hands every evening. Marceline had been paid a hundred and fifty
thousand francs per week, but she hadn't been happy because of the
crowding—people sleeping even in the chairs and on the sofas of the
world's most famous gambling palace. To Lanny the place meant Sir
Basil Zaharoff, who had owned it, and whom Lanny had met there as a
small boy. He was moved now to try another séance with Madame,
and heard the old munitions king of Europe lamenting the breakdown
of the world, especially those parts of it which he had possessed and
had been reluctant to leave behind him!

VI

The Golfe Juan was still blue in the deeps and green in the shallows,
and the sun set each night in glory behind the red Esterel Mountains.
The oleanders along the hedge were masses of white blossoms or pink,
and the scarlet hibiscus were small flaming suns. In the court the bees
made an endless humming in the flowers, and a new half-grown puppy
tumbled over himself trying to follow Marcel about. The Midi displayed all its midsummer lusciousness, and the playfolk, as distin-

guished from the working folk, went about in bathing suits all day. If anybody wept for the million and a quarter young Frenchmen who were prisoners of war in Germany and were being worked as slave labor, they did their weeping alone and kept a face of courage in public.

Of old, Lanny had come here to rest and to refresh himself with happy memories. But this time he came as a disturber, a herald of bad tidings. A day or two after his arrival he went into his mother's room and shut the door. "Old darling," he began, "we have to have a confidential talk, the most important ever."

"Yes, Lanny?" she said, and a scared look came upon her face, for his tone was even more grave than his words. She was sitting at her dressing table, doing her best to repair the ravages of time. Now she put down her tools, and he seated himself on the side of the bed, facing her.

"You must have been doing a lot of guessing about your son during the last few years, and you have been very good about not talking—or so I have believed."

"Never a word to anyone, Lanny."

"This time is the most important of all. Here is something about which you are not to breathe the faintest hint to anybody on earth. It might cost me my life, and more important yet, it might cost the lives of a great many American boys. I really haven't the right even to speak of the matter, but I am trusting to your tact and good sense. You have to take yourself and Parsifal and the child away from Bienvenu."

"Oh, *mon Dieu!*" she exclaimed. "The war is coming here?"

"You must never breathe such words, nor even think the thought. You are a lady of the leisure class, and you haven't had any sort of trip or vacation for many years. You have a whim to see some new part of the world, some place where food is not rationed."

"Where is the place?"

"I have been trying to think of one that isn't too far away or too difficult to reach. I have decided that French Morocco would be highly suitable."

"But Lanny! such a fantastic place! And I keep hearing that the war may come there!"

"Trust my judgment, dear mother. Marrakech is one of the most fascinating spots I ever visited. It is high up and reasonably cool in summer. There are elegant villas there, and you might find one to rent, and play the social queen if you have a mind to. Also, there are good hotels. It will be expensive, but don't try to save money at this time."

"And when do we have to go, Lanny?"

"I don't know the date, and if I did I wouldn't be free to tell it. But you have time to make your plans and build up a propaganda among your friends. It will be O.K. if you are out of France by a month from now."

"It is going to be so hard to make anybody believe that I am really interested in a trip to Morocco!"

"Put it on my account if you like. I have been there, and am going to be there again, perhaps for months. I have found a gold mine there—I mean, figuratively speaking. I have interested American millionaires in the marvelous fountains and floor mosaics which are in that country; they have become quite a fad in New York, as fascinating as jigsaw puzzles. You can say that I made several thousand dollars in a single month out of them, and that I want you to help me, inspecting and overseeing the packing and shipping. That's business, and you know how to talk about it as well as the next person. I have a book about Moroccan art, and you can pick up a few phrases and become an expert. I have photographs you can show to friends, and a letter from a millionaire ordering a fountain. With a little practice you can get yourself all steamed up."

"I suppose I could. What shall I do with Bienvenu?"

"Pick out some trustworthy French couple and put them in charge; pay them to take care of the place."

"And the paintings, and your library?"

"We just have to take our chances with all those things. If you started packing them it would certainly look like a flight, and that would be absolutely fatal. People would say, I have just been here and have told you something to frighten you. Don't take anything but what you would naturally take on a trip. Be a tourist, think like a tourist."

"What shall I tell Parsifal?"

"Tell him what you tell the others. It makes no difference to him where he is. There are many mosques in Marrakech, and he will study the Mohammedan religion and find out if they have any psychic experiences and what they make of them. Tell Parsifal that you have seen so little of me during the past few years, and I am going to be there off and on during the next few months."

"Shall we take Madame with us?"

"That would be too much of a burden. No one will harm an old woman here. But take a maid, of course."

"And what about Emily? Should we not warn her?"

"That is a painful decision. I simply dare not take the chance of having her leave at the same time that we do. Emily is an old woman, all but bedridden; the worst that can happen is that her home will be taken by the military and she moved into one of her cottages. I am sure she would not be interned."

"Oh, then it is the Germans who are coming here!"

"Nobody can say who is coming, dear. Only a foolish person would attempt to guess the result of the clash of forces. What I have tried to do is think of some place where there is little chance of your being caught in any fighting, or of being shut up in a concentration camp for the duration—and this war may have a dreadful lot of duration! It happens that I have special knowledge, and you must trust me. Play the game according to my rules."

"All right, I will take your word. One question more. What am I to do about that money I buried in the garden?"

"The best thing will be for me to dig it up and use it, and send a check for your account in your New York bank. It so happens that I have use for a lot of money in small bills, which cannot be traced because of being new and having consecutive serial numbers."

"Lanny, I have felt for a long time that you were doing something frightfully dangerous!"

"Others are doing far more dangerous things, Mother dear. Let it rest here, that I am doing something that counts, and that some day I'll tell you a lot of interesting stories!"

VII

Next morning the P.A. called his old friend Jerry Pendleton on the telephone. First he inquired: "How's business?" and when Jerry gave the expected reply: "Rotten!" Lanny said: "I have to go to Geneva to get a painting. Can you fix me up for the train tomorrow night?" The travel bureau man promised to attend to it, and Lanny added: "How would you like to play some tennis this afternoon?"

They played three sets, and then went for a swim from the rocks below the estate. Sitting in the hot sunshine, with the insurgent waves drowning his low voice, Lanny opened up: "Do you suppose your wife could run the bureau for a while, Jerry?"

"A child could run it," said the other. He was what the French call a *petit bourgeois,* and the Americans a small businessman; by either name his situation was unpromising.

Lanny looked at this good fellow who had once been his tutor, although only half a dozen years older. The Army had claimed him in World War I, and he had risen to be a lieutenant; but he hadn't bothered to come home, he had stayed and married a French girl and a *pension*, or so he had said, in his playful fashion. Now Lanny observed that Jerry's hair was turning gray. He remarked: "You are worrying, aren't you?"

"Well," was the reply, "it's hard to run a travel bureau when people can't travel and to run a *pension* when the cost of food goes up faster than the boarders' incomes."

"Have you thought about the danger of staying on here?"

"Of course; but what can I do? I can't afford to drop everything and take Cerise and the kids to America."

"I have an idea to suggest. I have come onto a fairly prosperous business, buying mosaics in Morocco and shipping them to New York. I told Beauty about it, and she has taken a notion to go in with me. She thinks she'd like to see Marrakech, and Parsifal wants to study the Mohammedan religion."

"Jeepers!" exclaimed the ex-tutor. "Isn't that a sort of dangerous place to be in? I keep hearing talk about our Army coming to Casablanca."

"Well, suppose they do? The fighting will be at the coast, and Marrakech is a hundred miles or so in the interior. From what I've learned of the French Army there they couldn't stand up against us very long even if they wanted to, which I don't think they will. And when they give up, any Americans who are there will be in America, and without the expense of crossing the ocean."

"You know the situation better than I, Lanny."

"I'd a lot rather be there than here when the fighting starts; for it's certain that if we invade any French territory, the Germans will move here. They have to do it, not merely to keep us from landing here, but to keep the French from helping us."

"Yes, and their first move will be to intern all the Americans, especially the able-bodied men."

"This is what has occurred to me, Jerry. You know Beauty—she has all the social gifts and can help by getting introductions and oiling the machinery, but she's not much good at the details of a business. I thought you might travel with the party as a sort of secretary, and when you get there, I could put you to work for a while and pay you enough to get along and have a bit to send back home."

"That's very handsome of you, Lanny. What is it, just kindness?"

"Not at all. I'll promise you plenty of work, maybe more than you

want. I put only one condition on it, that you don't say a word about
it until I tell you to come, and then you just tell Cerise that you are
helping Beauty on the trip. When you're safe in Morocco, you can
write her that you're staying a while longer. You understand, Cerise
won't be in any danger here because she's French, and the Germans
are behaving correctly. But if you were to tell her about it now she
might be tempted to tell her aunt, or one of the servants might over-
hear, and I can't afford to have my name talked about in this connection."

"Mum's the word," replied this dependable friend. And then with a
grin: "I wonder who Mum was."

VIII

The art expert was retracing his footsteps of the previous spring,
except that he visited Geneva ahead of Toulon. Among the conservative disciples of John Calvin he set to work to make his presence
known to art dealers and collectors; also he dropped a postcard to
"M. Philippe Brun" at the address which he had stowed away carefully
in his memory. "Just a line to let you know I'm in town. Bienvenu."
He went to the public library next afternoon and made connections
with Monck in the usual cautious way. In the evening they took a
long walk, and rested as before on the steps of the League of Nations
building, a mausoleum to them, the tomb of their hopes of past years.

The German had a lot to report. Colonel Donovan's organization
had sent a man to him, a young college instructor of German descent,
a man of keen intelligence with whom Monck was especially well
pleased. The agent had given him money, and later had produced some
apparatus. Monck didn't say what it was, but Lanny could guess that
it was a radio-sending outfit. There were hints that several other people
had gone to work; Monck didn't know the details, but he said that it
was encouraging to have such competent support. The anti-Nazi
movement of Germany was like a reservoir that had been drained almost dry; but now a new aqueduct was being constructed, and soon a
mighty new stream would be flowing in.

Monck talked more freely than he had done before; it was as if he
were preparing to come out from underground. Lanny had to warn
him not to become too confident; it would be a long time yet before
an American army could enter Germany. But they would be fighting
somewhere before this year was over, that much a P.A. was free to
tell his friend in confidence. Fresh from a visit to the Budd-Erling

plant, and from driving on Highway Number 1, he could testify that the sleeping giant overseas was stirring his limbs and getting to his feet. "As sure as tomorrow's sunrise, the Nazis are going to be knocked out." The old-time labor man and Social Democrat replied that these were the most pleasant words he had ever heard.

He reported on the results of his own inquiries. His "contact" had been in touch with a physicist, and it was true that Germany was making or preparing to make *schweres Wasser*. Indeed, the physicist had seen the blueprints of a very elaborate plant, but unfortunately he had never been told where the plant was to be located. "It is dangerous to ask questions in Germany nowadays, even of one's intimate friends." Oddly enough, the man went on to say, he had got some information about conditions in America, where there existed only a few quarts of "heavy water"; it was one of the scarcest products of the new physics.

The question of jet propulsion was not so ultra-secret, not because the Nazis didn't want it so, but because the job was far advanced and therefore had to have workers sharing the secret. There were a number, both Communists and Socialists, who had joined the Nazi party as a means of surviving, but who still kept the old faith buried in their hearts. Every day it became plainer to the workers that they were going to have to face a long war, and against fresh forces from the New World; if only the Russians could hold out through this summer and autumn, many of the German workers would become desperate and would risk their lives to tell what they knew. Said Monck: "I have sent out the call, and I'm waiting for echoes to come back. It isn't something that can be done in a few days. I hope and trust that people are working on it, and that some day I'll get answers, and possibly even the blueprints."

Lanny had no right to complain. He wasn't risking anything, but was staying in a palace hotel, the Beau Rivage, and strolling about looking at *objets d'art*. In the lining of his coat was a tiny oblong of paper with six words written on it, and this burned inward all the way to his heart; he longed so to use it, and was sure that if he were to address a note to Führer Adolf Hitler at the New Chancellery in Berlin, a telegram would come at once, followed by a courier and a plane, to bring him to the *Hauptstadt*, or to the Führer's *Hauptquartier*, wherever it might be. But what could Lanny accomplish, so far as concerned either atomic fission or jet propulsion? He was an enemy alien now, and would be watched every moment, no matter how plausible his story and how charming his manners; very certainly he would not be permitted to chat with any nuclear physicists or designers of supersonic projectiles. And anyhow, F.D.R. had said no, and until he said yes, Lanny would have to go on traveling *en prince* in neutral lands.

The best he could do was to pump this ex-sailor and ex-*capitán* completely dry of information concerning conditions in Germany and Switzerland. It was a mild night, and they were in an open place where no one could steal up behind them. They kept their voices low. Monck told about some of the comrades who had been helping him and who now were gone—these were the only ones he could mention. Some of them had been Trudi's friends whom Lanny had known in the old days that now seemed a hundred years past. "What fools we were!" remarked the Social Democratic leader. "We actually believed that the great cartelmasters would let us organize and vote them out of power!"

"And we thought the workers would stand by us when it came to a showdown!" responded the American. "We gave them credit for too much intelligence, Monck, and the capitalists for too little."

"Hitler is a cunning knave, you must remember."

"Part knave and part genius, *Genosse*."

"I suppose we have to admit that. It would seem as if some devil had constructed him especially to hoodwink the German folk and lead them to utter ruin and despair."

"The Pied Piper of Hamelin town!" said Lanny.

IX

Just before leaving Bienvenu the P.A. had stopped in Cannes and rented a typewriter of German make; at home he had spent several hours producing a document labeled: "Professor Zimmermann's Examination Questions." These questions, twenty-three in all, covered the points on which Lanny had received instructions from the young Jewish doctor of science. They represented the matters concerning which American physicists wished to ascertain how far the German physicists were informed; each question was one which Lanny had learned by heart and had kept reciting to himself ever since leaving the Institute of Advanced Study at Princeton. Several of the questions read: "What is the significance of the formula"—and then followed one of those assemblages of mathematical symbols which, so far as the layman was concerned, might as well have been ancient Hittite or modern Gujerati. Each formula contained carefully studied errors which would lead the German scientists astray if it fell into the wrong hands; but any scientist who really knew the advanced steps toward atomic fission would correct the errors. Dr. Braunschweig's last words had been: "Do not tell even your trusted agent that the formulas are wrong. The errors are a means of testing what comes back to us."

Coming from Bienvenu, Lanny had carried this document pinned to his undershirt, and he had slept with it. Now he unpinned it and laid it in Monck's hands, also the pin, and saw the German make it safe in the same manner. Lanny explained: "Professor Zimmermann is a top-flight physicist who happens to be an especially ardent Nazi. If this paper should come into possession of the Gestapo, they would call upon this learned gentleman to explain for whom his examination questions were intended, and this might cause at least a temporary slowing up of German progress in nuclear science."

Monck said: "I will put my man to work on it."

Lanny gave his comrade some of the money he had dug up from under Beauty's yellow oleander; after which he went to his hotel room and slept well. In the morning he typed out a report on what he had learned and took it out and dropped it into a postbox—he wasn't afraid to trust the mails in this six-hundred-year-old republic. He spent the day visiting his art friends, and purchased a portrait by Mary Cassatt of a charming tiny girl, intending it as a present to old Mrs. Fotheringay, his client in Chicago who had a mansion full of painted babies. Having thus established himself as an art expert and no spy, Lanny took the night train back to the Riviera.

He had only a few duties left: the first, to pay a call upon Emily Chattersworth and do what he could to cheer her up. This wasn't easy, for she said that her world had come to an end. And indeed it was so, the world that she had known and enjoyed was gone, probably forever. Beauty hadn't yet told her about the harebrained plan of buying mosaics in Morocco; Lanny didn't want to have to discuss the idea with Emily; he wasn't sure he could make it sound plausible to her shrewd mind. To flee and leave this old friend behind seemed cruel; but, on the other hand, to take a semi-invalid with them would be telling the world that Lanny had special information about events in the making.

He visited several persons on the Riviera who owned paintings and were living on the proceeds of their sale. Sooner or later the funds would be running low; and this was a cruel world, in which, when your funds were gone, nobody brought you any food, nobody prepared it for you or served it to you, and your friends had a tendency to cross to the other side of the street, for fear that you might start trying to borrow from them. But Lanny would be on hand and would say tactfully: "If you would care to put a price on that Ingres, I know a gentleman in New York who might be interested." Then he would say, even more tactfully: "I am sorry, but I fear that is much too high. I don't think I could advise my client to pay more than half the sum."

X

Lanny had written to "M. Guillaume Bruges" at Toulon, saying that he would soon arrive to inspect the sketches about which M. Bruges had informed him. There was a train that ran along this rockbound Coast of Pleasure, sometimes passing so close to the villas that you feared it was going to hit them. If you were rich and could afford *première classe*, you could be comfortable. Lanny with his carefully packed suitcases and little portable typewriter boarded the morning train, and a couple of hours later descended in Toulon and was driven in an old-style *fiacre* to the Grand Hotel.

All hotels were crowded, but there was always room for a gentleman who was known to be a friend of the military commandant of the port. Lanny made it a point to inquire of the hotel clerk what sort of transportation he could get to the mansion of the D'Avrienne family in the suburbs; he had come, so he said, for the purpose of giving further study to an art collection of which the city was proud. He had dropped a note, requesting permission, and now there was a reply awaiting him at the hotel, and he did not fail to refer to it.

Also, he asked whether any new art dealers had set themselves up in business since his last visit. He went out to look for them; and it was pure chance that he happened to be passing the bookstore of Armand Mercier. It was chance, also, that he happened to see on the stall in front of the shop a book that interested him. It was natural for a clerk to come out to see if he wished to make a purchase; and nobody heard the words which the clerk murmured: "Twenty hours, at the statue of the Genius of Navigation."

Lanny moved on, and inspected paintings in the shops, and admired them even though he found them commonplace. He inquired about old masters and made note of where some might be found; he did all this, knowing that rumors would spread and help to make him *persona grata.* The law required all foreigners to register with the police, and Lanny went and reported himself as on the way to Algiers; he was stopping by for a couple of days to find out if there was a possibility of obtaining examples of the art of painting, in which it was well known that the French excel all the rest of the world. The statement that "fine words butter no parsnips" had originated in England and would surely never have occurred to anyone who had been raised in the Midi!

XI

Promptly at the hour set, Lanny made contact with his friend, and they strolled in obscure streets, taking pains to make certain that no one was following. Their destination was the beautiful gardens of the hospital, out on Cap Cépet which forms one arm of the harbor. They found a quiet spot, in the open, there being sufficient moonlight so that no one could approach without detection. Speaking in low murmurs the ex-schoolman revealed that a man had come from Colonel Donovan's office, and that the little group of the underground were well pleased with what he had brought them and had promised.

Raoul himself hadn't met the man. "You know, Lanny, the fact that I am a Spaniard and worked for the Republican government makes me vulnerable. If ever the *flics* should take my fingerprints they would spot me, so I stick to my job and avoid the *rafles*, the round-ups in which they collect slave workers for Germany. I make friends among the workers, and listen, and try to pick out the honest comrades from the police agents and spies. It is dreadfully difficult these days; you have to guard every word you say, every gesture, and every expression of your face."

"I know," Lanny answered. "I worry about you; but we greatly need your help."

"You want to know about the Fleet. There is a civil war here, as everywhere in France. Partly it is the class war—three-quarters of the *marins* are for the Allies, whereas three-quarters of the officers are for tradition, that is to say, for obeying orders whatever they may be. Of course the situation is complicated by what the British did at Mersel-Kébir; a good part of the men hate them heartily for that; but few hate the Americans, and if the common sailors could have their way, the Fleet would sail out tomorrow and put itself under American command."

"That is unlikely, of course. The question is, whether they will let themselves be put under German command."

"That surely cannot happen, Lanny. There would be a mutiny on every ship."

"What is the truth about the Germans being taught how to run the machinery?"

"That is being done to some extent. The officers claim they cannot refuse to comply with German demands. There is an underground war going on over the issue. Wherever the Germans come, our *marins* of course know it, and they get together and agree to teach them wrongly as far as possible. They know what the Nazis want and hate their very guts. Naturally we make the most of the situation. I have written three leaflets that have been printed; many of the men have had a chance to read them. That is one of the ways your Intelligence man has been able to help us, with money, and now he has promised to get paper. That is scarce."

"Do you yourself need money, Raoul?"

"I can use some always; and so can Julie. She, being French, is not in as much danger as I. Believe me, I remember the months I spent in a concentration camp. The French are a grand people in many ways, but their treatment of the politically suspect—well, I'd get out of this country if I didn't see so much to be done."

"The critical time is near, Raoul. I don't know the day or the place, but I can tell you this much; the Americans are coming to the Mediterranean, and it will be this year."

"That is great news, of course; but it won't satisfy our little group; they want to see the Army here tomorrow! The fortifications of Toulon are powerful, but they don't extend very far to the east or the west, and landings could be made and the port surrounded."

"No doubt our military men have maps, Raoul. What you and your friends have to do is to save the Fleet, or at any rate keep it out of German hands. No one could exaggerate the importance of that. So long as the Germans don't have it, we can command the Mediterranean and can land at any place we select. The day we land on French territory, you can be sure the Germans will come down here in force, and they will use every stratagem they know to get the ships. That is when you must act, and put in everything you have. I probably won't be here, so I'm telling you now: get ready for the day. The fate of the war might depend upon it—at least for years."

XII

Raoul urged his friend to tell these things directly to the leaders of his group. There were differences of opinion, he explained, but all

three had been tremendously impressed by that little engraved visiting
card with the name of President Roosevelt on it. Lanny said: "I'm still
carrying it." At the same time he wondered, what would they make
of the other bit of paper which was sewed up in his coat? An appointment was made for the following evening, and Lanny returned to his
hotel. He discovered that his baggage had been gone through, not very
skillfully. He had left his correspondence conveniently on top, his
address list and his data on Moorish and Arab art. Nothing had been
taken.

In the morning he inspected the D'Avrienne treasures again, and
visited more art dealers, and took the trouble to get permission to see
another collection about which he had been informed. In the evening
he dined upon fish, newly caught in that old sea which had fed so
many human tribes for so many thousands of years. Then he went for
a "constitutional," and stopped to look in shop windows, and out of
the corner of his eye made certain that nobody else was stopping at
the same time. When at last he picked up his Spanish friend, they
walked separately around a couple of blocks in the Old Town before
at last they dived into the dark alleyway.

In the same dingy room were the three comrades to whom Lanny
had told his life story: Jean Catroux, the Communist, who wished to
be known as Zed; Soulay, the docker, tough and weatherbeaten; and
the mysterious young woman who had first been Mlle. Richard and
now was Mlle. Bléret. Zed was either the leader, or else the more
talkative; he said: "*Bonsoir, Camarade Zhone. Asseyez-vous, s'il vous
plaît.*" Comrade Jones took a vacant chair, and the spokesman continued: "We have met the agent you sent to us, and everything is
satisfactory. We don't know whether you know this man, or wish to
know about him."

Lanny's reply was: "I do not know him, and I much prefer not to
share any secret that is not necessary to my work. I only want to be
sure you have got what you want."

"We have, and we thank you."

"I have already told Comrade Bruges, but I will repeat for your
benefit, that there is to be an American invasion of the Mediterranean
area before the end of the present year. There was a conference of the
general staffs of Britain and America last month, and that was the decision. I have it upon the highest authority, and you may accept it as
settled. The exact place and date are still to be determined, but your
duties are the same in any case. You are asked to do everything in your
power to make certain that the French Fleet does not fall into the

hands of the Germans. That is the one absolutely vital thing that is within the field of your efforts."

"We have been told that, Comrade Jones, and we are doing our best and hope to do more."

"You should try to win the confidence of individual sailors and persuade them to organize so far as it can be done; you should also try to win officers; there are many who understand the principles of the Revolution, and are not under the Vichy spell. And not merely the sailors, but the arsenal workers, the dockers, the whole labor force of this port must be prepared to rise in a mass movement, to seize arms, and to make every building at the harbor a fortress to keep the Germans away from the ships."

"You are perhaps aware, Comrade Jones, that the Germans have compelled our commanders to reduce the fuel in the tanks, so that the ships cannot make their escape."

"I have been told that, and if that is the situation when the crisis comes, it will be necessary to sink the vessels. Men must be found with courage enough to open the seacocks, and then stand by and defend the ships while they sink. There have been such heroes in French history, I know, because my stepfather, the painter Marcel Detaze, was shot down in an observation balloon and had his face burned off; nevertheless, in the last desperate days of the second battle of the Marne, he took a gun and went into the fighting and gave his life."

"We know that story, comrade." It was the woman speaking, and Lanny turned toward her. She had been gazing at him intently out of her fine brown eyes, something he had observed on the previous occasions when they had met. She was an extremely attractive young woman, so Lanny had thought at the beginning, and he still thought it: slender and graceful, with sensitive features and an ardent expression. He had been interested to make her acquaintance; but now the circumstances had changed and he was a bit afraid of her. All his life he had been made aware that ladies "fell for him" easily, and he knew the world well enough not to attribute it altogether to his personal charms. He hadn't been more than six years old when Robbie had pointed out to him that he was the grandson of an American millionaire and might some day be the son of such a godlike being; the ladies would find that out, somehow or other, and for the rest of his days—young, middle-aged, or old—he would have to be aware of that special danger. Now, desiring no entanglements, he remarked:

"Let me tell you, comrades, that a few years ago I was married to a German artist of talent, a Socialist who did not give way to the Nazis.

She was seized by them and tortured to death, but she did not betray any of the secrets with which she had been entrusted. She used to quote to me the words of a German poem, supposed to be spoken by the Tirolese hero, Andreas Hofer: '*Wir sind all des Todes eigen,*' that is to say, '*Nous appartenons tous à la mort.*' Such is the spirit in which we have to work in these tragic days, men, women, and even children; we all belong to death. That is true of me, and also of my wife, for I have recently been married to an ardent comrade who would be here with me tonight, except that she is expecting a baby soon."

Without waiting to observe the effect of this statement upon the mademoiselle, Lanny turned his eyes to the sturdy dockworker with the well-browned skin and leathery hands. "It would be well, Comrade Soulay, if a few of you *enfants de la patrie* could get hold of some sticks of dynamite and plant them under the vital machinery of the arsenal before the Germans arrive. It would be better yet if you would study some of the bridges and tunnels and wreck them to delay the enemy's approach. This one thing you have to get clear, and don't let anybody persuade you otherwise—the instant they get word that an American soldier has set foot upon French soil, whether here or in North Africa, the Panzers and the parachutists will set out for Toulon. So don't let anything delay you; be ready to act the first night, because that may be the only night you have."

"*Que vous avez raison!*" said the horny-handed *enfant*.

13

The Yanks Are Coming

I

FROM Toulon to Marseille is another short train journey, and there the Pendleton Agence de Voyage had engaged passage for M. Budd on the same steamer which had carried him to Algiers the previous time. The great "midland sea" was still and the air was hot in midsummer, and again Lanny spent the night on deck. Late the next afternoon there loomed up that shining white city on the steep hillslopes, and once more a bus took him on the boulevard which runs along the shore, ascending slowly, and then turns and comes back in the opposite direction, still ascending. The bus continued into the suburbs until it came to a high, level spot which had been made into a beautiful garden, and here was a hotel prepared to provide a collector of mosaics with every comfort, provided that he could pay the high price.

The faithful Hajek had been notified and was on hand. He had been seeking new art treasures, and soon the visitor was immersed in those elaborate negotiations which he found amusing. They were the custom of the country, made him a great gentleman, and provided protection against espionage. Just as by going into a French café and ordering a cup of coffee or a glass of wine you had the right to sit and read all the newspapers in the place, so by bargaining over several fountains for ablutions and buying one of them Lanny could have the right to hold secret conferences with as many conspirators as he could find in Algiers.

Capitaine Denis de Bruyne came to the hotel and they sat under an arbor, conversing in low tones. Lanny told about his meeting with Charlot, and it was sad. Denis was not so bitter against his brother as the brother was against him. Denis took the position that Charlot was a strayed lamb whom he yearned to bring back into the fold. But Lanny couldn't hold out any hope; he had to report that Charlot had completely committed himself to the *collaborateurs* and could not be brought to hear reason. The older brother sat with his lips pressed together and the knuckles showing white in his clenched hands. "If only I could talk to him!" he lamented.

Lanny replied: "It would only add to the bitterness between you. You will have to leave it to events to change his mind."

"What events will do is to get him shot!" exclaimed the brother.

II

Lanny gave an account of his visits to Washington and London, and of the decision taken by the Allied Combined Chiefs of Staff. Denis, a man of honor, could be trusted with the great secret. Lanny told him that it was certain to be North Africa, and hardly possible that Algiers should not be one of the first ports taken. It was to be an invasion in force, and the troops would come to stay.

"It is most important for us to be sure of that," said the younger man. "We shall be staking our lives upon it. Our friends have been terribly discouraged by Dieppe."

He was referring to an event which had just been reported, of course with the high coloring the collaborationist press gave to all German successes. Some five thousand troops, mostly Canadians, had been thrown against Dieppe, and had managed to hold portions of the harbor for half a day. They had been forced to retire, and if you could believe the Algiers papers, they had lost several vessels of war, a great fleet of planes, and more than half the men who had taken part. The Germans had given them a bloody lesson and vindicated the claim that the Channel coast was invulnerable.

Lanny said: "It was a commando raid, Denis; a big one, but still a raid. It had to be undertaken because the Canadians were so impatient. What I am talking about is an invasion, with force enough to take and hold all French North Africa. You know how the Americans came last time, and the job they did; they are coming again, and in far greater force. We are building an army of eight million men, and the decision has been taken to open up the Mediterranean, destroy Rommel's army, and build air bases to put Italy out of the war. That is going to happen, and the Germans can no more stop it than they can stop tomorrow's sunrise."

The other replied: "I am ready to stake my life on my faith in you, Lanny; but you can understand how hard it is for a Frenchman to believe in success any more. For almost three years we have seen nothing but defeats, all over the world, and we have got the habit of despair."

"That is because you have to see the war through the enemy's spectacles. We in the outside world see it differently. The siege of London has certainly not been a defeat for Britain, and the sieges of Leningrad and Moscow have not been defeats for the Soviet Union. I am told by friends at home who are close to sources of information that we destroyed something more than a third of Japan's most highly trained flyers at the Battle of Midway, and we are destroying more every day in the struggle for the Solomons. Those things don't show up in the daily reports, but they are bound to have an effect in the long run."

"All that seems far off to us, Lanny. Here in North Africa we contemplate the fact that Rommel is only seventy miles from Alexandria, and that reinforcements and supplies are being poured in by way of Tunis and the other ports so close to Italy. I have been told that in Cairo there is a *trac*, a panic. The well-to-do residents are packing their belongings into their cars and preparing to flee to Palestine or to wherever they can go."

"That may be, Denis; but it is not the well-to-do residents who fight battles, and it may be they are encouraged to take themselves away and relieve the food situation by that much. What you do not hear about are the convoys we have been sending around South Africa and up through the Suez Canal. We have a new tank called the General Sherman that is believed to be good, and we have a self-propelled anti-tank gun that the Desert Fox isn't going to like a bit when he hears it go off. Don't forget, too, we have an airplane route established across the middle of Africa, and we are sending all kinds and sizes of planes to Cairo. I have no idea when the British will feel strong enough to attack, but I do know that they have been bringing up forces from all over the Middle East, and you can be sure that Rommel will have to do a lot more fighting before he gets to Alexandria, to say nothing of Suez."

III

Lanny was taken again to the apartment of Professor Aboulker, and had another session with him and the two Royalists, D'Astier de la Vigerie and the Jesuit Father Cordier. Lanny did not reveal to these three that he was positive about the Allied decision; he contented himself with saying that he had checked upon and verified his previous information, which was that the big attack was to come by way of the Mediterranean and was to be this year. Since Algiers was the most important French city in North Africa, it was fair to assume that it would be included in the program. Lanny was told that a representative of Colonel Donovan's organization had made contact with this group; the news pleased him greatly, for it meant that "Wild Bill" and his miscellaneous crowd were missing no openings. The Frenchmen professed to be satisfied with what they had got; the Americans were a wonderful people.

When this group learned that Lanny had been in London, they wanted to know if he had visited General de Gaulle. The truth was that he had kept as far from the French Joan of Arc as possible, for he had got the impression both in London and New York that the headquarters of this movement was beset with spies, intriguers, and publicity seekers. But he couldn't say this to Frenchmen in exile, who knew the General only by his radio eloquence. When they asked why President Roosevelt did not at once espouse this great leader's cause and place him at the head of the expedition, Lanny answered tactfully that the President was doing his best to distinguish between the winning of the war, which was the American task, and the future of *la patrie*, which was a problem for Frenchmen, and in which Americans had to exercise care to avoid even seeming to interfere. France was an ally, and all Frenchmen would be friends, save only those who had chosen to be friends of the Nazis. This statement pleased the group, and Lanny could only hope that when the Army came it would have some advisers who understood this touchy people.

Here in this apartment were five Frenchmen determined to work like all possessed for the occasion which the Americans oddly called "D-day." Their movement was spreading rapidly, and the different groups were at one in their desire to make as much trouble as possible for the enemy. Lanny promised to let them know what was coming and when; but they must understand that the Germans had many submarines, to say nothing of dive-bombing planes, and these constituted greater menaces than anything likely to be encountered on shore. Therefore every effort must be made to deceive the enemy as to the destination of the great convoy, and the friends of the cause must not expect definite information until the vessels were immediately at hand.

That didn't sound so good to the conspirators, and M. d'Astier remarked: "If our Chantiers de la Jeunesse take the key points of Algiers and then your troops don't come ashore, hundreds of French lads and all their leaders will be shot."

Lanny replied: "I will explain the situation to Washington, and no doubt Mr. Murphy will do it also. A code must be arranged, and you must know exactly what steps to take at every stage of the landing."

IV

The visitor inspected several fountains and made himself conspicuous as an art expert, telling about his achievement in starting a new fad among the American rich. This would have the effect of increasing the prices of what he hoped to buy, but under the circumstances he didn't mind that; his client, Mr. Vernon, would be making a contribution toward saving the lives of American soldiers. In the salons of the Algerian nabobs, in their town houses and their magnificent estates at the foot of the mountain range, Lanny discoursed upon the fact that they had treasures of art which they failed to appreciate; he rallied them because they were content with butchers' calendars for paintings, while the wealthy of New York were sending an agent to North Africa to snatch ancient Moroccan masterpieces from under their noses.

In one of these soirees he ran into the vegetable-oil king, and that gentleman, professing friendship, was hurt because M. Budd hadn't looked him up. Lanny went to lunch again at the Golf Club, and let himself be pumped dry concerning what was going on in New York and Washington, London and Madrid, Vichy and Cannes. He didn't mind it, for he told only what could do no harm, and he charged a good price for the service. M. Lemaigre-Dubreuil was a fountainhead of information about the leading personalities of Algeria, both French and German, to say nothing of American. He was a man to encourage, for he had great power and was ready and eager to make a deal for his own safety.

The son of Budd-Erling was the sort of person he could understand, and he asked anxiously what would be the policy of the American Army and administration to French capital in these colonial lands. He had heard so much about "That Man," and his dangerous prejudices against all "economic royalists." Lanny explained that F.D.R. was doing what he could to cut the ground from under the Communists by persuading the super-rich to part with some of their excessive gains. His New Deal was a milder set of measures than the British Tories had introduced two or three decades ago. This statement comforted the representative of the "two hundred families," now preparing to seek shelter under the Stars and Stripes.

Members of the *haute bourgeoisie* of Algiers were making money fast. They had found secret ways to undermine the Nazi system, by bribing individual officials of the Reichswehr, the *Partei*, or the various commissions which were looking out for German interests. "Some day the war will be over," a French high bourgeois would say to a Nazi big or little wig, "and then you will have nothing but your salary. Wouldn't it be the part of common sense to lay a little by?" This would enable the Frenchman to get hold of a block of stock in some bank or industry that was being acquired by the Germans, and then to transfer the shares to a newly organized holding concern in Switzerland or Sweden, Spain or the Argentine.

They whispered about these stratagems among themselves, and when they had come to know the son of Budd-Erling well enough they let him hear the whispers. They even offered to let him in on some of the good things, going fifty-fifty, of course. Lanny would smile amiably and say that whenever he had any money to spare he put it into his father's business; and he offered to let them in on that without any commission whatever. Some took him seriously and asked questions about Budd-Erling stocks; they had the most exaggerated ideas about the earnings of airplane shares, and equally exaggerated fears as to what would happen to such shares when the fighting stopped!

Lanny listened attentively and learned new things about both France and Germany. There were more tricks than you could shake a stick at, or even a whole bundle of sticks tied together with a cord and with an ax in the middle of them. Such had been the symbol carried before the ancient Roman lictors, proclaiming to the world their authority to flog backs and to chop off heads. The fasces, the bundle was called, and Mussolini and his gang had taken it over and used its name and its threat. Now Il Duce's sticks were falling apart, and if you could believe the big-business *émigrés* of North Africa, the Führer was struggling in vain against the same forces of disintegration. Every American knows the phrase, "Business is business," and every Frenchman knows "*Les affaires sont les affaires.*" The Germans had their version: "*Geschäft ist Geschäft*"!

V

A rather amusing episode arose out of Lanny's dealings with the vegetable-oil king. The latter said: "I mentioned you to Mr. Robert Murphy, and he expressed a desire to meet you. What do you say?"

Lanny had been carefully keeping away from the Counselor and his twelve vice-consuls—one of whom, according to the gossip now going the rounds, had fallen under the spell of a French woman who was revealed to be a Nazi spy! Lanny, a spy himself, didn't want to have anything to do with any of his fellow workers, whether German, French, or American. But he couldn't very well say that he was unwilling to make the acquaintance of the man who was his country's ambassador to this colonial world. He told Lemaigre that such a meeting would give him pleasure, and Lemaigre offered to arrange another luncheon. Lanny protested that it ought to be his turn, but the other answered that it was such a small matter they surely didn't have to talk about it; some day they would meet in America, and then it would be the American's turn to feed the Frenchman.

Lanny gave thought to this meeting in advance. He had heard about Mr. Murphy wherever he went, among rich and poor, for Mr. Murphy was a super-important person. Many of the farseeing French were looking upon him as soon to be consul, not in the modern commercial sense, but in the ancient Roman sense, the civil governor of a province. He was a person acceptable to the French because he was a Catholic, and also because he was genial and friendly, a democrat in the human sense of that word. The Americans had sent such a representative to France in the days when the young nation was striving to be born;

his name was Benjamin Franklin, and he had made a hit with the liberal elements of France both rich and poor. It was very probable that Mr. Murphy had read about this eminent predecessor, and would try in a modest way to follow his footsteps.

Lanny was bound to assume that Mr. Murphy, a career diplomat in Paris prior to the war, was nobody's fool. He could hardly have failed to have suspicions concerning a fellow countryman who traveled about so freely in wartime. Mr. Murphy received mysterious missives marked "Personal to the President, from Traveler," and he had orders to forward these promptly in the diplomatic pouches, which couriers bore by way of Tangier, the Azores, and Brazil. Could the Counselor have failed to note the fact that these letters ceased when Mr. Budd left North Africa and were resumed when he came back? Could the thought have failed to occur to him that his Chief had set somebody to watching him and his twelve subordinates? Mr. Murphy would have been less than human if he had not been curious about such a person; and he would have been less than a shrewd diplomat if he had not "pumped" the vegetable-oil king on the subject and hinted that a meeting might be brought about in a way that would not seem too obvious.

Lanny had been told by Roosevelt that he might reveal himself to the Counselor if he saw fit, but he had decided not to see fit just now. What the P.A. had on his mind were those six words which Hess had written on a scrap of paper, and the hope he was cherishing of taking them into Germany. If that should come about, the less he had had to do with American agents in North Africa, the better for him. He knew that the place was swarming with agents of the enemy's Armistice Commission. Now and then one of them sought out Herr Budd, who talked volubly about the charms of Arab and Moroccan architecture, and the wonders of Timgad which he had seen and of Volubilis about which he had been told. He expressed also the conviction that war was a sad and cruel thing, with which an art lover could not possibly have anything to do. And he was careful not to let any one of them get him alone in a dark alley.

VI

The career diplomat came to the Golf Club; tall, handsome, comfortably dressed, but not at all "high-hat." He was an agreeable talker, and Lanny liked to listen, but knew that he had not been invited there for this purpose. Presently the Counselor mentioned having been told that Mr. Budd had had the advantage of knowing some of the Nazi leaders. That was an invitation, and Lanny talked about the personal characteristics of Numbers One, Two, and Three, and told illustrative anecdotes. Mr. Murphy asked the art expert's guess as to the circumstances under which the war might end. When and how would the Nazis give up? To this Lanny said that Hitler was a fanatic and would die fighting like a rat in a corner; Göring, on the other hand, was a practical man and had sound military judgment; he would know when victory was no longer possible. Lanny smiled as he said: "I think he would be willing to surrender all Germany, provided that he was allowed to keep his castles, and the money he has deposited abroad, and above all, his art collection."

They commented upon that curious psychological complexity, a genuine love of beauty combined with monstrous greed. The Frenchman told a story about a refugee of his acquaintance, a German Jew who had been a great capitalist and had owned fine paintings. For a moment Lanny thought he might be talking about Johannes Robin, but no, it was another man, who had lived in Nürnberg. He had been put under house arrest, for his own good, he was told, to protect him against the anti-Semitic mobsters. The person who came to give him advice and to aid his exit from Germany was none other than the fat Marshal's wife.

"Emmy Sonnemann, the actress," Lanny remarked. "I had the pleasure of meeting her several times. She is a really kindhearted person and tried to help a number of the Jews."

"Maybe so," replied the vegetable-oil man. "The way she helped this particular Jew was by telling him that he had to sell his art works, his palace, and his shares in several big German companies, all for a few thousand marks. Emmy's husband was the buyer, and I have often wondered if Emmy got a commission on the deal."

"My God!" exclaimed Lanny. He was astounded, for he had thought that this stage star was really a kindly creature. Millions of Germans had thought so, too; she was built on a generous scale, the very archetype of Nordic blond beauty, praised by Hitler under the name of "Aryan." Lanny said: "I didn't think there was anything more for me to learn about the Nazis, but I see I was naïve." In his mind was the night which he and his father had spent in Karinhall, and in their bedroom Robbie had written on a scrap of paper, being afraid that the room might be "wired," a warning to his son not to be too cordial in manner to the Reichsmarschall's wife. Göring was known to be of a jealous temperament, and Robbie was afraid that he might resent even the ordinary social courtesies.

When the time came for the luncheon party to break up Lanny decided to make a brief "pass" at the Counselor. He remarked: "My mother is living on the Riviera, and she is talking about coming to Morocco this fall to help me in selecting some works of art for which I have orders. I don't know what to advise her. Can you tell me whether it is likely to be safe?"

There were only three in the private room, and certainly there wasn't any reason for caution in the presence of the vegetable-oil king. In his talks with Lanny this man of great affairs had made plain that he knew what was coming, and Lanny suspected that he had got it from his Irish-American friend. But perhaps Mr. Murphy didn't realize that Lanny had got that far with the French collaborator. What he answered was: "I wish I could tell you. I hear many reports, but I really couldn't say."

Lanny recognized this as the kind of skillful answer he had been taught to cultivate from his youth on. Mr. Robert Murphy hadn't made any false statement. No doubt he "wished" that he could tell, just as he wished many other good things—that the war was over, and that the world was a better place, with no gangsters and no gangsters' molls in it. Also, he heard many reports and read many, and he "couldn't" say—because he had been told not to. (He had just come back from a flying visit to Washington and London.)

VII

Lanny took a plane to Casablanca, leaving the faithful but too talkative Hajek to follow by the slower method of the rundown railroad. The P.A. had already written a note to General Béthouart, at military headquarters, saying that he was coming and hoped to have a chance to inspect the especially fine mosaic which the General had told him about. The General hadn't told any such thing, but Lanny guessed that he wouldn't be too dumb, and he wasn't. There came to the hotel a note making an appointment for the next day; and when the pair met they didn't talk about *objets d'art*, but about the American agents who were now at work in "Casa," and when was the Army coming, and in what force? There were several key persons whom the General could name, in the strictest confidence: persons whose help would be invaluable, but who would not move until they were certain that the great Army overseas was no dream. They were ready to climb onto the bandwagon, but not until they heard the music!

Beauty had written to Algiers, and now she wrote to Morocco.

Lanny had warned her not to say a word about her reasons for coming, or to ask any questions, and to this she carefully conformed. She said that good old Jerry had offered to escort them, not even asking for his expenses. Of course she was insisting upon paying these. "As you know," wrote this playful mother, "I have never failed to have a man to 'lean on' if I could get him, and usually I could. Parsifal, I fear, will not be much good for travel, because he is absent-minded and is apt to be 'saying his prayers' while the train conductor is asking for his tickets, or while the cusstoms man is 'going through' his bagage." It was a peculiarity of Beauty's epistolary style that she used a great many quotation marks, seeming to have the idea that they served for emphasis. Also, she was not strong on spelling, and the small dictionary which Lanny had bought for her always got covered up by other things. When he called her attention to errors, her answer would be: "Gertrude Stein writes as she pleases and gets away with it, so why shouldn't I?"

Anyhow, she was coming, and on a baking hot day Lanny went by the four-hour, overcrowded, dusty train to Marrakech and made hotel arrangements for the party. Incidentally he renewed acquaintance with the Moorish *caid* who owned an oasis and had presented him with a mosaic. Lanny had sent him in return a snappy chiming clock with bright-colored figures which came out and danced the hours. This gift was appreciated immensely, so Lanny had to attend another of those overwhelming banquets. He couldn't mention to this host that he was seeking a fountain, lest it be taken for a hint.

He put Hajek on the job, and very soon the word spread throughout the city, small in population but large in acreage. Partly it was an "old town," and partly a retreat for the rich, both native and foreign, with large estates planted in orange trees and date palms. They had very little interest in their native art and spent immense sums of money upon the crudest and gaudiest objects produced in Europe and America for colonial markets.

In this great center of Mohammedan piety, ritual ablutions were common, and fountains for that purpose were everywhere. Lanny inspected many and picked out one he wanted. He directed Hajek to start negotiations for half a dozen, and didn't tell the paynim Sancho Pánza which one he really meant to purchase. The elaborate negotiations went on day and night, and meantime Lanny collected military information and stowed it away in his mind, for he would never trust the mails of French North Africa. When the negotiations were completed, the fountain had to be taken apart and boxed piece by piece, an elaborate task, and Lanny would be glad when the family arrived so that the efficient Jerry could replace the somewhat bungling Mohammedan at this job.

VIII

The family arrived, decidedly worn after four days and nights on three trains and one steamship in hot weather. Beauty had brought her Provençal maid, grandniece of her old-time cook, to take care of little Marcel; she had also brought Madame Zyszynski, which had not been according to plan. "I just couldn't bear to leave her," the mother explained. "The Nazis have been so cruel to the Poles. It wasn't such a difficult trip after I had once made up my mind to it. But the visas were hard to get. It took a lot of 'drag.'" Lanny told the old woman he was delighted to see her, for to have done otherwise would have broken her heart. And besides, he could try some more experiments.

Living here was going to cost the family dear, but Lanny hoped it needn't be for too long, and, as he told his mother, it was no time to save when you might lose your life. Beauty had a thousand dollars a month which Robbie's secretary mailed to her New York bank account on the first day of every month unless it was Sunday; and she had sums which Lanny's colleague, Zoltan Kertezsi, kept adding to that same account for the Detaze paintings he was authorized to sell. Also, her man of God had a small income from investments he had made back in the State of Iowa; God had protected them as per request. So they could afford four thousand francs a day at the Hotel Mamounia, and the incidental expenses which were necessary to the happiness of a one-time "professional beauty."

It didn't take them long to get settled. Beauty had never failed to find people she knew in whatever part of the world she visited, and soon she was in the "social swim," which wouldn't completely stop its splashing for any wars. She was delighted with this unique Mohammedan city: the mud walls, the tall towers, the great market place with snake charmers and dancing boys from the Atlas Mountains. It was cold at night and hot by day; and strolling on its streets you saw not merely all the tribes of North Africa, but refugees from all Europe, French Syria, and even Indo-China.

As for Parsifal Dingle, he sat in his elegant room, sipping tea with various Mohammedan devotees who came to call, astonished and delighted to find an American gentleman taking a genuine interest in the technicalities of their Prophet's faith. So the two parents both had what they wanted; and Lanny could only hope that his judgment had been correct, and that Marrakech was a safer place for Americans than Juan-les-Pins. He believed that the fighting in North Africa would be on the beaches, and he knew that this city of mosques and millionaires was not equipped to stand a siege, even if the French had been minded for it. Of course if the "Yanks" were repelled, the Wehrmacht would come here, but the situation would be no worse than on the Riviera.

IX

Lanny put Jerry in charge of the packing of the fountain and left himself free to continue the gathering of information. Also, he had a little time for play, and took Madame to his room and seated her in a well-stuffed chair, where she could rest her head back and go into one of her trances. He had decided that her powers were waning, if not entirely gone, but he had to indulge her once in a while because she had adopted him in her heart as a son and must not be made to feel that she was put away on the shelf.

Perhaps it was that travel had stirred up her faculty. Whatever the reason, she gave a demonstration that reminded him of the old days. There came the familiar voice of Tecumseh, the Amerindian chieftain who said he had been an Iroquois, and much superior to the one known to history. What he actually was Lanny had never been able to decide, but he talked in character and his voice was sometimes like Madame's, sometimes not. For thirteen years the Polish ex-servant had assured the Budds that she knew about this voice only what other people had told her; she had never heard it in her life.

"So here you are again, young man!" boomed the "spirit." "Where have you been keeping yourself?" That a man of stone-age culture two centuries dead should be using modern slang was something you just had to guess about.

"You ought to know as well as I," bantered Lanny. They had treated each other in this fashion through the years.

"I am not nearly so much interested in you as you are in yourself. What is it you are looking for?"

"Nothing in particular, Tecumseh. Just the pleasure of a chat with you."

"You know you don't believe in me and never will. You just want to sit and make a lot of notes, and then what do you do with them?"

"I study them diligently, old friend."

"To what purpose? A ten-year-old child would know more. He would understand simple facts and wouldn't need such long words." Then, abruptly: "There is a man here, a foreign fellow. He speaks English badly, word by word. Why can't people learn a sensible language? I am tired of these queer ones who come crowding around you, always in trouble."

"I have lived most of my life in Europe, Tecumseh, and met all sorts of people. Ask the man his name."

"He says it is Hoo-go. Is that right?"

"I knew a man by that name."

"Is he an Indian? He gives the name Bear."

"He is a German. They spell it B-E-H-R. I remember him well. Ask him how long he has been in the spirit world."

"He says eight years. He says he went suddenly."

"No man could go more suddenly," declared Lanny, who held the event as one of the most vivid memories in his life. He had been driving the young Nazi in his car, and two Schutzstaffel men had driven up from behind, ordered Hugo out of the car, and shot him in the face, scattering his blood and brains over the pavement of a Munich street. Such things had been going on all over that city and also Berlin —it was part of the dreadful Blood Purge at the end of June and the beginning of July 1934. Adolf Hitler had become Chancellor upon a program of fundamental economic reforms, and after a year and a half his most sincere followers had realized that he had sold out to the cartelmasters and had no idea of abolishing "interest slavery" or breaking up the great landed estates. Adolf Hitler was getting ready for war, and the first thing he had to do was to rid himself of those "old companions," the *Sturmabteilung* men who had helped him to power and were clamoring for their reward. "National Socialists," they had called themselves, and they wanted the "Socialist" part, while their "Adi" was going to give them only the "Nationalist" part.

X

That was how Hugo Behr had been hurled suddenly into the spirit world; and now here he was, stammering poor English, trying to find out if Lanny Budd remembered and understood what had befallen him. Lanny answered yes to both questions, for somehow he didn't feel it necessary to continue his P.A. role in this strange limbo. Tecumseh said there were tears running down the German's cheeks as he lamented what was happening at present; the spirits were arriving by the thousand every day, and it was a most dreadful calamity, the murder of a whole race, the best in the world. It was that two-front war which all the military men had held to be the one inexcusable blunder; but Adolf Hitler, the ex-corporal or less, thought he knew more than all the trained minds of the *Generalstab*. "Send him over here, Lanny!" exclaimed the SA man.

"What would you do with him?" inquired Lanny, ever curious about this mysterious half-world.

But Hugo was vague, like all the others in that world. "Some still love him and some hate him," he declared. Apparently the German limbo was one vast clamor of controversy; all the spirits who hadn't been allowed to say what they thought on earth went at it eagerly now, and the German colony was what Germany itself might be expected to be when the Germans had been beaten—as Hugo said they were surely going to be.

When Lanny asked how he knew this, Hugo said, painfully through the mind and lips of Tecumseh, that his world was full of mentality in the same way that radio waves filled all space on earth. When Lanny asked why Hugo hadn't come to him before, he said it was like the problem of finding a receiving set on earth. He said that Madame was a battery that ran down quickly, and then there was no more power. He said it two or three times: *"Keine Kraft mehr,"* his voice dying away. There came silence, and then a sigh from the medium, and little moans as she came out of her trance.

"Was it good?" she asked, and Lanny told her it had been wonderful. He went off by himself to speculate, as he had been doing for years. Was there a fragment of the Hugo Behr personality floating about somewhere in space or out of space, in some universe of consciousness of which all our minds are part? Or was this an elaborate process of fictional creation which went on in the subconscious minds of some living persons, perhaps of all? Lanny hadn't thought of Hugo Behr for a long time, and there was no special circumstance connecting him with North Africa or with Lanny's present activities. Was this interview the product of Lanny's own subconscious fictionizing, and had some force in the mind of Madame dipped into his mind and taken this story, which surely he had never told to her or in her presence? Madame's mind had tied it up with her own subconscious fictionizing, which had to do with a stone-age man from North America. Was that man made out of some story told to her as a child, or picked up in some medium parlor which she had visited while in process of discovering her own gift?

This much could be certain, and only this: there were forces in our minds of which we had only the vaguest notion, and these forces went on creating mindstuff, in the same way that plants went on creating plants and animals creating animals. The process never ceased while life lasted; and whether it ceased then was a problem about which we had better keep our minds open—while life lasted.

XI

When the fountain had been packed and shipped, Lanny took his old friend Jerry for a walk and revealed to him the carefully guarded secret that for the past five years he had been working as a secret agent of the United States government. He was prepared to be told that his ex-tutor had guessed it, and this proved to be the case. "I never for a moment thought that you had lost interest in everything but buying paintings, Lanny. I knew it must be something serious so I never spoke of it even to my wife."

"That's fine, Jerry. And now here is the situation. The American Army is coming to North Africa before the end of the year, and it seems to me most unlikely that the Germans will fail to move into the Riviera. I was pretty sure you'd rather be in American hands than in those of the Nazis."

"I guessed that, too, and I'm very much obliged. I take it that Cerise and the children won't be in too great danger, for the Germans have shown that they want to conciliate the French. They've confined their murdering and raping to the eastern front."

"Exactly so. And here's the point: I have been authorized to pay out money to persons who are worthy of trust; and that means you. You know the French, and you can do first-rate work as an Intelligence man. You will have to keep up the pretense that you are working for me, and I have figured it out that it will be fair if I pay half your salary out of my own funds and half out of the government's. I don't know what Intelligence is paying, but I can find out. Meantime, would ten dollars a day and expenses seem right to you?"

"Very handsome, indeed; but I've no idea how to earn it. You'll have to tell me that."

"Don't worry; you'll be kept busy. The word is that the invasion is to be this year, and we have only three months before bad weather. I will tell you as much as I have already learned, and you can start from there. It will be your job to meet people who have information, and find ways to get it out of them. Of course if you have to pay them, that is O.K., and I will honor your account. My basic instruction is that we are trying to save the lives of our boys, and not to save money. The Nazis are printing it wholesale, or making the French do it. We want maps, we want photographs, everything of that sort. We want to know where military goods are stored, where the big guns are and their caliber, where the Germans have built their flak towers, every sort of military data. We want to know what is in the minds of the men, of the officers, the dockers, everybody."

"I'll do my best, Lanny, but I'm utterly lacking in experience."

"Nearly all our people are lacking, Jerry. We have to start from scratch. There will be other fellows working, and more and more of them coming. No doubt there will be a lot of duplication, but that's all right; what one man reports will check the next man's. And don't forget that wherever you go you are looking for mosaics and fountains and beautifully carved doorways—you are really looking for them, just as I am really buying them. If ever it happens that you get caught and questioned, whether it's by the French or whomever, you must swear that I employed you in good faith in connection with my art business, and that I haven't the slightest idea that you have been thinking about anything else."

"Sure thing, Lanny. All that goes without saying. Wild horses won't drag anything out of me."

"And one thing more, old man. Keep watch who is walking behind you at night, and don't let anybody lure you into a dark alley."

XII

So there was another secret agent, and it didn't take him long to get the hang of the job. A couple of hours questioning Lanny, and he was ready to go out and talk with Frenchmen and French-speaking natives, first about art works, then about politics and about the defenses of Casablanca. He would come back to his boss to report, and it wasn't many days before he had an interesting story. "Have you been to Volubilis?" he inquired.

"No," replied Lanny. "I saw the ruins of Timgad, and I imagine they are much the same."

"I've met a chap who has been studying Volubilis. He calls himself an archeologist and comes from Chicago."

"Name Faulkner?" inquired the other.

"Oh, then you know him!"

"I came over in the plane with him, the trip before last. Nice chap, I thought."

"Funny about him, Lanny. He's been to Volubilis, all right, and knows all about some new excavating the French did just before the war; but he isn't doing anything with his information so far as I can make out. What he does is to hang around and gossip with dockworkers and fishermen and people like that. He seems to have no end of time to make friends."

"I guessed that he was an O.S.S. man, Jerry. Our State Department isn't letting anybody over to study ancient ruins these days."

"He picked on me because he found I had lived half my life in France and knew the people. I've an idea he doesn't trust himself any too well. Seems shy."

"Another one who's lacking in experience!" remarked Lanny with a chuckle.

"He's been trying to find out everything I know, and of course I've been trying to find out everything he knows. We had a fine time taking in each other's washing."

"Well, you might combine forces, once you've made sure he's all right. He struck me as being very much the gentleman and scholar."

"I've a feeling that he's about ready to open up and propose something of the sort. I wondered what I should say."

"Let him do the talking. Tell him you're a patriot, of course, and would be glad to help in any way you can. But don't tell him you're an agent till you're absolutely certain of him, and don't ever let on that I know about it. Let it be that you're using my business as a camouflage. It might be that you could turn in your information through him, or he could put you in touch with his superior. I have to go back to New York very soon, and while I'm gone you might come on something that was too hot to keep."

"Just what I have been worrying about!" said Jerry Pendleton.

XIII

Once a week Lanny had been writing a letter to his wife. He told her about the art works he had inspected and about the scenery and the weather; he said that he was well, and so were the other members of the family, and that he loved her, and thought about her often, and hoped that her literary work was progressing, and that she wasn't overdoing it. All that, but not a word about the war, or politics, or anything approaching thereto; nor any strange words or mysterious statements which might excite the suspicion of a censor. Laurel, carefully warned, did the same; she informed him that she was well and moderately active, though she had come to a state where she moved slowly; she said that the weather was not troubling her; that she had been to visit his family, and also her own people in Baltimore; that the book was not so good as she had hoped, but she was trying to improve it. Assuming that the anonymous censor would be a human being, she had the boldness to add: "Marriage is a dreadfully bad habit; I miss you so!"

By the beginning of October Lanny felt that he had got as heavy a load of information as he could carry in one head. It was a question of flying back to Algiers and having it delivered to the office of Mr. Robert Murphy or of taking a trip home. Really there wasn't much difference, or so he told himself, and added that he could do better work if he had a chance to bring his mind up to date with that of his Chief. In the back of his head was the notion that he might win the Chief's permission to go to Switzerland and write a letter to Adolf Hitler, offering to bring him a message from his most loyal secretary and friend. In addition to all this was the desire to see Laurel, although he sternly told himself that the service of the country must come first and that his personal interest must never take precedence. Of course, if he could manage to make the two kinds of interest coincide, he would be glad to see a wife whom he missed as much as she missed him.

Things had worked out neatly in the matter of Jerry Pendleton. He had had a showdown with his Dr. Faulkner. (The archeologist had a Ph.D. from the University of Chicago, but was thinking of dropping it in Morocco because the natives knew the meaning of the word "doctor," or thought they did, and while he was measuring the dimensions of ancient Roman dwellings they would bring him cases of trachoma to be treated and tumors to be cut out.) Jerry had told this earnest scholar-turned-spy that he had a good salary as assistant to an art expert and had time to spare and would be glad to help him in the collecting of data useful to an army. So now Jerry had a way to turn in information and have it reach headquarters promptly, for Faulkner reported to one of the vice-consuls who had a concealed radio-sending set. Lanny gave Jerry several items which might be urgent, and Faulkner would get the credit for these and of course be made happy. This arrangement set Lanny free to take wing with a good conscience.

His procedure was to cable Robbie that he was ready to come home. A message to his father on such a subject would seem natural to any enemy agent who might have bought or exacted the right to inspect cablegrams out of French Morocco. Robbie would pass on the word to a man in Washington, about whom he knew nothing except the name, Baker, and a telephone number. The result was that a couple of days later a messenger from the consulate called at Lanny's hotel, informing him that a place had been reserved for him on the plane from Tangier to Lisbon, and from there on the Clipper to New York by way of the Azores and Bermuda.

XIV

So "Traveler" packed his belongings, leaving a bundle of summer clothing in his mother's care, it being no longer summer in New York. He wrote a few letters having to do with the business of art, letters which he wanted to come from Marrakech for the effect upon the clients, and also because he wanted censors and enemy agents to have a chance to read them. He bade good-by to the friends he had made and took a dilapidated train into Spanish Morocco. Two days later he went on board one of those luxurious flying boats that have nearly all the American comforts. It was shoved off from the Lisbon pier, its propellers began to whirl, and it went racing down the River Tagus. The waves slapped its underside, shaking it, and presently there were no more slaps and it was airborne, heading into the west, a crossing which in 1492 had taken the little caravels of Columbus a matter of seventy days, and which in 1942 could be made, without stops, in half a day. Such a difference when two numbers exchanged positions!

This flying boat was playing safe, and stopped at the Islands of the Green Cape, which the bold navigators of Portugal had taken long ago and which now the timid dictator of Portugal had rented to the Allies for a high price to save them the embarrassment of having to seize them. From there on to the still-vexed Bermoothes, which now had become an American naval and air station, to the embarrassment of staid citizens who had hitherto refused to recognize the existence of motorcars. Lanny's baggage was politely searched by the British authorities, also his clothing. He held his breath, wondering if they were going to find those two scraps of paper sewed up in the lining of his coat, scraps which were so oddly contradictory in their content! But the search was not that thorough, and whatever the name of Budd meant to the officials they gave no sign.

The Clipper was put down on the water of Long Island Sound, and after another customs investigation Lanny was free. His first act was to step into a telephone booth. He had been debating, in the words of a poem which schoolchildren learn: "Which shall it be? Which shall it be?" He had decided for duty instead of love; but as it happened, duty's telephone line was busy, so love had its chance. He heard the dear familiar voice and said: "Here I am, safe and sound!" She cried: "Oh, Lanny! Lanny!" There was a catch in her voice.

"Everything's jake!" he told her, "and I'll be home in an hour. Don't make any preparations, for I may be flying to Washington today." Such was the fate of a P.A.'s wife, who didn't even know what a P.A. was!

He telephoned Baker and was told as usual to call back in three hours for an appointment. Then to a taxi, and in due course he greeted the familiar elevator girl—all operators were women or old men now— and gave her a dollar bill so that she would be as glad to see him as he was to see her. He had left his key to the apartment with Laurel, so he had to ring the bell. Here she came, and what a spectacle! The bright eager face was the same, but the rest of her so different! He took her gently in his arms and told her it was grand and that he was tickled to death, and so on, and of course he was.

Thirteen years had passed since he had been through this same ex- perience. Irma had been brought up in smart society, where the young women of the twenties had done what they damn pleased and said it in that and other four-letter words. But Laurel had come of a Southern family and was old-fashioned in spite of calling herself a Socialist and feminist. She blushed when she saw her husband glance at that large protuberance, and as they sat on the couch, his arms about her, old- fashioned tears of happiness ran down her cheeks. What she said was: "Oh, do for God's sake get this awful war over! I can't stand it much longer!"

She had almost three years more of it yet to stand; but her husband didn't know that and couldn't tell her. The wisest men in the world could have given her only their guesses—"all different and no two alike!"

Printed in the United States
32943LVS00010B/23